Curse of the Flamingo

Copyright © Text: M E Gouws

Copyright Reg. Ref: 1556117698
Copyright © Cover Illustration:

ISBN 978-0-620-47832-8

marthieg@mweb.co.za

Cover illustration; Marli Beetge

Many thanks to the following:

To my long time partner Fanie, for always letting me follow my heart and for your dedication to help this story to be told.
To Marcia-Lize, for all your input and always believing in me.
To Caterina, for her love of stories and reading, and to Genevieve for keeping fantasy alive.

Mary Dunbar and Vicky Behling

To all the characters for allowing me to tell their story.

Chapter 1

Betrayal

"You stabbed me!" Egoragh clutched his chest and felt the warm blood between his fingers. Bewildered he saw his life spreading on the marble floor of the temple. He slowly lifted his head to look at the three men standing in front of him and fixed his gaze on the one holding the dripping blade.

"Why?"

The reply was cold and laced with malice, "Your birthright will now belong to me and I shall rule the worlds."

"That is why you put the dagger in my chest?" Egoragh whispered, "You are my brother!" His eyes blurred and he wondered if the pain he felt was from the terrible wound or the betrayal. His knees buckled and he fell to the floor. The marble felt cold against his cheek and from far away he heard his father's thundering voice.

"Am I too late?" Darkarh charged forward, knelt down and lifted his son into his arms. Blood soaked his clothes all around his chest. "My son," he cried, drawing him closer. "Don't leave, please don't leave." He picked him up and rushed to the long table where he swept the surface clear with his elbow and gently laid the limp figure down, pressing his hand over the gash in a vain attempt to stem the outpour of life.

"So much blood," he whispered. Desperate he looked up and roared, "The priest! Where is the priest?"

From one of the far sides of the temple a man in a grey robe rushed towards him. "What is wrong?"

"We must save him, he must not die."

"What happened?"

"It is a deed of jealousy and greed. Listen to me very carefully," he paused for a moment to make sure the old grey-haired man understood his urgency. "Do exactly as I ask. Take him to the lake – to the giant flamingos. Let them carry his soul to earth. You must hurry! If he dies, his soul will leave and we shall all be doomed."

Then he pressed the large seal ring on his finger to Egoragh's neck and spoke quietly, "As proof that you are my son, you and all your descendants will carry the beak mark." He bent forward, wiped the hair from his son's forehead and muttered. "You were the chosen and beloved one." He stepped away and waved his hand. "Go now. I will take care of the murderers."

The priest disappeared with Egoragh. Suddenly, evilness enveloped the temple. The kaleidoscope of color from the lead windows turned to black and grey as Darkarh, the god of the Magic World, unleashed his wrath and sorrow on his three remaining sons.

~

The deep frown and worried expression on the tall cloaked figure's face was barely visible in the moonlight as he searched the sky. The black lake seemed eerie, as if the stillness over the water had deepened, with only the silver path of the old moon stretching across its surface. A breeze swirled up. A large crimson-white feather fluttered past the man. His grey hair lifted from his shoulders and blew over his face. He shivered and drew his brown cloak closer, as icy streaks of mist swept over the lake and around him. The priest turned his head towards the horizon, his face flushed with emotion, and whispered, "He is here!"

A loud rumbling came from within the black boiling clouds that had gathered from nowhere and rushed towards him. Vivid blue flashes of lightning lit the heavens and the surrounding mountains.

He scrutinized the shadows trailing soundlessly through the air. The black formless mass passed and briefly veiled the full moon, causing the silver gleam on the lake to vanish. The mysterious shadows seemed to intensify as they drew nearer. Nerves strained to breaking point, Steukhon gazed up with expectation. Recognizing the thousands of huge, ghostly, bird-like shapes descending onto the water, he relaxed. A fleeting smile tucked the corner of his mouth. For several minutes he stood with scrunched, grave-blue eyes fixed on the mass of giant flamingos settling near the edge of the lake.

A cry cut through the night air.

Startled, the giant birds parted like two silver waves, revealing the naked baby that lay next to the water.

Steukhon's first instinct was to rush over to the child. He hesitated when a strong gust of wind blew a bundle of autumn leaves towards him. The leaves swirled, then passed by and danced around the little body. A vague sense of unease surrounded him. He realized that someone, or something evil was close and felt his pulse quicken. He looked back over his shoulder, but missed the half-human, half-animal shape that rose for a split second from the leaves fluttering around the tiny body.

Steukhon turned and moved forward cautiously. He knelt

beside the baby and scanned the little body, urgently seeking
something. When he saw the beak-shaped mark on the side of the
baby's neck, an expression of relief spread over his face and he
whispered reverently, "Your son Egorh has arrived, Darkarh!"

The child was wide-awake and the tiny limbs moved
energetically. The priest noticed how young Egorh clutched a
handful of crimson feathers and said with a smile in his voice,
"You rode the birds tonight as you used to ride your stallion:
bareback, clutching the mane with one hand!" He opened the
little fingers for the wind to snatch the feathers into the darkness
of the night.

Still sensing potential danger, Steukhon looked up and
scoured the nearby area. Satisfied that they were indeed alone,
he whispered to the whimpering baby, "We must hurry away
from here and get you to a safe place."

From his pocket, Steukhon took an amulet set with a large
black onyx and three black diamonds, which he hung around the
baby's neck. He smiled at the bulky jewel on the small body.
He removed his broad purple sash and wrapped the child in it.
A curtain of rain swept across the land. Steukhon looked up and
addressed the dark heavens. "Ah! Darkarh! You are making sure
your son cannot be traced!" Turning his wet face to the baby, he
spoke gently. "Come, we have to get you to your new home."
Steukhon left the lake hurriedly and disappeared into the forest,
cradling the precious purple-wrapped bundle.

Chapter 2

Chamber

The storm raged with full force over the land of Lark. To the north, the range of granite Black Mountains stood high between the vast lake and the land leading to the sea. In the darkness of night, the huge trees bent and swayed like young saplings under the storm's power. Astonishingly, the tempest had no effect on the autumn leaves that swept up the winding road towards the gloomy walls of the fortress, which lay hidden behind the massive Black Mountains. The leaves swirled around the weathered gargoyles that watched from each of the seven bastions. They passed through the entrance and continued down the badly lit passages to disappear through an enormous iron keyhole.

An unpleasant mustiness permeated the room. A long opening carved out near the top of one wall served as the only window in the area. A tattered deep amethyst curtain blew vigorously in the wind. Perched on the ledge, Khan, a black-crested eagle rested, unperturbed by the movement of the curtain and the raging storm. The layers of white droppings down the wall indicated that this ledge had been his residence for a long time.

The sound of thunderous snoring and the rattling of bangles against the large dressing table filled the room. A rustling noise came from the rusted keyhole as the red leaves were blown into the room and on towards a heavy, carved ironwood chest standing in the corner. They danced for a moment, as if pulled by invisible strings, and then disappeared into one of the hundred tiny drawers.

On the dressing table, a little worm-like creature with an enormous eye popped out of a yellow stone bangle that glimmered in the half-lit room. He turned and stared at the dressing table. "Hmmm ... new knowledge! *That's* the drawer that normally holds *important knowledge* from the outer world," he murmured excitedly.

Kep, the keeper of the Chest of Knowledge, was one of four genies, tiny but vicious. They were the helpers of Zinnia the sorceress. Each one lived in its own stone bangle and had only a single talent.

Consumed with curiosity, he swooped down towards the drawer and rubbed his little hands together, thinking to himself that Zinnia had been eagerly awaiting new knowledge from *this* drawer. Looking back over his shoulder towards the source of the loud snoring, Kep pursed his lips and muttered to himself, "I suppose I have to wake that moody old sorceress." He glided through the air to where Zinnia was in a deep slumber on the long, couch-like seat.

Her mass of thick dark reddish hair was spread wildly around her head, covering some of her face. Kep hesitantly called his mistress' name, "Zinnia! Zinnia!" but there was no reaction. He coughed and spoke louder. "Zinnia!" Still no response. "ZINNIA! There is new knowledge!" he eventually shouted.

Unhurriedly, a very long, gold-engraved fingernail pushed just enough hair aside to reveal a stone-cold evil eye that stared up at Kep suspiciously. He inched away to a safe distance, as he knew from past experience of Zinnia's foul mood when she was woken.

"This had better be good," she snarled from under her hair.

"The Knowledge-spirits have brought in new knowledge," Kep quavered.

"So what?" Her green eye glowered.

"They stored it in drawer number 99," Kep added hurriedly.

"What? When?" hollered Zinnia as she leaped up from her couch, which creaked under the sudden movement. She flicked her unruly locks back with both hands, revealing all ten nails.

"This very moment," Kep said more confidently, as he felt on firmer ground.

"Now? You mean, RIGHT NOW?"

"Yes," he nodded.

"Then tell me!" she shouted, trying to grab him.

Kep, expecting this, remained well out of reach. "I need the keys," was all he said.

Zinnia took out a small silk bag, which had been hidden inside her dress. She opened it feverishly and shook out a hundred small brass keys in front of Kep.

"Quick! Find the key! Where is Mem? MEM!" she shouted and another worm-like creature appeared. Mem, a little purple genie from the stone of memory, had one huge eye and three long eyelashes.

"There is new knowledge in drawer 99! Bring it to me!" demanded Zinnia, now fully awake. She pulled a yellow snake from the basket on the floor next to her and with it, tied back her wild, bushy tresses, revealing her face. The snake turned into a golden rope.

Kep flitted to the heap of keys and bent over to sort through them, searching to find the right one. He had two grey

10

hairs on the crown of his head, two wrinkles on his forehead, and was the only one-eyed genie that had two tiny arms with hands. When he found the key, he looked at it and ordered, "Find your knowledge!" He beckoned to Mem to follow him as he drifted towards the chest. The key swayed in front of the many keyholes, then slid into drawer 99 and unlocked it. The drawer sprang open. Kep glided to one side so Mem could peep into it with her big eye. She concentrated very hard. Once she had finished, Kep pushed the drawer back and locked it firmly.

Kep, still consumed by curiosity, whispered to Mem, "What do the autumn leaves do?"

She looked over her shoulder towards Zinnia, then whispered softly, "They catch the world's magical secrets as they travel, store them and bring them here so that I can decipher them for Zinnia. That is how she became so powerful. You know the old saying, 'Knowledge is power'?" Mem gave him a big wink with her long-lashed eye.

"Ahaa ..." replied Kep, savoring this new-found piece of information.

"Come on you two!" shouted Zinnia impatiently. "Stop dawdling. Tell me what you have found."

The two genies turned and floated back to her. Kep busied himself with the heap of keys, which he meticulously started to replace in the small bag, one by one. Mem rolled her eye then eagerly started to tell what she had just memorized. "Well, a child was born. His name is Egorh ... hmmm ... He's the son of Darkarh ... He was left at the lake and he has the mark of a flamingo beak on the side of his neck. A man found him and hung a black diamond and onyx amulet around his neck ... um ... oh yes! ... the child disappeared."

"Darkarh? Darkarh?" Zinnia mused aloud, "There were rumors about him. Something about him giving each of his sons a magical obelisk. Yes, that's it! To one son he gave an orinium obelisk. Yes! *That* was what the wizards talked about for many years. Do you understand what this could mean? With the power of the magical orinium metal in my possession, I could return to Xyltra. I could reclaim my position on the diamond skeleton chair!"

Zinnia stomped up and down, clacking her fingernails together so hard that sparks flew from the gold. "I must find out more. I must go to the Edifice!" she continued excitedly.

"The *Edifice of Secret Knowledge*?" the genies gasped in unison, "It is forbidden! No one is allowed in there."

"Oh, stop being so chicken-hearted," Zinnia snapped at them. "You two, find out about the entrances to the Edifice. I *must* get in." She continued mumbling to herself, "To think that they kicked *me* out! Apparently I was *too evil*. Well, if I can rule the magical world again, I will show them what *real* evil is all about!" She burst into raucous laughter, mirth that did not reach her eyes as she sneered, "They have never experienced, as I have, the intoxication of power!" Her eyes glinted as she imagined herself sitting once again high on the diamond skeleton throne in Xyltra, looking down as the sorceress-hood kneeled, bowed and begged for her forgiveness.

Kep found the key and he and Mem hurriedly sped back to the Chest of Knowledge, where Mem deciphered and memorized the information from another drawer about the entrances to the Edifice.

"Let me get dressed," Zinnia announced. She grabbed her leather belt from the chair and dipped her hand into a fat-bellied glass jar, where a poisonous turquoise-blue arrow frog jumped around. As Zinnia picked up the frog, it croaked indignantly before changing into a buckle. She clipped it to her belt, then tied it around the long burgundy dress that looked bright against her pale skin.

Behind her, Mem pronounced, "The Apse in The Edifice of Secret Knowledge has one small door that can be opened only from the inside. There are a few holes in the rock ceiling through which the golden hummingbirds move when they deliver messages, but Rockface guards these holes."

"Mmm ... the old Rockface contracts and closes the holes when he feels something on the surface." She continued to pace, then remembered. "Rock Venom ... I will have to use Rock

12

Venom!" Zinnia jerked her chamber door open and kicked the chubby red-faced dwarf who sat sleeping there with his pet owl, Hooter.

"Dwarf, call Arkarrah and tell him to meet me outside. We have work to do."

Although still half asleep, Dwarf, Zinnia's servant, grabbed his owl and scuttled away from her as quickly as possible. He knew a second kick would soon be on its way. Zinnia hurried into the room and threw her dark blue cloak around her shoulders, then walked towards three spider webs in the corner of her chamber. She held her hand in front of a spider with a huge yellow Charoite stone for a body. The spider, with its long red hairy legs, slowly crawled onto her hand and changed into a brooch which she used to fasten her cloak.

Zinnia spun round, ready to leave, and stopped. "I almost forgot something VERY important." She rushed over to a box filled with dusty little bottles and started to search through them. "Here we are!" She rubbed the dust off the labels and then read, "Rock Venom" and "Camouflage Serum." She held both bottles up and shouted with glee, "My days of glory will soon be here!" then slipped the bottles into her cloak pocket and left the room, slamming the door hard behind her. In the passageway she paused and shouted, "Come, bird!" Khan, her huge black-crested eagle answered with a loud shriek, then swooped from a high beam to perch on her shoulder. Zinnia disappeared. Outside the fortress the storm roared on without any sign of abating.

Chapter 3

Protector

Sir Matthew Bidault and a score of men were traveling through the vast Granilon forest on their way back to his estate. The Granilon forest curled around the mountains to the north, where it divided the vast hills and the surrounding land from the sea. It was known to host many dangers.

The riders traveled carefully and with great vigilance. The sudden, violent storm had passed and the pounding rain had left the road wet and muddy. Mist lingered in all the hollows and a moldy smell hung in the moist air. Dense fog slowly made its way in ripples and shut out most of the light from their torches. Aware that wolves had been following them for most of the evening, they were silent and uneasy, especially when they occasionally saw the glint of an eye nearby. The horses were nervous and tossed their heads, their nostrils flaring at the scent of danger. Instinctively, they knew that the sweat on their skin made them even more vulnerable.

Suddenly Sir Matthew jerked hard on the reins to stop his horse. In the middle of the road, ahead of them, three wolves stood growling. Alarmed, he leaned forward and peered into the gloominess. Something was lying there. Even at the age of forty, his eyesight was still faultless. He blinked when he saw a bundle of purple cloth next to the road. Suspiciously he reached for his whip and cracked it in the direction of the wolves, sending them scampering into the forest.

"Jake, see what that is," he ordered in a deep voice, pointing to the small heap. "The rest of you, stay alert!" Jake slid from his horse and cautiously moved to the little pile of wet cloth. He reached out hesitantly and slowly pulled the soaked fabric away. Stunned he stared at the tiny scrap of a child, drenched from the rain, then worriedly shouted over his shoulder. "It's a child – still alive!" Jake picked up the wet bundle and brought it over. Sir Matthew stared at the quiet but wide-awake baby, barely visible in the forest night. He scanned the area, wondering where the poor little soul had come from. "Get it to Marion the midwife and instruct her to take care of it," he ordered before spurring his horse into a trot. Jake mounted with the bundle and the rest followed without a word.

Sir Matthew's expression was troubled as he rode, deep in thought. Although he hardly ever smiled, he was a likable man who commanded respect from everyone who knew him. As a noble, he had a reputation for kindness and his judgments were always fair and honest. What on earth could drive a mother to abandon her young in a wolf-infested forest? He mused worriedly. "Did she know that I would be passing by?"

His mind drifted back for a fleeting moment to the frightful time when a plague had swept through the land and he had lost his own beloved wife and only son to its ravages. The memory of that time was still excruciatingly painful for him and he shook his head as if to rid himself of these feelings. As he pressed on through the dark forest, he was so deeply distracted that he missed the signpost, 'Welcome to

Old Falcon Place', which indicated the beginning of his large estate.

Once they arrived at the impressive house, Sir Matthew dismounted and took a decision. He turned to Jake. "I have changed my mind – bring the child into the house and warm it next to the fire. Call Joseph to bring something dry to wrap it in, then fetch the midwife." He walked up the stairs and pushed open the huge front door to allow Jake to pass. As he entered the hall, Sir Matthew was embraced by the warmth and familiar smell of his home. He relaxed his shoulders. It was good to be home after such a long, wet journey, he thought.

Sir Matthew was of medium build, graceful, with short dark-brown hair that had started to recede slightly at the sides of his forehead. He wore a neatly trimmed beard. The lines carved into his face reflected his strong character. He took a deep breath before he started up the solid, lavishly carved staircase, as he too was in need of dry clothes. Joseph would have to deal with this situation. He had always been a pillar of strength when it came to running the house. He would be the best one to care for the child till other plans were made, Sir Matthew thought as he disappeared into his bedroom.

~

A few hours later, Sir Matthew entered the richly furnished room and saw the crib next to the fireplace. He walked over and gazed at the infant, who was now warm, well fed and fast asleep. The memory of his own son brought a pang of emotion which he struggled to suppress. The only evidence of this was the sudden slight moisture that came into his eyes. The feeling of loss after so many years was still painfully strong. Looking closer at the sleeping child, he noticed a huge amulet around the tiny neck. Intrigued, he took it carefully in his hand to admire, but a movement from the window made him swing in that direction. A tall robed figure stood there. Sir Matthew tried to show no surprise as he held the outsider's gaze. How long the stern, grave-blue eyes had been watching him, silently evaluating him, he didn't know.

Around the stranger's neck dangled a large crystal. He was touching a big pearl ring. With a steely voice Sir Matthew said, "You came into my house unannounced?"

The robed man deliberated for a moment and his eyes swept the softly lit room, before they came to rest on the crib. "Do not be alarmed," the stranger finally spoke. "I am here because of the child."

Sir Matthew raised an enquiring eyebrow. "Are you coming to claim this baby that I found in the forest? A helpless infant – abandoned and about to be eaten by wolves? Who are you?"

The intruder's voice sounded deep and sure as he began to speak "I am Steukhon, high priest from the boy's past. For reasons yet unexplained, I cannot risk being seen around him. The wolves were temporarily in my service and would not have hurt the child. They were there to prevent others from harming him and I had been watching from nearby," he replied calmly.

Sir Matthew hesitated a moment before speaking again in a voice clothed with authority. "As the master of this house and you the trespasser here, I think an explanation is called for."

Steukhon took a deep breath, stepped closer to the crib and the crackling flames in the fireplace. Sir Matthew saw that his long robe was made of a fine, expensive grayish cloth. There was a long pause before he spoke. "You are a noble with many people in your care. You have shown compassion to the less fortunate and governed the land with fairness. The people who know you also recognize that you stand for truth and honor. More importantly, the gods have noticed all this." Steukhon paused.

"What has this to do with the abandoned young one?" Sir Matthew enquired, although somehow he knew something was to be asked of him.

"I am here to ask you to become the boy's father," Steukhon answered quietly.

"I cannot do that! I live alone ... I have no wife," he

protested and began to pace the floor. "No, it's impossible," he reiterated. "Tomorrow I will arrange for him to be taken to the monastery orphanage. That's the best I can do. He cannot stay here."

Steukhon watched as a range of emotions played on Sir Matthew's face and waited patiently before continuing. "This is no ordinary young one. Did you see the piece of jewelry around his neck? If abandoned, would he have been left with such a valuable bauble?"

"No – but how is any of this my business?"

Steukhon decided to speak plainly. "Just as he has a destiny, so have you. You have been chosen to be his protector. It is a great honor that is being offered to you."

Sir Matthew thought back to the feelings that had clutched at his heart just a few minutes earlier, when he'd gazed at the baby. It was undeniable that there was something special about the infant, and he felt a tenderness tugging at his chest. Steukhon waited quietly for him to regain his composure.

"I think you'd better tell me the whole story," Sir Matthew said finally.

Steukhon's eyes flickered hesitantly for a moment, and then he seemed to reach a decision. "Very well then. I shall tell you what you need to know. I knew his father, Darkarh. I was there when the child was given his name. However strange this may sound, I am asking you to trust me, for what I am about to tell you is all true. The child comes from another world, an ancient magical kingdom, unknown to earth."

"Magical?" Sir Matthew interrupted.

"Let me finish," Steukhon replied. He began to pace the floor. His voice was thoughtful as if his mind was somewhere else. "I can only tell you that which is of importance right now. Your open-mindedness and interest in the unknown will help you to understand." Steukhon turned back to the bundle and continued, "He was one of quadruplet-sons and his mother died giving birth to them.

"Darkarh loved his firstborn the most, because of his

gentle nature. He named him Egorhagh." Steukhon looked at the crib for a moment then continued, "As the sons grew older, Egorhagh's three brothers saw that their father favored him and they became increasingly jealous and greedy. Darkarh learned that his brothers were planning to kill Egorhagh. When he stumbled onto the scene, it was too late. To save Egorhagh's spirit, he sent it to earth to be reborn as a mortal at a specific time. He renamed him Egorh.

"How he came to earth is not important now. Darkarh made sure Egorhagh would never be found. Only I know the place, year and time of his birth. Egorhagh, his dearly loved son, was given the *mark of the beak,* to prove to all that he was the son of the god Darkarh."

"And this is the boy?" Sir Matthew asked with curiosity despite his confusion.

"Yes," replied Steukhon. Gently he turned the baby's neck to show the mark. "The danger is, he possesses an inherited magical metal that wizards, sorceresses, witches, in fact all in the magical world, want. They can never find it and they must be stopped at all costs. Only Egorhagh can do that."

"But he is just a baby," Sir Matthew protested.

"Yes, and you must know there is a great evil seeking him. Darkarh instructed me to give him this amulet for his protection. The black onyx and the black diamonds make him undetectable. There will come a time when his strength will outweigh that of the amulet. When that day arrives, he will be ready to fulfill his destiny. Until then he needs the guardianship and care of someone of your character."

Steukhon studied Sir Matthew's face for a while and said softly, "You have been chosen for this task ... to be his mortal father. If you are willing to do this, you must make sure that he is never without the amulet. Will you do this?"

Sir Matthew was overwhelmed by all he had heard but somehow he knew that he would accept this strange challenge to protect the young one and raise him as his own son. He nodded wordlessly.

"May I?" Steukhon suddenly asked, breaking his reverie and pointing to a pen and some paper on the desk standing in the corner.

Puzzled, Sir Matthew nodded and added, "Help yourself."

Steukhon scribbled a few lines on the piece of paper and rolled it up tightly. From his pocket he pulled out four golden hummingbirds, which hovered in front of him. He offered the scroll to them. One of the birds fluttered nearer and grasped it with tiny claws. "Take this to the Edifice and give it to Jerome to file in the secret book," he instructed the birds, then walked over to open the window to let them out. As they flew off he called after them, "Remember to take turns carrying the scroll!" He walked back to Sir Matthew and said, "I must leave now. I cannot be seen around Darkarh's son – our enemies are the same."

There was a sudden intensity in Steukhon's eyes and a chill in his voice as he continued, "If he does not grow up and fulfill his destiny, your world and mine will be ruled by evil. You must do everything in your power to be a father to him, protect him and let him grow up with love and security, to be the man his destiny demands him to be."

Sir Matthew, overawed, could only muster a whisper, "Why me?"

"Some lives are worth taking note of. They are documented so that others, if they choose, can learn from them or live by their example. Yours is such a life. Apart from being the fine man I know you to be, the gods and I also know of the void in your heart, left by your own son's death. My deepest hope is that you will allow this child to fill that emptiness and that you can give him the upbringing and love that is necessary for such a chosen mortal."

Steukhon noticed his purple sash drying on the chair close to the fire. He reached for it, tied it back around his waist and calmly said, "I must take my leave of you, but there is one last thing – Egorh will also have magical protectors: Dryads from the forest and mermaids from the sea." With a slight grin he nodded, "Anything else you would like to know, you will have to ask the gods yourself." He touched the large pearly ring on his finger and vanished.

Hearing a noise from the crib, Sir Matthew turned towards it and was surprised to find huge hazel-brown eyes staring at him. He bent down and took one little hand in his, feeling the tiny fingers gripping his firmly. He felt a tightening in his chest and the corners of his mouth turned up into a gentle smile. With a hushed voice he said, "Egorh, son of Darkarh, it looks as though the gods have decided. Welcome to my home, my son."

Intrigued and overwhelmed at the strange responsibility, he sat down beside the crib, deep in thought, wondering what the future would bring their way. He watched the little boy until he fell asleep, oblivious to the storm that once more roared in full fury. Sir Matthew stayed like that until the last of the logs in the fireplace had turned to ash.

Chapter 4

Edifice

The massive black granite cliffs looked like molten rock that had spilled over the rim of a giant cup, plunging straight down and disappearing into a valley of mist. The mist broke up sporadically, as if stirred by a gigantic spoon. Many shades of green forest could be seen. No birds had ever managed to perch on these smooth cliffs, although countless had tried through the aeons. Heaps of broken bird skeletons, piled up at the base of the cliff bore testimony to their failure. Millions of tiny vertical grooves pitted the rock's surface.

Over the ages this mountain had been given names such as, The Mountain of All Beginnings, The Vault of All Knowledge, but its true name was The Edifice of Secret Knowledge. Nobody could enter the Edifice uninvited and all its knowledge had to remain protected there. Should the unthinkable happen and a secret be stolen, any knowledge, once outside the

Edifice, would be immediately forgotten. This was The Law of the Edifice.

The Edifice of Secret Knowledge consisted of a small central chamber with a colossal hall on one side and a massive semi circular Apse on the other. Inside the colossal hall, conspicuous rows of huge round holes in the wall looked like living, breathing beings, as they expanded and contracted rhythmically. These were the origins of all metal ores such as gold, platinum, copper, iron and many stranger metals. It was from here that wealth was poured onto the earth. One cavity was not breathing. From this hole a mysterious white mist gushed up and a soft, deep, hollow sound could be heard. It was the empty hole of the orinium ore. The chamber of pulsating ores was such a magnificent and overwhelming sight, that it was rumored in the magical world that any intruders who saw the source of ores would be overcome and struck dumb for the rest of their lives.

In the Apse the walls were obscured entirely by solid floor to ceiling wooden bookshelves. Each shelf was crammed with thousands of volumes, some very old, some new. A vague, almost imperceptible mustiness lingered around the books. Intricately carved Wood-heads positioned on each shelf corner assisted in the mission to guard and protect the secret knowledge. These thousands of Wood-heads, with their gargoyle-like appearance, constantly rolled their huge eyes in all directions and sniffed the air for possible intruders.

A long, elaborately carved oak desk stood in the center of the dim and shadowy Apse. Next to the big oil lamp on the desk stood a row of nine old and strangely shaped bottles. On top, black silkworms were spinning diligently on the intricate shapes that were attached to each bottle.

"Have to be careful," muttered Jerome, who stooped over a large and very old recorded work that lay open on the desk. He was the Edifice's ancient gnome, as old as time itself. He was a peculiar character, with a grey ponytail on the top of his head. His long beard had two plaits with gold beads on either side. A large round gold earring dangled from his ear and his eyes were grey as moonlight mist. With shaky hands he carefully opened the scroll he had just received from the hummingbirds and began to pour the new knowledge into the book. His old eyes became watery with concentration as he watched the last word fall onto the page. Jerome sighed with relief and muttered, "Done! This is *very* important knowledge. Can't risk leaving *that* lying around." He closed the hard cover and ran his crooked old finger over the large embossed symbol. The shape of a flamingo head with a large beak was barely visible on the front of the cracked old leather cover. Underneath this mysterious symbol, the words *Sons of Darkarh* had been burned into it.

Jerome picked up the book and looked at the very long narrow ladder that stood against the shelves. I have to get up there with this work now, he thought resignedly, and sighed. It was a long way up for an ancient gnome, but duty was duty and the filing of such an important book had to be done meticulously. Jerome took his work very seriously and couldn't chance this task to magic.

For an instant the silkworms distracted him and he fumbled in his pocket for an enormous magnifying glass. He held it closely in front of his left eye and started to move slowly down the row of bottles, carefully inspecting the elaborate work of each worm. At the blue-green bottle he stopped and said angrily, "You are taking shortcuts again, Alfred. You are one of the most talented, but you are surely the laziest. I cannot use that bookmark if you spin it so sloppily! You have to spin every detail." Jerome removed the silk piece from under the worm, his face very close to it. He poked him with his short finger and said. "Now get it right this time, Alfred." He continued to inspect the other worms' work, grumbling and mumbling here and there. "It must be perfect ... Well done! You are behind schedule ... hmmm."

Satisfied, Jerome took a deep breath, clutched the book under his arm, gave his back a last rub and was about to clamber up the ladder when he heard cries of, "Scarab! Scarab!"

He swung around and shouted back, "What? ... Where are you situated? Give me your number, Wood-head!"

"Three thousand and fifty-two. Scarab – one with red eyes! Quick!"

Each Wood-head had a number and they had to guard the books to their left and right. When trouble was detected, they would spring to life and shout their numbers.

"Another break-in! It is the third time in such a short while. First the two silver moths now this beetle ... hmmm ... The same area again." Jerome's face creased and he tilted his head towards the rock ceiling. He saw that Rockface was sound asleep. His granite lips, nose and eyes dangled loose in the air.

I have no time for him now, Jerome thought with exasperation. He placed the book he had been carrying on a nearby shelf and dashed across the shiny floors, looking left and right, as he called up, "Three thousand and fifty-two?"

"Yes, up here, on this shelf. Three thousand and fifty-one also saw it."

Jerome stopped and rubbed his earring thoughtfully as he looked up, "Yes, it's just as I guessed. It's in the same section as before. Thank goodness for Wood-heads. It's impossible to guard all of the Apse's knowledge by myself." Following his exertions, he readjusted the broad leather belt around his waist. A wand, a big key and some tools protruded from a leather pouch that dangled from it. He grunted as he started to climb the long narrow ladder to find the intruder. "We know you are here," he called. His short ponytail bobbed on the crown of his head as he scanned feverishly between the books. "I know some wizard or witch has sent you to try to steal some knowledge, but you cannot, for I am the Guardian of the Secret Knowledge," he muttered.

"Aha! Wretched bug!" he blurted as he finally spotted the miscreant. The beetle skittered away and tried to hide behind another book but Jerome swiped it with one movement of his cupped hand. Dust swirled up from the shelf into his face and nostrils, causing him to sneeze violently. The long ladder started to swing from side to side like a giant pendulum and Jerome nearly lost his balance. He scrabbled for a hold on the shelf and just in time, grabbed it to stabilize himself. He peered down and sighed with relief. "Darn, *that* was close," he mumbled, "That floor seems horribly far away today."

The swipe had sent the scarab tumbling. It landed on its back on an old brown book on a lower shelf. Jerome started to clamber down the ladder to intercept the intruder. This time he swept the insect off the book, sending it down to the floor in a burst of dust. Concentrating hard on getting to the scarab, Jerome and his helpers did not notice the long snake, covered in camouflage serum that glided swiftly down from the ceiling holes, taking on the color and shape of everything it passed. The snake made its way silently and stealthily out of the Apse towards the tiny door of the middle chamber, and then disappeared through the keyhole.

"Game over," puffed Jerome, as he reached the floor and trapped the beetle. His attention snapped to the granite ceiling as he heard buzzing, whistling sounds. He looked up and thought, what are the birds up to now?

In the far reaches of the Apse, ten tiny holes, just big enough for the hummingbirds to pass through, allowed trickles of light into the Edifice. By this light a multitude of small golden birds vibrated their wings so fast that they became a haze, and their tiny bodies seemed suspended, wingless in air. As the light kissed their golden plumage, it was reflected, creating long golden rays of sunshine in the top of the Apse. These little birds were Jerome's messengers and he sent them to all the Worlds.

His face clouded with anger as he remembered Rockface. "You were sleeping again!" he barked up at the granite ceiling, "You are supposed to contract and close the holes at the sign of intruders!" A flat face appeared out of the granite and spoke, "I know, but there is something strange happening to me. It is as if my molecules are separating and a relaxing feeling is spreading across my surface. I cannot help falling asleep."

Jerome frowned and pulled on one of his beard plaits,

"This is very strange – a major problem I suspect. I shall have to seek advice immediately."

He took a brief look at the many narrow ladders resting against the bookshelves. "Well, I think I have everything under control for now. I must get that book back on the shelf." He turned and froze, the hair on his neck bristling. From nowhere, an alluring but evil-looking woman, wearing a long burgundy dress had appeared. A tall man followed, as she moved through the arch of the middle chamber into the Apse where Jerome stood. On her shoulder perched a black-crested eagle with peculiar-looking green eyes. Her wild hair was tied back with a golden rope and a huge spider brooch was pinned to her cloak. Jerome gaped at her. This can only mean trouble and danger, he thought!

The bird on her shoulder squawked, almost as if announcing their arrival. The woman's stone-cold green eyes matched the bird's. She stared at the gnome for a moment. Jerome shuddered and wondered which eyes were the worst, hers or those of the feathered creature. She had the longest golden-engraved fingernails he had ever seen and bangles of emerald green, ruby red and amethyst adorned her upper arm.

He shot a glance at the trapped scarab and wondered. Odd! First Rockface, then the beetle, now this woman ... What's happening here?

Chapter 5

Intruders

Jerome began to rage frantically, "Get out! Get out! What are you doing here? This place is forbidden. No one is allowed to enter the Edifice uninvited!" He waved his arms as he tried to drive the trespassers back from where they had come. The woman ignored him and scanned the area with huge concentration, then snapped, "Where is it?"

Without flinching, he retorted, "Where is what?"

"Where is the ore of orinium?"

Jerome ignored the question and resumed his shouting. "Get out! You cannot come in here, it is forbidden!" When he saw that she had no intention of leaving, he grabbed the wand from the pouch on his leather belt and cast a huge dome-like birdcage over the two intruders. Trapped, the bird on the woman's shoulder fluttered and then craned its neck to study the cage. Agitated, but nonetheless amused, she started to thrum loudly on the iron with one of her engraved nails. Good, thought Jerome. I have managed to rattle *her* cage.

She drew a long breath and hissed. "Do you know who I am?"

Hands on his hips, feeling a bit more secure now that he had trapped them, he replied, "No, but you have no business here and I can sense that you are evil. How did you get in?"

She glanced at the scarab still wriggling on its back and gave a sarcastic chortle. "Now then, nothing like a little Rock Venom to make a Rockface fall asleep, is there?" She started to inch her way around the cage as if searching the room for something, then turned to Jerome and repeated in an imperious tone, "Do you know who I am?"

"No. Should I?"

"I am Zinnia."

Jerome swallowed hard when he heard her name and thought, the sorceress! Many rumors were attached to that name – bad ones! He tried to keep a blank face. He was not going to allow her to know he felt intimidated. He spread his leather-booted feet firmly on the ground and replied, "You are breaking the Law of the Edifice."

She ignored him and continued to amble around the inside of the bars. She paused and gave Jerome a black look, while stroking her long gold nails, "Dwarf, do you know the power of *Emorph-z*?" she smirked.

"Should I?"

Zinnia scraped the iron with her nail. The sound rippled in waves through the Edifice, and intoned, "From iron to ashes!" In an instant the metal enclosure tumbled to cinders on the floor, leaving plumes of black dust hanging in the air.

Jerome's face fell. He had knowledge of this power, but had never witnessed it. Totally awestruck, he goggled at the pile of ash.

"Now let's get back to where we were. Where is the orinium ore?" the sorceress demanded again, only this time it sounded like a serious threat. She lifted her dress and stepped over the heap of ash around her and moved towards Jerome.

He took a few steps back. "All the orinium has been harvested ... long ago ... during the *Wizard Wars*. There isn't any here. The hole is empty," he blurted.

She bent down and hissed in a low voice, her face a few inches from his. "Those are rumors, but is it the TRUTH, dwarf?" Jerome did not flinch. She swung around and looked at the stacks of shelves holding the thousands of books, "I ..." she began, but stopped as she remembered Arkarrah standing behind her. Without blinking in his direction she waved her hand and said, "Oh, this is Arkarrah, my associate."

Jerome shifted his gaze to the man standing motionless behind her, only his beady black eyes moving. Fastened at the back, his straight, black hair was oiled flat onto his head. He acknowledged Jerome with a sneer and a nod.

"We are also here for another reason. We want information on the *past* of a certain family," Zinnia continued.

Still holding his ground, Jerome growled, "Then as a witch, YOU should know that all the knowledge in the Edifice is forbidden to outsiders like you. That's why it's named The Edifice of Secret Knowledge."

"I am *not* a witch," she spat. "I am a sorceress."

Suddenly, Khan flew from her shoulder to where the beetle was lying, snatched it from the floor and gulped it down. He fluttered up, landed on a shelf just above the big book Jerome had left there earlier, and wiped his beak.

"Ah yes, I remember, you are also the keeper of the Edifice," she scoffed.

"No! No! I am the *guardian* of the Edifice and I am a GNOME, not a dwarf!" Jerome corrected her with as much dignity as he could muster. After all, it was an honor to be the guardian of The Edifice of Secret Knowledge.

Zinnia arched her brows in mock astonishment and continued in a sarcastic tone, "If you are the guaaar...dian, I, that is, WE, need your help. We, have to find one particular book amongst all these millions." She leaned forward and smiled at Jerome menacingly then glanced at Arkarrah, "Or do we have to persuade you to help us?"

Jerome, sensing her meaning, did not utter a word. His throat felt very dry as he watched her cock her head and begin to read the titles of the books, gliding a long golden fingernail over the spines, while she waited for his answer.

When she stopped, Jerome knew this meant trouble and he held his breath. She retraced a few steps and hesitated at the leather cover with the embossed emblem, which was lying flat on the shelf where Jerome had left it.

He watched helplessly and felt increasingly frantic. "Rats!" he cursed silently, "I should have replaced it without delay ..."

Zinnia dripped with glee when she saw the book. She was about to pick it up but Jerome was quicker. He waved his wand at it and whisked it up into the air just before the sorceress could get hold of it. She stared at the floating book and realized that Jerome was not going to give up that easily.

She confronted him, the corners of her mouth dropping and her cruel gaze boring into the gnome. She hissed angrily. "So this is how it's going to be?"

"You cannot have the writing!" the gnome asserted with more courage than he felt.

She cackled, pointed and mumbled something which Jerome thought must be sorceress language. The book dropped a few feet from where it was hovering and then started to float towards her.

Again Jerome intercepted, this time moving the book further away from her fuming face. A tug of war began, which sent the volume reeling back and forth between them.

"Enough!" Jerome commanded and spun the book up towards the hovering hummingbirds. "Shield!" he yelled. In the wink of an eye, the birds swarmed forward and concealed the book, forming a golden shield-shaped ball all around it, desperately trying to lift it towards the ceiling and out of danger.

Furious, she threw a bolt of electric-red current towards the ball of birds, but they whizzed out of the way and the blast hit Rockface, almost causing his eyeballs to drop out of the rock. Again she tried to strike the golden bubble, but the birds managed to dodge once more.

Without warning, she threw two currents simultaneously. The birds avoided one bolt but rammed into the other. As the current hit with full force, the shield collapsed and the birds were thrown in all directions like golden sparks. Jerome, horrified, saw how the book came tumbling down, trailed by tiny dead golden bodies. Zinnia stormed forward to grab it but Jerome whisked it away just in time. With a single forceful movement of her hand, she then tossed Jerome across the chamber. He landed against the wall gasping.

"Not so fast, little *deformy*," Zinnia hissed.

"You cannot have it," Jerome rasped, fighting for breath. "It does not belong to you," he groaned desperately, his cheeks turning dark purple in anguish, then blurted, "Heads return to your beginning and protect!"

In a flash the gloomy wooden carved heads on each corner of the shelves tumbled down and collected into one massive ball of wood that turned into a huge tree, thousands of years old. The branches grew, spread out and collected all the volumes, including the *Book of Records*. As the branches touched them, they merged and became part of the old tree, leaving only empty walls.

Stumped, she watched as the many books and shelves disappeared. With a hideous sneer she cackled, "Clever dwarf! – but you underestimate me!" She twirled her hand six times to the right, then six times to the left and shouted, "Beginning, give me your end result!" This time Jerome watched in horror as the gigantic tree began to disintegrate and the shelves moved back onto the walls, followed by the books and the wooden heads. Before he could react, Zinnia snatched the book and hurriedly grabbed Mem, the amethyst bangle, off her arm and held it in front of the book. "Mem! MEM!" she shouted fiercely.

The purple creature wiggled herself out of the bangle and when she saw the ocean of knowledge in the chamber, her face sparkled and her eyeball grew larger.

"Mem, concentrate and look at this!" Zinnia demanded. "Look at the mark on the leather cover. Is this the same flamingo beak-symbol the leaves filed in drawer number 99?" Her excitement mounted.

Mem concentrated hard, and then gave a big wink. "Yes ... yes, it's the same."

She grabbed the book with both hands, her nostrils flaring with exhilaration. "I cannot believe my luck! Chance is on MY side for a change," the sorceress gloated.

Arkarrah, who'd been watching wordlessly, now moved closer, "Do you mean it's THE book, the one we came for?"

"Yes, yes! Look!" and she pointed at the title, *Sons of Darkarh.* "We have work to do," the sorceress continued.

Jerome had by this time dragged himself up from the floor. He waddled painfully over to Zinnia, planted himself in front of her and demanded, "Give it to me!"

She laughed scornfully. Realizing her indifference, Jerome pointed a gnarled finger to the shelves and dictated, "All between five thousand and eight thousand, come down NOW!" In a bat's eye, three thousand books came tumbling down from the shelves onto Zinnia and Arkarrah. The volume she had been holding slipped from her hand as she tried to cover her head. It skidded in between the tons that came tumbling to the floor. Jerome twirled his wand and ordered, "All between five thousand and eight thousand, return to your shelves!" The books collected themselves, floated in a huge pile and swooped away back onto the shelves. There was no way of finding the leather-covered work among the rows of volumes. From where Zinnia stood all the books looked the same.

Furious, she removed the golden rope from her hair and shrieked, "Tie him up!" She swung the cord to where the gnome stood. It spun around Jerome's body, tied itself into a knot and turned into a snake. Jerome looked helplessly at the reptile's flickering tongue not far from his face.

Zinnia flung the purple and yellow genie-bangles in the direction of the shelves and shouted, "Find the one with the flamingo beak-symbol!" Mem and Kep started to float up and down, left and right in front of the shelves, searching.

"Intruder! Worm!" a voice called from a shelf.

Mem skimmed over to the wooden face, lingered in front of it, her big eye rolling and hissed, "Not a worm – a genie. Be quiet or you will have your wooden skull split open!" Jerome's helper kept silent.

"Got it!" shouted Kep, hovering higher up.

"Brilliant," Zinnia yelled from below and held her hand out for the book, followed by the two genies. She took it and walked over to the long desk, where she sat down and cleared half the table with the back of her hand. She placed the two bangles close and the genies hovered patiently nearby, should she need them again. Without looking up, she ordered Arkarrah, "Go and see if the orinium ore is empty while I catch up on my reading. We must make sure the dwarf is telling the truth." Lost in the pages, Zinnia did not see or hear anything as she flipped rapidly, hungry to absorb everything. Her gold nail dragged over the words from left to right as she read. Bit by bit a look of excitement crept over her face.

Arkarrah ambled towards the chamber of ores, pulling his long brown cloak closer over his shoulders. He recalled the legend of *being struck dumb* should you sight the source of any of the metal ores, but his greed and curiosity pushed him on. He peeked around the corner, reluctantly and carefully, but when he saw the breathtaking holes, he snapped his head back behind the wall. Frozen with fear, he tried to swallow, his mouth suddenly felt very dry. A shriek and a movement from underneath his cloak startled him. He heaved a sigh of relief when he realized it was only Horris, his inquisitive pet bat. Annoyed, he pushed the ugly creature back inside. Cautiously he opened his mouth and blared, "Aaaaah ... Aaaah ..." to make sure he still had his voice.

Satisfied that his vocal cords were intact, he peeped around again into the huge chamber mesmerized by the holes that breathed and throbbed. His eyes gleamed when he saw the pulsing gold ore that Zinnia had promised him. He was about to investigate further when a hollow, mournful sound from further down towards the end of the chamber, numbed him. Remembering the legend he shuddered, "That's enough. I have seen all I want," and hustled back to where Zinnia was reading at the desk.

She jumped up when she saw Arkarrah. "I have found the information. I can rule at last!" she crowed. "The orinium obelisk exists! With my power I will be able to capture the magic metal. I will reclaim the skeleton chair of the Xyltra sorceress-hood. I will have every sorcerer, wizard, witch and high priest at my feet, everything will belong to ME!"

Arkarrah forced a cynical smile and ran the palm of his hand nervously over his flat oily hair.

"But first things first." Zinnia marched back and forth. "We must find the male that carries the beak mark. According to the records, he is the only one who can stop me. First I have to make a deal with the Haffgoss brothers and trade the obelisk for their resurrection from the Hap*Less* *S*phere."

"The Haffgoss?" Arkarrah asked.

"Yes, they are Darkarh's half-god sons. Secondly, I need thirty-thousand contented and willing humans, as well as thirty-thousand giant flamingos, for my plan to succeed!"

"Thirty-THOUSAND willing humans?" Arkarrah echoed incredulously.

"Yes, humans, that's the easy part. You should know, being a slave-monger yourself. The willing, we shall have to work on." She thought for a moment. "Maybe Iy can tell us where the beak-marked human might be." She took the emerald green bangle off her top arm, held it in the palm of her hand and called, "Iy!" but nothing happened. "Iy!" she tried again with a sharp note in her voice. Still nothing happened. She tapped her foot impatiently on the floor. "Iy! Iy!" she called again, even more harshly.

This time another worm-like creature, with a large head and one big dark green eye, became visible in the circle of the bangle. "What took you so long?" Zinnia snapped.

"My apology," Iy spoke in a weary, throaty voice, winking his big eye. "I was just looking."

"That is what you are supposed to do, you idiot." She took a swipe at him but Iy just floated out of the way. "You are the stone of sight. You must find the male with the beak mark. Look, here!" She showed Iy the symbol on the cover of the book. "You have to start working very hard. Search around every lake, forest and mansion, house or hole. I WANT THIS CHILD!"

Iy swayed and repeated, "Beak mark? Beak mark?" Squinting, he pursed his tiny lips together, moving his eye in all directions.

Zinnia leaned forward, waiting in anticipation.

Iy scanned in all directions, then winked and said, "I see nothing."

"Well, remember the mark and keep trying. It is important that you find him." She hid her disappointment and turned to Mem. "Come here. This is where we beat the system. As the stone-genie of memory, you are the only one able to memorize the information and to keep the knowledge once it's outside the Edifice. Make sure that you *do* remember everything!"

Mem started to sway on the pages, enjoying every moment. After a few minutes she had finished memorizing the new knowledge and winked her completion at Zinnia. Jerome had managed to waddle towards Zinnia, ignoring the hissing snake still tied around him. He raged, "If you take the book away, it will disintegrate. It's the rule of the Edifice!"

"I know the rules, dwarf. Maybe you're right or maybe you're wrong."

Jerome did not doubt the fierce intelligence that lurked in those spiteful green eyes and started to protest again but Zinnia cracked, "Oh, take your precious book!" and she flung it hard towards Jerome, hitting him in the stomach. He went soaring across the room, bumped his head against the wall and slid to the floor. The book fell at his feet and before darkness overtook him, he whispered, "Steukhon, you must come quickly."

"Let's go back, Arkarrah," she ordered. "I have work to do. I shall need to find the Sorrow-queen."

Arkarrah pulled a face and asked, "The Sorrow-queen? What's she got do with all this?"

"I will need her for my plan. I will explain later. Come!" She picked up the bangles and waited for the genies to disappear inside them, but Mem continued to sway around, rolling her big eye at the magnitude of information. "No, no," Zinnia protested, "you cannot read all these now. We have work to do." The little creature's mouth drooped into a sulk.

"We will come back, Mem. One of these days I will have control over all of this!" she reassured the little creature. She pushed Mem into the bangle and clipped it back on her top arm. Zinnia commanded the snake, "Unwind!"

The snake immediately freed itself, shot to her outstretched hand and turned back into a rope. She tied her unruly hair, spun around and disappeared with Arkarrah the same way in which they had come.

Chapter 6

The Message

The only light in the immense cave came from the tall candle on the large stone table. Steukhon, hunched over, was writing in an old book. He raised his head and brushed his grey curly hair away from his broad shoulders. He turned sideways and dropped the feather pen onto the page. Was that the gnome I heard calling from the Edifice, all the way here, to the land of Lark? He leaned back in his chair and absentmindedly rubbed the crystal that hung around his neck. It was an impressive piece, faceted into 29 angles, with a white light that radiated from deep within the heart of the stone.

On the opposite side of the table lay a golden-brown dog that was instantly awake and alert at the sound of Steukhon's voice. Its long ears were covered with blond satin curls and made the creature exceptionally beautiful.

"This is trouble. This is out of the ordinary. I must go

right away. Maximus, you know your duty," Steukhon muttered in alarm.

Maximus rose, stretched and moved to the book, where he curled up, his long ears covering everything that was written. A soft golden nimbus appeared and surrounded his whole body. Steukhon knew that there was no one alive who was strong enough to dislodge Maximus from his written work. It would be safe. The priest closed his eyes, touched the big pearly ring on his finger and vanished.

~

Hardly had Zinnia and Arkarrah left the Edifice when Steukhon appeared, still touching his ring. "Gnome, did you summon me?" he asked with his deep voice, but there was no answer. He looked around and called, "JEROME!" wondering where the gnome could be. He saw the ash and frowned, then noticed Jerome lying on the floor.

Rushing over, he shook him by the shoulders and asked, "Gnome, what happened here? Is the *Book of Records* in trouble? What happened?" Jerome slowly regained consciousness and opened one eye. When he saw Steukhon he struggled to his feet and shook his head to clear it, causing the gold beads in his beard-plaits to tinkle. He began to wave his arms and the words tumbled from him in a rush, "The ...the ... sorceress Zinnia was here," he managed and pointed to the book on the floor. "She r...r...read it. I could not s...s...stop her. She is v...very powerful."

"Slowly now, slowly. Take a deep breath and start again," calmed Steukhon.

Jerome gasped and went on, "She is l...looking for orinium and somebody with a b...beak mark," he stuttered.

Steukhon picked up the book and paged through it to

see if anything had been taken. "Hmmm," he said thoughtfully and fixed his gaze on Jerome. "That is what I was afraid of. She probably knows now what happened to Darkarh and his Haffgoss sons. She read about the laws that can reinstate them, so she must also have read about the orinium obelisk. This is a frightening situation. Ever since she was banished from Xyltra, she has accumulated power in the hopes of taking back her place on the skeleton throne. With orinium in her possession she will be able to do that."

"How do you know this?" Jerome asked.

"I am the priest who wrote the *Book of Records*." A slight frown came to his face as he looked around, "How did she get in here?"

"I had just finished pouring the new knowledge you sent me into the book and was about to replace it on the shelf, when one of my heads spotted a scarab intruder. I placed the book nearby, then sought to get rid of the insect. The next moment they seemed to have appeared as if from nowhere. I insisted they leave but she ignored me, so I cast the birdcage over them. She mentioned something about having a power, e...*emorph-z*, something like that ... I can't remember. She destroyed the cage," Jerome snapped his fingers, "just like that!"

Steukhon rubbed his chin, "You say 'they'? She was not alone?"

"No, there was a man with her. She called him Arkarrah." He was struggling with his words and still very upset. "Maybe they picked my lock," he fretted. "I have to make a new lock immediately."

I wonder what devilish plot she is hatching, Steukhon thought and a shadow of uneasiness came into his eyes. She was clever. She used the stone genies to steal the knowledge. They do not fall under the same rules of the Edifice. "Jerome we must act," he said decisively. "In the forest, the rainbow maidens congregate once a month. Find them and let them pass a message to the two larger Dryads, Mirk and Kirk, who live in the backwoods. They are the fastest of the Dryads. They always travel together with their bulldog ... I mean Bull*frog*. Instruct the maidens to tell the Dryads to locate the boy with the beak mark. They will find him at Old Falcon Place. The Dryads must follow and protect him, from this day on until the time comes. If anything out of the ordinary happens to him, they must let me know without delay." Steukhon thought a little longer, then added. "Send the same message to the seven mermaids living in the waters of the *Algo* zone. They too must ensure that the boy is safe if ever he travels on water.

"Jerome, if we want both the magical and human worlds to survive, we must act diligently and tirelessly." Without another word, Steukhon touched the big pearl and vanished.

~

Jerome scribbled the messages on two pieces of paper, rolled them up and waved his arms towards the ceiling. At once golden rays formed as a new group of hummingbirds dropped down to hover before him. "Hummingbirds, you heard the priest. Take these messages to the rainbow maidens and the mermaids."

Two birds from the glowing cluster, grabbed the rolled up messages. They all swept up to the ceiling, fanned out and vanished through the holes.

Outside the Edifice, like a shooting star in the sky above the backwoods, the same golden rays dropped down to earth and sea.

Jerome, hands on his hips, looked in disgust at the ashy floor. This was one thing that he was very fussy about. It had to be clean and shiny. The books could not be dusted – the titles might be destroyed or fade over time, but his floor *must* shine. He clicked his fingers towards a pair of enormous, beige, woolly slippers neatly stored under the table and said, "I know you have already done the cleaning but this cannot wait until tomorrow." The slippers reluctantly walked out from under the table. Jerome said firmly, "Right! If the floor shines within the hour you can have a day off." The slippers started to dust and rub with enthusiasm.

"Ah! I have to replace the door's lock." Jerome rushed off uttering, "Call me when you have finished. I will let you out to empty yourselves."

As he passed the black silkworms, he noticed that they had already woven some of the ash into their delicate pieces of work. He plonked himself down and with his chin on his hand, said with disappointment, "Their shapes are spoiled. It has taken the worms a lifetime to finish this work."

Jerome, alone with his thoughts, pondered on the day's disturbing incident. "What does it all mean?" he wondered to himself, "Is it an omen? Is something great or something terrible going to happen?" He rubbed his aching head at the mystery of it all.

Chapter 7

Forest Nymphs

Egorh sat on one of the tall stone gateposts of the imposing gateway. The well-known name "Old Falcon Place" was chiseled into the left post. The estate could only be approached by a broad, winding dirt road, lined on one side by ancient trees and on the other by a green valley that stretched into the mountains.

He was excited; it was his eighth birthday and Sir Matthew was due home after a two-week trip. Egorh was sure he would not have forgotten his birthday and would bring home a present – he always did. Chewing on the soft end of a blade of grass, shading his hazel-brown eyes against the bright sun, he scanned the road for any sign of riders.

When the evidence of a thin dust trail became visible he stood up. He was sure it was his father and he waited anxiously for the riders to come closer. Confident it was them, he scrambled to the ground with the agility of a spider and ran towards the group. With tight fists he pumped his arms as he raced forward.

Out of breath, he came to stop in front of Sir Matthew. He noticed the bay stallion that trailed behind his father's horse.

Sir Matthew dismounted to greet Egorh, "It's the big day today," he said in a light voice, smiling. Egorh nodded, unable to tear his eyes away from the spirited horse tugging at the reins. Sir Matthew could see Egorh was burning with curiosity. He blocked his sight to the horse and asked, "What have you been doing while I was away?" Egorh did not hear the question and peeped around him to gaze at the animal.

His father shook his head smilingly. He could see Egorh was fixated on the horse. There was no way that he would be able to prolong the moment. He laughed and tossed the bay's reins to Egorh, "Your gift, young man." The horse neighed loudly. He was a magnificent dark brown creature with a long black mane and tail.

Egorh beamed, "Do you really mean it – my own horse?" He bubbled with excitement.

Sir Matthew just nodded, proud and fascinated by the boy's reaction. "I bought him from the Duke, John Bronbeck, at Crimson Lake. It's from one of his best lines."

"Can I ride him now?" Egorh asked, his eyes huge with hope.

"Without a saddle?" Sir Matthew frowned, but before he could say a word, Egorh had grabbed the stallion's mane and had vaulted onto its back. He pressed his heels lightly into the animal's sides and nudged him, urging him into a gallop.

Egorh's excitement knew no bounds as he lay flat against the horse clinging to its mane with one hand, his auburn hair blowing wild in the wind. His father chuckled as he watched his son hurtling down the road until only a scrap of dust was visible.

"Jake," he said, "give him some time with his new friend, then find them and bring him home. He's ridden many lively horses but none the likes of this." Sir Matthew shook his head and thought, what a wild eight year old. Amused, but slightly worried about Egorh alone in the forest, he mounted and steered his own horse in the direction of the mansion.

Deep in the forest, Egorh stopped at a clear stream. His horse's neck was lathered. He dismounted and hunkered down beside the animal as it began to drink. "Just a sip now," he said. His cheeks flushed with excitement as he gazed into the animal's dark eyes. "That was the best ride ever!" The shiny coat quivered under his touch.

"I will call you Vector – that's right – Vector," he said, softly stroking the animal.

"That's a good name," Egorh heard a voice behind him say.

Startled, he leapt to his feet. He was astonished to see two strange creatures standing not far from him. Long blond ponytails reached down to their waists. The huge ocean-blue eyes stared at him. They were handsome and impressive creatures with ivory skins and chiseled features.

"Who are you?" Egorh asked curiously. He could see they were about two heads taller than he.

"I'm Mirk and that's Kirk," said the one with his hair only partially tied, the rest hanging like a mane around his face.

"This is Bullfrog," said Kirk and he lifted the huge toad off his shoulder and set it on the ground. "He's my pet and he travels everywhere with us."

Egorh could see that it was not a normal toad. It was huge and had red eyes and lime green patches of moss on its back.

"Where do you come from?" Egorh asked.

"We are forest nymphs, better known as the giant Dryads," said Mirk. "We have always been here."

"Well, except for once when they took us away," said Kirk.

Mirk elbowed Kirk and hissed, "That's not important now."

They were fascinating mystical beings, with their large deer-like ears and Egorh stared at them, suspicion mingled with awe.

"What do you do here?" he asked

"We look after the forest," Kirk said, staring thoughtfully at Bullfrog.

A sudden noise alerted the Dryads and they stood attentively. Egorh watched how their ears turned in the direction of the noise.

"You have to go back with your new horse now," said Mirk. "We will meet again tomorrow and tell you more."

"We will show you our forest if you like," said Kirk before he scooped up the toad and placed it on his shoulder once more.

"How will I know where to find you?"

"Don't worry, we'll find you."

Egorh liked the idea. That would be exciting, he thought, always ready for adventure.

Just then Jake came weaving through the trees. "Young Egorh, your father said I must escort you back home."

Egorh looked at the Dryads but Mirk just said, "Don't worry, he cannot see us. Humans don't see us very often." Egorh watched in amazement as they disappeared into the forest with unbelievable speed. He pulled himself up onto Vector and nudged him to follow Jake back to the estate. He was sure his birthday cake was ready in the kitchen by now.

This is a great birthday, he mused as he trotted beside Jake, "My own stallion and these strange new forest creatures ... Dryads!" They were not humans but he liked them. There was something about them that made him feel comfortable in their presence.

Since receiving the message from the Edifice, the giant Dryads had been Egorh's constant protectors in the forest, always at a distance, until today, his eighth birthday.

The next day, Egorh entered the forest with great excitement and curiosity and guided his stallion towards the stream where he had met the Dryads. As they moved deeper into the woods it became very quiet with only the sound of leaves crunching beneath Vector's hooves to break the silence. Then a face dropped down in front of Egorh, jolting him in his saddle. It was

Kirk, dangling from a branch, his long ponytail almost touching the ground.

"Told you we would find you," he smiled, unhooking his legs and landing effortlessly on his feet. Nearby, Mirk sat on a fallen tree trunk chewing on some roots.

"Come," Kirk gestured with his long hand.

Egorh slid off Vector and followed Kirk. He noticed that their suits were made of some type of skin and he asked, "Your clothes – what are they made of?"

"Discarded lizard-tail skins. The pieces are glued together with spider web, making them sticky enough to latch onto any surface. Sleeping in trees is easy for us. You can touch it if you like," said Kirk.

Egorh walked closer and rubbed the material. Immediately his finger stuck to the surface.

"Its dyed bright red with two-thirds cranberry and one-third wild red-fig," Mirk muttered with his mouth half full with root. "The buttons are carved from the front teeth we collect from the beaver-graveyard."

"Want some root?" Kirk offered.

"No thanks. Have you always been in the forest?"

"Always, except once for a cycle of twelve moons," Mirk said and began to explain their history to the fascinated Egorh.

"There was a period in Earth's history, when we were poisoned by the heartless wizard, Ardor. During this time he managed to steal the great wizard book of spells and potions from the Dryad King. The poison changed us into ruthless and villainous nymphs. We caused destruction and turmoil in the forest, leaving the animals terrified and in a constant state of bewilderment." Mirk's huge eyes stared sadly into the forest.

"We were caught by the rainbow maidens and sent to the goddess of Nature where we were imprisoned. After we had been fed pure food and water, it was discovered that we had been poisoned. Under the guidance of the goddess, we again became pure in spirit and found compassion in our hearts. We learned to embrace the forest and all that lived in it, and so again became its dependable and loyal protectors.

"We were given the status of the color red. Only the fastest and bravest of Dryads are allowed to wear this color. It's an honor that a Dryad has to earn."

"What happened to Ardor?" Egorh asked astonished.

"He was punished with blindness and still lives in the Blue Mist Mountains."

Egorh followed them further into the forest, leading Vector. He confronted Kirk and Mirk with many questions until late that afternoon when they parted and he returned home.

Egorh had discovered many things about his new friends: Their light ivory skins were a result of always being in the shade of the forest. In darkness, their fascinating blue eyes changed to pitch black, adjusting their vision for night. The peculiar looking dark blue bottles that swung from thin leather straps across their chests were filled with magical oil given to them by the goddesses to heal injured forest creatures. They were the purest of the nymphs and where there were bad vibrations and impure thoughts, Dryads were absent. Only humans with pure thoughts could move into their dimension and meet them.

At first, Egorh had not believed Kirk when he told him this, but a few weeks later he had come to the forest with Sir Matthew. Proud of his friends, Egorh had tried to introduce Kirk and Mirk to his father, but when he saw the questioning look on Sir Matthew's face, he realized that the Dryads had spoken the truth.

It was that day, later in the evening, that Sir Matthew called Egorh to join him in his study. Wide eyed he peeped around the door and immediately sensed Sir Matthew's seriousness. He swallowed and hoped he was not in trouble because of his friends that his father could not see, but when he saw the tall glass of warm milk and one of Marion's bulky rusks waiting next to the chair, he relaxed.

"Come in young man. Don't look so worried. I want to talk to you before I leave for up North tomorrow."

Egorh's face fell slightly but then visibly brightened as he thought, maybe now I will have more time to spend with Mirk and Kirk. Normally Sir Matthew's absence would upset him but with his new friends he was sure the time would pass very quickly. He walked over to the big leather chair, sat on the edge and then wiggled himself back into the seat, his legs quite a distance from the floor. He loved these special times alone with Sir Matthew.

"You are growing up so fast, becoming a fine man." Sir Matthew smiled, "Before long those legs will reach the floor."

With his lips tightly closed, Egorh gave him a huge grin.

"I see that you are spending much time with Vector in the forest. Is it with the friends you tried to show me today?"

A flicker of uncertainty came into Egorh's eyes and he hesitated but then nodded, "Yes."

"Tell me about them. What do they look like?"

Egorh jumped from the chair and started to explain, his arms waving. Sir Matthew could only watch in awe, impressed by the child's excitement.

"The one's name is Kirk and the other Mirk. They are a little taller than me," he gestured with his hands. "They have hair hanging down to here," Egorh indicated his waist with the side of his hand. He squeezed his eyes closed for a moment to emphasize his next point, "And they are FAST!"

Sir Matthew sat in silent admiration, not wanting to spoil the moment by interrupting. Egorh's mouth became dry and he settled again into the chair to take a sip of the milk that had long since become cold.

"Do you know why I cannot see them?"

Egorh nodded, his mouth so full of rusk that he barely managed to say, "They live in another dimension. They told me that just as our world exists, there also exists a magical one unknown to most, but that I can experience both these worlds."

For a moment Sir Matthew looked thoughtful, then he got up and came to sit in the chair next to Egorh. He stared down at his hand and rubbed his knuckles. "You are different, Egorh."

Egorh swallowed and carefully put the other half of the rusk back on the table. He looked at Sir Matthew and asked with curiosity, "I am?"

"You have met magical friends that others cannot see and you will probably meet many more. That makes you special but it also makes you vulnerable to evil in a world I cannot see and protect you from. Just as evil exists in our world, so does it in the magical one. Because of your link to the mystic world, you were given this amulet for your protection on the day you were born."

Egorh stopped chewing and stared at Sir Matthew with his huge hazel eyes. He felt a sudden tightness in his stomach and an uneasiness that began to crawl up his throat as he listened wordlessly while Sir Matthew explained.

"One day you will be strong and powerful. Until then it is the amulet with its magical power that will protect you. You must always wear it. The blackness and shape of the onyx stones deflect all evil and as this evil bounces off the surface, the diamonds absorb it."

Egorh rubbed the big black jewel and uncertainty and awe rippled over his face.

"Promise me that you will take this very seriously," said Sir Matthew.

Egorh nodded solemnly.

"Then come, let me walk you to your room."

Egorh slid out of the chair and asked, "Did you know my mother?" He had wanted to ask Sir Matthew this question for a long time and tonight the words just slipped out.

The sudden question surprised Sir Matthew and he hesitated for a moment, then said, "No, unfortunately not. The man that asked me to be your father knew her well. He said she was very beautiful and loved you dearly. You might meet him one day and he will be able to tell you more about your mother."

He nodded silently and with Sir Matthew's arm around his shoulder he felt very safe and the uncertainty of a moment ago slipped from his mind.

After Sir Matthew had tucked him in and closed the door, Egorh got up to sit by the window. He stared at the thin clouds throwing shadows on the moon and Sir Matthew's words whirled in his head for some time. The words that his mother had loved him dearly brought a certain joy to him and he would always keep them close in his heart.

Protected by the innocence of an eight year old, he did not know what lay ahead. He crawled back into bed and his last thoughts were, I wonder where Mirk and Kirk are sleeping tonight. Do their eyes really become the same as the owl-apes' at night?

Chapter 8

Destiny Begins

The afternoon sun was hot and Egorh tried to blow the thick, auburn hair away from his sticky forehead. He sat on the sidestep of the carriage waiting for Joseph. He juggled two small stones he had picked up from the side of the road, just to pass the time. In his twelfth year, he glowed with health, his sun-browned skin emphasizing his white teeth and bright hazel eyes.

Although Egorh had been raised in opulence, Sir Matthew was strict and firm with his upbringing. At the rebellious young age of twelve, Egorh viewed the world as a place of much uncertainty and perplexity. He found comfort in the many hours he spent practicing with his sword and bow.

It had been a day of festivities, as archers and fencers from afar had gathered to compete for the title of champion. Egorh recalled the day's contests. A glint of triumph crossed his face as he thought how thrilling it had been to fight the older boys. It felt so good! He had walked away with the title for the third year in a row. He grinned when he remembered the humiliation of one of the contestants – a full head taller than himself. His challenger barely got the chance to defend himself and failed time after time to avoid Egorh's blows. His rival's expression was dark with embarrassment as he hissed sharply, "You bigheaded fool – I'll get you."

Repeatedly Egorh's blunt game-sword had struck. First his arm, then his back and after the third direct contact, the contest was over and Egorh was declared the winner. Driven by pain and shame, the loser tried to sneak in a cowardly blow but Egorh merely sidestepped and brought his hilt hard down on his opponent's shoulder. The blow rocked the older youth; he fell back and dropped to the ground. The fight won, Egorh ignored his humiliation, merely tilting his head and walking away.

Egorh's thoughts were interrupted by jeering. He looked up and recognized some of the boys he had beaten in the contest, sauntering towards him. "Hey! You with the necklace!" Jim, a tall youth with greasy blond hair sneered, "You think you're so great with a bow and sword? How about a real fight?" Egorh could see his closely set eyes were hungry for trouble as were those of the others. They nudged each other, laughed and yelled more insults at him.

He ignored them. Sir Matthew had taught him self control. In public, to keep one's pride was important. The blond youth however, would not be ignored. His lip curled as he slapped Egorh mockingly on the cheek. Egorh flushed with fury and clenched his fists, ready to wipe the arrogant smirk off his pimpled face, but curbed his temper.

"Come on Jim, show him you don't need swords and arrows to prove yourself," Jim's supporters taunted. Jim loosened his shoulders, bent his neck from side-to-side and surged forward. He threw a straight punch at Egorh. Then the two of them were rolling in the dirt and Egorh could hear the other rabble-rousers cheering, "Get him Jim!" Another rushed forward and kicked Egorh in the chest, winding him. Egorh regained his composure, leapt forward and managed a strong blow to Jim's head. He heard a loud crack and saw the bully cover his nose, his cupped hand quickly filling with spurting blood.

"You broke my nose!" Jim yelped like an injured puppy, pain making his eyes well with tears.

"In two places, I hope!" Egorh muttered through clenched teeth.

Jim roared with fury as he saw the flush of triumph that washed over Egorh.

"Get him! Break every bone in his body!" Jim shouted to the others.

They stormed forward and tackled Egorh. Two of them held him on the ground with their knees and pressed his face into the dirt. Egorh yelled with rage and struggled wildly, but the dust smothered him as they held him down. Soon he was coughing and choking. Egorh managed to twist his body and grab one of his assailants by the throat. The boy punched madly at Egorh to make him let go. Fists hammered down on Egorh's head from every side. Egorh fought back but could not reach to do any real damage. As his vision blurred and black spots exploded in front of him, he could hear ringing in his ears. Vaguely, he heard a deep roar from far away. He recognized Joseph's voice and felt his attackers release him.

"Useless thugs!" Joseph yelled after them as they fled. He pulled Egorh up and dusted off his clothes.

Egorh looked terrible. His jaw was swollen, a lump stood out on his temple and there was a gash above his eyebrow. He ignored the pain, drew himself up to his full height and spoke as formally as he knew how. "I could have handled that myself, Joseph."

Joseph searched the youngster's face. Egorh's blood was boiling with humiliation as he glared back at him.

Joseph was a quiet, even-tempered man who breathed loudly through his nostrils and pursed his lips when he was serious.

"You were outnumbered," he said quietly.

"They were clumsy," Egorh responded hotly.

"You know I don't doubt your courage, young man. I know your skill with weapons, but it is your street-fighting ability that I doubt. Maybe we should ask your father to get you a tutor in the art of thuggery, if one could call it an art?" Joseph raised a quizzical eyebrow.

"You won't tell him about the fight, will you?" Egorh pleaded using the back of his hand to wipe the blood running down his face.

Joseph ignored the appeal. "As your father's heir, you are expected to learn the responsibilities and duties of being a nobleman. When he visits the city, he expects you to behave in this manner, not as a rascal involved in common brawls. What would I have told him if I had found you maimed or dead today?"

"You could tell him I fell from my horse." Egorh suggested sullenly.

"Ha! If I am prepared to lie for you, promise me there'll be no more fights," Joseph retorted.

Egorh nodded miserably.

The rumbling of a speeding carriage made Joseph look up. He was just in time to grab Egorh by the arm and pull him out of its way as it charged past leaving them in a cloud of dust. Joseph recognized the blond boy on the back seat glaring at them with face bruised and his nose swollen. Joseph was familiar with the crest on the carriage door and frowned.

"Did you see them? They tried to run us over." Egorh yelled angrily.

"Yes, they're the nobles from up East, hooligans known for the bad blood that runs in their family. Always running in a pack like wild dogs, making trouble wherever they go. Come, we must get home and have someone look at that cut." Joseph smiled inwardly. He knew it was Egorh's pride that was hurt more than his body.

Joseph did not dare to confess that he was glad Egorh had

stood his ground against the four trouble makers. He felt warm inside. The boy had become like a son to him in the twelve summers that he had known him.

Egorh leaned back on the seat of the carriage, still too upset to catch the hint of pride in Joseph's eyes. He was quiet on his way back to the house but inside he was angry. Angry at being shamed, angry for not being strong enough to beat those bullies, angry for not having a mother and angry for not knowing why he must still wear the stupid amulet. He was just simply angry for being angry.

For the next few days Egorh spent the hours from first light to sunset practicing among the tall trees of the forest. First he would train using his sword, endlessly striking the air in single strokes. When his wrist began to burn with fatigue and his clothes dripped with sweat, he changed to his bow and arrow. Arrow after arrow he sent into an ancient tree until it bled with streams of gum. The blisters on his fingers turned into calluses from drawing the bowstring back hour after hour, until his muscles were numb and his anger had subsided.

He was not aware that Kirk and Mirk had been watching him from a distance, patiently waiting for his rage to subside.

~

Kirk and Mirk were not only Egorh's best friends, they were also his tutors. After the embarrasing experience in town with the older boys, Egorh realized that there was a sudden shift in their training. From that day on, their casual lessons became serious and intense. They had made it their business to school him and pass all their skills in weaponry on to him, including the practice of thuggery. Whenever Egorh entered the forest, they relentlessly attacked him. They pounced from among the branches and sent him plummeting from his horse. They would sneak up from behind and tackle him. He had to agree to endless challenges of *free fighting,* as they liked to call it. They confronted him with sticks, chains and any possible weapons they could find.

Initially Kirk and Mirk won all the bouts, but as the months passed with many bloody noses and bruises to show for their battles, Egorh became the true champion. He became as fast as a deer and as agile as a wild cat. It was on one of these occasions that Egorh challenged Kirk with all the confidence of youth, "Come Kirk, let's fight for something. If I win you must show me those Pesos spiders that you told me about."

"And what do I get when I win, which I'm sure I will," snorted Kirk.

"Make your choice," Egorh grinned boldly.

Kirk thought for a while then looked at Egorh and smirked, "You must put both feet in the center of the black wolves' lair."

"Kirk no, that's too dangerous. They have cubs now," warned Mirk. "The mother will be there."

"I accept," interrupted Egorh eagerly.

Kirk's eyes narrowed, "How will you do it?"

"Easy. I will lower myself down from an overhanging branch with a vine. Do you accept?" his eyes shone with excitement.

Kirk scratched his head thoughtfully.

"You're crazy Kirk," mumbled Mirk.

"Why?" asked Egorh

"Ardor, the relentless wizard we told you about, seeks the Pesos spiders. Some time ago a few of them were stolen from us and the story spread to every corner. Ardor has been obsessed in finding the spiders ever since. He needs them to spin him a magical falcon's eye that will return his sight and also enable him to decipher the book he stole. We have had many confrontations with him but have never been able to get the book back." Mirk displayed a horrible looking scar on his ribs. "The old wizard has bred and trained strange creatures to seek out and bring him all spiders in the areas he believes the Pesos to be. In his hope to find a Pesos spider, he has almost wiped out the entire spider species, creating an alarming imbalance throughout the forest. But he will never find them as they are kept in another dimension. To move and expose our Pesos spiders will be too dangerous," Mirk warned.

"I can bring only one, the youngest, whose powers are far from fully developed and I will be very careful. It is important that Egorh gets to know more about the magical world anyway," Kirk said, nonchalantly shrugging his shoulders.

Mirk had an uneasy feeling, but Kirk liked challenges like these.

"Kirk if you fail, you do realize the consequences could be disastrous?"

"I know."

"You accept then, Kirk?" Egorh prompted.

Kirk nodded and they stormed towards each other. It was a tough wrestling match, but before long, Egorh got the better of Kirk and managed to pin him down.

Kirk was a bad loser and got up very agitated. While dusting his clothes he muttered, "What do you expect from a son of Darkarh who has been given great skills?"

Mirk suddenly hissed at Kirk, "Keep quiet Kirk! It's forbidden to talk about it!"

It was the first time he had ever seen either of his two Dryad friends furious and he felt uneasy, yet excited.

"What do you mean?" Egorh asked. "What are you talking about? Who is Darkarh?"

Mirk answered curtly, "Leave it, Egorh. One day you will find out for yourself." Egorh wanted to know more, but the two Dryads disappeared abruptly into nowhere. He had shouted after them and promised that he would not ask any more questions. The forest crackled and they returned, Kirk's ill humor now spent. True to his word, Egorh did not ask anything more about this curious exchange, but he stored it in his memory. The two

Dryads acted as if nothing unusual had happened and chattered to Egorh about his victory prize.

Chapter 9

Bunkums

Barely dawn, Egorh sneaked slowly down the staircase, boots in one hand and the other sliding along the solid wooden balustrade. He tried to make as little noise as possible. At the bottom of the stairs he held his breath and tiptoed past the study into the hall, where he sat down and quickly yanked his boots on. These were his favorites as they gripped to any surface almost as well as his bare feet.

"I must hurry," the excited boy mumbled to himself. He caught a glimpse of his reflection in the tall mirror on the opposite wall. The sudden sparkle from the amulet hanging around his neck caused him to stop. A frown appeared and his hazel eyes narrowed slightly. He looked at the flamingo birthmark at the base of his neck, then back to the amulet, clenched his jaw and grumbled, "WHEN will my power be greater than yours?"

He grabbed the amulet and dropped it down the front of his shirt. He laced up his leather jerkin, tighter than most other days and mumbled, "I don't want you to be in my way today."

With his fingers, he carelessly combed his short auburn hair into some sort of tidiness.

He thought of the incidents in town when the boys had teased him for wearing the diamond amulet. There were many times when he'd rebelled and felt like dropping the jewel into the river.

He lifted his sheathed blade from the brackets on the wall, rubbing his thumb over the engraved silver hilt. It was a gift from Sir Matthew who had it specially made for him. He strapped it around his waist and slipped the bow and quiver over his shoulder, then reached for the large brass door-knob, turned it and slipped quietly out the back door of the mansion. He made for the stables, taking care that neither Joseph nor any other staff members saw him.

If Joseph finds me sneaking off to the forest again, he will as always, insist that someone accompany me and that will spoil my plan, especially today when I meet with the Dryads, he thought.

His hands worked fast as he slipped the bridle over his stallion's head. The steed blew noisily through his nostrils then gently nuzzled Egorh as his fingers checked the straps once more. "Shh ... Shh, Vector. We can talk later," he tried to calm the excited mount. "Today I will ride without a saddle," he whispered and with one leap he landed on the stallion's back and nudged him towards the stable door. Egorh's balance was perfect as he galloped with reckless speed towards the forest. He smiled as he held his stallion's mane with only one hand and felt the wind on his sun-browned skin. It was a bright day and he was glad to be out, happy that no one from the house had stopped him.

He had had so many adventures with the Dryads over the years. He had helped to spring traps that were intended for wolf, deer, rabbit and many other forest animals. When forest fires started, the Dryads would blow warnings, using the horn of the rare mountain goat. They healed the sick and wounded animals with magic oil.

Memories of his childhood played across his mind's eye as he rode low, almost flat against the stallion's neck. "I am fortunate to have the Dryads as my friends," he whispered in the animal's ear. Egorh reveled in the euphoria that he felt as the animal strained under him. The meeting with the Dryads promised an exciting day!

He slowed down when he found himself in the dense forest of ancient trees. Suddenly Vector came to an abrupt halt and Egorh grabbed the mane to prevent a fall. The animal whinnied and shook his head. He followed the horse's gaze and spotted the big toad sitting in Vector's path.

"Bullfrog," Egorh mumbled. "If the toad is here, they are here."

He peered up into the dense forest canopy and thought he saw a movement above him.

"Mirk!" he called out. "I know you're there, you almost sent me flying into the bushes." Mirk peeped from behind a branch. The beginnings of a smile crinkled his gem-like eyes as he jumped down.

"It's good to see you again Egorh. You would have made my day if you had fallen into that bush of poison ivy behind you," Mirk joked.

"Not likely! Come on! Where's that spider you promised to show me?"

"I'm expecting Kirk anytime now," he replied.

"Did he get it?"

"Patience, my friend!" Egorh watched as Mirk swarmed up the face of the tree trunk, like an agile stump-tailed lizard, his long pearly white ponytail swaying around his waist. He craned his neck to see if Kirk was in sight yet.

"Here comes Kirk now."

Kirk came swinging through the branches with a leather pouch dangling at his side. The corn silk streaks in his white hair shone where they caught the filtered sun through the trees.

It was easy for the Dryads, with their remarkably long hands and feet, to move around with exceptional speed in the forest. Egorh still marveled at their tunnel-shaped ears that could detect the slightest sound over a long distance.

"You're nice and early," said Kirk brightly. "Did you bring some bait?"

"Yes, I took some of the fat grumblers from the stables," Egorh replied. He leaped lightly from his horse, tethered it to a nearby tree and took a small jar from his pocket.

Mirk swung down and stood next to Egorh. The two of them were almost the same height. Egorh could barely conceal his eagerness. Mirk remained on watch in the trees. He felt uneasy and looked around. "Are you sure you were not followed?"

"Yes, I'm certain. I gave a few fast turns then snaked my way along a few winding courses to throw anyone who could be following off my tracks," assured Kirk. Sensing Egorh's keenness, Kirk slipped his hand into his pouch and pulled out a monstrous hairy spider, the size of a man's palm. "He's magnificent, isn't he?"

"Wow!" said Egorh with a smile, his big eyes alive with wonder. "That's the youngest of them?"

"Yes, one of the eleven." Kirk puffed his chest out proudly and held the huge spider on the back of his long hand. The ends of all eight legs were of deep purple crystal. He dug again into the leather pouch and pulled out a purple web. "Mirk, come down and help me with the web. Let's spread it between those branches."

Mirk descended from his branch. When the web was tightly stretched, he sprang back into the tree where he could be on guard for any danger.

Kirk let the spider crawl onto the web and said, "Watch this. Give Purple Legs the grumbler and see what happens."

Egorh placed a grumbler in front of the strange creature, which moved forward and started to secrete the most exquisite purple silk thread he had ever seen. The creature maneuvered the grumbler in all directions, covering it completely with the purple spider silk. Egorh gazed in awe as the grumbler turned into a purple jewel.

"The spider captures the life and characteristics of the specific insect and the stone becomes magical. This purple stone is the stone of memory, thus its magic will be such that it will be able to climb, fly and walk like this insect. If a dragonfly was trapped, it would also be able to hover in the air," explained Kirk to the awestruck Egorh.

"We told you a few were once stolen. A sorceress from the land of Lark in the Black Mountains captured tiny genies in the magic stones," Kirk added, entertaining the young boy with his story.

"With great effort we managed to get the Pesos spiders back," Mirk snorted, but before he could continue, the ground beneath them began to tremble.

"Trouble!" bellowed Mirk from his lookout. "It's the Hog-bunkums! They found us." At that moment gigantic round balls with protruding spikes rolled wildly down the track towards Egorh and Kirk, sending moss and fern in all directions.

"Quick, save the spider!" Kirk yelled.

Mirk leaped from above and covered the spider and the stone, then disappeared instantly.

"What are they? EXPLAIN, Kirk!" shouted Egorh, ready with his sword, as more enormous spiky balls appeared. They started to dart erratically and aggressively around Egorh, watching him with their black, orange-pupiled eyes. Their large mouths with protruding teeth were hideous. They closed in from all sides.

"They belong to the wizard Ardor, the creatures he bred to sniff out the spiders. They must have followed me here," Kirk yelled. "They are the devil's own! Half-breeds! Porcupine and hedgehog – and stupid. It will take them a while to realize that the spider has gone, but they will try to kill us before they leave."

"Look at the size of them," Egorh whispered. He and Kirk crouched down and tried to move back but were too late. The

Hog-bunkums had encircled them, ready to attack.

"Be careful! They snap like wild dogs, and the old wizard could have dipped their quills in poison," warned Kirk.

Egorh realized that there were too many Hog-bunkums to kill and the only way out was to climb into the nearest tree – and quickly. He looked around and saw a vine draped over a branch five paces away. He slid his sword back into its sheath and shouted, "Kirk, we have to jump and grab the vine. I will take the left end and you go for the right, but we must grasp it at the same time to balance."

They jumped, gripped the ends of the vine and started pulling themselves up. As Egorh reached the top, he slipped his arm around the branch, but then heard a snap and saw Kirk fall back onto a bare patch of ground, his piece of the vine still in his hands.

To his surprise, he saw the Hog-bunkums milling around but not attacking Kirk. As he pulled himself onto the branch, he realized that Kirk had landed in mud, concealed by leaves, small ferns and patches of damp moss. A movement rippled over the surface, as the mud pool produced a downward sucking force around Kirk, pulling him deeper.

"Don't move, Kirk! Sit quietly!" Egorh yelled. "I will get you out. Just hold still!"

Kirk, still dazed from his fall did not register where he had landed. He tried to get to his feet, but with a shock discovered that his legs were held in a strong grip. With every movement he made, he sank further down into the bog.

Kirk realized he was in trouble and called out, "No, stay there, Egorh! You cannot come down, the Hog-bunkums will kill you!"

Egorh looked at the hostile creatures waiting for him below and felt a worm of fear in his stomach. He looked down at Kirk and saw how rapidly he was disappearing into the mud.

"Don't move, Kirk! I am coming!" he yelled.

"This is no time to be noble, Egorh! Save yourself! Mirk will return soon." Kirk was worried. The mud was like a hungry demon around him. He could not permit the Hog-bunkums to cause the death of the son of Darkarh. The Dryads were supposed to protect Egorh, not endanger him. Kirk yelled again, "Egorh! Wait! Stay there or you will be killed!"

Egorh suddenly felt a wave of compassion for the trapped Dryad and silently vowed that he would not let his friend die. Black with anger, he looked down at the evil spiked balls and shouted, "I will not die!" He took a long dive from the branch and landed near to where Kirk was. The Hog-bunkums scattered in all directions but then spun around immediately and rushed forward. As he hit the ground, Egorh drew his sword and slashed the life out of the first charging creature. He had just enough time to grab the point of the vine and pin it into the ground with an arrow, embedding it as deeply as he could.

"Pull yourself out with the vine, Kirk!" Egorh yelled loudly, noticing the mute desperation on his face. "I will take care of these devils." Kirk was already up to his arms in the mud when he grabbed the vine.

Egorh dropped to one knee and avoided the pounce of one of the Hog-bunkums, sending it tumbling over his head. As he rose, he felt the creature's quills piercing his thigh. He spun around but a strange numbness started to spread through the muscle. Again he dropped to one knee and spilled all the arrows from the quiver onto the ground in front of him.

With immense speed he fired arrow after arrow, leaving many of the creatures dead. There was no fear in his eyes, only anger. The excruciating pain in his leg turned to paralysis. After the last arrow was fired he managed to balance on his good leg. With a mighty effort he swung the sword before him with all the strength he could muster, cleaving another Hog-bunkum in two. He grabbed another by the quills and lifted it into the air, swung it around and then flung it into the others.

Egorh's heart leaped as he saw that the arrow attached to the vine was unable to hold the weight of Kirk and the clinging mud.

His arms and legs were numbing, the paralysis spreading.

He kept himself upright by sheer will and then fell onto the vine, clutching it with both hands. He managed a kick out backwards and sent a Hog-bunkum tumbling, then felt how another quill pierced through the sole of his boot.

"Grab my hand!" he shouted to Kirk and locked his grip around Kirk's hand. With one mighty pull he managed to free his friend from what would have been his tomb. Kirk stood coated with filth and took a deep breath to calm himself, as relief washed over his face.

Egorh's eyes blurred as he tried to stand, his poisoned leg buckling under him. Kirk snatched the sword and swung wildly at the remaining attackers. Just then, arrows started to rain down from above them.

Kirk glanced up and was relieved to see Mirk standing on a branch, picking off the Hog-bunkums one by one.

"Get onto the horse," yelled Mirk. "I will cover you. It will be the quickest."

Kirk steadied Egorh and they stumbled towards the panic-stricken Vector. The forest echoed with the cries of the dying creatures. With Kirk's help, Egorh mounted Vector who was frantically neighing and pawing the ground. A Hog-bunkum suddenly rushed forward from the shadows and shook a number of sharp quills into the animal's chest. Bewildered and in pain, Vector spun around and took off into the dense forest, with Egorh and Kirk clinging on desperately. Egorh did not see the branch that hit him full across the chest, sending him flying into a tree trunk. In the confusion he did not notice his amulet had caught on a small branch and was ripped from his neck. Kirk, being a Dryad, could escape more easily and landed light-footed on a branch. Egorh lay stunned and dazed on the forest floor.

The few remaining Hog-bunkums, as though answering some distant summons, started to melt back into the forest. Some lingered for a while but soon they were all gone.

"What's happening?" Egorh rasped painfully.

"They've finally realized that the spider escaped them," sighed Kirk, muddy and relieved. Just then Mirk arrived on the scene, fearing what he might find. His face relaxed into a faint smile of relief when he saw that the two had escaped.

"Let me rub some magical Dryad oil onto your wounds, then call your mount," Mirk insisted. Egorh soon felt the pain and swelling draining from his leg. Relieved, he whistled for Vector who came limping back. Spikes were embedded in his chest and some dangled from his leg. Egorh tried to keep him calm while Kirk removed the painful quills. Kirk and Mirk then rubbed a few drops of Dryad oil onto the animal's wounds, healing them.

"Go home now Egorh," Mirk said. "This day has delivered more than we had anticipated." Egorh knew better than to argue. He stiffly mounted, nodded to his friends and turned towards home. He rode at an easy canter but remained wary of every sound, the images of the creatures still rushing through his mind.

Kirk looked at Mirk with relief. "That was the closest I have ever been to becoming part of Mother Earth for good. The son of Darkarh saved a Dryad today. He has become my protector instead of me being his," he said quietly.

"Yes," Mirk concurred. "If it was not for the secret of the son of Darkarh that had to be kept from the world, we could have sent the message to the outskirts of the forest and beyond, but it is not yet time." The two Dryads cautiously made their way back into the forest.

~

Egorh was tired from the day's excitement and not even the smell of his favorite dish, lamb stew with whole carrots and young potatoes, could keep him in the kitchen. He went to his room early that evening. Sir Matthew had been away for several weeks, visiting the city and his old friend at Crimson Lake, but would be back the next day.

In his room he removed his shirt and realized with a stab of despair that he had lost his amulet.

"It must have happened with the fall in the forest," he surmised "What now? Sir Matthew will be very upset with me for losing the amulet. He has always been so adamant about it, reminding me never to take it off. I will have to call the Dryads for help." Egorh walked over to a chest and searched in a drawer for a thin bronze pipe. "Mirk said I must use this in an emergency and this certainly IS one."

He walked over to the window and blew as hard as he could on the small pipe. No sound came from it, but Egorh waited.

The moon was bright but clouds scudded across it, throwing the area around the house into darkness. The night deepened as he waited for his friends. "Maybe I don't need the amulet anymore. Maybe I became stronger than it today," he thought as he paced up and down. Somehow he couldn't convince himself that this was the case.

The trees around the mansion moved in the rising wind. Egorh sat waiting for what seemed like hours at the window. Eventually he could not keep his eyes open any longer and fell asleep in the chair.

A tapping sound on the window followed by a croak woke him and his heart leapt as he quickly moved to open it.

Kirk stood on the windowsill with his pet Bullfrog clinging to his shoulder. His blue daytime eyes had now tuned pitch black. His ivory skin looked pale in the moonlight.

"You called?" Mirk drew himself up onto the ledge and into a crouch, oblivious of his precarious position.

"Thanks for coming!" gasped a relieved Egorh. "I need your help. I have lost my amulet! It must have happened when I fell from Vector today. Can you find it? I cannot be without it." Egorh was unable to keep the note of panic from his voice. He saw how Kirk's night eyes darkened even further and a shadow of disturbance flickered across his face.

"This certainly means trouble – big trouble."

Egorh had never heard Kirk speak in such chilling tones, but before he could ask for the reason there was a growl of distant thunder. Kirk looked up into the dark night. "We must hurry before our footprints are washed away. I will go with Mirk and look for the amulet right away." Without another word, they dropped back from the ledge, making a long jump to a nearby branch and another enormous leap into a tree further on the estate's grounds.

Relieved, Egorh fell back on his bed to wait for their return. His mind replayed Sir Matthew's voice: "There will come a time young Egorh, when your own strength will be greater than that of the amulet, but until then, promise me that you will always wear it. We don't always understand or know what the future holds. Only know this – for now your life depends on it."

"It will be a miserable night until they get back," Egorh muttered and drifted into an uneasy sleep, unaware that being without the amulet, he had alerted the forces of evil. Before the night was over he would have been discovered.

Chapter 10

Sorrow-Queen

"Damn!" Zinnia cursed as she bumped her foot against the corner of a headstone. In the pitch dark, Arkarrah followed right behind and her eagle flew from gravestone to gravestone.

"Where *is* this place? Kep told me I must look out for the big tomb with the two large ornamental pots on each side of the door. Apparently the Sorrow-queen lives in one of them. Arkarrah, are you looking out for it?" she hissed.

"Why do we need the queen?" Arkarrah snorted irritably.

Zinnia stopped, waved her long fingernails and snapped vehemently.

"The book clearly stated that we need willing, loving people for the Haffgoss resurrection to work. How will you get humans to be like that Arkarrah?"

"Take their sorrows away?"

"Exactly. The Sorrow-queen must take their sorrows away so that I can use their hearts." She continued to search between the neglected graves and fretted to herself, "My plan is almost complete, except that I cannot find the baby with the beak mark. What if the leaves made a mistake? Impossible! They have *never* been wrong. What if he is dead? No, I must just be patient and continue my search for the baby, or boy by now, I am sure." She snapped again, "Arkarrah are you searching?"

"Yes!" His voice held a tremor of fear. "Is this not something we can do by day? Why does it have to be at night?" he whined and shuddered as a cloud made the moon disappear for a few seconds.

"The Sorrow-queen will only speak to us at night," Zinnia retorted with barely concealed contempt.

He whirled around as he heard a fluttering behind him. But it was Khan, and he gave a sigh of relief. "Stupid bird – made my bones feel chalky."

"Don't call him stupid or he will beg me to let him peck out your eyes," she spat.

"Oh, so now, with the full moon, he turns from an eagle to a crow," Arkarrah mumbled sarcastically and thought to himself, she is so excessively rude and impatient. If it was not for the promised gold ore, which I have seen with my own eyes, I would not be here tonight. He jumped with fright when Horris, the bat, crawled out from under his cloak and disappeared with a shriek into the dark night. Arkarrah considered himself a brave man, but only during the day.

Zinnia continued to move slowly from tomb to tomb, highly irritated with Arkarrah's grunting and muttering behind her. She stopped, swung around and glared at him. "I will tell you about the Sorrow-queen, but only to stop your complaining." She turned back to follow the weed-strewn path between the headstones. "The Sorrow-queen was punished by the elders and thrown out of her kingdom for snickering. Laughing is forbidden. When a Sorrow-queen laughs, a sorrow is returned to its origin or even worse given to an innocent. Her penance was to collect enough sorrows to fill the silver-glass box she carries with her. That would prove that she is worthy of being a Sorrow-queen."

Zinnia stopped, narrowed her eyes and searched the grounds. "So now she stays here. Apparently she spends all her time in the graveyard collecting sorrows from the mourners." Zinnia started off again but stopped when a movement caught her eye.

Eight long, bluish fingers appeared over the rim of a huge, urn-shaped pot nearby and two large hollow eyes peeped over the rim.

"Why are you looking for me?" a plaintive voice whispered, "What do you want?"

Zinnia smiled sweetly and with a quick nod said in her friendliest voice, "Sorrow-queen, I'm *so* glad to have found you. I have a proposition for you."

"Why?" the sorrowful-looking creature asked as she started to climb out of the pot. She was a ghostly grey, with the saddest eyes Arkarrah had ever seen, the corners of her mouth turned down and hung past her very pointed chin. Her hair was a cloud of mist, floating about her head.

Zinnia continued, "Well, rumor has it, not that I listen to rumors of course, that you are not doing well with the collection of sorrows around here."

The Sorrow-queen looked up at the moon and then back at her two visitors, her hollow eyes, two pools of mercury, and gave a deep sigh.

"Yes, you heard the truth, I am without luck. Most of the mourners that come here want to keep their sorrows to themselves, so that they can wallow in them for the rest of their lives," and with that she disappeared back into the pot.

"No! Wait, don't go!" Zinnia wheedled in as sweet a voice as she could manage, "As I said, I have a proposition for you."

After what felt like an age to Zinnia, the eight long, bluish fingers appeared over the rim of the pot again and the Sorrow-queen slowly re-emerged.

"What sort of proposition?" she demanded petulantly.

"Well, if you come with me, I shall assure you of plenty of sorrows," Zinnia answered with a clipped voice, barely able to conceal her intolerance.

"Then I must leave my pot? I cannot just leave my pot," the Sorrow-queen wailed.

"I will give you a better and nicer pot to live in," Zinnia countered in a silky voice.

"I will be sorry to leave my pot."

"Well, now you have another sorrow. Why don't you grab it for yourself?" Zinnia replied, and thought, this is so frustrating! I could gnaw a chunk of marble from a tombstone.

"Are you *sure* there will be sorrows?"

"Yes, oh yes, *thousands* of them," Zinnia promised blithely.

The Sorrow-queen thought for a long while, her huge eyes roving from the graveyard to the moon and back. All Zinnia could do was to conceal her impatience from this tiresome creature and wait. Finally the sad voice droned, "All right, but I must get my sorrow box before we can leave." The Sorrow-queen disappeared back into her pot. Zinnia stomped between the graves as she waited. Eventually the Sorrow-queen reappeared and joined them. They started to leave the cemetery, the Sorrow-queen floating above the ground behind Zinnia and Arkarrah.

"I must be careful of her." Arkarrah thought warily, "I like to wallow in my sorrows, especially with a bottle of rum."

"Perfect!" Zinnia mumbled to herself. "I have made a deal with the greedy Haffgoss and now I have the spook! My plan is coming together."

In the dark, the genie Iy, suddenly popped out of the bangle around Zinnia's arm and yelled, "I see him!"

Arkarrah jumped a few steps back and looked around nervously.

"What? Who do you see?" snapped Zinnia.

"The boy with the beak mark!" Iy replied.

"Where is he? Quickly! Show me!" she yelled.

Iy swayed and blinked and in the moonlight, the face of Egorh appeared in Iy's big eye. The image melted into another that showed two rivers, a mountain peak, a huge estate and a young boy standing at a bedroom window, as if waiting for something.

"Where is this place?" Zinnia spoke excitedly. "Arkarrah, come here at once!"

She summoned Khan, stretched out her arm for the bird to perch on and then held him in front of Iy, so he could see the image too. "Find this boy and take Arkarrah there," she ordered. The eagle's green eyes scoured the image, then blinked in acknowledgement at Zinnia.

"Excellent! The boy has been found!" she crowed." Arkarrah you must leave immediately. Remember, I want the boy dead. That is the deal. Don't forget to bring his corpse as evidence to show the Haffgoss.

Chapter 11

Attack

Egorh heard the tapping again. There was no trace of the tempest that had raged most of the night over Old Falcon Place. The first blush of day barely lit his room as he hurried, half asleep, to the window. He caught a glimpse of a long ponytail and realized it was the Dryads. He fumbled to open the window. The crisp air nipped his cheeks as he pushed his head through the opening and asked eagerly, "Did you get it?"

Kirk was already crouched on the wide ledge, waiting for Mirk to arrive. He appeared, pulled himself over the ledge, and stood next to Kirk. Mirk took the amulet from his neck and handed it to Egorh. "We found it in the tree where you fell."

Egorh's worried face broke into a smile as he took back the precious stones. "Thank you a thousand times."

Mirk bowed his head then looked away. "Glad we could help," he replied curtly. There was no doubt that he was deeply troubled. The priest had warned them that the evil that sought Egorh was strong and would take advantage of the slightest opportunity. Maybe *this* had been such an opportunity.

Kirk, sharing Mirk's concern, looked thoughtfully down at his long hands. His face suddenly seemed colder than the early morning chill. There was a long pause.

Sensing the Dryads' uneasiness, Egorh shrugged, "What? The amulet has been recovered. It's safely around my neck."

The Dryads remained without a word for some time.

"Tell me – what's the matter?" Egorh asked, his stomach in a knot.

After a while it was Mirk who replied, his blond mane blowing over his face, "Use the pipe-whistle if you need us. We'll be around. Come Kirk."

They left without another word and Egorh watched as they leaped away at breakneck speed, to disappear into the shadows without looking back.

The first rays of the morning sun chose that instant to break over the ancient treetops of the forest and light the land. Egorh did not notice the sweet scent of jasmine that drifted into his room. He struggled with the icy feeling that clutched at him. He grasped the amulet and felt anger, mingled with fear, rising from his gut. It's come back to me. I am not strong enough! When will I be ready for what I need to confront? Who is this enemy that forces me to stay unseen? Egorh held the precious amulet in one hand, absentmindedly touching the mark on his neck with the other.

~

It was mid morning when Sir Matthew returned to the estate. He was in a good mood. The storms were gone and had left the fields greener than ever. The weather seemed too fine for him to worry about the future. He'd had a good trip and enjoyed the visit to his old friend Duke John Bronbeck at Crimson Lake.

An uneasy feeling had been gnawing at his insides

for some time. There should be a plan for young Egorh's future, should anything happen to himself. He knew that Duke John was a man of solid character; a responsible man who seemed particularly caring towards young Egorh. Sir Matthew trusted the Duke implicitly and decided to reveal the boy's history to him. At first, he had been very reluctant to share this knowledge with anyone, but John had promised him that he would keep Egorh's identity a secret. I've done the right thing, he reassured himself.

They had both lost their wives to the plague. A close bond had formed between them during those difficult times and John was like a brother to him now. He knew his friend would take his place as a father, should something happen to him.

He smiled and spurred his horse. He had missed the youngster and was eager to see him again.

~

For years there had been a ritual when Sir Matthew returned from a trip and Egorh's eyes shone as he waited at the door. The reunion always started with a mock battle. It was almost lunchtime and Egorh's stomach rumbled as delicious smells drifted from the kitchen. Marion must have warmed up the leftover lamb casserole but today I will ignore my growling stomach a little longer, he thought. He watched as Sir Matthew entered the hall, sniffed and mumbled, "I am starved." He rushed up to his father as he removed his coat and said, "I'm glad you are back, Father. How was your trip?"

Sir Matthew turned to him and Egorh could see the affection in his eyes. "It's good to see you too, Egorh. My visit to Duke John and the city was everything I had hoped it would be, thank you. Have you spent the weeks of my absence wisely?"

"Yes, I've been training," Egorh nodded eagerly.

"You will have to prove that," Sir Matthew smiled.

Egorh studied his father and asked excitedly, "Are you going to give me the chance to?" He drew his sword and examined the blade casually, turning it back and forth in his hand, the worries of the previous night forgotten.

"What more could you have possibly learned in the short time I have been gone?" Sir Matthew teased and handed Joseph his coat. "I have won all our challenges so far."

"Let me show you, Father," he beamed, balancing slightly with bent knees.

"I am starved but the old falcon will first teach the young chick a lesson." Sir Matthew smiled, amused by his son's enthusiasm. He drew his sword, jabbing and prodding with the blade a few times to tempt Egorh. "Come, let's see if I have been wasting my money on your trainer."

Joseph rolled his eyes and shook his head. "Not again," he grumbled under his breath and took a few steps back. "Another ruckus, demolishing the house, I wish they would take it outside!"

Egorh attacked robustly and Sir Matthew just managed to evade his sword. He kept his eyes locked on Egorh and became aware of a swiftness and agility that had not been there before. He must have spent the entire time practicing with his invisible friends from Granilon forest, he thought.

Egorh's eagerness to impress Sir Matthew made him careless and before he knew it, Sir Matthew had managed to knock the sword from his grip and sent it clattering across the marble floor.

Egorh flushed with irritation.

Sir Matthew shook his head. "Always remain calm, young man. There is nothing wrong with your skill, balance or reflexes but your rage and impatience undo all that." Sir Matthew was always ready to instruct.

"Then I will have to practice more," Egorh replied solemnly.

"A trained mind is more important in battle than just skill

with weapons," Sir Matthew continued. "Let me see what you can do."

Egorh knew that the friendly skirmish would not stop until Sir Matthew was satisfied that he could not be provoked again and he picked up his sword. He didn't mind. Somehow when they sparred together, Sir Matthew always managed to channel his anger and rebelliousness in other directions.

The duel that followed was fast and furious around the pillars and among the tables and chairs of the lavish hall. Joseph followed behind at a safe distance, catching vases, straightening paintings, replacing cushions and trying to restore order as the two sword-fighters left havoc in their wake as they battled to outdo one another. Time after time, Sir Matthew had the upper hand and he searched for any sign of anger on Egorh's face.

Egorh fought hard, but Sir Matthew managed to drive him up the staircase to the passage on the next floor. He smiled politely and glowed with the excitement of the challenge. He flung his sword high and caught it with his left hand, then leaped onto the balustrade, balancing on the handrail on the balls of his feet. He held the sword mockingly in the guard position and teased, "Come Father!"

He saw how Sir Matthew measured the distance of a fall to the bottom, faking a blank expression and merely grumbled, "Show off!" Egorh smiled broadly at his father's remark.

"Get down from there," his father insisted.

Egorh leapt down with ease and slashed forward. Sir Matthew managed to ward off the thrust and Egorh's sword slammed into the wooden handrail, forcing out a wedge and sending it flying down to where Joseph caught it. He inspected the piece of wood and grunted, "Clean cut! It will be easy to glue."

Breathing heavily, Sir Matthew barely managed to drive him back past the many rooms leading from the passage and into his room at the end. Once in the room, Sir Matthew laughed, lowered his sword to catch his breath and wiped the perspiration from his forehead.

Egorh flicked the thick auburn hair from his face and acknowledged his father's hard-won victory with a deep bow and they slid their swords back into their sheaths.

Sir Matthew smiled proudly as he looked at young Egorh. A model of a perfect son he thought.

A sudden flapping movement outside the window distracted Egorh. He glanced up and saw a black-crested eagle with weird green eyes and claws that seemed too large, staring at him. It was making repeated and almost unbearably loud screeching calls.

A shiver ran down his spine but Sir Matthew quickly closed the heavy drapes. Egorh could see from his expression that something was wrong. "What is it Father?" he asked quietly, a prickle of apprehension passing through his young body.

Sir Matthew tried to look unconcerned, "Nothing's wrong, Egorh, nothing at all. Just my imagination. Come let's go and eat!"

"Will you be home for long this time?"

"A few days, perhaps a week. I wish it was longer but the people up north need me to help with a strategy against the increased attacks by the slave traders."

Egorh couldn't help but feel disappointed and his expression tightened. Sir Matthew sighed and put his hand on his shoulder, finding his gaze. "You do understand that it's necessary to keep evil from our lands?"

He nodded. When his father was away he missed their evenings of conversation in front of the fireplace. Sometimes they would talk until the early hours of the morning about the philosophies of life. Sir Matthew would also tell tales of great battles and the brave men who fought them. He again would entertain his father with reports of his adventures in the woods with the Dryads and their skillful training.

Sir Matthew ruffled Egorh's hair, "Come on, don't look so glum. I have a good piece of history that I have been saving to tell you."

Egorh forced a happy expression, "I also have a good story to tell you."

"Then we both have something to look forward to tonight."
Sir Matthew smiled. "But with an empty stomach no man can
think. Let's find the source of that delicious aroma."

He grinned as he felt his father's arm around him. Although
Sir Matthew was generally a strict man, his patience and strong
beliefs were an endless source of strength for him. He admired
Sir Matthew's great wisdom and hoped that someday he too
would acquire such knowledge.

~

Arkarrah pushed the branches slightly apart and screwed
up his sly face trying to see any movement from the big house
in the distance.

"No one yet. Why are they taking so long? It was a simple
task," he grunted and turned back to the men who were gathered
in the forest just out of sight of the main house. The bunch were
wrapped to their ears against the cold but still shivered. They
had been waiting all night for two of their group to return from
their mission.

"Horribly cold night," shivered Arkarrah as he blew hot
breath onto his hands, agitated and frozen to the marrow.

It had been a trying wait with no fires allowed in case
they should be spotted. He knew his men would give anything
to stuff their empty bellies with greasy meat and cheap wine, to
drive out the cold. Two had set out for the big house under the
cover of darkness with the intention of finding someone they
could bring back to question.

A noise broke from the bushes and Arkarrah's men jumped
up, ready to fight. But they relaxed when they saw it was the two
returning, dragging a gagged old man between them. "He is a
gardener at the house," they announced, pleased with themselves,
as they hauled him before Arkarrah.

"Good," Arkarrah smirked as his black beady eyes raked

the old man. He bent forward and ripped the gag off. "I hope you have what I want."

Above, the black-crested eagle gave a ghastly ear-piercing cry and the gardener shuddered with fear.

"See, even Khan is happy you are here," he sneered.

"What do you w-w-want?" the man whimpered.

"Information," Arkarrah said tapping his fingertips together.

Unable to hide his distress the man stuttered, "I know n-n-nothing! I just work in Sir Matthew's g-g-gardens,"

"Mmmm." Arkarrah flattened his oily hair with his palm and grinned, showing his yellow teeth, "I will help you to remember," he snapped over his shoulder, "Sojun, give me the bag."

Sojun stared cruelly from under pencil-thin eyebrows at the gardener as he passed a bag to Arkarrah. The countless wrinkles on his face were barely visible under the brim of his straw hat.

"SO – let's see what we have here to loosen a tongue." Arkarrah pulled out an enormous scorpion, held it up by one of its legs and dangled it back and forth very close to the gardener's face. He kept it well away from himself, to escape the creature's grasping, fear-inducing stingers. The man paled as the two tails swirled aggressively and dangerously near.

"Repulsive-looking creature, isn't it? Perilously poisonous! This is a rare one. It has two tails. Death Stalker, they call it. The men can tell you, they have seen many victims' limbs turn black in only a few minutes, followed by a painful death!"

Muddled by fear, the poor old man licked his dry lips.

The gang had been watching the terrified gardener and the pantomime with the scorpion so intently that no one had noticed the young hunter peeping from behind a tree, holding a rabbit that he'd just caught in a trap nearby.

"Where's the boy?" Arkarrah spat. The gardener lowered his gaze from the scorpion and started to stutter.

"H... h... he's in the house with his f-f-father."

"Who else is there?" Arkarrah demanded, bringing the creature even closer.

"Joseph the m-manservant and three servants."

"Where is the lady of the house?"

"There is no lady, she died l-l-long ago."

Arkarrah dropped the scorpion back into the bag Sojun was holding and instructed, "Tie the wretched old man to a tree. If he lied, we will come back for him."

Arkarrah began a serious conversation with the rest, planning the attack. No one spotted the wiry youngster untying the gardener and the two of them slipping silently away into the forest.

It was much later when Arkarrah discovered the disappearance and bellowed. "He's gone – the gardener is gone! Who was responsible for tying him up?"

Someone pointed to a one-eyed man. Arkarrah walked over to him and hissed, "Useless fool!" He drew his sword and drove it through the man's chest.

With the body at his feet, an irate Arkarrah roared, "Do not take my orders lightly!" He glared, making sure everybody had heard him, then wiped his sword on a broad leaf from a nearby shrub.

"They could have been warned by now. Gather the horses. Hurry!" he barked. "Sojun, take the bats and the scorpion to the camp and make sure there is enough nectar to mark the slaves." He mounted, followed by his men, and raced towards the house.

Sojun began to head off in the opposite direction with his mule, moving deeper into the woods where he knew he would find the ingredients for the deadly salve he had to mix. On the mule, a battered cage, partly covered with a black cloth, was fastened with a leather strap. Inside the cage, two enormous white-winged vampire bats dangled upside down. A distinct stench identified their presence as they moved deeper into the forest. Now and again shrill calls from within the cage caused many other bats, clustered around in the high trees, to flutter and react with sharp shrieks.

"Shut up!" barked Sojun as he slammed his hand hard on the cage. "We don't want to be followed."

Chapter 12

Escape

It was early and Egorh was keen to get to the stables and take Vector up Creek Hill. He had heard that a local boy had spotted wild mountain cats up near the falcon's nest the day before. He wanted to make sure the breeding pair was still around. Falcons had rarely been seen for the past few years at Old Falcon Place and he wanted to make sure that the cats did not get to them.

He frowned as he heard Sir Matthew yell. His father's steps pounded hard as he came charging up the stairs to his room.

"Egorh!" The door burst open and Sir Matthew stood there, his face flushed with emotion.

"There is danger! We must hurry! We must leave the house immediately!" he panted.

Egorh was startled by his father's frantic outburst, "What's the matter, Father? What has happened?"

"Joseph," he gasped, "Joseph just informed me about a planned attack on the house. He thinks it's the slave traders.

Some thugs kidnapped the old gardener earlier this morning and forced information from him, but fortunately someone in the woods helped him slip away and raise the alarm."

He had heard many stories of the brutal and cruel slave traders and the thought of a possible attack enraged him. "Father, we can fight them. You, Joseph and I," Egorh said with complete confidence in his voice as he reached for his sword.

"NO Egorh! There are too many of them! We stand no chance. It appears that there's a group of more than twenty men, all heavily armed. Today you cannot be a hero. Let's go! Now!"

Egorh turned to argue but Sir Matthew grabbed him by the arm and hurried him down the stairs as fast as he could. They raced out the front door and scrambled into the waiting carriage. Joseph whipped the horses madly to reach full speed as they sped away from the house.

In the distance, he saw a group of riders tearing towards them. Joseph tried his best to stay ahead but the mob was faster and it was not long before they caught up. Flames burst out everywhere as burning arrows struck the carriage. Egorh could hear the attackers' shouts. Shocked, he saw Joseph slump forward and tumble from his seat to the ground, an arrow deeply embedded in his chest. Flames and smoke filled the carriage. Sir Matthew tried in vain to open the door.

The flames horrified Egorh. His face twisted with anguish, the smoke burned his throat and he started to cough and gasp for air. He felt Sir Matthew's grip on his arm, "Egorh, you *must* escape. Do not let these men capture you, no matter what happens next. Do you understand me?" Sir Matthew shook him, urging a response. "Don't *ever* take the amulet off. Remember that!"

Egorh, battling to breathe, could barely grasp his father's words and nodded mutely. Sir Matthew managed to kick the door open and pushed Egorh out. He rolled down the side of the steep embankment. The driverless carriage lurched violently, causing the door to slam shut again before Sir Matthew could follow.

Thorns and bushes tore at Egorh's skin and he landed, breathless and bleeding in a ditch. He struggled upright and scurried for cover behind a nearby tree. Powerless, he heard Sir Matthew's frantic attempts to escape. In the roaring and raging of the inferno, a strong wind suddenly came out of nowhere and fanned the flames even more furiously.

In their panic, the terrified horses managed to break loose and the burning coach overturned. From his hiding place, Egorh watched in horror as the flames engulfed the entire structure. He screamed for his father but he knew it was in vain.

The nearest trees were scorched and shriveled, as the burning wreck filled the forest with smoke.

"Father! NO!" Egorh screamed in anguish. His heart told him that Sir Matthew would not escape. He stood, horrified by the cruelty of what had just happened. The young boy clenched his jaw and swallowed hard. His eyes blurred with tears.

He became aware of galloping hooves and screaming men. He glanced in that direction; then fell back behind a tree for cover.

The horses' hooves kicked up dust as the thugs circled and tried to get closer, but the leaping flames were too fierce. Egorh's knees felt weak with panic, he knew he had to remain hidden if he wanted to survive.

A man in a brown cape approached the burning coach, trying to protect his face from the heat with his hand. "Where is the boy? I'm sure I saw a man and a boy climb in. Find him! I cannot tell the sorceress that I have lost the boy. Search every inch of the area!" he shouted. His men fanned out but could find no sign of anyone.

Gnawing at Arkarrah's insides was the thought that the boy had been burned alive but he needed proof. Zinnia said she wanted the body as evidence or the Haffgoss brothers would not believe her.

"Kill the flames! Bring wet branches, sand, water, anything

you can find. I have to search inside," yelled Arkarrah. Pacing to and fro in a state of impatience and agitation, he waited for the flames to die down. He climbed on top of the overturned coach and kicked the door in. His mouth twisted in revulsion at the sight of the burnt corpse.

"There is only one body and it's not a child's." His snake eyes darted in all directions. Lifting a thin lip he snarled, "Find him!"

Egorh hearing all this, moved from his hiding place, and slipped into a crevice of a nearby rock. He sat deathly quiet, his knuckles turning white as he clutched his amulet. For the first time in his life he hoped and prayed that it really *did* possess the magical powers he had been told about. The men sounded close and Egorh scarcely breathed as they combed the vicinity. His heart fluttered when someone close called, "Arkarrah, let's go back to the house and search there. Perhaps you're mistaken; maybe it was a decoy, a trick to deceive us." But the brown-caped man was reluctant to leave. He walked up and down and sniffed the smoke-laden air. "Keep looking!" he roared.

It felt like forever, before Arkarrah gave up the search. When Egorh heard their voices become more distant and the pounding hooves receding, he crept out of his hiding place and approached the smoldering carriage.

In his path, out of nowhere, a monstrous black wolf appeared. A curl of steamy breath flowed from its wide nostrils, its watery yellow eyes glinted as it stared viciously at him. Egorh's hand dropped to his sword but found it was not there. Vaguely he remembered there had been no time to take it when they fled the house. He tried to move away but the wolf began to circle him.

A glitter of gold appeared in the beast's eyes, a reflection of the last of the glowing embers of the fire behind him. Paralyzed by fear, he heard a growl escape from the creature's mouth as it opened its jaws. The sound was faint but vibrated a rage that reached deep into every corner of his mind.

The animal's eyes mysteriously became two huge black pools of liquid that melted together and lingered in front of him, like a moon that had dropped from the sky. Images began to appear of flames that flared up, buildings crumbling and hoards of crimson-pink birds taking flight.

The images were old but familiar and, as he stared, he realized there was something else, some act of violence. He felt panic squeeze his throat, slowly choking him. He heard an anguished cry and saw the silhouette of a man holding a knife dripping with blood. Egorh felt undeniably part of the scene. His heart pounded as he felt death all around. His body trembled. He covered his ears and shut his eyes tightly, willing it all to go away.

Gradually the images began to melt, the round space faded and the beast's eyes turned yellow again. The wolf lowered its head and snarled with yellow fangs. There was a dangerous challenge in its leer as it leaped towards him. Egorh stumbled back and fell onto the dirt. The wolf passed him like a ghost and vanished through a thick tree trunk, as if recalled by some unseen force.

Egorh felt drained. He stood up and searched for any trace of the animal, then turned and ran towards the burned-out rubble, not daring to look back. He was unaware that Sir Matthew's fiery death had awakened an ancient memory of his past in the image of the wolf. That very image had crawled into the deepest corners of his heart, from where it would torment him until it could be conquered.

His face was taut, dirty and tearstained as he stood gaping in horror and disbelief at the carnage before him. He was unaware that blood oozed from a gash on his forehead as he stared at the smoldering wreckage. He dropped to his knees, his eyes dark with grief. "Don't leave me, Father," he whispered.

The skirmish they had enjoyed earlier that day flashed through his mind; how his father had smiled at him. He knew his father was proud of him and that he loved him. Holding back the wave of sorrow that threatened to devour him he muttered, "What will I do without you?"

He did not know how long he sat there. It was only when rage began to burn deep within him and the nails of his clenched fists drew blood from his palms that he yelled in anger, "I will find them! They will not get away with this!" He swallowed his sobs. "I am sorry, Father! It is all my fault. I lost the amulet." He clutched the amulet as tears coursed down his cheeks and mixed with the blood already there, the dark drops staining his leather jerkin. He was unaware of the black-crested eagle with the green eyes that flew from the tree above.

Vaguely Egorh became aware of approaching hoof beats. Fearing a return of the slayers, he hid once more in the underbrush. There was murder in his heart, but without his bow or sword he could do nothing. He would have to wait. Relief washed over him when he recognized the horses and coach that pulled up alongside the burnt-out wreck. He scrambled up and rushed towards his father's friend.

Surprisingly agile for his fifty-six summers, the Duke jumped out and approached the terrible scene. He hesitated when he saw the destruction. With a groan of misery, he realized that Sir Matthew and Joseph had not survived.

Hearing a sound behind him, he turned and saw his friend's son in a shocking state.

"Egorh, thank the gods you're alive! Are you alright?"

Egorh nodded mutely.

"I heard rumors of slave traders in the area," he explained, "and came to warn your father. The servants told us of your sudden flight but we were too late. We followed you here. I am *so* sorry." The Duke shook his head in despair. His slanting eyes smoldered like coals beneath his low brows as he breathed heavily in anger.

Duke John gently took him by the arm and said, "Come on

my boy. I'll take you to my home. We have both lost someone special today."

"No sir," Egorh managed to say. "I have to get my sword and bow, and Vector my horse. I have to find those men, sir!"

"I know, I know," he soothed, "but now is not the right time. It will be too dangerous for you to go back. You will stay with me until we have found out what they were after. We need someone to look at your wound. My men will take care of your father and Joseph's bodies for you. I will instruct one of them to fetch your horse and weapons. We *will* find whoever is responsible for this dreadful deed."

Still numb with shock, Egorh allowed himself to be helped into the coach and somberly whispered, "Thank you." His brown eyes were sad and dark. He was glad that the Duke was there.

Chapter 13

Eye of the Flamingo

Egorh's white shirt was torn and stained with blood. His tears had left thin lines on his dirty cheeks.

"Here, Egorh, use my handkerchief to wipe your face," Duke John said in a strong voice that could not be ignored.

Egorh took it without saying a word and looked out of the window. The pale spring sun of Old Falcon Place hung low on the horizon as he felt the wheels starting to turn in a direction that would be new to him. His misery deepened at the thought that he would never see his home again. As the sun dipped, colors of pink, peach and gold exploded around the silhouettes of the moving clouds, unnoticed by him. His mind became blank as he retreated from reality.

John took pity on young Egorh. He could see there was strength in the young boy's frame as he sat wordlessly. His eyes fell on the strange beak mark on the side of Egorh's neck. Matthew had informed him about the mark and the bizarre history of the child. If it had been anybody else telling the story, he would have laughed it off as rubbish, but Matthew Bidault was a solid and dependable man. John swallowed hard, immensely saddened by his loss, and muttered, "Don't worry old friend, I will keep my promise to care for young Egorh. I will not let you down."

For the next three days the carriage sped through hills and forests, the driver watchful for possible attack. The days were bright but the nights chillingly cold. The coach driver seldom stopped. When he did, it was only long enough for the horses to rest a few minutes and drink from the clear mountain rivers they passed, while they themselves nibbled on dried meat and bread that was wrapped in cloth. Throughout each day, Egorh watched the land speed by and studied the man sitting opposite him. Duke John was of noble birth and the fourth generation of respected horse breeders. Training young colts was his hobby. His skin was weathered from the outdoors and a small wry grin was about the only smile you would ever see from him. Egorh thought he looked kind and he liked this man.

Despite his anguish and grief, Egorh managed to sleep for short periods. At night, the swaying, dim oil lamp inside the coach would hypnotize him into a restless slumber. With his closed eyes, the Duke was unaware that Egorh was cursing the haunting image of the brown-cloaked man silently. "Keep him alive!" he whispered, "so I can find him one day and kill him to avenge my father's death."

~

It was late afternoon on the third day when they rumbled through the gates of the massive Crimson Lake Estate. The house stood among fenced green meadows where herds of fine horses grazed and young stallions tried to outrun one another. Egorh caught a glimpse of a vast lake ahead that shone like gold in the setting sun. On the lakeshore, a wave of red movement grabbed his attention and made him lean forward in his seat. For the first time in three days, his eyes became bright with interest. Hundreds and hundreds of red legs moved beneath the pink bodies of the beautiful birds that were gathered around the edge. Large groups were taking flight.

"These are the birds!" Egorh said out aloud and stared in disbelief. The scene in front of him was almost identical to the image of the birds he had seen in the eyes of the black wolf he'd encountered.

"Giant flamingos, incredible sight, aren't they?" he heard Duke John say. Unaware of the real cause of Egorh's curiosity, he looked in the direction of the flamingos and added, "There are many of them today, more than usual."

Egorh stared at the birds without saying a word.

The coach came to a halt in front of the impressive entrance to the mansion. The Duke climbed out first, then turned to Egorh and said, "We will have dinner in one-and-a-half hours. My staff will look after you. Go with them and freshen up. I will see to it that you get clean clothes. We will talk later."

Still intrigued, Egorh cast a glance back at the lake before he started to descend. He looked up at the house and noticed a young girl who came rushing through the doorway towards them. Egorh stopped and the girl smiled at him. She was the most beautiful thing he'd ever seen and her striking blue eyes held him captivated for a heartbeat. Something tugged inside him and he felt his face redden. He quickly lowered his eyes to his dusty boots and continued his way up. A sudden loud honk behind him made him swing around. A group of flamingos had gathered as if from nowhere and were moving towards him, bills down and heads shaking from side to side. Some were pumping their necks, calling out with loud gabbling sounds, their scapular and back feathers raised, wings flapping. Egorh stood motionless. He wasn't going to show any fear of the birds – not before Duke John and especially not in front of the girl. He took a slow breath, kept his expression as blank as possible and stared at the birds, now almost within reach.

Duke John moved to stand next to the girl. "What is happening Father?" she asked, somewhat concerned.

"I have no idea Kayrin. I have never seen the flamingos behave like this before."

An enormous male seemed to be the most aggressive, beating its wings and throwing its head back, as if about to attack with its pitch-black bill. It lowered its wings and moved proudly but stiffly, closer to Egorh. He is huge, Egorh thought calmly. Strangely he did not feel threatened. The bird's head was so near that he could count the eyelashes. There was a challenge in its eyes as it studied Egorh, almost as if it was searching for something.

John moved slowly to take the whip from the carriage driver, preparing to use it. He felt his daughter's hand on his arm, "Relax Father. I don't think it means any harm. Let's wait a few moments," she whispered.

The male bird approached Egorh and began to circle him, examining the boy carefully. Egorh's dark eyes followed the bird's movements intently. The flamingo paused when it saw the beak mark on his neck, as if it had found what it had been searching for. The feathered creature cocked its head and dipped its bill a few times. A strange tranquility descended on the scene. No one spoke; there was no birdsong, nor any noise from the other flamingos. There was not even a breath of moving air.

Egorh felt strangely compelled to speak to the bird. He whispered softly, "We have met before. You know it and I know it, although I do not know when or where. I am sure time will tell." The flamingo appeared to be listening sharply. Egorh swallowed and spoke again, "Go back to the lake now."

"I have never witnessed such behavior!" the Duke whispered to his daughter. "The boy is fearless. He spoke to the flamingo as if it were tame. It appears as if they understand each other."

There was no movement anywhere for a few anxious moments, then the bird turned its eyes away and gave a thunderous trumpeting call. A sign of agreement, or contentment?

96

Egorh wondered. Without warning, the male turned to the other flamingos, stretched its neck high and flagged it from side to side. It opened its wings and started to beat them, while uttering more blaring calls. As if this was a signal, the other birds joined in and there was a deafening noise as small groups of birds took flight. Soon all of them were in the air, creating a crimson-pink cloud. Egorh watched as they circled a few times and then, one by one, descended to the far corner of the lake. He thought to himself, I have seen this before. Somehow I am part of it.

"Amazing," John marveled, as he accompanied his daughter into the mansion. Does this affinity with the flamingos have something to do with the flamingo beak mark? What can it all mean? he wondered.

Egorh, somewhat dazed by what had just happened, did not dare to look at the girl again. He followed them up the steps to the doorway, mystified by what had just occurred.

The bedroom he was shown to was spacious and adequately lit with oil lamps, though rather high ceilinged. The walls were painted in soft beige to match the darkish brown marble floor, which was scattered with a few woven rugs. A chilly blast of wind came from an open window with large ledges and Egorh felt how the cold bit deep into his bones. A heavy curtain stirred at one side and he walked over to close the window. From there the flamingos could clearly be seen around the lake.

The room was very elegantly furnished and most comfortable. He had a long bath and changed into the light shirt and trousers a friendly servant had brought him. I do not feel like dinner, he thought, as he walked down the stairs to join Duke John and his daughter in the dining room. The table was set with tall crystal glasses and lavish silver and gold plated dinnerware. During the meal, Egorh was very sombre, confused by the day's events. He listlessly moved his uneaten food around the plate with his fork. Constantly he felt Kayrin's penetrating glances towards him, but he did not dare look in her direction in case he would flush with emotion again. As he stared at his plate, he remembered her eyes, as blue as the breeding plumage of the indigo bunting bird. Having grown up with neither mother nor sisters, Egorh was unsure of how to behave towards Kayrin. It would be some time before he would feel confident enough to look her squarely in the eye.

The Duke and Kayrin tried their best to make him feel welcome, but it wasn't long before he asked, "Please excuse me, I would like to go to my room. Thank you for your hospitality." He rose to his feet and gave a small bow towards Duke John and the girl, without looking at her. As he walked away, he was aware of her eyes following him. Her smile showed that she was intrigued by the young boy with the handsome face and dark hazel-brown eyes.

~

Dinner finished, Duke John retired to his study, closed the door and walked over to a table where some decanters were standing. He poured himself a stiff cognac before he dropped into the big leather chair and sighed. He twirled the glass a few times, staring at the crystal tumbler, savoring the color of the golden liquid. He took a warming sip. A frown furrowed his brow as his mind drifted back over the past few days. The murder of Matthew and Joseph, finding Egorh alive, their journey home and today the strange incident with the flamingos.

The study was effectively lit and spacious. The floor was of dark wood, accented by a dark Persian rug. John never smoked himself, but he liked to keep the rolled tobacco for some of his visitors, which accounted for the faint cigar smell that lingered in the air. He pulled an envelope from the drawer of his heavy, solid wood desk and broke the seal. He took out the pages of the letter that his old friend had given him on an earlier visit.

He started to read its contents slowly. 'My dear old friend,' it began. 'When you read this letter, I most probably will not be alive and as we have discussed before, you will now be the new protector of Egorh, the son of Darkarh. The secret is yours to keep. This young man carries the beak mark as proof of his lineage. You know what to do and I know you will raise him well. Remember the importance of the amulet; he must *never* be without it. It will protect him *until the time has come*. Please be sure to enforce this.' John sat for a while deep in thought as he tried to make sense of it all.

Reaching a decision, he rang the bell for a servant to ask Egorh to join him in the study. A few moments later, Egorh appeared and Duke John showed him to a big leather chair opposite him. Egorh, despite his exhaustion, could see that his father's friend was preoccupied.

"Egorh, the past few days have been very difficult for you and you would probably prefer to rest, but there are some things I need to tell you." Duke John tapped the letter he still held in his hand. "Your father asked me to take care of you should anything happen to him and I made that promise. You know he was like a brother to me. You are the sole heir of his estate – Old Falcon Place now belongs to you. I will take care of the land until you are ready and able to do so yourself."

"But I am ready Sir. I can take care of it myself. Marion is still there." Trying to be convincing, he leaned forward, his hands on his knees.

The Duke shook his head. "You cannot go back there for now, in case your father's murderers should return."

Egorh sat in silence for a moment, then asked, "Did my father say anything else?"

"Only that in time things you need to know will be revealed to you." Duke John was not finding his task easy but the boy's self-control, rare for someone so young, helped slightly. He changed the subject. "I hope you will, for now, make my house your home. There are many diversions here to amuse a young lad like yourself. But I need to ask you not to go into the woods alone. We have had an increasing number of raids recently by the slave traders and the woods are not safe."

Egorh remained silent, then said placidly, "Thank you sir

for your kindness in taking me into your home. One day I shall repay your generosity. May I return to my room sir?"

"Of course, my boy, of course. Try to get some sleep. Goodnight." Egorh bowed and left the study.

On the way to his room, he experienced a strange feeling. He did not know what it was, but knew he had to go to the lake. He opened the large front door and stepped outside.

The full moon was reflected by the water and he could see the flamingos massed around the lake. The birds were restless, moving their thin legs up and down as if they were dancing. He walked towards the edge and bent down to see his reflection in the mirror-like water. The beak mark on his neck was barely visible and he instinctively touched it.

"Who am I?" Egorh softly asked. "What evil forces are searching for me? Who is responsible for killing my father and Joseph? Why do I feel this powerful attraction to these strange and beautiful birds?"

He stood up and felt an almost unbearable throbbing pain in his chest. In an anguished voice he cried out, "WHO AM I?" His voice carried over the lake. He crouched back down, leaned forward with his face in his hands and once more desperately asked, "Who am I?"

For a moment nothing moved and there was silence over and around the water. Then he became aware of a large flamingo. It appeared to be the same bird that he had encountered that afternoon and it slowly approached him. It came so close that he could see the yellow of its eye. He stared at the bird without blinking, breathless, not knowing what to expect. The flamingo lowered its neck and the pupil of its eye slowly widened, the yellow iris disappearing as though a curtain was being drawn. Egorh felt himself pulled into the bird's eye. A vague terror possessed him as he felt himself sliding down a formless mass of black fog, his heart thumped with fear in the strange darkness.

Gradually, the blackness disappeared and he saw in front of him, not the lake and its birds, but a huge vertical cliff with an old door set in it. He closed his eyes and thought, am I dreaming? Slowly his trembling ceased and the sense of terror left him. He opened his eyes and the mysterious door in front of him swung open. He felt compelled to enter.

Chapter 14

High Priest

Cautiously Egorh moved towards the open door and saw a tunnel with many steps leading down to somewhere far below. In the distance an owl was calling. He slipped through the doorway and down the steps. All the way down, the wet stone walls were illuminated by oil lamps. The pungent smell of ancient wet soil hung in the air. Not knowing what to expect he walked down carefully. Reaching the bottom he saw an opening ahead that lead into a huge, granite-domed chamber. It was a mystical place. Tiny golden birds skimmed the air and sucked nectar from purple flowers.

"This must be a dream," he murmured.

In a corner of the room, an imposing-looking man with grey curly hair falling onto his shoulders sat at a long stone table, writing by the light of a tall candle. On the other side of the table, a dog with the longest blond curly ears Egorh had ever seen was fast asleep. One ear spread across the table and the other hung down, almost touching the floor.

There were many passages leading from the large domed room to more halls and chambers. In the vast granite chamber, natural springs fed into a big pond. At the edge, a huge flamingo with bright crimson feathers twisted its neck and scratched under one wing, paying him no attention.

The man looked up from his work. The shadow of the flickering candle danced over his face and grave-blue eyes. He raised his eyebrows as he stood up. He was tall and now looked even more imposing. Egorh's head was spinning. He swallowed hard and asked with as much courage as he could muster, "Who are you?"

"You asked a question at the lake, young Egorh. Remember?" the man spoke in a deep voice.

"How do you know my name? How did I get here?" Egorh tensed and took a few steps back.

The grey-haired man ignored his questions and said instead, "Your question at the lake is why you are here. I am Steukhon, a priest from the Magic World. I will try to answer your questions." He walked towards Egorh, toying with the large crystal that hung around his neck. Egorh noticed that the dog had moved to lie upon the scroll which Steukhon had been writing in, as if to protect its contents.

Steukhon followed Egorh's stare and said, "Ah, the dog. His name is Maximus. He is the protector of my documents. Even here I must be wary. There are thieves everywhere these days. One cannot be too careful." He turned his attention to Egorh. The child had grown into a fine youngster, he thought. From an early age, much news of Egorh had reached his ears; his bravery in saving a Dryad's life and his eagerness to train with sword and bow. Steukhon also knew about the anger that never seemed to leave him and saw the same piercing eyes of those of his father, Darkarh.

"I am going to tell you a tale. It might sound strange and far-fetched, but I hope that when I am finished it will bring some calmness to your heart and mind. By now, you must have realized that you are not like other children," said Steukhon.

Egorh only nodded.

"You play and talk with Dryads, see things other humans don't and you have exceptional skill with weapons for your age."

"You know the Dryads?"

"Yes, I know Mirk and Kirk."

"But I thought no one else could see them."

"Well then, it seems we have something in common." Steukhon's eyes sparkled with amusement. He continued in a serious tone. "Your question was, 'Who am I?' Well, you come from the Magic world, now fallen because of greed and jealousy. There was an ancient god named Darkarh, who fell in love with a beautiful mortal woman, Nerifa.

"Darkarh loved Nerifa dearly and built a magnificent castle in her honor, with hot and cold springs for her to bathe and a glorious garden for her enjoyment. He created thousands and thousands of giant crimson-pink birds to entertain her by the water and called them flamingos. When they danced at sunset, the masses of moving red legs looked like glimmering flames. It was a magnificent kingdom.

"Then, unexpectedly, Nerifa died, while giving birth to her four sons. To each of his sons, Darkarh gave the power of a true element and an obelisk of astonishing magic. The firstborn, he named Egorhagh and bestowed upon him the true element of fire, strength of achievement, bravery and skill with weapons. His obelisk was made of the magical orinium metal. The other brothers were less favored and received lesser gifts."

Steukhon walked back to the table. Egorh followed, sat down and waited. After a pause Steukhon continued, "Having knowledge of Egorhagh's magical obelisk, they planned to murder him and claim it. To save his favorite son's spirit, Darkarh cast it into a giant flamingo, one of the thousands around the castle's lakes and urged all the birds to take flight. Egorhagh's spirit was sent to earth to be reborn as a mortal.

"Distraught at losing his son, Darkarh destroyed his land

104

with fire and cast his three evil sons into the HapLess Sphere - a region of doom and hopelessness."

Steukhon's hand made a twirling motion in the air and a pink cloud appeared. In the mist, a picture of masses of birds in the sky, burning buildings and tumbling mud could be seen. The sky looked as if it was on fire with all the thousands of birds and the smoldering land below.

"It was impossible to find Egorhagh in all the destruction." Steukhon muttered. As he lowered his hand, the picture vanished.

Egorh gasped and thought, that's what I saw! In the wolf's eyes, the birds ... thousands of birds! He trembled at the thought.

Steukhon went on, "So that no one would be able to trace Egorhagh on earth, by searching the flamingos' eyes, Darkarh changed their beautiful blue eyes to solid yellow. So that no one could ever ask them of his whereabouts, he silenced their lovely voices. All they do now is make a trumpet sound and keep mostly to themselves. Finally, Darkarh instructed that his earthly son be named Egorh and be given the mark of the beak, to prove to all that he was his son. From that day on, every soul from that bloodline would be born with a mark in the shape of a flamingo beak." Steukhon paused, "Like the one you carry Egorh," he added quietly.

Egorh touched the mark. "Me?" he whispered in disbelief. "What do you mean? Am I ...?"

"Yes Egorh, you are Egorhagh the son of Darkarh."

"But my father ..." Egorh struggled to get the words out. "My father was burnt alive!"

"I know and I am so sorry for your loss. I was responsible for your birth on earth and Sir Matthew was chosen by Darkarh to be your earthly father. I was the one who took you to him the day you were born. Darkarh was your real father."

He waited in silence for Egorh to process all that he had heard. His strong voice broke into Egorh's whirling thoughts as he continued, "There is a great deal more you should know. Now you understand why the flamingos are interested in you and why they will always seek your presence. You are spiritually connected."

"Was Nerifa my real mother? What was she like?" Egorh asked eagerly.

"Yes. She was beautiful and kind and loved the birds Darkarh gave her. She was a very special person."

"And Darkarh?"

"He was strong and powerful and I can see that his spirit runs through you. You can be proud to be his son."

Egorh felt pleased that he had learned something about his parents and wanted to ask many more questions, but Steukhon interrupted.

"You had one other question. Why are you here? Well, when you asked the question tonight, 'Who am I?' there was so much desperation in your voice that the flamingo sensed your pain and just this once, opened his eye to enable you to find the answers, by bringing you to me."

He stared at the confused Egorh. Shadows flickered across the boy's face and he said with concern, "Egorh, you have had a terrible experience. It is important for you to embrace this experience so you can conquer the evil of it. Only then will you be able to find peace."

The priest turned away from the silent boy, sat down, picked up the feather pen and resumed his writing.

Egorh raised his eyes and said, "The wolf I saw at the attack – has it got something to do with all of this?"

"You saw a wolf?" the priest scowled.

"Yes, what does it mean? It has come back to torture me in my dreams."

"You were afraid of the flames. Demons always enter through the door of fear. You will have to fight it."

"When?"

Steukhon held his gaze for a long time and then said, "The demon will challenge you when you need to fear him the least."

Egorh stood rapt from all he had heard, "Tell me more ...
I need to know much more," he began.

Steukhon looked up from his writing and answered
seriously, "You have a destiny, young Egorh. Let's leave it at
that. For now you have to attend to the business of growing up.
When the time comes, all will be revealed to you. But remember,
always wear the amulet for your protection."

"But ..." Egorh started, when suddenly he found himself
back at the lake with the flamingo still very close to him. He
looked around, wondering if he had fallen asleep and had been
dreaming. He stared at the bird and then asked, "Could you
speak in the times of Darkarh?" The bird uttered a soft honk.
"Then what I just experienced was not a dream, but reality?"
The bird lowered its long neck and gently honked again as if to
agree. Egorh watched mutely as the flamingo moved away. He
turned and walked slowly back towards the house.

He was completely alone in the darkness. In the dim light
of the moon, his mind was spinning with everything that had
just happened.

~

In his study, John had heard Egorh's cry echoing over the
lake and had gone to the front door to watch over the tormented
boy from a distance. He knew the child would only find peace
once all his questions had been answered. As Egorh reached
the doorway, he placed his strong hand on the boy's shoulder,
"Try to get some sleep Egorh." He closed the front door behind
them.

In his darkened bedroom, Egorh lay on his back thinking
of everything that had happened that day, until his mind settled
on Kayrin's beautiful indigo eyes. He smiled at the recollection
and drifted into a deep sleep.

It was just after midnight when Egorh let out a raw cry and
sat up in bed. He wiped the sweat from his brow and his heart

hammered inside his chest as he felt the burning flames and smelled the charred flesh all around him. He sat rigid with fear until he realized it was only a nightmare. He got up, splashed some cold water over his hot face and climbed back into bed where he slept fitfully for the rest of the night. He did not know that the demon of fire and flames had come to visit him that night.

Chapter 15

Rescue

Pale with agony, the boy's brown eyes searched the top of the walls anxiously for any movement. "Anybody there? Heeeelp ...!" he cried. There was desperation in his hoarse voice as he yelled. He shook his head wearily as his cry faded into the air unheard. How many days have I been in this living hell-hole? he wondered with despair. He had been out hunting when he had fallen straight into a wolf trap. "It's your own fault, Daniel," he muttered to himself, "you were careless." He peered up at the hole his body had made in the wooden lattice of the trap and saw distant treetops silhouetted against the sky. He trembled uncontrollably. I have been along this path so many times before. There wasn't supposed to be a trap here. It must have been freshly dug. Darn poachers! Trapped a human instead of a wolf. Daniel was furious at himself and angrily wiped away the sweat dripping from his forehead.

On his third attempt, he had managed with great effort to pull the monster clamps away from his badly injured leg. Each of the previous times they snapped back, he felt the steel teeth plough deeper into the flesh around his ankle. He had staunched the blood with a piece of cloth torn from his sleeve, but the wound was deep and throbbed painfully.

He had tried to climb the steep walls of the pit, but with his injured fingers it was agony and he kept sliding back. Daniel groaned. His eyes could hardly focus on the badly swollen fingers he held in front of him. He was in a bad way.

All he could do was to pray that the poachers would return soon. They would at least either help him or kill him. Whichever way, he would be better off than he was now with flies buzzing around his painful wound, and the thirst and hunger. He felt appallingly weak, his lips were parched and he was breathing fast. His body was burning up with fever and he started to tremble violently. He struggled to his feet again but the rain had made the inside of the pit muddy and slippery and he fell back. He covered his head with his hands and fought against despair. He sobbed in his misery and eventually drifted into a feverish unconsciousness. The breeze carried his soft moans further into the forest.

~

Egorh woke when the sun threw a long ray of light through the small gap in the curtains onto his bed. He was still drowsy but suddenly leaped up, as if someone had thrown a jug of ice-cold water over him. It had been three weeks since his terrible ordeal. A week had passed since the funeral and last night his personal belongings had arrived from Old Falcon Place. The realization of where he was and what had happened resurfaced. He feverishly began to search for his most precious items in the container. When he found his sword, bow, quiver and the Dryads' flute, he swallowed hard, fighting to hide conflicting emotions. The recent funeral was still vivid in his mind. Finally, after all the trauma of the past few weeks, he held something from his old life in his hands again. The thought of his horse, Vector, waiting in the stables made his somber mood lift slightly.

Steukhon, my destiny, the eye of the flamingo. It all seems so unreal now, Egorh thought as he recalled his arrival at his new home. He dressed quickly, eager to see Vector. He made sure the amulet was hidden under his leather jerkin, yanked on his favorite boots, strapped on his sword, grabbed his bow and quiver and hurried to the stables where the stallion stood, ears pricked to the sounds of his new surroundings.

The Duke's love for horses was quite apparent. His stables were as impressive as his mansion and held fifty of his finest breeding stock. The smell of fresh straw and dung filled Egorh's nostrils pleasantly. Over the past weeks he had drawn comfort from the company of the thoroughbreds and had spent most of his time with them as a release from melancholy thoughts.

He greeted Vector with a slap on the flank, ran his hands down the horse's legs and checked him everywhere. Vector snorted as if in reply, pawed the ground and neighed loudly. Egorh grabbed a brush and spoke softly to the horse as he began to groom him. "Vector! At last we are together again. We are lucky to have a good home, but I promise you that one day we will go back to Old Falcon Place." Vector shook his head as if he understood. The horse's shiny coat quivered under the grooming brush as Egorh continued, "But right now I must find Mirk and Kirk. I remember they spoke of the 'Son of Darkarh' once. I wonder why they didn't tell me what it all meant? I know Duke John warned me not to go into the forest alone, but the Dryads will surely be there."

Egorh stopped as he heard a soft voice behind him. "That's a first-class stallion." It was Kayrin. He dropped the brush clumsily and without looking at her, stooped down to pick it up. He felt his face redden and he wondered what she wanted. With renewed vigor he resumed the horse's grooming, ignoring the girl altogether.

There was an uncomfortable silence between them and Egorh thought he could feel her indigo eyes burning into his back. The air suddenly felt thick and the noise of the many horses around him seemed to fade.

Kayrin tried again. "I watched you practicing yesterday. Everyone here is talking about your skill. Father mentioned that he would like you to join him and his men in their fight against the slave traders. He said he could do with someone like you at his side." There was an awkward silence before Egorh heard her continue, "They say your skills are driven by anger."

Egorh still did not speak but Kayrin could see a small muscle moving in his clenched jaw and she wondered if she had said too much.

She looked solemnly down at her folded hands when no answer came from him.

"I am going to live in the city to further my education. I will be leaving later today."

Egorh wanted to scream, No! But he crushed the word before it could pass his lips. The girl's black hair, the intensity of her eyes, the milky skin and the sparkling laugh had haunted him since the day he had arrived at his new home. If only he had the courage, he would follow her like a puppy dog all day long. She had made him look forward to each day, even if he could only watch her from a distance.

With forced control, he stopped the brushing and turned around, with a blank masked face. "I am happy for you. I believe there are good tutors to be found." Egorh knew those were the most futile words he had ever uttered but his mind would not allow him to think. He looked away and remained stiff and distant, concentrating on the straw-dust trapped in the sun's rays.

"Yes," she replied disappointed. He did not see the sadness that came into her face as she started to move away, thinking that he did not like her for some reason.

"Goodbye Egorh. I hope my home will become your home in time," and she left quickly.

A part of him wanted to stop her. He lifted his hands but then dropped them, as another part of him feared the hurt he imagined such a friendship could bring.

How could he explain to her that the blood of Darkarh ran through him? That a priest had told him he had evil brothers from another world who sought his death. That he was still not strong enough to protect himself and needed the protection of an amulet? If he should lose it again, how would he be able to protect her? Sir Matthew's death had proved this. He would have to wait until he was ready. His father had told him once that desire causes weakness and that to avoid such desire would make you strong. Getting to know Kayrin would have to wait until he became the warrior he was destined to be. He remained in the stables for a long time until he felt Vector's muzzle nudging his back. He turned, quickly mounted the stallion, grabbed his mane and steered him with his knees to the stable doors.

The morning was quiet and the land seemed empty to Egorh as he raced mindlessly across it. He passed the impressive hordes of giant flamingos around the lake and failed to notice the group of men standing in the green field not far from the road.

Duke John's dark eyes stared proudly at a newborn colt and he beamed with delight. It was the first one of the new bloodline he had introduced a year ago. He looked up when he heard the sound of thundering hooves and with scrunched eyes he gazed in the direction of the dust cloud that swirled up around the horse's legs.

He saw the rider holding effortlessly onto the animal's mane with one hand, using the other to give him perfect balance. Horse and rider passed by at full speed, looking neither left nor right. John shook his head and murmured, "There's no doubt about it – he is no ordinary child." A slight shadow flickered in his eyes as he thought, I cannot stop him. It's the first day with his horse in some time.

Matthew had told him that Egorh had friends in the forest who looked out for him. They were his true teachers and greatly responsible for his extraordinary skills. He was not to be too worried when Egorh sometimes visited there. Duke John watched with interest as the rider veered off the road into the dense trees. He knew the forest with its dangers and could not suppress an uneasy sense of foreboding. "I will leave it to the gods to protect him today," he shrugged.

~

The stallion's speed and power helped to clear Egorh's head. He was oblivious to the crisp air and spray of water that spattered on both sides, as Vector's hooves cut through the shallow river. It was only when some of the spray splashed onto his face that he became aware of his surroundings. He slowed down and once they had reached the other side of the river, he paused and looked back in the direction of Crimson Lake. He shuddered, trying to rid himself of the feelings Kayrin had stirred up within him at the stables.

After a few moments he urged Vector into a trot. He followed a narrow trail that wound between the giant trees. The woods were older and denser than those at Old Falcon Place and he had to move slowly. Decades of damp humus and lush vegetation made the air rich in oxygen and easy to inhale.

Egorh felt eager to see his forest friends again, despite Duke John's warnings of the dangers. He smiled as he reminded himself that the Dryads' greeting was always a test and he sat alert, ready for anything. His heart surged when he saw the familiar huge toad leap from a tree to the ground. The next moment Vector snorted as he felt Kirk slap him on his rump.

"No tricks today?" Egorh asked as he dismounted.

"No, we will welcome you first to this part of the forest," Mirk said as he leaped down from a branch. Egorh could sense that the Dryads felt uneasy and could not look him in the eye.

"You heard ...?"

"Yes. We are so sorry for your loss Egorh," Mirk said, his eyes peering far into the forest.

Egorh watched Vector, where he snuffled amongst the dead leaves. Time was lost as the three friends each toiled with their own thoughts.

"I met the priest Steukhon." Egorh broke the silence.

The Dryads stared at him and Kirk's long hand shot up in a gesture to be quiet. "Shhhh ... Not another word," he said sharply.

The Dryads' ears twisted as they listened intently. Mirk was the first to speak, very softly, "It is forbidden to mention that name around you. The woods have ears."

"But ..." Egorh protested.

Mirk shook his head and frowned, "You were told everything you needed to know. It is crucial that we do not speak of it again." Kirk held up his hand, signaling to be quiet and moved a few steps deeper into the woods. He turned his head in every direction until he was satisfied there was no one around. Kirk always claimed he had the sharper eyes of the two.

Suddenly, they heard a muffled cry and all three jerked their heads in that direction.

Something was out there. Egorh came to stand next to Kirk to search the forest shadows. After a while Egorh whispered, "It sounds as though someone is in pain."

"Could be a trap," Kirk replied.

"Maybe, but let's go and look," Egorh dropped his hand to his sword and whistled softly for Vector to follow.

The Dryads glanced at each other and then followed him. Their cobalt eyes scrutinized every moving branch and leaf as they followed the faint cries through the trees, visibly troubled by the thought that they were to have unwanted company.

It wasn't long before they stood at a hole covered with a broken lattice and they could hear the anguished sounds from below. Egorh cleared the hole, crouched on its edge and stared down. "It looks like a young boy. He's badly injured," he muttered to the Dryads who also stood stooped over the pit.

"He must have fallen into the wolf trap," Mirk added.

"Looks as though his leg is badly hurt," Kirk frowned.

Egorh lay on his stomach and peered down. His gaze hardened as he saw the boy and the black, blood-drenched cloth around his leg and said, "He is in a bad way." He noticed the boy's filthy clothes, swollen fingers and apparent fever that caused his black hair to drip with sweat as he shivered. The boy's eyes were wide open, his lips swollen and cracked. Egorh inched forward again and called down into the hole but there was no answer.

"Quick! I don't think we have much time. Help me to cut the lattice. We will tie him onto it with vines so we can pull him up," Egorh instructed and brought the blade of his sword hard down on the lattice. It was easy for the Dryads to move in and out of the hole. They quickly tied the boy to the piece of grid and Egorh started to pull him out.

Daniel whimpered as he felt the movement. Faintly he heard a horse snort and saw shadows move. He moaned again in agony. A spark of hope that he would live flared up before he drifted away.

Egorh looked at Mirk questioningly. Mirk knelt down and removed the cloth from the gaping black wound.

"He will lose the leg," Egorh grunted.

"I have enough magic oil for the bone but not for the whole injury," Mirk commented. "If we can heal the bone, then you can take him to the house to be cared for there."

Mirk and Kirk took the blue bottles from their necks and started to drip the bluish oil onto the bone of the gaping wound. Egorh was speechless at the healing power of the oil. The blackness slowly disappeared around the gash as it became new with fresh blood. Kirk tied some flat, dark leaves he had stripped from a nearby shrub over the wound. Together they picked up the almost lifeless boy and heaved him onto the horse. He stopped groaning when he sat behind Egorh, tightly fastened with young forest vines.

"You must hurry back. That wound is serious," Kirk said.

"I will," Egorh nodded and nudged Vector back the way they had come.

The Dryads leapt away into the forest canopy and Egorh heard Mirk say, "We must fetch more oil."

~

It was three days later that Egorh walked into the room where the household staff were nursing the injured boy slowly back to health. He had told his nurses that his name was Daniel and he was from a nearby village, where he lived with his elderly grandmother. She had been overjoyed when she heard the news that her grandson was still alive, after being missing for six days. The cleaned, dressed wound was healing extraordinarily well and the boy's fever had broken.

Daniel was propped up on pillows in bed, still looking pale, but with a hint of color returning to his cheeks. Egorh introduced himself to Daniel.

"I am Egorh. I found you in the wolf trap."

Daniel, a little self-conscious, grinned wryly and tried to lean forward to stretch out a hand, but he was still too weak.

"Not to worry. I came to see that your wounds were healing all right. That was a nasty business in that trap. You almost lost a leg there."

Daniel's grin faltered and he nodded somberly. The young man that saved his life radiated strength and character and he could sense a great deal of liveliness in his spirit. He was polite and had an easy way about him. Daniel immediately felt that he would like him.

"Thank you, sir. I don't know what I would have done with only one leg."

"Well, maybe if you had a wooden leg you could have pushed that into the wolf's trap and saved yourself a lot of agony." Egorh grinned trying to ease the boy's seriousness.

Daniel shook his head then looked straight at Egorh. "My father told me once that if a man saves your life, you are forever indebted to him."

Egorh smiled at the earnest orphan, only two years younger than himself and nodded. His behavior was open and his brown eyes sparkled with intelligence.

"Does that mean you owe me?" Egorh asked.

"I guess so," he said cheerfully.

"We'll see." Egorh turned to leave, thinking ... undeniably a friendly heart.

At the door he turned to Daniel and smiled. "You can start by calling me Egorh."

Chapter 16

Revelation

The tall forest trees next to the road offered a welcome barrier between the group of men and the scorching afternoon sun, as Crimson Lake appeared in the distance. Egorh was tired but the expression on his strong, sun-browned face was that of satisfaction. It had been one of the hardest clashes against the slave traders since the day he started to ride with Duke John four years ago. This had confirmed Egorh's fears that the slave traders had lately become more aggressive and bold. The group of strong and hardy men from the estate had managed to send them scattering into the Granite Mountains. Behind the riders, fifteen horses trailed, loaded with belongings that they had taken from the slave camp. They had set thirty captives free before burning it to the ground.

Egorh glanced at Duke John and they exchanged smiles as they listened to the men's friendly arguments, laughter and embellished tales. Daniel was riding just behind Egorh, as he had been since the day he had recovered satisfactorily from his ordeal in the wolf trap. Initially it had jarred Egorh to be followed and waited on by Daniel, but in time the two young men had become good friends, although Daniel saw himself more as Egorh's servant. He was a wirily built young man with pitch-black hair, and devoted to Egorh. He had proved himself someone to be trusted, riding at Egorh's back.

Egorh turned his head as they trotted past the outskirts of the lake, alive with the presence of thousands of crimson flamingos. His hazel eyes darkened slightly as he thought, the giant birds still manage to stir these strange emotions in me, causing my soul to surge like a tempest to the deepest corners of my being. His thoughts went back to the meeting with the priest.

They had traveled long and far and the smell of sweat was strong amongst the men. Egorh longed to plunge into the pool below the waterfall – his favorite place.

Duke John glanced at Egorh. At sixteen, the young man had become something of a legend, fighting the slave traders. A glint of pride flickered in his eyes as he saw how Egorh sat with such ease and confidence on Vector. There was much anger still burning in him, but he had managed somehow to turn the emotion into a weapon that drove him to unmatched courage. Some called him the *perfect warrior*.

Egorh narrowed his eyes as he noticed a rider coming their way, long black hair trailing behind in the wind. His heart gave a jolt and his hand clenched the reins. There could only be one person who loved to ride that fast and with such disregard – the Duke's daughter. Kayrin had been coming home from the city regularly but Egorh had chosen to avoid her most of the time. They had brief discussions several times and he had occasionally felt her earnest eyes fixed on him, but he had always guarded his emotions fiercely.

"It's Kayrin!" John called out and spurred his horse into a gallop to meet her. She was laughing as she waved. Her elegant riding clothes fluttered around her. Egorh and the men caught up with the two and each man dropped his gaze in respect to greet her. Egorh did not meet her eyes and turned them instead to Duke John. "I'm certain that you and Lady Kayrin have plenty to discuss. We'll go on ahead if you don't mind, sir." His voice was stronger and had deepened since the last time she had seen him.

John grinned as he nodded his assent and thought with amusement, our fearless young hero, always running away from his own heart's longings! Egorh did not notice the deep look of disappointment in Kayrin's eyes as she watched him and a few men challenge each other over the last stretch of road to the stables.

Kayrin fixed her gaze on the lake and thought, still the same avoidance. Will I ever get to know him truly? He had been in her mind and heart from the very first day he came to Crimson Lake. She knew then that there would be no room for any other and that she would wait for him for as long as it took. Many young men in the city had tried to win her heart, but she had no interest. Today, her heart felt too big for her chest as she saw him sitting so painfully straight in the saddle. His wide shoulders were very noticeable and she couldn't help noticing the muscles on his forearms as he held the reins loosely with both hands. His brown hair had grown long and he wore it tied low on his neck. The epitome of strength and health, she thought. Could any man be more handsome? Kayrin blushed at her thoughts and sighed helplessly. Egorh was already all the man he would ever be – she loved him desperately.

Her father asked her many questions about the city and her studies as they slowly made their way home. For a while she managed to shift her thoughts about Egorh to the back of her mind. They were almost at the estate when she decided now was the time to talk to Egorh. She would ask him outright why he always fled when she was around. She needed answers. She left her father's side and guided her horse along the trail to the waterfall where she was sure she would find him.

She saw him as he pulled on his boots, his wet hair falling loosely around his shoulders. She hesitated briefly but then dismounted and walked up to him purposefully.

"You swam?" she asked in a gentle voice.

Egorh, somewhat surprised to see her alone, nodded politely and started to fiddle with the buckle on Vector's halter. A slender hand interrupted his actions, her soft voice persisted, "Was the water warm?"

"It was warm."

"I need to ask you something."

He looked up at her with a guarded expression. His heart began to beat faster when he realized just how close she was.

"Egorh, I need to know … is it something I've done? You have been avoiding me since the day you came to live with us – four years ago."

He looked at her for a long time without saying anything. The silence was almost unbearable. His heart lurched when her beautiful eyes once again reminded him of the indigo bunting birds swaying on the long grass in the wind, shining like blue jewels as their breeding plumage caught the sun. He blinked slowly as her perfume, deliciously soft and penetrating, drifted to him. When at last he spoke, his voice trembled, "No, Kayrin, you have done nothing wrong. I have a history, a past. It is dangerous to care." He looked down and started to pick on a callus caused by his bowstring. "My father was killed because of me."

"You cannot believe that!" Kayrin moved closer.

"It's true. There are people looking for me and they will not give up until they have found me. My destiny is to do battle with them and this would endanger you. You must understand it is better that we do not become friends." He spoke with a forced calmness, his face set and unreadable. But when Egorh saw Kayrin's eyes brimming with tears, his resolve crumbled and he reached out to her. He took her hand gently, and pulled her towards him.

Egorh's heart fluttered, he tried to breathe but his lungs would not obey. Every nerve in his body seemed like a strained harp string ready to snap and he could not speak. He leaned forward, drawn like a moth to a flame. Kayrin unresisting, knew that he wanted to kiss her and she closed her eyes. His hands cupped her face and he kissed her soft lips.

She gently pulled away from his embrace and spoke the words she had for so long dreamed of speaking. "I love you Egorh. I've loved you from the very first minute we met." She closed her eyes, afraid of what he might say. Her heart beat with suffocating speed that left her with very little self-control.

When she opened her eyes, his face was close to hers and he nodded slowly, his breath warm on her cheek. "Beautiful Kayrin ... I cannot remember a day when I did *not* love you." His voice was hoarse and when their lips touched again, Egorh knew he had tempted fate. There was no turning back now and he would accept the added responsibility of protecting her against all the evil that was pursuing him.

A long time had passed when he gently released her, held her hands and asked passionately, "In two years, after my eighteenth year, will you marry me, Kayrin Bronbeck?"

She looked deep into his eyes and her happiness knew no bounds. All Egorh's defenses were down and heart leaped to heart. She could not speak and slowly nodded.

Chapter 17

Hunt

Deep in the forest, Mirk and Kirk were fast asleep in a giant tree, each on a branch snoring away, unmindful of their surroundings. On the ground, at the foot of the trunk, sat Bullfrog, also soundly asleep.

Mirk awoke as something wet dripped onto his cheek. When he realized it came from Kirk's drooling mouth, he jumped up and shouted, "That is so disgusting. Close your mouth when you sleep, Kirk!" He wiped the spit from his cheek.

Kirk opened an eye, then turned nonchalantly onto his other side to continue with his nap. Mirk sighed, still tired and wanting to carry on sleeping. He shut his eyes but again felt something tickling his cheek. Opening his eyes again, he saw it was Kirk's long ponytail dangling from the branch above.

"That's it! That is as far as my patience stretches this morning!" he shouted. "Next time *you* sleep at the bottom or in another tree."

He looked into the forest. A thick mist had settled between

the tall trees barely allowing the weak sun through. He grumbled, "It's early but Egorh should be here soon." The previous day Egorh had confirmed that the boar was definitely infected with the mad disease. They agreed that together they would track down the dangerous animal.

Maybe I could get some root to chew on while I wait. Mirk leaped to the ground. A distant sound made him tilt his head. "It's them Kirk," he called up when he heard Egorh and Daniel's muted footsteps. "Come, it's time to track that rogue beast before he causes more destruction."

Kirk stretched then bounded to where Mirk stood waiting.

Egorh, followed closely by Daniel, entered the forest very quietly. The wet soil and soft leaves beneath their feet muffled all sound. They had been following the wild boar's tracks from the village, where it had last been seen. Egorh knew the sounds of the forest and listened intently for the slightest change. He scanned the tracks with a practiced eye. Daniel grunted as he stumbled over a root from one of the forest giants and Egorh frowned with irritation, gesturing for him to be quiet. Daniel shrugged his shoulders apologetically. Egorh's thoughts went back to the time he had found Daniel in the wolf trap. I can't blame him for walking as if the forest bed was an eggshell, petrified to death as he inspected every footfall. Daniel's fear made him a clumsy partner to hunt with, but his lack of interest in the forest suited Egorh. It gave him many opportunities to visit the Dryads by himself.

Nearby, Mirk and Kirk were watching from a giant redwood tree, their large toad lurking in the underbrush.

Egorh looked up when the leaves above him moved and he greeted the Dryads, who peered silently down from the branch where they stood, with a silent nod. Since Daniel was there, communication would be limited. They watched as Egorh pressed on with the hunt. They had noticed a change in him; he was now much taller and had grown in strength and authority. The way he held himself in his eighteenth year showed an inner force he had not displayed before. The lightness had gone from his voice and when he spoke, his tone was firm and authoritative.

Egorh pointed to some fresh droppings that suggested the boar might be nearby. Kirk dipped his head and with two fingers signaled that he would scout further on. A few seconds later, he was back and indicated that the animal was just ahead. Egorh tensed visibly with a prickling sense of danger and he reached for an arrow from the quiver that hung from his shoulder.

Danger hung in the air and Egorh moved forward cautiously. He knew that if the sick boar injured him, he would be infected and that could mean his death. He had seen the mad disease make the spines of strong men snap in half as they curled back in pain. The old women called it the 'devil's disease': any man or animal infected died a horrible death. His mouth tightened as he moved forward slowly, but with intense focus. He drew the arrow back in the bow and noticed that the Dryads were also ready with their arrows.

Coming around a tree, Egorh saw the boar. The sides of its mouth were flecked with foam, its overlarge nostrils dilated as it sniffed the air, grunting. Before Egorh could release the arrow, he caught a movement to his right. A large black wolf stood a few feet away, growling. With its tail pulled tightly down and its huge head hanging low, it was ready to attack. Egorh stopped and paled to the bone. He had forgotten what fear felt like as it churned in his chest. An eerie silence fell over the forest. Small beads of perspiration started to form on his forehead as he turned and aimed at the wolf. He remembered the eyes that changed to frightful black holes, filled with nightmares from long ago. Leaping flames, destruction and haunting images of thousands of crimson-pink birds in the sky weaved in front of him. Egorh faltered as he stared, transfixed and terrified.

"Egorh, KILL the wolf!" Daniel shouted frantically. As the wolf leaped through the air towards him, Egorh's instinct took over and he released the arrow. As the shaft slapped into its chest, the animal clawed the air before dropping lifeless at his feet. Egorh reached for his sword and hacked off the animal's head. It was not so much the creature but rather the lingering images he wanted to kill.

Just then Egorh saw that the squealing boar was almost upon him. There was no time to raise his sword. He fell back, trying to avoid the beast. Before the possessed boar could attack, Mirk's arrow slammed into the animal. The hog slumped, tearing at the ground with its tusks in its death throes, leaving deep furrows, before it finally lay still.

Daniel gawked from wolf to boar and asked in disbelief, "How did you get that right?" but Egorh did not hear him. He remembered the priest's words, "It will challenge you when you need to fear it the least." An incredible stillness came over Egorh as he realized that it was his own demon that had come to haunt him again from the depths of his heart where it always lay waiting. He snapped back to the present, lifted his eyes to the trees and breathed. "Thank you."

Mirk knew those words were for him and he nodded from where he balanced on the branch.

"I will fetch the horses, sir." Daniel said very quickly, ready to flee the scene. Egorh grabbed him by his shirt, "Not so fast. I need your help to burn the boar."

Daniel began to collect dry wood and leaves to cover the animal. He pulled a face of disgust when he saw blood running from the animal's mouth and thought, why ask me to do this? He knows I hate blood, but he knew not to question Egorh's actions. Egorh saw Daniel's face, repulsed by the sight of the dead animal, but chose to ignore him as his mind was still with the wolf.

Suddenly the pounding of hooves filled the forest as riders approached them with loud cries. Egorh heard Mirk shout from his lookout, "Slave traders!"

As the riders came thundering past, beating their horses as if pursued by the devil himself, Egorh grabbed Daniel, dropped back behind a tree and readied his bow with lightning speed. He let loose a barrage of arrows that tore into the horsemen, sending them tumbling to the ground. There was no room to hide and the slave traders were trapped as arrows ripped through their numbers. Egorh took aim at the brown-cloaked leader who had stopped when he heard the cries of his men, but then spurred his horse to move on. The arrow missed the rider and found its way into the horse's shoulder. The animal stumbled and sent the man to the ground with a thump. Panicking, he leaped up and grabbed the reins of another horse, whose rider lay unmoving nearby. Before he mounted, he looked straight towards Egorh. With bewildered horror Egorh froze as he recognized the man from that dreadful day when his father had been killed. This was the murderer they had called Arkarrah.

The moment of recognition passed and Arkarrah remounted. He heard Arkarrah roar, "We are being slaughtered here! Let's go!" Egorh furiously renewed his attack as the villains fled.

"Quick, Daniel, get the horses! I have to follow that man," he shouted as they disappeared into the woods.

But Daniel and the Dryads stood frozen in amazement at what they had just witnessed. Kirk elbowed Mirk and whispered in awe, "Did you see it? The talent Darkarh has blessed him with?"

Mirk answered, "Yes – and the devastating speed with which he drew and shot those arrows?"

Egorh angrily spun around to scold Daniel, but then heard the sound of more horses approaching. He recognized Duke John and his men, who were in pursuit of the slave traders.

They reined in their horses beside Egorh. "It is not safe to follow," the Duke warned. "Let them go. We've had a long chase and the horses are tired. It is best we all go back." He noticed the troubled look on Egorh's face and asked, "Are you all right?"

"I recognized the leader of the group. I am convinced it is the same man who murdered my father."

"Are you sure?"

128

"Yes, I will never forget that face. I *have* to find him."

"Not now. There might be an ambush ahead."

Egorh cursed in anger.

"We must first determine why he is in this area and with how many of his men. I will arrange for a new search party and fresh horses when we get back," Duke John tried to reassure him. Egorh frowned in frustration but realized he was right.

The Dryads, still perched on a branch, had followed the whole conversation. Mirk grabbed Kirk by the arm. "Did you hear that? We have to get a message to Steukhon that Arkarrah is here. Quick, let's get going ... grab the toad!"

Chapter 18

Crow

Hatred surged as the face of his father's killer burned Egorh's mind like a hot coal. If Duke John had not stopped him, he would have avenged his father's murder today. For six years he had examined the faces of every scoundrel they had fought on the slave trail, even those of the dead. Reason told him that the Duke was right, warning about the danger of possible ambush. He could have been responsible for the death of good men.

His expression softened slightly as he recalled a lesson learned many years ago from Sir Matthew, "A man filled with emotion cannot win a battle."

Egorh was not new to the tactics of the slave mongers. They were cruel and ruthless men, who would stop at nothing to cram their pockets with gold in exchange for lives. Duke John had managed to cripple their evil work twice during the past month and he had become a thorn in their flesh. Was it out of desperation that they came so close to his land? Egorh wondered.

As the sun passed its highest point of the day, the men

moved out of the forest and made their way back to the estate. They were exhausted from the chase and sat in silence on the tired horses. When the grounds of Crimson Lake became visible, Egorh's spirit lifted at the thought of meeting with Kayrin later on. At the stables, he slid from Vector and turned to Daniel. "Daniel, please let Lady Kayrin know I will be waiting at the lake within the hour. Tell the stable boy to rub Vector down and then turn him loose for a while, but have him saddled again."

"Yes sir," replied Daniel, aware of Egorh's troubled expression. He handed Vector's reins to the stable boy, gave him the instructions and made his way to the mansion.

The long passage was sunlit as Daniel walked to find Kayrin. The wolf and boar images still played in his mind. He did not notice the floor with its intricate design of tiles that he usually found so imposing. A breeze came through an open window and Daniel stopped when the light ivory curtains blew in front of him. Female voices came from the room ahead and he was suddenly reluctant to face them. He sucked through his front teeth as he considered what to do. Soft footsteps behind him made him spin around and he drew a relieved breath as he recognized one of the maids.

"What are you doing here, Daniel?"

"I have a message for Lady Kayrin. Can you pass it on to her please? I am in a hurry. It's from Egorh. He said he will be at the lake within the hour."

The maid nodded, smiling wryly to herself, fully aware of the young man's unease. She pushed the double doors open, made a small bow and closed them behind her again. Daniel scurried back down the passage out of the house towards the stables.

Egorh followed the stone-paved road that led towards the rock bridge not far from the house. The experience in the forest was still troubling him and he tried to relax his muscles.

As he shrugged his shoulders, a sudden feeling of foreboding washed over him. What has this day brought? he wondered. Was it coincidence or forewarning that the wolf and Arkarrah both crossed my path this same morning? He frowned, struggling to find the calm he needed.

A sudden gust of wind chilled his face, warning of the change of season. From the bridge that crossed the bottom of the vast lake, the familiar sight of the giant crimson-pink birds could be seen coloring its shore. The lush gardens on the opposite side featured a series of elaborate fountains and reminded him again of a similar image, the picture the priest had stirred up many years ago before it changed into burning, tumbling buildings. Egorh shrugged, then placed one foot on the lower end of the bridge overgrown with moss and waited for Kayrin.

He stood lost in thought. A sudden loud honk startled him and he looked up. A group of flamingos, making their usual noises and dipping their beaks, had gathered around him. He had sensed a restlessness in them lately that puzzled him. Each night he had stood and watched them for hours from his bedroom window, as the thousands of red legs pounded the mud in a frenzy of tiny steps. Their bodies had constantly moved as if locked in a mystifying dance by the light of the ghostly moon.

The birds' curiosity no longer daunted Egorh. He watched as a big female came so close to him that he could count every tiny wrinkle around her yellow eye. His thoughts jumped back to that night when he had somehow passed through the male flamingo's eye. He took a deep breath and rested his hands on his knee. His connection to these giant birds felt more intense lately than ever before.

Rapid footsteps made him twist around and he watched Kayrin approach. Her smile was bright and her long black hair shone in the sunlight as it trailed in the breeze.

"Admiring the birds again?" she teased.

Egorh's dark mood lifted and he smiled with happiness as his senses were filled with the soft intoxicating smell of white lilies that surrounded her. He took her hand, "Come, let's forget about the birds. We have something important to discuss."

Kayrin chuckled, "And what may that be?" Egorh took her face in both his hands, kissed her gently and murmured, "I love you."

"And I you," she smiled.

Egorh's face was serious as he spoke. "Kayrin, I know our wedding is next week, but I want us to take our vows today, alone, just you and me at the waterfall."

"Today?" For a moment she lost her light manner as she looked into his hazel eyes and sensed a sudden urgency.

"I want the day of our betrothal to be a special day, one that belongs only to us," Egorh added in a rush, but paused when he saw her searching his face questioningly.

"Our day to remember, Kayrin," he whispered softly.

Her eyes moved to the lake as she considered his request. Marrying him was what she had always lived for, but his request was startlingly sudden. "What will my father say?" she frowned and held his gaze for a while before answering, "He has planned a wedding."

"It will go on as planned."

"Why not? Yes ... Just you and me! Our day." Kayrin agreed.

"I have arranged for the monk Raleigh to meet us at the waterfall and to marry us within the hour. He will hear our vows."

"How did you know I would agree?"

"I did not, but I knew your heart would."

Kayrin smiled happily. He whistled and Vector trotted towards them. Egorh's heart filled with joy as he vaulted onto the horse and pulled her up in front of him. He nudged the stallion with his heels and guided him in the direction of the waterfall.

The secluded waterfall was still their favorite, special and private place. This is where they talked about their future and shared pearls of laughter. They had spent many hours there together swimming, feeling the falls' soft mists on their bodies and watching the ripples that smoothed out before reaching the pool's edge.

Egorh and Kayrin had just arrived when they heard swearing and stumbling noises as somebody approached through the forest.

"Raleigh!" Egorh exclaimed when he saw the monk whose face was red and puffy, swaying on his feet. Nearby, Uwak, his crow, flew up to a branch close by, imitating some of his master's drunken curses.

Egorh felt his temper rise and asked scornfully, "Are you drunk again Raleigh?"

"I am not drunk, just happy for the two of you," the monk replied with a slur in his speech.

"Could you not at least have stayed sober for this occasion?" Egorh struggled to restrain his anger but decided he would not allow the old fool to spoil this special day.

"Let's begin then," Egorh ordered. He had never liked the monk with his fleshy lips and shifty eyes.

Out of breath from the extra weight he carried around his waist, Raleigh fumbled in the pocket of his dirty brown robe for a small book. Planting his feet wide apart to minimize his swaying, he coughed to clear his throat, opened the book with shaky hands and began to read them their vows. Egorh interrupted and said, "Wait." He ran to pick a few wild Arum lilies and gave them to Kayrin. "You have to hold flowers, my bride."

The Dryads had been watching the service from the treetops. Kirk pretended to gag from the soppiness, but Mirk wanted to get a better view. He loved ceremonies and especially weddings. He thought it was *so* romantic.

In spite of Raleigh, it was a beautiful moment. When it was time for the exchange of rings, Egorh's eyes sparkled and he softly said to Kayrin, "In one week's time, we will we take our vows again and I will put a ring on your finger for the whole world to see, but to remember this day, a golden chain around your ankle will remind you of my undying love."

Egorh took an unusual and delicate golden chain from his pocket, knelt beside her and fastened it around her ankle. He rose, held her tenderly and kissed her. They fell silent to allow the memory to linger in their minds.

Their sacred time was shattered when Raleigh coughed expectantly. His throbbing head prevented him from sharing the couple's happiness. Egorh impatiently, took two pieces of gold from his pocket and handed them to him. "Thank you for your services. Go now and leave us."

Raleigh started in the direction of the woods but looked back and addressed Kayrin, "You must come and choose one of my rare flowers as my wedding gift to you. It has taken me twelve years to grow this plant and it is only starting to flower now."

"Thank you Raleigh, I will surely do that," she replied.

Raleigh staggered off into the woods. He felt less concerned about his drunken state now that he had made his offer to the bride.

~

With the monk gone, Egorh and Kayrin lay embraced on the soft grass. The waterfall's soothing sounds added to this most perfect of moments. Kayrin could see that Egorh's brown eyes were clouded with emotion and she trailed her finger over every line of his handsome features in admiration. She whispered softly as she gazed up at his face.

"Tell me ... tell me what I must know?"

He took her face between both his hands and with a

135

tremble in his voice softly said, "Kayrin Bidault, I will always love you."

She closed her eyes and when he kissed her, her lips felt like velvet petals.

"This moment belongs to us, Kayrin, and is ours to keep. Hold and treasure this memory. If somehow fate tricks us, send a message with the wind for me to catch and I'll be there."

"Thank you for this special moment, Egorh. I bless the day that you came to us and into my heart."

They stayed holding each other in silence, lost in their own thoughts.

Suddenly Egorh broke away, clambered onto a large rock at the waterside, and to Kayrin's delight, jumped into the deep pool, shouting, "I am married! I am married!" As he came to the surface, he did not realize that the chain bearing his amulet had snapped with the impact and was slowly drifting to the bottom of the pool.

He climbed out and joined her on the grass. Suddenly he became serious as he said, "I killed a wolf today."

Kayrin looked surprised and replied, "You killed a wolf? What about the rogue boar you were tracking?"

"Yes, the boar was killed too, but the wolf was a strange experience."

He rolled onto his back, his clothes and hair dripping. "It awakened a strange feeling of turmoil in me – something I cannot explain, a feeling from deep within." He reached out with a sun-darkened hand and marveled at the contrast of her milky skin. The gentleness of her clasp made him look up at her and he lost himself in her eyes, those dark blue pools, which had no surface, only depth. Their love for each other was caught in an unbreakable web of iron.

A sudden high-pitched shriek cut through the air and made them both look up with a start. Egorh searched the treetops and saw the head of a black-crested eagle as it turned back and forth on a nearby branch. He sat up quickly as the bird flapped its wings and its green eyes burned fiercely into him. The bird stretched its neck and screeched again with a wide-open beak as if it had found its prey. A shiver ran down Egorh's spine and his hand felt for his amulet.

With a shock he realized it was missing. His mind spun to the previous time he had lost it. Egorh ran to where he had jumped into the pond, he searched the rock, the water and surrounding area. He looked everywhere, but he could not see the jewel anywhere. For a moment he stood rooted as fear washed over him and he thought, is this the day the old priest spoke about? The day I would no longer need it? First the demon wolf; then my father's murderer; now the amulet. I must protect Kayrin. I have to take her home. She cannot be with me.

His expression was dark with concern as he walked back to where she sat. With a guarded face and only the little muscle in his jaw betraying his turmoil, Egorh took Kayrin's hands and pulled her to her feet. "Come my love, we must go back. It is getting late."

"Egorh, you look worried. Is something wrong?"

"Let's go." He tried to keep his voice light. "We must go home now, the woods are not safe." He looked up and saw the dark shadow circling high in the sky. He gave a long whistle and Vector trotted over.

Kayrin realized something was dreadfully wrong but followed him without saying a word. Night was approaching as they crossed the bridge and Egorh again noticed how restless the flamingos had become. He felt uneasy as his thoughts went to Duke John, Daniel and all the others he cared about.

~

After the marriage ceremony, Mirk and Kirk had moved back into the woods to give the couple some privacy. Their attention was grabbed by the loud shriek of the eagle.

"It's Khan, the sorceress's eagle." Kirk muttered. His expression was troubled as he saw the evil stare of the bird.

"What is *he* doing here? How did he find Egorh?" Mirk's voice was grave.

The Dryads had noticed Egorh's agitation as he frantically searched around the pool, then gave up and swiftly left with Kayrin. Kirk jumped off the branch and called to the toad, "Come quickly! He has lost his amulet." From the edge of the pool Kirk could see the silver chain lying at the bottom. "Fetch it, fetch the silver chain!" he shouted.

Bullfrog leaped into the water and swam for all he was worth, to where the amulet was lying. He curled his tongue around the chain and turned to swim back. The toad surfaced and Kirk grabbed the amulet with a sigh of relief.

He held it in his hand and read the glyphs inscribed on its back: "Protect the mark of the beak." Suddenly, he felt the wings of a bird almost touching his face, and the talons tore his palm as the amulet was snatched from his hand. Kirk looked up, "Oh no! It's Raleigh's crow, Uwak! Come back you stupid bird, come back!" he shouted, waving his arms.

"It's mine, it's mine," shrieked the crow as it flew off with the amulet dangling from its talons. Impressed with his trophy, he headed straight for the tall cliffs to hide it.

"What are we going to do now?" Kirk jumped up and down frantically, shaking his fist at the bird.

"We must leave at once and find Steukhon's helper, Bubba," Mirk replied. "Remember what Steukhon said. There would be a time when the gods decide that Egorh must fulfill his destiny and the amulet will lose its power. Maybe the time has arrived. Bubba needs to know what has happened so that he can tell Steukhon. There's also the news of Arkarrah and the appearance of the eagle. There's no time to lose."

"You're right, let's hurry!" Kirk replied.

The two Dryads disappeared into the forest.

Chapter 19

Discovered

Zinnia frowned as she paced the granite floor, her mood bordering on hysterical anger as her eyes flickered from Arkarrah to the bangles lying on the long stone table. Ancient dusty oil lamps on the walls struggled to light up the spacious hall deep within the mountain. Bats flew around the heavy granite pillars that disappeared into a high ceiling. The sorceress's head snapped upwards when the death shriek of a bat caught her attention. Khan had just snatched it in mid air and swooped down to settle on a nearby chair. A grim smile twisted her lips as she watched, entertained by the bird pulling long strips of flesh from the live, squealing bat and gulping them down.

Two wide stairways led from the room to the huge iron doors above. On one of the stairways sat Dwarf teasing his pet owl Hooter, and keeping one eye on Zinnia as she walked back and forth. From his chubby fingers he dangled a small white mouse in and out of the irritated owl's sight. Watching the owl's head bobbing sideways and up and down, its wings flapping as the mouse squeaked, he fell back onto the steps, rolling with laughter.

Zinnia stopped her pacing and slammed her fist down on the stone table. Irritated by the dwarf's antics, she bellowed, "Where is he? Why can I not find him? Who is protecting him? I am Zinnia! I *must* be able to find him!"

Khan, sitting on the chair next to her, startled by the sudden outburst, flapped his wings and dropped the rest of his meal on the floor.

"My plan is almost complete, but I cannot find the man with the beak mark." She reached for the golden water carafe on the table, only to find it empty. "There is no water, dwarf!" she shouted. "Arkarrah, take that dwarf and feed him and his owl to the eagles, then find me a decent servant on your way back."

Fearing Zinnia's black mood, the dwarf grabbed Hooter and scuttled up the stairs, saying hurriedly, "I am sorry! I will fetch your water immediately!" Zinnia addressed Arkarrah.

"You *claim* you have searched everywhere, so why can you not find him?"

Before he could answer, a rattle from the emerald green bangle on the table caught her attention. Zinnia stared icily at the genie that appeared and asked, "What? Have you news?"

Iy blinked his big eye and nodded confidently. "I see him, the man with the beak mark."

"You do?" Zinnia's mood soared at the news and she moved closer.

Arkarrah took a step forward and in Iy's eye he saw the reflection of a wedding ceremony. "Raleigh?" he sounded surprised. When Egorh's face appeared, it was as if he had been hammered by some unseen force and blurted, "So *he* is the one, I should have known." Zinnia swung around. "You knew about this man all these years?"

He fell back a step as he felt her angry breath on his cheek. He tried to explain. "No, I did not know! This man is absolutely lethal. I have not seen anything like it. He is no ordinary man."

"Did you think it would be that easy? If it was, I could have asked my pathetic dwarf to find him. Why do you think I promised you the gold ore? You should have already killed him when he was young, as I instructed you!" Zinnia hissed, her green eyes piercing Arkarrah. The only thing that prevented her from killing him was that he was a necessary pawn in her scheme. Now was not the time to cause an upset. She needed more hearts and there was no time to find another corrupt and ruthless thug like him to do her work.

She turned from him and sneered, "So what is it that makes the son of Darkarh *so* different?"

"He is a legend in battle. He has speed and skill with weapons never before seen. I have witnessed him kill five of my henchmen, single-handedly, in seconds. You cannot get close to him or his men that easily."

"He is a mortal, flesh and blood, and can be killed." Zinnia glowered at him, her skin flushed and her jaw clenched in fury. "Find somebody he cares about – a woman, a father, a child, a mother, ANYBODY," she barked.

Arkarrah swallowed. "We killed his family a long time ago, remember."

Zinnia clenched her fists in pure frustration. Suddenly the ruby stone bangle's genie appeared. Zinnia whirled to pick it up, since she did not often see this little creature. Her furious expression faded and she asked, "Aart, what are *you* doing outside?"

The peculiar-looking red genie with its pink eye answered, "He has a *luvur*."

"What? Are you *sure*?"

The genie winked slowly with her long-lashed eye. "*Luuk*," she said.

Zinnia, with Arkarrah behind her, gazed into Aart's eye and saw Kayrin laughing with Egorh at the waterfall.

Zinnia, delirious with excitement yelled, "Khan!" She held out her hand for him to perch, then moved him in front of the genie. "Find out where they are," she ordered the eagle. Khan screeched.

"Arkarrah, follow the bird. You *must* get the girl and bring her to me," Zinnia commanded, ignoring his pet bat as it dropped from the high ceiling, landed on his shoulder and crawled into his coat pocket.

"If he loves her, Darkarh's son will be sure to follow and I will deal with him myself. Go now. If you fail me again, you will pay the price of incompetence."

Arkarrah avoided the cold ferocity of her green eyes and stepped back to follow the eagle down the passage. He glanced sideways at the life-sized statues standing at the feet of some of the pillars. He had known many of the faces personally, before Zinnia had unleashed her wrath on them and turned them to stone.

~

The sound of Arkarrah's footsteps had hardly faded when Zinnia's attention was drawn to the top of the broad stairway on the left. A grey cloud formed and three men in long robes emerged. She saw the eyes of the newcomers staring at her as they descended. When they stopped silently before her, their faces hard and strained, Zinnia dipped her head, feigning surprise, "Sons of Darkarh? I am honored," she said as politely as she could. DAMN – I must have left the vortex passage between our worlds open, she thought.

Even though they could not remain in the earthly world for long before being forced back to the HapLess Sphere, she did not have time for them, especially now that she had found Egorh. She tried to refrain from being rude and told herself to remember the orinium obelisk. "I did not expect you! It has been a long time indeed," she said, unable to keep the sharp tone from her voice.

Since falling from their father's favor, they had lived in the HapLess Sphere as fallen gods, the Haffgoss, only the dark side of their elements remaining. This made them extremely dangerous.

The tallest, Arugh, was the first to step forward, bowing his head stiffly as if the gesture was unfamiliar. "We are tired of waiting. We had an agreement and we demand a final time for our return from the region of doom and hopelessness. My brothers and I think that you are purposely delaying this matter." The only thing to spoil his striking looks was his small, close-set eyes.

"Delay?" Zinnia colored with anger.

Air was his element. She knew he was very unpredictable and clearly on the warpath. She could not trust him. Like a scorpion, he would sting from behind.

She forced a smile in his direction but before she could answer, Warogh grunted in an unpleasant tone, "Yes, your promises are worthless."

From his hiding place, Dwarf could see how Zinnia's knuckles whitened as she clenched her hands. Warogh was the smallest of all the brothers, the most repulsive, annoyingly talkative and reflected his restless element of *water*. He flowed in any direction his brothers demanded of him and was extremely destructive. Given the chance, he would ramble on pointlessly, always wringing his hands. He looked weird with his grey aquamarine-striped robe, short blond hair and a seahorse carved out of bone dangling from one ear.

Eragh joined the others and started to parade in front of Zinnia. With a rock-hard voice he ridiculed, "You have betrayed us. You said you were the most powerful sorceress. It was a lie! How is it possible, with your supposed powers, that you have not been able to find him? We think you are conspiring with our brother against us."

Zinnia glowered at the three and waited for them to finish their blustering and yelping. She smiled a tight smile and her tone was deadly as she spoke, "How dare you speak to me like this!" Her eyes did not leave the man who prowled in front of her. His reddish brown hair fell in curls onto his shoulders. Around his neck hung a broad leather band embedded with all the precious jewels found on earth.

"I AM the mightiest sorceress. Who are YOU to come uninvited into my fortress to insult me and to make demands? You need me, not I you. I will let you know when I am ready."

Eragh stiffened slightly and Zinnia wondered if the fool felt insulted by her words.

How dare he address me as if I was beneath him, while he is the one to bow to me? She wondered briefly if she should remind him of his position, but thought better of it as her ultimate goal, the diamond skeleton throne and the kneeling Xyltra sorceresses flashed in her mind.

She did not move, just glared at them, letting her long fingernails click together to show her displeasure. Eragh was strong with his *earth* element, bombastic and arrogant. If she allowed her temper to erupt, an awful clash could ensure. He was a bully and used his brutal force to intimidate both his brothers into insignificance.

The Haffgoss seemed anxious and Eragh spoke again. "Up to now, you have proved nothing. Where are the thirty-thousand hearts? We want to rule again and you are wasting our time. We are considering approaching another sorcerer, one who could fulfill his promises in exchange for the orinium."

The atmosphere was thick and explosive. The Haffgoss were no strangers to malice but she was more callous than they could comprehend. Zinnia threw her head back and snapped, "Who will want to deal with fallen gods that murdered their own brother and tarnished their father's name, only to be condemned by him? It is only I who am prepared to work with such outcasts as yourselves." She raised her hand and hurled them crashing into a pillar.

Grunting noises erupted as extreme anger and humiliation overtook the brothers. Their bodies started to transform into their beast forms, whose moods were notoriously vile.

"So you want to challenge us?" hissed the now-winged Arugh. He arched his neck, relishing the challenge and strutted in front of her, leaving white marks on the granite floor as his razor-sharp talons gouged into the stone.

Warogh and Eragh, now also dreadfully transformed, slowly closed in on Zinnia with intimidating noises. Arugh flapped his large wings to show his anger, stirring up a strong gust of wind. Zinnia's hair and clothes flapped around her, but she ignored his aggressive moves. Silver and gold scales covered his legs and his head resembled that of a vulture, with enormous black eyes.

Zinnia fell back a few steps before Warogh's horrendous wet tail could strike her, as it swept the floor. Black and aquamarine scales covered his entire body, with light stripes down the sides. The abalone shell-fin on his back flashed as he moved and the bone seahorse earring swung around his fish-like face. His short legs and arms were shaped like those of a lizard. Of all the Haffgoss, he irritated Zinnia the most because the slime he oozed dirtied her floor.

"Wait!" The Haffgoss flinched at the venom in her voice as Zinnia's enraged roar filled the room. "We are fighting the same war here, remember?"

"You have insulted us!" snarled Warogh, with a curled lip.

"I will give you proof, but only if you control your tempers. I ..." but before Zinnia could finish, Eragh asked sarcastically, "Proof? What proof?" His yellow beast eyes glared with aggression as he padded around. The scales on his body were thick and square. Layers of bulky loose skin hung around his neck, partially hidden by his broad leather collar. His head was massive and curved fangs showed dangerously at the sides of his mouth. Zinnia stood tall, took a deep breath, her face set and unreadable as she attempted to control her intolerance.

"Well, let me speak." She sauntered away from the beasts, "I have just discovered where your brother is hiding."

"You lie! It's just a ploy to buy some time," shouted Arugh. There was savagery in their eyes as they stomped back and forth.

"I can prove it!" she hissed.

Zinnia's patience ran thin but she knew she had to control the volatile situation and clenched her fists as she glowered at them, "You make the choice, brothers. We can fight or we can rule! If you fight, you lose the thousands of hearts that lie waiting for you and I will not tell you where your brother is. What's it going to be?" Again she waited and slowly the brothers pushed the darkness of their elements away and turned back into their human form.

"Let me show you."

"How?" Warogh snarled.

Zinnia took Iy off her arm and put him in the center of the long table. "Come and look into his eye and you will see your brother."

They stared but nothing appeared.

"Iy! Iy! ... Come out immediately! I have no time for games," Zinnia hissed through her teeth and a slight flush appeared on her neck.

Arugh jeered, "See, I told you she is just playing for time." When Iy came out and looked in their direction with his big eye, Zinnia breathed a sigh of relief.

The brothers pushed and shoved to get a closer look into the eye and became very quiet when they saw Egorh with Kayrin crossing the bridge at Crimson Lake on Vector.

"That is our brother?"

"Yes, the one with the beak mark."

Zinnia grabbed Iy and put him back on her arm, knowing she was in control of the situation again.

"I am almost done," continued Zinnia, unable to keep a note of triumph from her voice.

"Everything is in place. Just before you came, my genie Aart discovered Egorh and his woman. Arkarrah is already on his way to kidnap her. Your brother will definitely try to rescue her. We will set a trap for him and I shall do what needs to be done once he has been captured. I only need a few more hearts to complete my part of the deal, another shipment arrived this morning. Very soon you will have *his heart* as proof." With a ghost of a smile Zinnia gloated, "We will see each other before the second quarter of the moon."

The three Haffgoss whispered amongst themselves and Eragh nodded, "We are satisfied." His words sounded oddly false but Zinnia accepted them. "Until the second quarter of the moon then." The three bowed sheepishly and disappeared into their grey cloud.

Zinnia exhaled slowly at the thought of victory. Her mouth twisted into a sneer, she threw back her head and her raucous cackle echoed through the large chamber.

Chapter 20

Old Herb Kitchen

Bubba was busy in the old herb kitchen and walked over to the ancient bulky stove where steam swirled from the bubbling, simmering pots, their lids rattling away. A peculiarly sharp but nauseatingly sweet aroma lingered in the air. Bubba could never decide whether he liked or hated the thick ever-present smell. He rubbed an itch at the end of his nose. The area in front of the stove was hot and he wiped beads of sweat from his forehead. He was a slightly built but lean young man and wore a brown robe, as most monks in training do.

His superior, the monk Raleigh, had instructed him to keep an eye on his brewing concoctions, while he gathered more herbs from the bushes around the so-called monastery. The kitchen was grimy, with dirty pots piled up next to the stove and cockroaches scuttling across the floor. Bunches of dried plants hung from the ceiling. Leaves and flowers were stacked in heaps. In the corner of the room was the monk's old worn-out rocking chair covered in red velvet, with tatty, dirty armrests. The old monk usually took his naps here when he drank himself blind with liquor and, more often than not, could not find the way to his bedroom. Right above the ragged chair, on a beam just below the ceiling, was the messy nest of Raleigh's crow, Uwak.

Bubba leaned forward, his interest aroused by a jar packed with crawling black scorpions. There were glass jars of all shapes, sizes and colors filled with varieties of insects, reptiles and objects stacked on the dilapidated shelves. Some of the contents could barely be seen as the outsides of the bottles were covered with a thick layer of dust. Bubba looked up from the pots and squinted as he tried to decipher some of the labels.

Hmmm ... these are peculiar labels, almost unreadable. Looks as if a drunk fly fell into the ink and dragged itself across them, he thought.

Bubba did not notice how the boiling concoction he was stirring began to take on the image of a green chubby face with big round eyes like pheasant eggs. With a menacing expression, the face looked up to the corner shelf where a trapped grumbler was trying to escape a spider's web. He then turned his egg eyes to the lip of the pot, snapped another grumbler off the rim, with a long tongue that appeared from nowhere and disappeared with a smirk back into the green slop.

Bubba stamped his sandal as he felt something crawling over his foot. He looked down and saw several large cockroaches scurrying across the floor in the grime, seemingly playing a game of hide-and-seek between the dirty pots. Have fun, he thought irritably. Soon you will be part of Raleigh's brew.

He sighed and returned to the steaming pots with a troubled expression. He started to hum a song he remembered from his childhood. He lifted the lids of the other pots and stirred aimlessly here and there. The song was an old one and there was longing in his heart.

His mind went back to the dreadful day the slave traders took his sister from their home and the senseless killing of the many people who tried to escape. His mouth went dry when he recalled how he had fought back. It was the ugly man with the snake eyes that had struck him down. Weak from his injuries, he was left to die.

Bubba drew his mouth into a thin line as he remembered how he had watched helplessly as scavenging crows hopped closer and closer to him. Unexpectedly, a tall man with long grey hair had appeared and said softly, "I will help you. Try to stay alive." The stranger had taken him by the wrists and Bubba remembered the big milky ring on the old man's finger as he tried to raise him to his feet, but Bubba was too weak and could not stand on his own. The old man had knelt and looked at Bubba's blank eyes, "I am Steukhon. You are safe with me. Close your eyes and try to sleep."

When he awoke, he was in a different place, together with the long grey-haired man and he had no idea how he had gotten there. Steukhon spent many days carefully nursing him back to health. As the months passed he became like Bubba's second father.

During the time they spent together, Steukhon came to trust the gentle Bubba and revealed the story of Egorh's destiny. Bubba became part of the greater plan. He was to be the messenger between Steukhon and the Dryads, destined to work with Raleigh, the pathetic drunkard that collaborated with the sorceress at his so called monastery. He had to be the eyes and ears for Steukhon and to report everything concerning Egorh's life.

Shortly after he came to Raleigh, he recognized the frequent visitor Arkarrah, the slave trader who had captured his sister, murdered his people and left him for dead. Countless times he had contemplated poisoning him with Raleigh's concoctions, stabbing him to death, or ripping his heart out and feeding it to the barnyard owls, but Steukhon told him to restrain himself, for by doing so, he would be serving a greater cause, the destiny of Egorh. It had often been difficult for him but with the guidance of Steukhon, he had managed it. Whenever he felt revenge and hatred bubbling up from his soul, he sang or hummed this same old song.

He was snapped out of his reverie by the death shriek of a mouse as one of the owls sank its talons into it while scurrying across the floor.

"Damn owls," he muttered agitated, as he saw the predator flying back to the beam with the dangling mouse, to where the other owls awaited the food. They had been here since he came and they had long since decided that in-house hunting was much easier than outside hunting.

Distracted, he didn't notice a small green hand slip from one of the pots, grab his fingers and pull them into the boiling liquid. "Dragons' nostrils!" he yelped. "That hurts!" he shook his hand and blew on the burns, trying to cool them down. He did not see the green chubby face chuckle, causing the pot to boil over.

He was heading towards the water pail when he became aware of a movement at the kitchen door. He saw the big toad sitting in the doorway. "The Dryads are here," he muttered. "There must be trouble again somewhere and they need to communicate with me."

Holding his burned fingers in the air, Bubba bravely tried to greet his visitors as if nothing was bothering him.

"As always, I am honored," and he nodded in the direction of Bullfrog. "I have not felt your presence for a long time. I gather something is wrong and that is why you're here."

Kirk looked at Mirk and said, "Bubba burned his hand."

"I will put some oil on it," Mirk said and he opened the small blue bottle hanging from the leather belt across his chest. Bubba's hand was too high for him to reach, so he jumped onto the table, took Bubba's hand in his own and poured a drop of oil on each finger.

Bubba could not see the Dryads and tried not to look alarmed when he felt a firm grip on his hand and a drop of oil slowly spreading on each blistered finger. Steukhon had told him of the many miracles the Dryads could perform. In awe he watched as the blisters healed and the pain subsided.

"Amazing! Thank you! You have no idea how painful that was."

His discomfort relieved, he craned his neck to see where Raleigh was. The window was too dirty to see through, so he cleaned a small area with his sleeve. "I gather you have some important news for me to pass to Steukhon. We must be careful – Raleigh is just outside and may come in at any moment. Time is of the essence and we will have to communicate in writing. I will fetch paper and ink," he went into the next room.

Bubba returned with paper made of pressed bark, a small bottle of black ink and a quill. He placed them on the long wooden table. He kept checking as he spoke to make sure Raleigh was still busy in the garden. "Try to be quick before the monk comes. Write down what you want to say," Bubba said softly.

Mirk could sense Bubba's urgency but he was not used to writing, so it took some concentration for him just to hold the pen, trying it in different ways in his long hand. Eventually the quill was dipped into the ink and the ancient letters started to form on the paper. Being a Dryad, Mirk only needed to write the first letter of his thoughts, the first letter would then inform the next letter of what it should be, then the next, until all was done.

Bubba stood alongside the table and watched the moving pen with sharp interest. He tried to decipher the intricate handwriting on the paper as the letters tagged each other, one after the next. It read:

Ψου μυστ γο το Στευκηον. *(You must go to Steukhon.)*

Ιγοῃ Σαω Ἀῃκκαῃῃαħ ιη τηε ωοοδΣ. *(Egorh saw Arkarrah in the woods.)*

Εγορηэσ αμυλετ ωασ στολεν βψ τηε μονκэσ χροω. *(Egorh's amulet was stolen by the monk's crow.)*

Τηε βλαχκ–χρεστεδ εαγλε ωασ τηερε. *(The black-crested eagle was there.)*

Ηε ισ δισχοϖερεδ! *(He is discovered!)*

Bubba grunted, shook his head and felt a burning anger as he saw Arkarrah's name written. "I'll have to find the crow and the amulet immediately then." He peered out of the window as he heard a crow caw in the distance.

Chapter 21

Raleigh's Crow

The last of the season's hot sun scorched down and, with his sleeve, Raleigh wiped the sweat from his face. He looked at the sky and blew from his puffed cheeks. The winter rain was still a few months away and he was glad, as some of the dried herbs still needed harvesting. Crouched, the monk painstakingly searched through the leaves of a low bush in the monastery grounds. A loud squawk made him stand upright. He almost lost his balance as Uwak swooped right over him and landed nearby.

"Stupid bird!" he cursed. "You gave me a fright. Where have you been the last few days?" Just as Raleigh was about to chase the bird, he noticed something dangling from the crow's claws. Raleigh's eyes widened as he saw the sparkle of magnificent jewels in the sunlight. He did not breathe his normal heavy breath, but spattered with a maddened calm, "How did you get this? It's an amulet! Give it to me," Raleigh demanded. He cautiously approached the bird, but the effort of protecting the shiny object in the cliffs made Uwak take off in the direction of the monastery kitchen, shrieking, "It's mine! It's mine!" before Raleigh could snatch it away from him.

Raleigh dropped the herbs and rushed after Uwak, shouting and waving his arms, "Give it to me! Drop it!" He knew the value of such diamonds and his eyes sparkled. The bird disappeared through the back door of the kitchen, flew directly to its untidy nest of twigs and feathers and sat on the amulet trying to hide it.

Raleigh was completely out of breath when he reached the kitchen, wheezing like a pair of bellows. The veins on his nose and cheeks protruded like red cobwebs. As he held onto the doorframe trying to catch his breath, he heard the sound of horses approaching. From a distance, he recognized one of the riders as Arkarrah.

"He must be coming for a shipment of *nepenthe* again," he reasoned.

He inhaled heavily and stumbled into the kitchen, his face now pink and shiny with sweat. "I must get the amulet from the crow and hide it before Arkarrah arrives," he muttered. He hurried over to the red chair from where he could just reach Uwak's nest that reeked of rotten meat.

He knew the crow would not give up its prize without a fight. Uwak shrieked again, "It's mine! It's mine!" as he pecked Raleigh's hand with his sharp beak. Losing his patience, Raleigh managed to yank one of the twigs from the nest and swiped at the bird. Uwak surged from the nest irate and joined the owls on their beam still shrieking, "It's mine! It's mine!" Out of sheer frustration he pecked at the owls next to him.

Raleigh grinned when he saw the amulet in the nest and grabbed it. He weighed it in the palm of his hand and wondered where the crow had stolen it. It must be from a wealthy noble. An itch of worry sprang up from within as he admired the diamonds. The writing on the back of the amulet was unfamiliar to him and he rubbed it thoughtfully for a moment with his stocky thumb. He decided to ignore the warning voice in his head and climbed down from the chair. Hurriedly, he moved over to the shelves to look for a glass jar in which to hide the amulet.

He saw one with four red scorpions inside and thought, Aha, Arkarrah will think twice before he puts his hand in *this* jar. He tried to hide the jar behind the others, for he knew that nothing escaped Arkarrah's beady eyes.

Raleigh had been in such a hurry to get to Uwak and the amulet that he had not noticed Bubba standing at the kitchen table, watching in silence. He became aware of his presence and rudely ordered him out of the room, saying, "Get out! I have some important business to attend to."

Bubba turned to grab the paper and ink from the corner of the table but was unable to as Raleigh pushed him outside and slammed the door. He waited, uncertain what to do.

"What if the letter is discovered?" He quietly prayed that the Dryads would make a plan to remove it, or do *something*. He pretended to be busy in the garden, out of sight but not far from the open kitchen window, so that he could hear what was happening.

~

The door flung open and Arkarrah strode in with a grunt. "My good man Raleigh," he said loudly.

Raleigh cowered, a dim smile touched the corners of his mouth. "Arkarrah! I did not expect you so soon."

Arkarrah threw himself down into a chair and swung his boots onto the table with so much force that a few glass bottles fell to the floor. "Oops" he grinned mockingly. He reached for a bowl of grapes and stuffed some into his mouth but quickly spat them onto the floor, grimacing. "Can you not grow sweeter grapes? These set my teeth on edge." He shivered with distaste, opened his coat and held a grape just outside his pocket. "Horris! Come my little creature, I have something sour for you." Disturbed, his pet bat crawled out but scurried back when noises erupted from the barn owls.

"Oh, those bats, they smell so bad," Kirk muttered from where he was sitting, wrinkling his nose.

"Zinnia needs more potion, the potion to *forget sorrows*. The same as always and I hope you have it ready." Arkarrah reached into his pocket and took out three gold pieces, which he threw carelessly onto the table.

"Yes, yes, it's almost ready," replied Raleigh and rubbed his hands nervously together. "I just have to bottle it." He started to collect five empty green bottles from the shelf.

Arkarrah turned his head and noticed the piece of paper with the peculiar writing on the table. He tilted his head and tried to read it. The paper started to move slowly towards the end of the table. Puzzled, he looked around to see what was moving it. He glared at Raleigh who was standing in front of the stove with his back towards him. Arkarrah looked under the long table but still saw nothing. He sat motionless for a moment and watched the paper continue to move slowly away from him. Before it disappeared over the side of the table, he pinned it down by quickly thrusting his dagger into the wood.

Mirk, sitting in the windowsill, was watching Kirk have a bit of fun with Arkarrah, but when Arkarrah renewed his efforts to read the message, Mirk realized that he might *just* make out what had been written and that could be dangerous. He quickly leaped from the window sill and spilt the bottle of ink over the paper to cover the writing. Arkarrah jumped to his feet cursing, as the ink spattered the sleeve of his coat.

Raleigh quickly picked up the bottle and mumbled, "I am sorry. Bubba must have brought it in here. Come, here is some water."

Arkarrah moved over to the water beaker and then caught sight of the amulet in the jar on the shelf. "And this?" he asked, reaching for the jar.

"Do not touch it!" exclaimed Raleigh. "It is the mad witch's stone that she gave me to soak in oil of devil's claw. If you touch it, it will bring you eternal bad luck. That is, if the scorpions do not sting you to death first."

Arkarrah jerked back his hand.

Raleigh secretly prayed that he would lose interest in the amulet. Arkarrah angled his head to try to see more of the object but decided to rather leave it and moved away. Raleigh, weak with relief, forced himself to act with studied indifference.

"I have another task for you," said Arkarrah.

"Me?" asked Raleigh and tried to dart past him.

Arkarrah's beady eyes missed nothing and he quickly stepped into Raleigh's path, forcing the monk to halt.

"What is it Arkarrah?" he asked.

"I heard about your meeting with the two lovebirds at the waterfall."

"Yes, I had to marry them. Why does that interest you?" He turned to the stove to start filling the bottles.

"I want you to lure the girl into the woods," Arkarrah said, hoping that he would not meet with too much resistance from Raleigh.

The monk held himself very still as he considered, then replied. "No, no, I cannot do that! I am already afraid the Duke will guess what I am doing and if Egorh finds out I will not live to see another day. Why her? You can get enough other people."

"The sorceress is willing to pay."

The monk watched closely as Arkarrah untied a bag from his belt and emptied it disdainfully onto the table. One glance at the heap of gold was enough to cause sweat to break out on the monk's round face. The sorceress must be desperate to pay that amount of gold, he thought, his eyes fixed on the shiny gold pieces. The prickle of warning was back and Raleigh hesitated.

Arkarrah grabbed him by the shoulders and snarled, "It's not as if you have any choice. Maybe I will just take all the gold pieces back, you greedy old fool." He released Raleigh and looked around, "Or maybe I should just burn all of this down."

"No! Wait, I'll do it," He gazed at the gold. He could retire and have more time to sit in the chair. "I will do it. It so happens that I offered the girl one of my rare flowers as a wedding gift and she is coming here tomorrow to fetch it."

"Hmmm ... Splendid," drawled Arkarrah.

"Why is she needed?" Raleigh asked weakly.

"The less you know the better. Just do it." Arkarrah grabbed the potion bottles from the table and was about to leave when he spotted a toad near the dirty pots, ready to catch a cockroach.

He stopped, smiled, then kicked Bullfrog across the floor and watched as he landed against a cupboard. He laughed and left slamming the door behind him.

Raleigh looked at the toad and wondered where it came from. He shook his head and mumbled, "This place is getting too busy for me: rats, owls, crows, frogs, people and tonight the three witches are coming for their brew." He gave a disheartened sigh, fumbled in his pocket and took out a bottle of cheap rum. He quickly uncorked the bottle and with shaky hands, put it to his thirsty lips. He drank greedily, staring at the huge lifeless toad.

Suddenly it disappeared before his eyes. Raleigh stared at the empty space. He rubbed his eyes in disbelief and took another large swig from the bottle. He slipped it back into his pocket and returned to the stove.

Kirk leapt up from where he had been sitting, ran towards Bullfrog and picked him up.

"Bullfrog, are you alright?" As Kirk shook the toad, it opened one eye, coughed and drew a deep breath.

Kirk put it on his shoulder and fumed, "I'll have to teach that pig a lesson."

Mirk put his hand on Kirk's arm, "Let it go Kirk! Think about the outcome. We have work to do in the forest. We know we can trust Bubba to retrieve the amulet, warn Egorh and get the message back to Steukhon."

Kirk nodded with a clouded face, then reluctantly followed Mirk into the woods.

"If the Duke knew what business I was running, he would most surely have me hanged, but then again, the money is so good," Raleigh mumbled, as he filled a big jar with the green concoction that had burned Bubba. He sealed it with a cork dipped in bees wax and scribbled on the label, "When the new moon appears, take the potion for two days, at exactly one minute past midnight. The wicked spirit will reveal itself on the last night of the full moon at precisely two minutes past midnight."

Raleigh took the glass jar and placed it outside in the garden, under a giant redwood tree. He looked up at the sky and thought, it's getting late. Soon the witches will be here for the potion. He quickly fetched an empty cup and placed it next to the jar for the witches to drop his money into. The green chubby face rolled his egg eyes from side to side, pressing his nose flat against the inside of the jar. Raleigh ignored him and mumbled, "After midnight someone will drink you and you will be free to run in their veins. The witches will be happy." He closed the door behind him and fumbled eagerly in his pocket for the bottle.

Bubba had overheard every word that had been said. After Arkarrah had departed, he quietly walked to the stables to find his mule. He whispered softly into the animal's ear, "We have to travel, but first I have to wait for Raleigh to drink himself into insensibility so that I can get the amulet. We must leave as soon as possible." Bubba threw a saddle over the mule's back, his hands trembling slightly as he checked the girth. His eyes were troubled as he prepared for the journey.

He quietly left the stables, leading his mule to the back of the house, closer to the kitchen. From here he could peek in to see when Raleigh had passed out from too much of his home-brewed rum.

It was not long before he heard loud snoring from the chair. He sneaked into the kitchen and tiptoed to the shelf where he had seen him hide the amulet. But the jar was empty and the red scorpions were loose, exploring the shelf. Bubba scratched his cheek and murmured, "What did the old fool do with it? Where has he hidden it now?" Glancing around, he saw the amulet dangling from Raleigh's clenched fist. I hope he's very drunk tonight so I can get it and be on my way, he thought.

As Bubba approached, the crow suddenly cawed loudly from his nest above, "It's mine! It's mine!" Raleigh sat up straight. His eyes were red and glassy from the drink, his face mottled and puffy as he looked straight at Bubba. Caught off guard, Bubba quickly collected himself and calmly pointed to the water jar and said, "I brought you some fresh water for the night." Raleigh relaxed, nodded blearily to him and slumped down to sleep. Forgetting that he had been clutching the amulet, Raleigh let it slip out of his hand but Bubba caught it before it could hit the floor.

As he left through the back door, he heard chuckles coming from under the redwood tree. He looked around and saw the mule had gone. "Damn those witches! They've scared my mule away. They must have come for the monk's concoction." From under the tree he heard one of them cackle, "Don't lose your shadow now."

"I have it safely tucked away," replied Bubba, while thinking to himself, I have no time to start a conversation with those three, even though they are my favorites. He quickly walked in the direction he thought the mule would have taken.

Soon he came upon the mule, then slipped into the saddle and nudged the animal in the direction of Bronbeck's mansion. He had not traveled far when he heard voices and realized the road to Crimson Lake was already blocked by a line of dark riders. He spun his mule around and headed east for Crow Shore and the great slave markets. Bubba sighed. Above his head the stars were clear and bright as the crescent moon slowly rose.

His mind filled with anger at the thought of the slave traders. He prayed softly for their failure.

Chapter 22

Trouble

With the picture of Arkarrah still torturing his mind, Egorh remained visibly strained all morning. He and the men had been out combing the land to the South. He had searched the woods every day for the past four days, but his father's murderer seemed to have left the area. He gritted his teeth in irritation.

As summer ended, the ground was dry and dusty. Egorh looked at the sky and longed for rain. Far above his head a falcon circled, its head turning slowly back and forth as it hunted. He shrugged and tried to throw off his dark mood. He envied the falcon's freedom as it soared. It reminded him of Old Falcon Place. After the wedding, he planned to move there with Kayrin and raise their children.

A frown creased his forehead. He had not smiled since the loss of his amulet and his mood was somber. He could not prevent the overwhelming feeling of darkness constantly washing over him. Had he endangered Kayrin by loving her?

The mist was thick and made it difficult to move along

the tortuous trail that ran against the mountain. The search was abandoned when they were forced to turn back earlier than usual. As they reached the dusty road that led to the estate, the riders spread out to catch some of the early sun. The men's conversation grew lighter and louder with laughter.

Daniel was arguing with one of his companions about something unimportant, just for the sake of arguing, to see how much he could tolerate without losing his temper. Usually the others would bet on how long such an argument would last. It often landed Daniel in trouble, but he always seemed to escape unscathed.

They entered the grounds of Crimson Lake, which rang with the sounds of laughter and merriment. A mood of celebration and festivity was everywhere. Everyone in the neighborhood had been invited to Egorh and Kayrin's wedding.

The jubilant mood was contagious and Egorh felt his spirits lift. He pushed all thoughts of his lost amulet and Arkarrah to the back of his mind.

Egorh smiled as he recalled the previous night at the dinner table. Duke John had given his daughter a long blue velvet box. "The traditional gift of something old," he'd said. "It belonged to your mother. I gave this to her on the day you were born." Kayrin had opened the velvet box carefully and gasped with delight when she saw the magnificent chain and its large diamond. She'd jumped up and embraced her father.

"I know your mother would have given anything to be here on your special day," he said quietly. "In memory of her, I wanted to give you the piece of jewelry that she loved most."

"Thank you, Father. I will cherish it for the rest of my life." Kayrin had asked Egorh to fasten it around her neck. His heart swelled with happiness as he thought of their secret marriage and how beautiful she looked.

Later that day, approaching the stables, Egorh sensed that

something was wrong. One of his scouts came running towards them gasping for breath. "There are slave traders in the woods," the man managed to gasp.

"Where?" Egorh demanded.

He pointed towards a road that disappeared into the forest.

Egorh frowned in that direction, "Damn! They must have slipped past us by making a circle to the East."

"There's more, sir." The poor fellow stood for a moment panting with his hands on his knees. "Lady Kayrin has gone that way!"

Egorh felt his blood run cold. "What! Why would she go into the forest?"

"Someone at the house said she had gone to Raleigh for flowers." The man wiped his hand across his sweaty face.

Alarmed, Egorh spun his horse to head in that direction. He waved for his men to follow and they quickly reassembled, setting off at a hard gallop. His pulse leapt when he saw Kayrin's horse coming towards them riderless, with stirrups flapping. "She must have fallen and could be badly hurt. We must find her quickly." It was the only thought Egorh allowed himself.

The group followed the tracks of Kayrin's horse back into the woods and soon reached a stretch of road roughened by many hoof and boot marks; a sure sign that a struggle must have taken place.

Egorh dismounted carefully and scanned the vicinity for a possible ambush. He strung his bow by feel, never taking his eyes off the underbrush that could hide a number of armed villains. His team followed silently, weapons drawn. They searched deeper into the forest, watching for the slightest movement. Every sense was heightened as they prepared for an attack. They found nothing and relaxed. Then unexpectedly, one of the men called out, "Here! A piece of cloth hanging from a shrub."

Egorh walked towards him, took the scrap of material and examined it. "This is from her dress." Rage kindled in him as he recognized the color. "I will kill them," he whispered swallowing the bitterness that rose in his throat as he rubbed the cloth between his fingers.

"Come let us follow." He took a firm grip on the reins and swung his leg over Vector's back. "The thugs could not be far away," he muttered and spurred his horse. A thousand thoughts rushed through his mind. What if she's dead? No, then there would be blood ... a body ... more evidence ...

"There!" Daniel shouted as he saw something fluttering on a branch. Egorh halted, examined what Daniel had found and realized that it was a piece of lace from Kayrin's sleeve.

No one spoke as they followed the tracks. Throughout the day the hoof prints grew fresher and easier to see. Egorh knew that they were closing in on their enemy. The kidnappers had made little attempt to hide their trail and that thought nagged at him.

"If they are heading for a large camp sir, we could be outnumbered," Daniel confided. He had also noticed that the trail seemed too easy to follow. "Maybe one of us should fetch more men ... or we could all be killed."

"They will not escape us, Daniel. One way or another I will hunt them down." Egorh's face was tight and he struggled to keep his emotions under control.

~

It was late afternoon when they heard the sound of laughter. Egorh signaled his men to dismount and slowly they crept closer, taking care not to alert the thugs. Egorh strung his bow quietly and nodded to his men as they prepared themselves.

Around the fire, a group of ruffians were laughing and joking, bragging that they had escaped anyone looking for the girl. Egorh's sharp eyes took in every detail of the group but there was no sign of Kayrin. He adjusted his grip on the bow, realizing they were outnumbered two to one.

The kidnappers were armed with long swords and short daggers. As Egorh slowly moved out from behind a tree, he saw a man on the other side of the fire holding a bottle of rum and laughing loudly. Just then a guard spotted them. He roared an alarm, "They're here!"

The arrow left Egorh's bow, traveled through the flames and pierced the enemy's throat. The wounded man staggered forward, dropping the bottle of alcohol into the fire, before falling into it himself. In an instant, the flames had engulfed him.

The stench of burning human flesh sent shivers down Egorh's spine. He paled as he felt a peculiar paralysis wash over him. His arms dropped to his sides and beads of perspiration began to form on his forehead. The smell of burning flesh and flames instantly brought back the memory of Sir Matthew's murder, and the ancient fear of fire exploded in his mind. With tortured face he stood there, his chest heaving, hypnotized by the flames swimming viciously before his eyes, keeping him locked in fear, oblivious to the fighting men.

Daniel was not a skilled swordsman but tried to outmaneuver his opponent with the swiftness of his feet. He fought desperately but felt the attacker slowly overpowering him. He saw Egorh frozen, staring at the fire and shouted, "What's wrong, sir?" He ducked the sweeping blade of his opponent.

He noticed a man approaching Egorh with his sword held high and again he shouted, "Egorh, watch out!" but there was no reaction. Egorh was in the tight grip of his fear. "Egorh!" Daniel thundered. Egorh heard the frantic voice of Daniel calling his name and as it finally penetrated his consciousness, he felt his terror slip away. He gasped and became aware of the fierce fighting around him. He saw the armed man rushing towards him and instinctively drew his sword and drove it through his assailant's chest, killing him instantly.

Daniel, confused at Egorh's behavior, lost his concentration for a few seconds. He felt an excruciating pain as the blade of his attacker slashed his forearm. He bent forward, grabbing the wound and saw that his opponent had lifted his sword to deliver another blow. He twisted and barely managed to escape the swinging sword.

Daniel heard Egorh behind him and saw him block the thug's attack, just before the blade could strike. The man grinned, showing his decayed black teeth. Kayrin's chain was dangling from his neck. Enraged, Egorh grabbed his dagger from his belt and thrust it into the man's throat, sending him lifeless to the ground. Egorh rolled the body over with his boot and removed Kayrin's chain. He looked up and realized the fighting had stopped and the rest of the gang had fled, and Daniel was clutching his bloody arm. The rest of his men also seemed unharmed.

He desperately scanned the area and his stomach twisted. Feeling Kayrin's necklace in his hand he whispered, "She is not here. They purposely led me up the wrong trail," and started to pace. "How could I have been so stupid?" In hindsight he realized all the signs were there. They were following a false trail. "I have been blinded by my own emotions."

Daniel tried to reassure him. "You care, sir."

"How does that serve her now, Daniel?"

He could feel the eyes of his men on him, thought for a moment, then spoke, "We must go back and follow another trail. We have been tricked. "Daniel, bandage your wound before we leave."

Daniel pressed on the wound to stop the oozing blood. "What happened, Egorh ... back at the fire? You could have been killed."

"I don't know." It was not the right time to explain to Daniel what had happened. He glanced at him and softly said, "Thank you. You saved my life."

Daniel shrugged awkwardly, "Glad to ..."

Egorh held his gaze then said, "I guess we are even now."

Daniel studied him for a moment, "I guess so." He watched Egorh walk away to mount Vector and wondered what the reason could be for his strange behavior. First it was the wolf and now the fire.

Egorh mounted his horse and turned to his men. His voice was low and firm when he spoke, "The slave traders will be heading for a place where they can leave undetected with their cargo. If Kayrin is with them, and I fear she might be, we must try to stop them before they leave the shore. We must hurry." Egorh dug in his heels and Vector leaped forward. They followed the road that led to the dreaded Crow Shore.

Chapter 23

Camp

The giant trees became less dense and it seemed that they were nearing the forest edge. Kayrin heard the sound of waves in the distance.

Arriving at the encampment they saw small groups of men sitting around smoky fires who glared blearily at her as she was roughly pulled from her mount and shoved towards a group of frightened-looking people. They were mostly young men and women, sitting on one side of the camp, all tied together with ropes. No one dared to speak and she could see their lips were dry and cracked from thirst. One of her captives pushed her brutally to the ground and bound her hands behind her back.

Kayrin pulled her knees to her chest and the day's dreadful happenings flashed through her mind. What a fool I've been, she thought, tears brimming. I should never have gone into the forest by myself. I was warned so many times. How could I be so headstrong? All this for Raleigh's flower ... Kidnapped by ... who knows? My father and Egorh must be frantic with worry by now.

She looked up when she heard the thunder of approaching hooves and a loud voice. She recognized him as the man who had led the ambush. His snake eyes roamed the camp, taking in every detail. He had to make sure everything was going according to plan. Kayrin forced herself to sit up painfully straight as he strode towards her. She shuddered slightly and hated herself for the sign of weakness.

He regarded Kayrin with sharp interest, then bent down and roughly made sure her hands were tied properly. She smelt his foul breath, shrank back and turned her head away. With rough, sword-hardened hands he grabbed her chin and forced her gaze back towards him. Her own anger broke free and she flashed him a black look. Filled with rage and hatred she hissed, "Egorh will find you and kill you all. He will leave your corpses for the wild dogs."

The man seemed amused by this outburst and crouched at her side. He grinned and said, "Hmmm ... spirited *and* beautiful. It's a pity Zinnia wants you for bait or I would have kept you for myself." He stood up and his voice was forceful when he continued, "We have all been waiting for him for a long time. The sooner he comes, the better."

Kayrin had overheard his instructions that afternoon. He had entrusted her chain to one of his thugs and said, "Use this if you need to prove that she's been taken. If you are clever, you can bargain with it and save your life when you meet him."

Arkarrah turned away and bellowed, "Where is Sojun?" The sinewy old man got up from the group by the fire and approached. He stared from under the brim of his straw hat and sucked at the back of his teeth, where a piece of meat was trapped. Arkarrah nodded his head in Kayrin's direction. "Make sure you do not overlook this one with your *special treatment*. She's important but trouble. I don't want to have to look for escapees in the forest. They know too much and we have no time to waste." Sojun nodded in response.

Arkarrah yelled at another man. "You there, go to Crow

170

Shore and report back when the ship has arrived so we can load the captives." Arkarrah, knowing Egorh's reputation, could not help feeling uneasy and was eager to leave as soon as possible.

"Close your eyes against the crows," Arkarrah warned. "If they get to you I will leave you behind. There is no time or place for the wounded on the ship." He turned to join a boisterous group who were drinking by the fire.

~

Kirk and Mirk had witnessed Kayrin's capture and were following Arkarrah and his men. In the glimmer of a ghostly moon, the two Dryads sat in a big tree on the outskirts of the camp, cloaked in their invisibility. They followed all the activity in the area closely. They had hoped Egorh would have arrived by now. They did not know about Arkarrah's decoy group, who had led him away from the camp. They were becoming anxious.

"Mirk, this man Arkarrah is evil. I suspect a trap," Kirk whispered worriedly. "Why isn't Egorh here?"

~

Shrieking sounds emanated from an old and dilapidated cage, half covered with an old blanket next to Sojun. Four ruby red eyes stared from the inside. The two huge white-winged vampire bats hanging upside down began to flap their wings, showing their sharp white teeth. They were ugly animals, covered in brown fur with white tipped wings and shiny black ears. A distinctive stench hung around them.

"Be quiet! I am still busy with the mixture," Sojun snapped at them.

Sojun had been out all day searching deep in the forest

to find the haunt of the night civet cat. The musk left on the bark of the trees by the male was an important ingredient in his ointment. He also made sure nobody followed him to the old *Aquilaria* tree, which he had discovered many years ago. From a large wound in the tree, precious *Argar tears* oozed out of its heartwood, as it continuously tried to heal itself with its sap over many years. *Argar tears* were known for their mysterious and pleasing odor and were another vital component of Sojun's blend.

The fire cast erratic light on his wrinkled features as he mixed the slimy scrapings of musk secretion together with the *Argar tears* and *neroli* oil. He added a few drops of resin from the gum tree to complete his powerful concoction. He knew the potent odor of the brew would send the bats into a frenzy, making them vicious hunters.

"Come, my little sacrifice," Sojun murmured, as he took the rabbit he had caught earlier, out of a bag. "Let's give our valuable viewers a demonstration of what would happen if they tried to escape." He smeared the rabbit with some of the sticky substance and let it go. The bats in the cage went into a mad fury, beating their wings and shrieking horribly.

"Go, my beauties!" said Sojun and opened the cage. The rabbit started to zigzag across the clearing, half blinded by the flames of the fire. It paused, then frantically continued. Before it could reach the edge of the clearing, the two bats attacked it, tearing at its flesh. Screeching noises from all around the trees grew louder as hundreds of bats appeared from nowhere.

As if summoned by an invisible demon, they joined in the feeding frenzy. In a heartbeat, the rabbit was stripped clean, leaving only bones. A shrill sound pierced the air as Sojun gave a long whistle through thin lips. The two huge bats immediately flew back into their cage. Realizing the feast was over, the remaining bats returned to their nests in the trees. The night became quiet again.

Arkarrah had been watching the hunt with amusement. He fixed his scowl on the terrified prisoners. "You will all be marked with the same special mixture. The bats will hunt you down if you try to escape. They will kill you and devour your flesh, leaving only your dry bones just as they did with the rabbit. You have been warned." Some of the captive women wept and Arkarrah smiled cruelly as he rejoined the men around the fire. He looked up when he noticed something move. He cocked his head but relaxed when he saw it was just a huge toad that had disappeared into the low bushes.

~

"These are evil humans, Mirk," Kirk muttered in thin-lipped fury. He stood transfixed with horror at what he had witnessed. "We must help Kayrin to escape!"

Alarmed, Mirk looked at Kirk and said, "You saw what happened to the rabbit!"

"But we are the protectors. We *must* find a way," Kirk replied worriedly.

"And if she is eaten by the bats, are *you* going to inform Steukhon?" Mirk asked.

"Well, put like that ..." Kirk replied. After a pause he added, "If she doesn't escape, at least Egorh will have a chance to follow and save her."

"Look what that wretched old man is doing now!" interrupted Mirk and pointed at Sojun.

The two Dryads watched as he dipped a stick into his mixture and started to mark the captives one by one, wiping a small amount of it onto their backs, where it would be difficult to remove. Following Arkarrah's orders, Sojun paid special attention to Kayrin, dabbing her twice. The sweet scent of the mixture made her shudder. With his face almost touching hers, he whispered with his appalling breath in her ear, "The bats will kill for this." Kayrin pulled her face away and said sarcastically, "I wonder which would kill me first, your breath or the bats."

There was a hollowness in Sojun's laugh as he shuffled away, leaving the nauseatingly sweet smell lingering in the air.

The Dryads watched helplessly and prepared for a long night.

Chapter 24

Fleeing

The starved captives were served a very thin, barely edible soup. Exhausted, they soon started to drift into restless slumber. The campfires flickered and only the subdued talking of a few, mixed with the sounds of sleep, could be heard.

Kayrin fought off her drowsiness as she worked on a plan. I must try to escape. It is important that I remove these scent-marked clothes and leave them behind, she thought.

She tugged at the rope around her wrists. The moon had reached its highest point, bathing the encampment in ghostly light. After what felt like hours of working at the knots, she felt the rope finally loosen. The camp was silent now, except for three men still gambling around a fire, sharing a bottle of rum.

She prayed silently that she would manage to slip away undetected. She removed her tainted cloak and slowly began to crawl towards the edge of the camp, keeping her eyes on the gamblers. She managed to slip behind a tree but the sharp crack of a dry twig snapping under her feet, echoed in the still night.

The tallest of the men lifted his head. She did not wait any longer, but bolted into the forest, not knowing whether they had seen her or not.

A warning cry arose from around the campfire: "Someone has escaped!"

The camp erupted. A furious Arkarrah ran towards the prisoners. "Damn, it's the wench that has escaped. Follow her!" he ordered, but the men hesitated for fear of what lurked in the forest.

Arkarrah disgustedly paced and said, "She can't go too far. There are many wild animals around. She will have to find shelter somewhere. We will send the bats out at first light. If they go now, they will finish her off. I need her alive, or at least half alive. Although," he added after a thoughtful pause, "it is the man Egorh we *really* want. Even if the girl is slain, he will not know it. He will still come searching for her." He smiled to himself, "We must be sure that there is no evidence left anywhere if she *is* killed."

~

Kayrin felt the bushes tug at her clothes as she ran. Her only thought was to get as far away from the camp as possible. After what seemed like an eternity, she slowed down. Exhausted by her efforts, she sank to the forest floor and leaned against a tree, the nauseating smell of the sticky substance the old man had smeared on her cloak still lingered around her.

She remained there, curled up all night. Wide-eyed and alert, she listened to the unfamiliar sounds of the forest. For a fleeting moment, panic tried to take over but she fought it back. "I *have* to be strong. Egorh must be near. I know he is looking for me." She reassured herself. As she stared into the dark, a pair of glowing eyes appeared, coming closer and closer.

There was a sudden loud yelp, the sound of branches breaking and an animal taking flight. Kayrin was paralyzed with fear and she drew herself into a tight ball.

Above her Mirk asked, "Did you get him?"

"Yes, bang on the nose. He will be gone for some time," replied Kirk, as the wolf's yelps echoed in the night.

"Mirk, I think you should go and look for Egorh. I will stay with Bullfrog to watch over her."

"You're right. I have had the same thoughts. There must be some sort of trouble; the road to Crow Shore is difficult."

Without another word, Mirk leapt into a tree, his ponytail shining silver in the moonlight as he disappeared through the forest canopy.

At first light, Kayrin rose and started to run deeper into the forest, a direction she hoped would be away from the camp and Crow Shore.

Kirk followed quietly, invisible in the trees above.

Chapter 25

Danger

Egorh sat poised and alert, looking up at the grey sky. The forest had become much darker and the smell of damp pine needles hung in the air. Streaks of mist drifted in from nowhere and moisture dripped from the foliage. It was going to be a moonless night and that would force him to slow down. He quietly cursed under his breath.

"Light the torches," he shouted to his men, "We cannot stop."

The narrow trail forced the riders into single file as they trotted along. The flames from the burning torches held above their heads hardly managed to light the way ahead of them. They were uneasy and their eyes darted from side to side, searching for any sign of movement.

Egorh held up his hand for them to stop as they came to a large green grassland where rock pools shone dark in the grass.

His attention was drawn to the far side of this clearing, where the trail disappeared again into the forest. Dark shadows skimmed the distant treetops and with narrowed eyes, he tried to make out their origin. The moving shadows were erratic, not smooth like that of any owl or night bird he knew. He tilted his head one way, then the other for any sound but heard none. Sensing danger, he started to inch forward. His men instinctively moved closer to each other.

"This doesn't feel right sir," Daniel whispered as a deadly silence enveloped them.

"It would be better to travel in daylight."

"We cannot stop," reprimanded Egorh softly. "We have no time to lose. We *must* catch the kidnappers before they reach the boats."

Unable to tear his eyes away from the shadows that now swung across the plain towards them, Daniel glanced at Egorh and could see that nothing would make him slow down. He fell into an uneasy silence, staring at the shadows that seemed to have increased.

"They are probably just night creatures, Daniel, and our torches will scare them away," said Egorh. He urged a reluctant Vector forward.

The horses nickered nervously and the men formed a line on both sides of Egorh. Suddenly, the strange shadows changed direction and flitted through the dark sky above them, barely missing their heads. A dull, hairy body broke away from the shadowy mass and dropped. With a high-pitched screech it smashed into the flames of the torchbearer slightly ahead of Egorh. Silver dust exploded from the creature and engulfed the rider and his horse. The man froze in horror and his hand clawed at his throat as he gasped for air. His face twisted in agony as the poison entered his skin and lungs. Speechless, the others watched as both horse and rider collapsed to the ground.

"Fall back!" Egorh yelled and yanked the reins to swerve away. He drew his sword as the heavens darkened with innumerable shadows. In the chaos he did not see the figure that came dogtrotting, crouched across the dark field with a drawn bow held low to the ground. Vector reared and Egorh rose in his stirrups, holding his sword high, ready to slash at whatever had spooked his mount.

Surprise flickered across his face as he recognized the familiar voice that spoke urgently from the ground beside him. "Quick! Tell your men to throw down the torches. The flames attract the toxic moths."

"Mirk? What are you doing here?"

"HURRY!" Mirk shouted.

Egorh felt an arrow from Mirk's bow fly past his head and a creature dropped from the sky before it could get to the torch nearest him.

"Egorh, do it NOW!"

Hearing the Dryad's urgency, Egorh yelled, "Throw the torches away, as far as possible, then fall back quickly! These creatures are drawn to the flames!"

Standing half-crouched, Mirk sent shaft after shaft into the shadowy attackers, to give Egorh and his group time to drop the torches and move out of danger.

There was pandemonium as the riders tried to get away. The clang of swords mingled with their panic-stricken outcries. The men were brave fighters, but they could only perceive the strange creatures skimming above as an attack from a diabolical source.

Mirk leaped onto Vector's back and sat perched behind Egorh, balancing as they hurriedly galloped away.

The moths swarmed the sky. Poisonous dust clouds boiled and raged as they dived into the flames of the torches. Out of danger and earshot of the others, Egorh slowed Vector to a trot, and twisted in his saddle. "What are you doing in the grassland? You never leave the forest."

"I was looking for you."

"Why?"

"I have news," Mirk went on. "We followed Kayrin and her kidnappers but when you did not show, we knew something was wrong, so I came looking for you."

"Kayrin?" fear clutched his heart and Egorh gasped, "Is

she safe?" Coldness settled in the pit of his stomach.

"Yes, she is unharmed."

Egorh heaved a sigh of relief and said, "Then, my friend you have brought me good news tonight!"

"That's not all," Mirk gravely continued. "Kayrin has managed to escape her captors for now, but she remains in great danger. She is in hiding and Kirk is guarding her."

The cold feeling in Egorh's stomach intensified and he slowly asked, "Tell me who is responsible for all of this, Mirk."

"A nasty looking piece of work, who calls himself Arkarrah."

"Arkarrah? That son of a worm-minded serpent! It is me he wants, not Kayrin."

"You're right ... I overheard him telling her that she was being used as bait."

There was a long silence before Egorh nodded slowly and spoke quietly. "It has begun, Mirk. Evil took my life when I was the son of Darkarh and it has taken the life of my earthly father." He looked into the moonless night and muttered. "Now it has touched the life of my beloved Kayrin."

Mirk waited in silence, sensing Egorh's turmoil.

Egorh's fists were clenched, his voice was rough and his dark eyes blazed when he eventually spoke again. "I never wanted this battle but I have had enough of the amulet's veiled existence. This malevolence that seeks me – I swear I will find it and destroy it forever!"

Mirk left him alone with his thoughts for a moment before he asked, "What took you so long to get here?"

"We were led on a false trail."

Mirk chewed his bottom lip, "You are still on a very dangerous trail. This one leads past the narrow valley of the upside-down-ear people."

"Upside-down-ear people? You mean ..." Egorh started.

"They have been cursed with upside-down ears. They sacrifice the vocal cords of birds to the Hollow-hole. They believe that one day the Hollow-hole will find a song on one of the vocal cords which will please it, the curse will be lifted, and their ears will become normal. The rock pools you saw back in the open field are tears shed by the nightingale queen when they caught all her nightingales."

Egorh shook his head in disbelief. "She wept all those pools?"

"Yes, there was a boy named Bubba who saved some of her birds. As a reward she gave him her singing bowl before she disappeared to another part of the forest with her remaining birds."

"That explains the strange and eerie silence."

"Yes, most of the birds are gone."

"And the moths?" Egorh asked.

"At night, they guard the entrance to the land of the upside-down-ear people."

"Should I be worried?" Egorh asked already knowing the answer after the clash with the moths.

"Since the curse they have never allowed strangers into their territory and will attack if they feel threatened in any way." Mirk went on, "When I left the slave monger, the captives had made camp not far from Crow Shore. You can avoid the upside-down-ear people by taking another road, but it will lengthen your journey by two days."

Egorh lapsed into silence again as he thought of the new obstacles he must overcome, then shook his head slowly.

"No, we cannot delay."

Mirk glanced at him and saw that a strong, determined look had settled on his face.

"We will have to fight or talk our way through."

"Then I suggest you send your men home. These strange people might not feel threatened by one outsider and may let you pass unchallenged."

Egorh thought, it's worth a try. I will speak to them.

"I will be waiting in the forest."

"Is there anything more I should know about these upside-down-ear people?"

"They hunt with nets and arrows and are extremely

182

accurate archers. They can bring down a tiny bird in flight. Nothing escapes their aim. They can also see into the fourth dimension, so I will be visible to them." Mirk fell silent then said, "See you in the morning." Before Egorh could ask another question, he had disappeared silently into the forest.

Egorh spurred Vector to rejoin Daniel and the riders waiting at the edge of the forest. He could see the fear on their grim faces. They were hard men, good men and had fought the slave traders with courage, but this was no ordinary fight. Mirk was right, they should go home.

"We will make camp and rest here tonight," Egorh said as he leaped lightly from Vector. "We are out of range. The moths will not trouble us again."

The men murmured their agreement and began to make a fire just large enough to remind the forest's predators to keep away. They drank water and nibbled on the last of the dried meat from their saddlebags. They were silent and uneasy.

It was later that evening that Egorh came to crouch by the smoldering logs of the fire, wanting its warmth to take the chill out of his bones, and he decided to speak to his men.

He looked at each one and then began, "You will go no further than this. I want you to return to your homes and your families in the morning. It is better to travel the road to Crow Shore alone. I have reason to believe that unfamiliar dangers, stranger than the one we have met with tonight, lie ahead. Alone I could move faster and more unobtrusively."

"We ..." one of them began, but Egorh held up his hand. "You are good men and I am proud to have fought with you, but my mind is made up. We go our separate ways in the morning and we will meet again in a few days at Crimson Lake."

The faces in front of him were hard to read in the dim firelight but Egorh thought he could detect a certain sense of relief among them. He took Kayrin's necklace out of his pocket and walked over to Daniel.

"Daniel, give this chain to the Duke. Tell him I *will* bring Lady Kayrin home."

Daniel stared at the chain dangling from Egorh's hand, the jewel at the end sparkling. He smiled grimly, then shook his head and spoke resolutely.

"You know, sir, I will not leave your side. Long ago, when you saved my life, it was decided that I would follow you whatever happens. Give the necklace to someone else to take back to Kayrin's father and let me go with you. I will not return with them."

Egorh knew it would be futile to argue this time. He turned to another, gave him the necklace and the message.

"Thank you, Daniel," Egorh said quietly, moved by his friend's determination. He addressed the men again, "We must try to sleep. We all have long journeys ahead of us in the morning."

They had not brought anything in the way of bedding, so they dug sleeping hollows, filled them with dry leaves and slept side by side around the fire.

Somewhere deeper into the forest Kirk was chewing on a root, troubled as he tried to sleep.

Before dawn, the men mounted their horses and dipped their heads to Egorh and Daniel. As their hoof beats dwindled into the distance Egorh looked at Daniel and said, "You can still change your mind."

Daniel just shook his head.

They both knew that a bridge of trust and understanding had developed between them over the years and Egorh was proud to travel with him. They turned their horses towards the clearing.

Chapter 26

Upside-Down-Ear People

Retracing their steps from the previous evening, Daniel was the first to see a dead wolf near the body of the poisoned man and his horse. Realizing just how toxic the moths were, they could not risk touching the bodies. They covered them with rocks and thick branches before moving on.

Nearing the opposite side of the grassland, Egorh noticed clusters of huge hairy creatures clinging to the trees. Only a slight tremble here and there proved them alive and he presumed they were the moths from the previous night. With drawn swords, they moved past, making sure not to disturb them.

They entered the forest, but the dense undergrowth forced them to dismount. Egorh wondered where Mirk could be. He relaxed when the low growth thinned and was about to remount when he heard Mirk shout, "WATCH OUT!" He looked up as a net came falling down. Immediately both of them were wrapped up tight in the mesh and jerked high into the air.

"Darn, Mirk! Couldn't you warn us earlier?" Egorh shouted, struggling to escape.

"The net was concealed, I did not see it."

"Whom are you speaking to?" asked a bewildered Daniel with his knees pushed way past his ears. Egorh did not answer but looked down and saw five young men standing beneath them. Their naked torsos were smooth with oil and shone like polished bronze. They looked strange with their upside-down ears, long straight noses and thin lips. Long black hair dangled in thick plaits from the crowns of their shaved heads. They glared up at Egorh and Daniel with strange, yellow, owl-like eyes.

"We are in deep trouble, sir!" muttered Daniel.

They held large, peculiar looking iron discs in their hands. Axes hung from the belts of their baggy pants.

Egorh whispered from the corner of his mouth, "Must be a weapon, of some sort. Be ready, Daniel, I am going to cut us out of here. Try to land on your feet and make for the horses."

Egorh managed to reach the dagger in his boot and hacked at the thick net, making an opening for them to slip out.

As they landed on the ground, they were surrounded. More groups of shiny bodies swarmed in and began to encircle them. A young man in the first row snapped his disc open and revealed a sharp, half-moon blade. An unpleasant smile twisted his upper lip.

"Wait!" Egorh shouted, but the young man gave no sign that he had heard and the mob moved closer. "We come in peace. We lost our trail and came to ask for safe passage through your valley," Egorh tried again, but the first six men stormed towards them with their blades held high. Egorh drew his sword and leaned forward. Every nerve in his body strained, the muscles in his forearm quivered as he waited for the attack.

"Stay close!" he yelled to Daniel.

Egorh ducked when the first blade whirred past his head with blinding speed and sank deep into the tree trunk behind him. A few men were swinging small nets in circles ready to throw them but Kirk dashed between Egorh and his attackers and collapsed each swinging net, causing confusion and chaos.

Yelling, the strange figures charged and Egorh could see that they were horribly outnumbered. He punched the first reaching him with such ferocity that the bronze body stumbled back into the others. Three more fell to his stabbing blade. Arrows from Mirk's bow injured many. To one side, Egorh became aware of Daniel fighting bravely. He could see the boy was in agony and hoped that the blood on his shirt was not from the wound on his arm that had opened or even worse. The fighting raged back and forth and sweat drenched Egorh's body as he managed to hurl another bare-chested man through the air into the advancing enemy.

Another assailant leapt forward, holding a dagger. Egorh took a few steps back, tripped over a root and fell. Blades whizzed towards him. He thought that any one of the weapons would certainly strike him in the head but at the last moment, the closest one swung off course and struck a tree, missing him by a hair's breadth. He heard more weapons being snapped open and felt how the blades sliced through the fabric of his clothes and pinned him to the tree, leaving thin cuts on his skin. Daniel had been captured and was being held down. To the right stood a row of fifty archers with arrows aimed at Mirk.

A sudden quietness settled over their enemy and Egorh watched helplessly as a grizzled older man with a covered torso walked towards him. A gold ear dangled on a chain from his neck and Egorh presumed him to be the leader. His dark eyes stared at Egorh while he repeatedly flicked his weapon open and closed, revealing the sharp half-moon blade. Egorh did not flinch and matched the enemy's gaze.

"Why are you here?" the man growled.

"We were headed for Crow Shore and lost our way."

"Where are the other men hiding?"

"There are no others, only us." Egorh tried to say convincingly.

"You are lying! There were many torches last night."

Egorh's gaze did not falter under the old man's scrutiny as he answered, "I have sent them all home."

"Why?"

"The quest from here is mine alone. My friend Daniel is my only companion."

"You killed our moths," the elder snarled.

Egorh chose his words carefully, "We had no choice. They killed one of my men."

The man assessed him thoughtfully. His gaze fell on the beak mark and his eyes widened. He raised his hand and a silence came over the attackers behind him. Pinned to the tree and helpless, Egorh watched as the old male moved closer. He lifted his half-moon blade and slid Egorh's shirt away to inspect the mark.

Egorh stared at the aged warrior as he stepped back. He detected a change in the man's expression. The emotion flickering in his eyes could be respect or approval, Egorh did not know, but his manner was no longer threatening.

In a strange tongue he snapped some words to a young boy nearby. A soft muttering, like whispering leaves, swelled up among the bare-chested army. The boy bowed and rushed away. The leader opened his arms wide, signaling for the crowd to move back, then turned to Egorh.

With a small bow he spoke, "My name is Ukar. Our people can see into the fourth dimension. We can see your Dryad friend. Fifty of my finest archers have him at arrow point. We do not want to kill him, so order him down. If he obeys, he will not be hurt."

Egorh looked at Mirk and the row of archers. He knew this was no time for a standoff. He nodded for Mirk to conform. Mirk lowered his bow, slipped the arrow back into his quiver and leapt down to stand next to Egorh.

Within moments the crowd parted and a group of women appeared carrying long spears tipped with white bone. The female in front, carried no weapon and moved smoothly towards Egorh, her posture strikingly perfect. She stopped before him, proud and tall, her perfect bronze body outlined by the white robe that clung to her. Her yellow, owl-like eyes were intense as she searched him, until they rested on his flamingo beak mark.

"My name is Varkin," she said softly. She glanced at Ukar and ordered, "Release him."

The upside-down-ear people quietly obeyed this command and removed the blades that had pinned him to the tree.

"It is said that the mark you bear is proof that you are the son of Darkarh. Is this true?"

Egorh stood tall and she sensed the quiet strength in him. It was the first time he had been asked to admit this and he replied, "The truth cannot be hidden." He did not know if this answer would mean his death or his release.

"There is a sorceress who seeks your death." Varkin continued.

"I know evil pursues me," Egorh replied, meeting her gaze. He wondered who the source of her information might be.

With her peculiar yellow eyes, Varkin held his gaze for a long while before she turned to Ukar and they exchanged words in their strange tongue.

Egorh gasped in awe as he saw that her bare back was tattooed with two magnificent wings. The incredibly intricate tattoo started at her shoulders and ended just above her slender hips, quivering on her skin as she moved.

Sensing his incredulity, the woman said, "We were cursed by the same sorceress from the land of Lark, who seeks your death. She had learned that we are exceptional archers and we have quivers that never empty. We had heard of her evil and refused to help her. She turned my people's ears upside-down and trapped our wings beneath our skin. Like the moths, we could also fly at certain times of the year. She told us that to break the curse, we would have to seek the song of a bird that the Hollow-hole desires and offer it to him as a sacrifice. This was a trick, for up to now we have not found such a bird. If you can destroy her, the curse will be broken."

Egorh's eyes fell on a young boy who appeared at her side and handed her an unusual carved quiver, holding only one arrow fitted with snow-white feathers.

As the group watched Egorh she handed it to him.

"If you will help us, we wish to honor you with one of our never-empty quivers."

Egorh took the gift and said, "Thank you. It is for many reasons that I seek to destroy this evil and if I can add your suffering to my cause, it will make my reason for revenge even stronger."

"Prove to me that you are worthy of this honor," she whispered

He took his own quiver and handed it to Daniel, then slipped the gift over his shoulder. Varkin smiled and stood aside for them to pass. Egorh bowed, picked up his sword and walked over to Vector.

Daniel and Mirk followed close behind. Egorh could see that Daniel was puzzled and confused by what had happened.

Mirk made for the forest trees. "I am going to find Kirk." From the top of the trees he warned, "I see no smoke from campfires, only thousands of bats swarming around about three hours' ride from here. It could mean trouble. I will go on ahead to see," and with that he disappeared at Dryad speed.

Egorh and Daniel mounted their horses and set off. When they heard bird-song again, they realized they had left the valley of the upside-down-ear people. Egorh paused to glance back at the valley and he thought about the significance of his beak mark.

Daniel was silent. He could not understand why these strange people had not taken their lives, why Egorh was treated like a god and then ... then there was the curious business of the person he could not hear or see whom Egorh called Mirk.

"Come, Daniel, we must hurry," Egorh said, interrupting Daniel's thoughts. "I will explain everything to you later. Now is not the time." They urged their horses in the direction of Crow Shore.

Chapter 27

Bats

"Send the bats!" Arkarrah shouted, kicking the old man who lay fast asleep under his soiled blanket. Arkarrah had had a sleepless night and his mood was explosive. The young woman's escape would not be easy to explain to Zinnia and he was haunted by thoughts of a surprise attack by Egorh.

All around the camp, men stirred from their night's sleep. They milled around, yawning and stretching, their eyes bleary from the smoke or from too much alcohol. They prepared for another day in the saddle.

"On your feet!" Arkarrah shouted, prodding the old man again with his boot. Sojun sat up, his wrinkled mouth puckered in irritation. He rose to his feet, displeased at the way he had been woken. He cleared the phlegm from his throat and spat with displeasure. Arkarrah watched this performance with contempt, as he paced to and fro, chewing his lip nervously. Just then one of Arkarrah's cronies appeared, holding Kayrin's discarded clothing.

"She left this behind sir. It has Sojun's markings on it."

"What?" shouted Arkarrah and grabbed the cloak. "How will we find her now? I have no time to track her down." Anger flared in his eyes.

Fuming, Arkarrah turned to Sojun, who seemed disinterested as he fiddled with the bats' cage door. Not meeting his eyes, Sojun mumbled, "I made sure she got some of the mixture on her hair. She *will* be found." He gestured in the direction of the forest.

A horrible grin spread over Arkarrah's face, "Well then, let the hunt begin."

Sojun slammed his hand hard on the side of the cage and the vampire bats hurtled away swiftly, shrieking loudly. Free from the cage, they shot into a sky still pale with the earliness of the morning. He had trained them well. They knew how to find their prey and followed the scent of his concoction. A sudden flutter came from the inside of Arkarrah's coat as Horris crawled out and followed with a frantic squeal.

As the large white-winged bats darted through the sky, their screeching sounds traveled through the forest, causing a stir among the forest bats high up in the trees. Suddenly, the dark gathering began to unravel and a black cloud of bloodthirsty, shrieking creatures joined the hunt.

"Let's follow!" Arkarrah yelled.

~

With hardly any sleep the previous night, Kayrin had been waiting impatiently for daylight so she could run deeper into the woods. Loud chatters began as the forest started to wake long before first light. She rubbed her tired eyes and waited nervously, then started to search where the sweet scent came from. She felt the stickiness on her head and realized with shock that the old man must have rubbed some of the stuff in her hair as well. When the forest bed became visible she started to run, suspicious of any movement around her. Her features were anxious.

As she paused to catch her breath, the cacophony of bat shrieks reached her ears. Panic-stricken, she realized that they had picked up the scent in her hair and had followed her after all. Leaving her scent-marked cloak behind at the camp was fruitless. Her only thought now was to seek cover.

She frantically looked around her and saw a giant tree with a hollowed trunk not too far away. She raced towards it. She was not quick enough and the first bats began to attack. Their tiny razor-blade teeth dug into her flesh. She lashed out madly at the aggressive creatures, but the more she tried to beat them off, the more they attacked, driven to frenzy by the smell of blood. She eventually stumbled into the hollow trunk but some of the bats followed and as they latched onto her they dug deeper into her bleeding wounds with teeth and claws.

Kirk joined by Mirk shortly before daybreak, followed Kayrin. There was no time to brief Kirk on Egorh's situation. The Dryads did not waste time and sprang into action. "She's in trouble! Let's block the entrance with branches." They leaped to the ground and dragged as many branches as they could in front of the tree's entrance, hoping to stop the bats' attack.

Inside the huge hollow, Kayrin struggled to free herself from the greedy, biting bats that had followed her. She was terrified and the pain from the tiny teeth that hacked into her flesh was excruciating. She screamed in fear.

"I will help her deal with the bats inside," gasped Kirk. "You stay outside to see that no more follow."

Once inside her hiding place, Kirk grabbed the bats from Kayrin and smacked their heads together with vicious speed, leaving a heap of dead creatures. With the last bat removed, Kirk looked at Kayrin in horror as she cringed, whimpering inside the trunk. Her arm, shoulder and one side of her face were shredded. For a moment Kirk stood looking helplessly at her as she slumped to the ground and faded into unconsciousness.

He shouted to Mirk outside, "Kayrin looks bad and is unconscious. What must I do?"

"We must keep her alive, Kirk. Egorh *must* have a chance to save her. She *cannot* die. Apply some oil to her wounds."

Kirk took the blue bottle that hung across his chest and cautiously dripped the liquid onto Kayrin's wounds. "This will stop the infection at least," he muttered to himself.

"Hurry, Kirk! We must leave! I hear the sound of horses coming this way. Leave the bottle of magic oil in the pocket of her skirt."

"How will she know how to use it? What happens if she drinks it?"

"Whisper in her ear and she will remember when she sees the bottle. Hurry!"

Kirk knelt beside her and whispered into her ear, "Put the oil in the blue bottle on your wounds." He stood, reluctant to leave her, then crawled out and leaped to where Mirk perched on a branch above.

"Did you find Egorh?" Kirk finally had a chance to ask him.

"Yes, I found him but I am afraid he is still a long way behind, at least three hours."

"That's not good news. We'd better watch and see what happens next." The two Dryads, cloaked in their invisibility, waited.

Arkarrah and his pack arrived within minutes and stared at the hollow tree, surrounded by angry, swarming bats. A piercing whistle cut through the air as Sojun called his white winged bats like hunting dogs. The Dryads watched as the creatures returned to the cage. With their leaders now caged, the mass of smaller bats drifted back to their treetop colonies. The hunt was over.

From where she hid, Kayrin gradually became aware of her surroundings and struggled to sit up. She stifled a scream when she remembered what had happened and looked around fearfully. She shivered and rubbed her arms but cringed with pain when she touched the open wounds. Recalling the black velvety creatures that had attacked her so viciously, she shuddered. She rested her head against the trunk, but a heap of dead bats near her feet made her jerk her legs up quickly. She became aware of voices outside the tree and knew it must be the men coming for her but she was too traumatized to care what happened next.

Kayrin heard a rough voice outside shout, "Bring her out, we have wasted enough time." The branches at the entrance to the tree were removed and two men reached in and dragged her out into the open.

Arkarrah looked on triumphantly. "So, she is not dead then?"

"No," replied Sojun glumly, puzzled that the bats had not finished her off.

"Take her away," Arkarrah barked. They picked her up and threw her over the saddle in front of one of the riders, then headed back to camp.

Chapter 28

Crow Shore

It was late afternoon when they arrived back at the camp. A few had stayed behind, cleared the site and packed the horses. Arkarrah strode through the area to make sure nothing was left behind and barked a few more orders before he mounted. There was a sudden urgency amongst all of them to leave soon. The captives were pushed to move faster in the direction of the distant sound of waves.

Kayrin fought against the pain as they pushed forward to the place she heard them call Crow Shore. She rode in a daze, drifting in and out of consciousness. When the horses stopped again, she heard the sound of waves close by. She smelled the salty air and felt it sting her wounds.

When they stopped, Kayrin was pulled roughly out of the saddle and thrown over a bulky man's shoulder. She was carried to a small boat that waited at the water's edge and dumped among the captives who were already sitting there, bundled together, wide-eyed with fear.

Despite her pain and humiliation, Kayrin's attention was

drawn to hundreds and hundreds of black birds cutting shadows across the sky. Some plunged down and strutted around on the rocky shore, screeching and pecking ferociously at one another, squabbling to get to the center of the huddle. She tried to see what the fighting was about and realized with horror that the crows were ripping at the flesh of dead bodies. All along the shore, bleached bones that had been pecked clean long ago lay scattered among the rocks.

There was activity everywhere on the shore, which was sheltered on both sides by enormous outcrops of grey rock. These barriers, which stretched from the tree line to the sea, had created a secluded half-moon beach. The huge headland formed a natural breakwater against the high swell of the open sea. As the waves smashed against the rocks, they fizzed and sprayed, leaving a calm lagoon between them, a perfect loading bay for the slave mongers. The dreaded Crow Shore was the place of departure for all traffickers and their cargoes. It was a dangerous spot, where, on occasion, rival slave traders would fight each other.

Bad weather had suddenly swept in from the ocean, pushing thick fog over the boulders and beach, deep into the woods. With patience running thin, burly armed men shoved the shackled captives viciously towards the water, where more small boats waited. Their blank faces showed no remorse for having chosen a life of kidnapping and plunder. Some of the boats were already pushed into the breaking waves, heading towards the large ship anchored in deep water.

Fear rose in Kayrin's throat as she felt her boat moving. Her eyes darted hopefully back to the forest. There was nothing, only the hordes of scavenger birds on the shore. She watched them despairingly as the wind howled, making their black feathers stand straight up in the air.

Her attention was drawn to Arkarrah when she heard him shout, "Cover the horse's eyes before the crows get to them, then take them to the old man. Tell him we will be back with the next full moon. He can take two horses as payment but not of the best. I want to find them in good condition when I return." A few men hurriedly gathered all the horses and shielded the beasts' heads from the pecking crows. Sensing danger, the jittery horses were driven with cracking whips further up the coast. Clouds of crows fluttered up before their pounding hooves and skimmed the shore before they noisily returned.

In all the confusion on the shore, no one noticed a man slip in amongst a group of captives. Bubba's eyes searched desperately for Kayrin. He kept his head low to avoid drawing any attention.

The small boats were rowed towards the ship and as they neared it, Kayrin could hear the crew on board shouting for the anchor to be raised. The shackled prisoners found it difficult to climb the rope ladder and many felt the whip burning on their backs as they struggled. Once on board the ship, they were herded into a corner like animals. Bubba who had seen Kayrin, tried to move closer to her as they were boarding.

Kayrin dropped down onto the deck with the others, panic-stricken and trembling. She pulled her legs up to her chest, let her forehead rest on her knees and let her thoughts travel back to the man she loved.

She looked up when she heard someone calling her name.

"Can it be Egorh? Has he come for me?" she thought frantically. She tried to get up but a whiplash on her shoulder made her fall back.

"Get down woman," the guard shouted. As he lifted his whip again, Bubba used his little blowpipe to shoot the guard with a tiny thorn dipped in the oil of poison ivy from Raleigh's kitchen. The man felt a sting on his neck and slapped at it. He walked away cursing loudly.

Still burning from the whip, Kayrin thought, it must be my mind playing tricks on me … that voice was so distant and faint … we are now too far away from the shore. She lowered her head and sobbed quietly.

She slipped her hand into her skirt pocket for a handkerchief but felt something else, something hard. Puzzled, she stared at a little blue bottle. "How did this get here?" Then vaguely she recalled a voice ... a voice that sounded very faint away, telling her to put the oil on her wounds.

She frowned and thought, my mind is playing tricks on me ... all these voices. But something made her unscrew the bottle and drop a little of the oil onto the wound on her forearm. She lay back and closed her eyes. Slowly her pain eased.

She was amazed and began to put oil on all her wounds: her arm, forehead, lips, cheek and her badly swollen eye. She felt the pain drain from her body. With all her heart, she silently thanked whoever had given it to her. Visions of her childhood, her father, her life at Crimson Lake and her beloved Egorh ran through her mind and for a moment, she found peace.

~

The horses had not been spared as Egorh and Daniel raced towards Crow Shore. Egorh prayed that he would not be too late and that somehow Kirk and Mirk had managed to hold back the slave traders.

At last they arrived at the shore, deserted but for the black scavenging birds. The burnt out remnants of campfires oozed thin tendrils of smoke into the wind. Egorh glanced with horror at the crows and their grisly work. He looked to the sky where vultures drew circles as they flew, patient and slow against the wind, waiting to descend to share in the feast. He rushed over the rocky shore towards the lagoon, sending hordes of crows into the sky as Vector forced a path among them.

Egorh's eyes darkened with despair as he gazed over the water. A chill of hopelessness tugged at his insides.

"Daniel, we are too late!"

The distant ship with all sails already unfurled, had

weighed anchor and was sailing away.

Out of sheer desperation, Egorh spurred Vector into the sea and shouted, "Kayrin! Kayrin!" His voice carried over the water and he waited in vain for her answer. He realized the situation was hopeless and watched in silence as the ship moved further out to sea. Egorh sat frozen on his horse, staring at the disappearing vessel. His lips hardly moved as he whispered, "Kayrin ... I will come for you. I will seek you until I draw my last breath. I cannot lose you!"

He watched until the ship had completely disappeared before he turned his horse back towards Daniel, who did not speak. Egorh's ravaged expression told its own story and he waited patiently for him to break the silence.

It was with a firm voice and renewed conviction that Egorh finally spoke. "Daniel, we must follow. We will ride further up the coast to the city's harbor. *Someone* there will have information on the course of that ship. Are you still with me or do you wish to return home?"

"My place is here with you sir. I have no wish to leave you, none at all!" Daniel replied simply.

"Then let's not waste any more time."

~

From the edge of the forest, Kirk and Mirk had watched helplessly as the slave vessel left.

"I should have killed him," Kirk muttered darkly.

Mirk understood his feeling and replied, "Kirk, think of who you are and what you will become. Don't let the evil of our past find a pathway through your hate. We have too many to serve and protect."

Kirk swarmed up a tree and plonked himself down on a branch. Taking a scorpion he caught earlier from his pocket, he began to play a game, not saying a word. He knew Mirk was right as always.

Their hearts were heavy, for Egorh had not saved Kayrin, but their spirits lifted when he and Daniel eventually arrived. They heard his anguished cry to his beloved. They strained their ears to hear his plans to follow the trail further.

Once they saw the two riders leave, Mirk said, "Let's go. Our task has ended. Bubba is now watching over Kayrin and she has our magic healing oil, so her wounds should not trouble her. The seven mermaids and Steukhon will take over now and help Egorh fulfill his destiny."

"We must get more oil and attend to the forest," Mirk tried to distract Kirk. "I saw the white termites moving into the large oak tree, the one where the rainbow maidens meet. Did you give them permission to work there?"

"No, never, They cannot! We must immediately remove them," snorted Kirk.

He scooped up Bullfrog and they disappeared into the forest with their usual Dryad speed.

Chapter 29

Slave Trail

The harbor city of Melsat was five hours' hard ride north of Crow Shore. It was an ancient slave city, hostile to any newcomers. It was well known that one could buy their way into the heart of the city with enough gold. Many came here to hide from the law or trade in forbidden goods. There were few women and some skinny children and the noise and activity came from the men who crowded the streets.

The air was hot and windless when Egorh and Daniel arrived at Melsat. The market place reeked of rot and filth. Egorh watched with disgust as stray dogs sniffed around in the waste that had accumulated on the shoreline, carelessly dumped overboard by the docking ships.

He had scoured the docks and tensed. "Do you see what I see, Daniel?" Egorh murmured and indicated at the bustle on the dock to their left. Between all sorts of stuff that was being loaded, a group of shackled people were being herded aboard a ship that was in the last stages of loading and preparing to leave.

"We are in luck. There is only one place a vessel with that kind of cargo would be bound: the same place they have taken Kayrin. We *must* board."

"The local tavern," Daniel spoke excitedly. "That's where we must go. Tongues are always loose and we might get some information."

So as not to attract attention, they strolled towards a group of men who stood nearby, arguing loudly and waving their arms, while stuffing their mouths with meat cooked at a nearby stall. When Egorh cleared his throat, they stopped in mid sentence and turned with raised brows to him.

"We are thirsty. Can you direct us to an inn?"

There was an uneasy silence, which Daniel thought much too long. The tall, dark man, who had granted himself no time to swallow in the heat of the argument, motioned with his head towards a scruffy building further up the street. Egorh nodded his thanks and veered towards the inn, where he hoped he would find the information he needed.

A scruffy sailor stood at the door of the noisy inn and Egorh spoke quietly, "Daniel, I will go in alone. You must stay with the horses. If we leave them, we will never see them again."

Daniel nodded. "I'll keep them ready, just in case, sir."

Egorh moved towards the wooden door, but the sailor quickly blocked his path and said testily, "Any business here?"

Egorh barely concealed the surge of anger that rose within him and spoke softly. "My business is with your captain."

"And what *is* your business?" Egorh heard someone say from within the tavern.

Peering into the room, Egorh answered, "A safe passage on your ship for two. I can pay."

A slight pause followed, then he heard someone bark. "Let him through."

The sailor stepped aside and Egorh walked to a table where a few men sat drinking. A craggy featured man leaned forward and squeezed his brows into a frown.

"Are you the captain of the ship that is preparing to sail?" Egorh asked.

"In Melsat, information is not given to strangers, it is sold." The man's nostrils flared as he breathed his beer breath and stared at Egorh. The captain, from his earliest memories, had lived a wandering life, mostly aboard his ship and he knew trouble when he saw it. But when Egorh tossed some gold coins in front of him, his greed overcame most of his suspicion.

They exchanged glances as the captain tapped his bulky fingers on the table, inches away from the gold, "I don't want trouble. My vessel is a merchant ship with a cargo of spices and textiles."

"I will add two horses," Egorh's heart sank at the thought of losing Vector. "I will come back for them, and if I find them in good order, I will double the price."

The captain looked again at the coins, then swept the pile off the table into his hand and nodded at two men in the corner.

Moving the coins from one hand to the other, he leaned back and glowered from beneath bushy eyebrows. "There are conditions. You are to remain on deck. No walking around, no questions asked and only dry bread and water."

Egorh nodded, keeping his face blank.

The captain growled to his crew, "Take the horses to my stable and see the new passengers aboard." Egorh left the inn and signaled to Daniel to approach with the two mounts. "Trust me, it was the only way," he whispered to an unhappy Daniel.

Vector jerked his head as the man led him away, freed himself and trotted back to Egorh. Egorh grabbed the animal's reins, rubbed Vector's nose, swallowed hard on the bitter taste that had suddenly risen in his mouth and whispered, "I will be back, my friend." He handed the reins of the snorting animal back to the surly man with great reluctance, and silently they followed the sailor.

As they walked along the quay, Egorh noticed that the waterline of the ship was slightly below the surface indicating that the vessel was overloaded. He was more than ever convinced that the hold was crammed with slaves.

They were led up the gangway and onto the deck where the sailor indicated a corner near a large heap of tackle, which would be their place during the journey. Without another word, he turned his back and walked away. Egorh did not trust any of the unsavory-looking crew and kept his hand close to his sword. They settled as best they could against the ropes. Egorh adjusted his new quiver to fit under his arm and clutched it firmly to his side.

Once they left the sheltered curve of the harbor, the wind seemed to grab the baggy sails and Egorh turned his eyes to the wake of the boat, saddened at the thought of Vector.

As the ship's bow ploughed into the waves of the open sea, he fell back against the ropes and closed his eyes. Daniel let out a long sigh and tried to find a hollow for his back against the prickly heap of tackle.

With the ship far out at sea, Egorh's mind raced with thoughts of Kayrin, his demon and Varkin. He glanced at the quiet Daniel between the tackle and knew he owed him an explanation. Since they left the upside-down-ear people, Daniel's mind had been troubled and he felt it important to tell him the meaning of all that had happened.

"Daniel, I have something to tell you."

Daniel opened his mouth to say something but was unsure what to say and kept quiet.

"You chose to follow me and therefore I owe you the truth. Back there at the upside-down-ear people I spoke to a Dryad. His name is Kirk. He has a companion named Mirk. They live in another dimension or world if you can call it that. Not many humans can see them."

"Ghosts?" Daniel swallowed.

"No, they are real like you and me, only a little different. Their true mission is to protect the forest. Most of what I am about to tell you will sound absurd, but you have to trust me on this and believe all I tell you to be true. I met these strange creatures on my eighth birthday in the forest and they have been my friends ever since. On that day they told me that I am part of the magical world as well as the world you and I both know. They have been my constant companions most of my younger years and I have experienced many magical things with them." Egorh looked at the awe struck Daniel and continued, "It is to them that you owe your leg. That day in the wolf trap, they were the ones who pulled you out and used their magical oil to heal the bone."

"Are you serious?"

"Listen carefully. I will try to tell you all."

Egorh's face was hard to read in the dim moonlight as he crossed his legs and began to tell Daniel about his young life with Mirk and Kirk, the hidden amulet, the visit to the cave and the tales of the priest and his destiny, his secret marriage to Kayrin, the lost amulet, and the appearance of the green-eyed eagle. "I guess what I really want to explain is that I belong to the mortal as well as the magical world."

Daniel's eyes were dark pools as he soaked up everything Egorh had said. He asked; "Have you worked with magic?"

"No ... only seen it done."

Daniel nodded silently, trying to digest the bizarreness of it all.

"I am afraid I have endangered Kayrin's life. I always prayed that she would not become part of all this, but destiny it seems, has its own rules," Egorh said gravely.

It was hours later when he fell silent and Daniel stood up to fetch water. The two men, deep in thought, listened to the waves and the creaking deck as they sipped the water. The journey suddenly became treacherous. At times the ship bobbed and swayed, whipped by brutal winds, as storms raged on and off for three days. They clung to the ropes not to be washed overboard by the angry waves that crashed onto the deck. Egorh had no opportunity to test his suspicions, as the crew kept a close watch on them and the hatchway was heavily guarded. He decided to stick to the captain's conditions and not attempt to investigate. They could follow the slaves once they had disembarked.

On the fourth night, the clouds parted and they looked up into a sky that was sprinkled with millions of stars. There was a chill in Egorh's heart as he thought of Kayrin.

~

Duke John stood beside his fireplace at Crimson Lake. He had been pacing the floor for many hours that day. His eyes were clouded with worry and his knuckles whitened as he clasped the poker to stir the logs, though they were burning well and did not need it. He thought of Sir Matthew's tale of long ago and the strange tale of the son of Darkarh. His beloved Kayrin was missing and Egorh had set off in pursuit. He was almost beside himself with concern. He hoped that she would not become part of Egorh's destiny. He walked to the window to stare at the empty road, then squinted as horses suddenly burst out of the trees and raced towards the house. He recognized them as his men and rushed outside to meet them.

The men that stood in front of Duke John did not bear good news. He frowned as the speaker stepped forward, shook his head and uttered the words he had been dreading. "I'm sorry, sir, we could not find your daughter. The attackers used two teams to throw us off their tracks. We managed to kill one group. Egorh and Daniel went on alone."

John tensed and his stomach felt hollow when the man held out Kayrin's chain and said, "Sir, Egorh sends this. He said to tell you that he *will* bring her back." With difficulty, the Duke controlled his emotions, nodded wordlessly and turned from them.

Inside, away from all, he closed his eyes, held the chain to his chest and prayed, "Please God, let him save her!" He looked again at the chain and whispered, "The time has come."

Kayrin could not keep track of time and was only aware of the constant heaving and pitching of the vessel as it battled through the ocean, causing ever-present nausea.

~

207

"Water! Water!" shouted a round-faced man in front of her, holding a dirty leather bucket. She shook her head in refusal, repulsed by the foul smell of the tainted water.

"Drink!" he ordered, dipping a tin mug into the liquid. "There is no food."

Anger flared in Kayrin and her blue eyes were icy as she snarled, "Drink your own rotten filth!"

The sailor snorted and without taking his eyes off her, slowly sipped the water. Kayrin shuddered in disgust as she saw him filter it between his rotten teeth, live cockroaches sticking to his gums. She retched and looked away. The sailor spat the cockroaches over the rail and swaggered away.

As the morning star disappeared from the sky, Kayrin heard a loud voice shouting from high up on the mast, "Drakens Harbor!" At once bodies crawled from every hole and the deck became alive. Instructions and orders were bellowed, the sails came down and it wasn't long before they started to glide smoothly into harbor.

Thick mooring ropes tied the ship to a broad timbered pier.

"Where to now?" she wondered. Before long, the captives were herded towards a rope ladder and forced down onto the landing stage.

"Take this miserable bunch to the slave market and wait for me there," Arkarrah instructed from the ship's rail. He noticed a man slip away from the group of captives and disappear into the crowd.

"That man! There! He is escaping!" Arkarrah shouted and pointed to where Bubba had just melted into the crowd. "Catch him and bring him to me! He has a brown robe. I want to know who he is." A few of Arkarrah's men dashed after Bubba but they were too late; he had vanished.

"Damn ..." muttered Arkarrah. "How did he get on board? Who can he be?"

Kayrin and the captives were being steered across a bridge, one of many leading to the mainland, in the direction of the harbor city. Just like her, the others were now hungry, thirsty and weak. The cracking whips all around them and the angry shouts of Arkarrah and his men, forced the prisoners to move faster. The harbor city was busy, but none of the people passing even glanced in their direction. With eyes pinned to the ground, they seemed afraid to look at them. The captives were kept very close together and away from the crowds, making communication impossible.

Kayrin looked at her surroundings but cringed when she heard the crack of a whip above her head. "Keep your eyes down and follow," a man shouted from behind. "I don't want any trouble."

The city of Drakens was old but busy, the dusty streets crowded. Merchants and street traders were everywhere. The place was very noisy as everybody tried to speak at the same time, some shouting and some arguing. At the roadside, scores of vendors were trying to sell all sorts of goods: live or cooked chicken, fruits known only to that land, and colorful fabrics hanging from poles anchored in the ground.

As they neared the end of the street, they were bunched together and ordered to stay next to an open raised area. Some prisoners were pushed onto the raised level and Kayrin recognized faces from the ship.

A bell clanged and Kayrin looked up. The group standing nearby wearing rich, colorful clothes was doubtless the potential buyers of the helpless captives. They abruptly stopped their conversations and moved closer to the platform, as did Arkarrah.

The buyers lingered in front of the frightened prisoners, inspecting them like animals, while noisily shouting offers. They used a strange language Kayrin had never heard before. One of them looked in her direction, pointed at her and then spoke to Arkarrah, but he just shook his head, indicating that her group was not for sale.

After some noisy trading at the slave market, the harbor city lost some of its mad energy as men and women returned home. New masters took the captives away, now as slaves. Kayrin and the others in her group remained where they were.

"Come!" Arkarrah summoned his men and gave each one a piece of gold. As he shoved the leather pouch back inside his pocket, a shrieking noise exploded from within. The man closest to him leaped away, landing on his back in the dust. Embarrassed, he got up as his companions roared with laughter.

Arkarrah smiled gleefully and tapped the outside of his pocket, displaying his yellowing teeth, "Horris, my gold protector, protesting the disturbance of his sleep. Think twice before attempting to rob me of my gold. Bring that wretched group but give them bread and water first, for the journey is long," he instructed and leaped into the saddle of a nearby horse that his men had brought.

Their journey was arduous, the route hard and rocky. Kayrin's feet were soon covered in blisters and hurting. Pain and gloom showed on all their faces. They traveled most of the day towards the huge dark cliffs of the grim Black Mountain.

~

Bubba, hungry and tired from the long journey, was happy to see Steukhon again after so many years. "Bubba!" Steukhon called with outstretched arms. "It has been a while and it's good to see you again. Come sit and tell me everything."

"Well, the Dryads told me Egorh lost his amulet and Raleigh's crow stole it. The black-crested eagle arrived which means Zinnia has discovered him," Bubba blurted out in a rush. "Here is the amulet. I managed to take it from Raleigh before I left."

Bubba told how Arkarrah's accomplices had blocked the entrances to the estate and how he had managed to slip onto the ship. "I kept an eye on Kayrin. The bats had wounded her badly but thank goodness for the Dryads' healing oil. I stayed near to her but she was so closely guarded that I could not do anything to help her escape."

Steukhon looked at the amulet and said thoughtfully, "It is regrettable, but it is time ..."

"Will he come?" asked Bubba.

"Yes, it is written. You must go and wait for Egorh at the harbor and bring him here. Give him the amulet as proof that we know him. Soon the amulet will only be a magnificent piece of jewelry, worthless as protection since Egorh's powers will be fully developed. Till that time comes, we must insist that he wears it. I do not want Zinnia to know his whereabouts, for if she does, we will all be discovered. Hurry back to the city, Bubba."

Chapter 30

Curse

The convoy of weary victims had slowed down to a snail's pace, the uneven terrain making it impossible to progress with much speed. It had been many hours since they had left Drakens Harbor. Kayrin could see the Black Mountain ahead. Below the track, a massive lake glimmered. On the edge, long necked crimson birds moved around gracefully in their thousands. Under different circumstances, it would have been a sight of great beauty.

Arkarrah suddenly stopped his horse, looked back along the line of captives, his face twisted with irritation, and barked impatiently, "Take their shackles off and tie their hands behind their backs." He added, "Then use your whips. I need them to move faster." The men yanked savagely at the shackles, causing some of the prisoners to cry out in agony where the metal had eaten into their flesh.

The rocky road eventually ended against a vertical cliff reaching skywards. Arkarrah bellowed, "Give the signal!" A wiry man took a small object out of his pocket and held it against his mouth. A shrill sound, like that of a bird calling, filled the air and from high above, a bird echoed the same call. Kayrin recognized it as an eagle when it swept down from its high patrol. Most of the captives who had been walking with eyes down and slumped shoulders, jerked their heads skywards when, as if from nowhere, more eagles appeared, swooping through the sky just above their heads. The birds looked vicious and the prisoners instinctively lowered their heads.

From an opening far above in the high cliff, a man peeped out and Arkarrah signaled to him, making a circle in the air with his hand. The guard disappeared and a loud grinding sound began. The massive rock split open, allowing just enough space for the travelers to pass through into a large area and more cliffs appeared, almost like a mountain within a mountain. Kayrin looked back and saw that the entrance had closed behind them.

In the rock of the second mountain, stairs led up to an impressive entrance with solid columns on each side.

"Bring them," snarled Arkarrah. Once they moved through the entrance into the mountain, she could see a wide passage that ended in a long granite stairway, leading up to a higher level. On both sides, oil lamps cast fluttering shadows on the floor. A chill ran down her spine as she saw that the lamps hung from the claws of life-size eagle sculptures, carved in the finest detail from the same granite as the floors. They looked terrifyingly realistic. Some had outstretched wings, their cruel talons visible; others had wide-open beaks, as if the birds were calling out.

They were forced into a huge hall with magnificent pillars. Slants of light came from wide rectangular openings carved on both sides of the walls. From here eagles were flying in and out. Kayrin caught a glimpse of someone sitting at a long table. Before she could make out anything more, they were pushed into a smaller chamber and the doors slammed shut behind them.

A row of larger-than-life flamingo statues, with huge bills stretched high and wings spread half open, stood along the walls. Flat wide bowls filled to the brim with fluids rested on the backs of the flamingos. As the bowls bubbled and sputtered, thin trails of vapor spread through the entire room and soaked the air with an aroma of putrid sweetness.

At the feet of some of the flamingo statues, men dressed only in loincloths sat or lay, motionless, their skin so tightly stretched over their bones that they looked like skeletons. Kayrin could not, at first, make out if they were dead or alive but then some moved and rose to their feet. They began to shuffle in her direction. She fell back a few steps in alarm as the hollow-eyed people came closer.

A noise from somewhere nearby startled her and she spun around. Two large, grey-blue eyes peeped halfway over the rim of the tall urn next to her. Eight long bluish fingers, with protruding knuckles, clutched the brim.

A flat voice spoke. "Don't be afraid! They won't hurt you. They are not dangerous. They will help to untie you."

Kayrin unnerved, asked, "Who are you?" and pulled away as she felt someone behind her start to untie her ropes. She couldn't help to think that she had stared into the eyes of a dead man.

"I am the Sorrow-queen."

"The *what*?" asked Kayrin and rubbed her wrists, barely noticing the deep wounds that the ropes had made. Around her, the rest of the captives were also being released. She turned to the skeletal man who had untied her and thanked him softly.

"These poor souls are addicts of the *nepenthe*," continued the Sorrow-queen expressionlessly, ignoring Kayrin's question. "Zinnia's slaves."

"Addicts?" Kayrin watched how the men huddled forward over the bubbling mist in turn, eyes closed, to inhale the slow plume of lime green vapor.

When they turned away, their eyes where red and clouded. Their facial expressions had faded into nothingness. They dropped to the floor where they lay under the illusion of their dreams.

"They live on the smell of the *nepenthe*. They don't get

hungry and they never eat," the Sorrow-queen simpered on, her huge eyes and taut face now fully emerged from the urn. "When they expire, Zinnia replaces them with new addicts."

Kayrin became aware of a blurry sense of tranquility. She no longer felt afraid and a wonderful feeling of joy slowly saturated her being. Her fellow captives were also succumbing to the drug, the harshness of their recent ordeal instantly forgotten. Kayrin forced herself not to give way to the effect of the drug.

"What place is this? Why are we here?" she asked.

The Sorrow-queen stared at Kayrin in silence.

"Can you at least tell me what we are doing here?" she tried again.

"Don't do that," the Sorrow-queen snapped, drooping her mouth down.

"Do what?" Kayrin asked, puzzled by this strange creature.

"There, you did it again. I don't like badgers." The Sorrow-queen slipped back into the urn. From inside her voice echoed, "I don't get involved and I don't like questions."

"But who is Zinnia?" Kayrin urged.

Slowly the fingers and eyes reappeared. "You mean you really don't know who Zinnia is?"

"No."

Gradually she re-emerged. "She is a powerful sorceress."

"Oh … and what are we here for?"

She ignored Kayrin's question and asked, "Can I have your sorrows?"

"What for?" Kayrin asked incredulously.

"Zinnia needs happy people with happy hearts. You will feel *very* happy once I take them."

Kayrin, now very intoxicated replied meekly, "Yes, take them."

"Thank you," the Sorrow-queen said cheerlessly and slipped out of the urn. Between her bony hands she clutched a glass box. She moved forward and wrapped her blue-grey hazy body around Kayrin. When she unwrapped herself again, Kayrin saw that she had poured something invisible into the glass box and tucked it under her arm.

Kayrin followed this strange creature as she went from one captive to the next, speaking sweetly and asking for their sorrows. As she had done with Kayrin, the Sorrow-queen wrapped herself around each person, then poured nothingness into the glass box. When the last one was done, she took the glass box and disappeared back into the urn.

Suddenly the door burst open and Arkarrah called to Kayrin. "Come here and follow me." Submissively she followed him.

"Wait here," he ordered at the foot of the broad granite stairway.

~

Through the openings behind the long stone table where Zinnia sat, eagles flew in and out with loud cries. The rectangular openings were large, almost nine arm lengths in width. A bad smell rose from a mixture of bird droppings and rotten pieces of flesh. Rodent skulls, rabbit rib cages and a mixture of bones and pieces of dried skin littered the floor along the ledge.

Zinnia looked intimidating in a black dress heavily braided with gold. Her extravagant chair was not far from where Dwarf sat playing with Hooter on the stairs. She was in a foul mood, digging and scraping with her long gold fingernail in the bowl in front of her, in search of a soft piece of meat. Her jealousy of the sorceress-hood had gnawed deep into her mind the past few days and had robbed her of sleep the previous night. She was still bound to the labor of taking hearts from slaves, when she should be sitting in the diamond skeleton chair, looking down on the Xyltra sorceresses as they bowed to her.

"I hope these flamingo tongues are edible, Dwarf," she snapped and glanced in his direction.

Sensing Zinnia's explosive mood, Dwarf thrust Hooter under his arm and nodded vigorously. "Yes, yes, they are tender, just as you like them." He tried to sound as convincing as possible.

She found a piece of meat but after chewing it only once, spat it back into the bowl and snapped, "No, they're not! You killed the old ones again. Remove it and bring me a bowl to wash my hands. You know I hate tough tongues." She lifted up the gold water jug but found no water in it. As Dwarf reached for the bowl of tongues, she grabbed his hand, her green eyes blazing and hissed, "You are a lazy dwarf!" She reached over to a container of long porcupine quills and pulled the longest one from the bundle. Without hesitation, she jammed it right through Dwarf's hand, pinning it to the table.

Dwarf cringed and his eyes clouded with agony but he willed himself not to cry out.

Zinnia ignored him, pulled another porcupine quill from the bundle, relaxed back into her chair and started to pick the meat from her teeth. "No water ... tough tongues ... dirty floors ... why don't I just change you into something else, like an owl or a statue?" She waved at the life-size human statues that stood against the walls and continued. "They too disobeyed me at some point in their lives."

But her amusement was interrupted when she heard the sound of boots and saw Arkarrah coming up the stairs. She noticed there was lightness in his walk and a sparkle of triumph in his snake eyes. Forgetting about Dwarf pinned to the table, Zinnia sat upright, her eyes slanted slightly as she watched him approach.

It was only when he made a small bow that she said. "Ah ... Arkarrah, at last! I hope you have good news for me."

His mouth twisted into a sneer of victory. "She is here. They call her Kayrin."

"Kayrin? The girl? Are you sure?" Zinnia could barely conceal her excitement.

"I *personally* took charge of this task and I can assure you it is her."

Zinnia leapt up from her chair, her face alight. She clattered her long gold nails so hard together, that blue sparks spattered in all directions. "Brilliant! Excellent! Soon the son of Darkarh will follow. We must be ready. Fifteen hearts, one death, that's all I need to claim the title of high priestess. The magical world will bow before me, sacrificing anything I demand to honor me!" Cruel laughter erupted from her mouth.

"See that the girl is prepared by the Sorrow-queen, then bring her to me."

"It has already been done. She is waiting down there." Arkarrah indicated with his chin at Kayrin, standing uncertainly at the foot of the stairs.

"Did you bring more *nepenthe* from the monk?"

"Yes," he handed her the small green bottles.

Zinnia flushed with excitement. "Bring her to me! Go to the guards. Tell them to be ready and on the lookout for Egorh. The genie has been tracking him."

Arkarrah walked back to Kayrin and pushed her up the stairs to where Zinnia stood, then spun on his heel and left.

Dwarf yanked the quill out, rushed down the stairs and disappeared around a corner, clutching his painful hand.

Zinnia cast her gaze over Kayrin, her mouth twisted in a grin when she saw her dream-like state, the result of inhaling the *nepenthe* mist.

She lifted her chin and said, "I am Zinnia."

Kayrin turned her dilated pupils to Zinnia and asked blearily, "A sorceress?"

"THE sorceress," Zinnia vented.

She started to circle Kayrin, then stopped. "Ah, you poor thing. I see that the bats got hold of you." Her expression grew a fraction less terrible but the evil remained as she purred, "Did you try to escape? Did Arkarrah not warn you?" She moved closer and scrutinized Kayrin's scars. "Your wounds have healed miraculously fast, I must say. Those germ-ridden teeth and claws can be lethal."

Zinnia clicked her nails as she spoke, "You must be

wondering why you are here. Let me tell you. There is something I want. It belongs to the man you were frolicking with around the waterfall."

"Egorh?" Kayrin asked dreamily.

Zinnia bent towards Kayrin, her face laced with malice and said, "You should understand that my war is not with you, but with *Egorh*." she sneered. "But to complete my task I *do* need your heart."

"You're going to kill me?" Kayrin struggled against the fog in her mind.

"All humans die," Zinnia replied, "but for willing hearts, I change humans into magnificent giant flamingos."

"If I die, Egorh will avenge me," Kayrin managed to say.

Zinnia stood upright and clicked her nails together again, a spike of irritation flaring at the girl's resistance. "I see you are not completely willing yet, but I cannot waste a heart."

The sorceress took a small green bottle from the table, snapped it open and swirled the lime green vapor beneath Kayrin's nose. "Come, smell the wonderful aroma of the forest!"

Kayrin tried to pull away but Zinnia shot out a hand, grabbed her wrist and hissed, "It has to be a willing heart. Breathe in!"

Kayrin's mind tried to resist, but the undiluted fumes that escaped from the bottle overpowered her. She staggered slightly when her wrist was released.

"That's better," Zinnia muttered when she saw Kayrin become more compliant.

She reached out and took Kayrin by the shoulders, then shifted one hand to her chest. Kayrin felt Zinnia's nails burn into her. She felt the threat of death, but nothing seemed to matter any more. She was unable to utter a sound or make any movement, so strong was the power of the drug.

Zinnia's eyes blazed as she intoned, "From flesh to stone! From flesh to flamingo!" She stood back, sweat glistening on her face, lost momentarily in a trance with arms spread wide, waiting, her senses heightened to the point of ecstasy.

Kayrin watched mutely as a mysterious crimson mist started to swirl around her. A knot of horror sprang to her throat. She tried to scream but no sound came out and her eyes filled with tears. Her arms fell limply to her sides and she knew she could not escape. She slowly turned her head towards Zinnia. A red glow started to spread over Kayrin's chest. Zinnia reached forward and scooped out a red stone in the shape of a heart, from deep within her ribcage. Holding the heart-stone high, Zinnia cried triumphantly, "The curse of the flamingo! One step closer to victory." Inspecting the heart-stone she continued, "The heart of the loved one!"

Still ecstatic, Zinnia put the heart-stone into a gold bowl standing on the table.

A thin stream of blood trickled out of the hole where Kayrin's heart had been and slowly the crimson-pink mist increased around her and engulfed her whole body. Her clothes fell to the floor. Out of the mist a large bird with soft crimson-pink-colored feathers appeared.

Zinnia triumphant, said, "Now there is a magnificent example of the greater flamingo." She leaned towards the bird adding, "I hope, my beautiful bird, that your *man* will soon be here!"

She picked up the bowl with the heart-stone and shooed the flamingo away saying, "Go! Leave me."

The bird didn't move.

Impatiently she called, "Dwarf! Chase the flamingo to the opening." She then left through a large door. Dwarf noticed the chain that was twined around the bird's webbed foot, hidden beneath the discarded clothes. He gave a shrug, then gently ushered the flamingo towards the opening. It spread its wings and flew to join the other birds around the lake. As Dwarf picked up the clothes a blue bottle rolled onto the floor. He picked it up. The content spilled onto his hand. Astonished he saw it heal before his eyes. He heard Zinnia yell, "Dwarf! Tell Arkarrah to bring me the others. We must finish!"

Chapter 31

Shadow

It was just before sunrise when the sails were lowered and they slowly glided into the harbor. Egorh prayed that this would be the place where he would find Kayrin. Nobody noticed the seven mermaids who swam quietly back to the open sea, satisfied that Egorh had arrived safely. Any ordinary man would have mistaken them for dolphins. Only the sheen of their wet tails revealed their presence as they periodically broke the surface of the water and dived, leaving ripples on the watery red path of the rising sun.

The silence of the dawn was broken by the shouts of the sailors on deck as they prepared to dock. It would not be long before the wooden stepladders were lowered to the jetty below.

Egorh and Daniel were among the first to leave the ship. "Daniel, we must remain close by. I am still convinced there are captives on board and we'll need to follow them. Keep your eyes peeled."

Daniel realized that he was starving. "Please, let's get some bread."

Before Egorh could answer he saw two bulky sailors push a group of chained men down the lowered ladders. "The greedy old scoundrel ... I knew it! The ship *was* carrying slaves," Egorh muttered through gritted teeth.

"Sir, *please*, we must eat," Daniel begged, bone tired and very hungry.

"Yes, yes, go and get some bread," Egorh answered distractedly. "But hurry! I am going to follow that group."

Daniel, nose in the air like a dog following a scent, started to chase the smell of fresh bread. Luckily the source of the smell was close by and he pushed to the front of the line at the stall, ignoring the objections of those around him, while keeping an eye on Egorh.

"Sorry, but my master is about to leave," he apologized, when the woman vendor ridged her eyes into two identical peaks at his bad manners. She gave him the hot bread. Famished beyond control he took a huge bite. A voice nearby asked sarcastically, "Hungry, boy?" Daniel looked up, straight at Arkarrah. For a moment, fear twisted the young man's face but he quickly smoothed his features, took a deep breath, hurriedly paid for his bread and turned to leave the stall.

For a split second Arkarrah wondered, "Now where have I seen him before?" He looked back but Daniel had disappeared into the crowd, like a rabbit into its hole.

~

"Wow! That was as close as I have ever been to a conversation with the devil himself. I made the quickest exit ever!" Daniel was out of breath as he excitedly told Egorh about the close encounter he'd just had, handing some bread to him. "He is here! I saw him!"

"Who is here?"

"Arkarrah!"

Egorh was startled. "Are you sure?"

"Yes, he asked me if I was hungry."

"Did he recognize you?"

"No, I don't think so."

"Now we know that we are in the right place." Egorh spoke with new hope in his voice.

They followed behind the group of prisoners as closely as they dared. The packed dirt path was hemmed in on both sides by houses and other buildings, which started to thin out as they moved away from the town's center. Egorh wondered where the slaves might be going and whether Kayrin would be at the end of their journey. He became aware of a brown-robed man, who seemed to be shadowing them on the other side of the street. At first Egorh thought it was nothing, but when the man kept on staring in their direction, it unnerved him slightly. He had hoped that they could trail behind the slaves unnoticed.

He leaned closer to Daniel and whispered, "I think we are being followed. There's a hooded man behind us and he's getting closer." A short while later Egorh felt a hand on his shoulder. He froze in mid-step, spun around and freed his sword with one smooth pull.

The man held up his arms in defense and studied Egorh, measuring if he could say what he wished to.

"What do you want?" Egorh demanded.

"Please, sir, put your weapon away. It will attract unwelcome attention." The hooded man glanced up and down the road, then urged, "We cannot talk here. Follow me!" He turned and walked away.

Egorh was suspicious. "Do I have any business with you?"

Bubba stopped and muttered, "Put your sword away and I will explain." Before Egorh could object further, Bubba continued, "I know you are looking for Kayrin, the lady with the indigo blue eyes." He walked away hurriedly.

Egorh, dumbfounded for a second, quickly recovered and charged forward. Not far around the corner he managed to catch up with him. Egorh grabbed him by his clothes, spun him around and hissed, "How do you know of her? Where is she?" Daniel pulled at Egorh's arm and begged, "Please, sir! Let's avoid any attention. Let us hear what the man has to say."

Egorh, realizing he had caused a commotion, which they could ill afford, calmed down. Bubba pulled his hood back and spoke softly. "My name is Bubba and I have been sent here to await your arrival."

"You? I have seen you before. You are the young man who works for Raleigh. I have seen you in his kitchen. What are you doing here? What do you know about Kayrin?"

"Shh! Not here! Come with me." Bubba turned and walked down the road away from the main street and the crowds, covering his face with his hood.

Egorh hesitated, sheathed his sword and followed reluctantly. In a more secluded place, Bubba stopped and fumbled around to find the deep pocket in his robe. "Wait. I need to give you something immediately. It belongs to you." Egorh could not believe his eyes when he saw the amulet.

He was immediately suspicious. "How did you get it? I lost it at the waterfall."

Bubba nodded. "You must put it on now. It is important that you are not discovered."

Egorh took the amulet from Bubba and hung it around his neck. He had heard those words many times in the past and now he was hearing them from this stranger.

"There is no more time for talk. We must go."

As Egorh fell in next to Bubba he asked, "Where are we going?"

"I must take you to someone who will help you to find her, an old friend," replied Bubba.

"Friend? I have no friend in this place," Egorh said apprehensively.

"I am taking you to the one who instructed me to find you. He has been waiting a long time for you."

"What do you mean?"

"Come," was Bubba's only reply as he walked on quickly, ignoring all questions. Egorh kept beside him with Daniel following behind. Bubba progressed from a walk to a faster pace, which Egorh matched. They moved out of the town, past the last of the flat houses. They climbed a hill and a stretch of dry dusty land lay before them. Far ahead were the imposing Black Mountains and to the right a smaller jagged edged mountain with a green forest at its foot.

They kept moving all morning and into the afternoon, pausing only to drink the water Bubba offered. Something was bothering Egorh about Bubba. Suddenly he stopped and said, "That's it! You have no shadow! How is this possible?" Egorh took a few steps back, unable to keep the sharp tone from his voice as he said, "All things under the sun cast shadows. How can I trust something that does not?"

Daniel looked down and searched for a shadow, his eyes wide with confusion. "This is trickery," he muttered.

Bubba shrugged and crushed a sudden spike of irritation. There was no time for lengthy explanations. They had to get to the cave as soon as possible, but he knew that the truth of his absent shadow could not be hidden.

"I know I am shadow-less. I carry my shadow in a tiny box with me. I helped three witches to resolve a dispute about their brooms. I resolved the matter and they were so grateful that they caught my shadow and gave it to me as a gift."

"What?" retorted Egorh amazed.

"I know it's hard to believe," Bubba replied, "but let me show you." He reached into his pocket, brought out a tiny silver box and snapped it open. Immediately Shadow slipped out and stood by his side.

Egorh relaxed and grinned. "Of all the things I have ever seen, this is the strangest."

"Yes, I can understand that. It's very handy, I must say. But we have no time to talk more about it now. Perhaps later," Bubba hurried on.

It was late afternoon when the three turned away from the

huge Black Mountain range with its high cliffs. They followed a more obscure route into the dense forest. They came into a secluded clearing where Bubba paused in front of the steep side of the mountain.

He fumbled in the bag that was slung across his chest and took out a small round copper bowl and a wooden mallet. He started to move the mallet anti-clockwise around the rim of the bowl, producing incredibly rich and beautiful sounds. Egorh's mind went back to what Mirk had told him in the forest, about the nightingales and the singing bowl, and he realized that this was the man he had spoken about. Egorh and Daniel watched, speechless.

Daniel jumped back as a huge door suddenly appeared in the granite as if by magic. It swung open with a loud creak.

"All right, let's go," said Bubba and he took a burning torch from the wall at the entrance to light the narrow stairs going down.

Daniel's eyes were full of dread as he looked back and saw the huge door slam closed behind them and disappear back into the granite. He stared at the solid rock and said, "That's *really* weird."

Egorh tensed. He could not escape the sense of familiarity that suddenly washed over him.

"That door ... but it was in the moonlight ... can it be? I feel I have been here before. Yes, it was ... it was the day I arrived at Crimson Lake, after my father was murdered. I *was* here!" Egorh stood quietly for a moment as memories crept into his mind. "It was at the lake ... the priest ..."

"Hurry!" Bubba's words interrupted Egorh's spinning thoughts.

Chapter 32

Meeting

The steps were wet and slippery and the three men proceeded cautiously.

"Keep moving, we haven't much time," Bubba urged, looking back to the top of the stairs. "Hurry up, Daniel ... you're falling behind," Egorh warned.

Daniel mumbled, "This is no place to crack my butt-bone or any other bone for that matter."

Egorh almost collided with Bubba, who had stopped and cocked his head.

"Wait" said Bubba and pushed Egorh and Daniel back a few steps with one arm. Egorh frowned when he felt a trembling in the stairs beneath them.

"What's happening?" whispered Daniel as he felt a low vibration in his bones.

"Move back more ... they will quickly pass," Bubba replied tersely.

Abruptly, a creature plunged through the wall and hurtled forward, a large, round-headed thing, slimy and smooth. It smashed into the opposite wall, as if the stone was of no consequence at all, and vanished as quickly as it had appeared. Hundreds more fat, worm-like creatures burst through the wall. As they disappeared into the opposite side, the only evidence of their presence was the slime that oozed from the holes they had left.

"What the devil?" Egorh muttered.

"They are giant earthworms. They're harmless but you don't want to get in their way." Daniel looked milk-pale. His heart hammered in his chest and he could not help cursing under his breath. They waited in silence for the tremors to fade, then Bubba spoke again,

"Come on, we haven't much time," he indicated to the top of the stairs. "We don't want to be trapped in the mountain."

They gaped as they saw that the top of the stairway had started to dissolve. Egorh grabbed Daniel by the arm and they stormed down the stairs behind Bubba.

The stairs curved and opened into a great vault-like cave. Bubba looked back as the last step vanished into the solid wall behind them and, relieved, blew out of puffed cheeks.

Egorh stopped, his eyes scanning the vastness of the cave and its contents. A large spring-water pool bubbled like a boiling pot, forcing water over its brim to create smaller streams and ponds further down. A blanket of steam hung around the surface as the water gushed up from far below.

Bright beams of sunlight poured from large cracks high up in the granite walls. Patches of the purple *Amara* flower grew between the flat rocks. Hundreds of golden hummingbirds made a spectacular sight as they darted around, feeding on the sweet nectar.

"I know this place," Egorh whispered to himself as he felt the familiarity of the cave tugging at his memory. From the immense cavern, five openings led to more caves and passages. At the far end of the big pond, a magnificent flamingo, long necked and graceful, ruffled her feathers.

"There's the flamingo with the bright crimson feathers ... just as I remember it," Egorh whispered in amazement.

Daniel, who stood right behind him, was in awe and asked, "Was this what you spoke about on the ship? This is where you have been before?"

"Yes, a long time ago."

A number of golden hummingbirds hovered in front of them, blocking their way.

"Don't worry," Bubba reassured, "they love strangers with good energy. They will soon disperse."

Daniel who had never seen anything like this, asked doubtfully, "Are you sure they are not overgrown bees about to sting us?"

Bubba smiled, "They mean no harm and are Steukhon's messengers." The birds returned like a moving ray of sunlight to the purple *Amara* flowers.

"Follow me," Bubba said and he led them up the steps to a higher level. More ponds bubbled in this upper chamber. In a corner, barely visible between stacks of books, stood a long stone table with a tall candle on top of it. There sat the man Egorh remembered as the high priest. He was deep in concentration and unaware of their presence as he wrote in the thick book in front of him. It was only when Maximus, the golden brown dog snarled, that Steukhon lifted his head. His face lit up when he saw Bubba.

"Bubba, you are back! You have traveled safely! I am *so* pleased!"

"Master Steukhon, here is the young man you await." Bubba bowed and backed away, leaving Egorh and Daniel alone with Steukhon. Egorh sensed the scrutiny of the priest's grey-blue eyes as they flickered up to meet his.

Steukhon was surprised by Egorh's height. He was taller than his father Darkarh had been, taller than any of his brothers. He was sun-browned with strong muscles that radiated with youthful energy.

"You are the man ... the priest I met after my father was killed?" Egorh asked.

"Yes."

After a long moment Egorh spoke, "I am here to find Kayrin. Bubba told me you have news of her."

Steukhon nodded. "Yes, I do." He stood up, moved from behind the table and circled Egorh. He was as he remembered him. When his eyes fell on the mark on Egorh's neck, he relaxed and returned to the table.

He tore out the page he had been writing on before the visitors came. He rolled it up tightly and reached for a candle to seal the scroll with wax.

As he lifted the candle, he was not particularly careful and a stream of wax flowed onto the table. Daniel looked at the mess and thought, mmmm... I can see he has done that before ... there is more wax on the table than on the candle.

Steukhon was quiet as he meticulously completed his task, then clicked his fingers. Five golden hummingbirds appeared and hovered in front of him. He held out the rolled sheet to the birds and said, "Take this to the Apse of Secret Knowledge and give it to Jerome. He will know what to do with it." The birds left immediately, disappearing through a crack high up in the cave wall.

With a gesture, Steukhon invited Egorh to take a seat.

The priest stared at him intently, uncertain how he would react after so many years. Does he have what his destiny demands ... the strength and courage of his ancient father? he mused. I have watched him grow into the brave young man he is now, but how will the son of Darkarh fare when the time comes?

A sudden splash in a nearby pond made Egorh and Daniel whirl around. The face of a young woman appeared above the surface of the steaming water. She took in the scene with mystic, ocean-blue eyes. When her gaze fell on Egorh, they gleamed slightly before she moved them questioningly to the priest.

"Thank you, Zukressa, he is here. You can go back now."

Soundlessly, the fish-like creature melted back into the hot water.

Steukhon focused on Egorh and asked in a deep voice, "Can you remember anything we discussed that night, many years ago?"

"What have I just seen?" Egorh asked.

"We have much to discuss so I will be brief on this matter. Zukressa is one of the seven mermaids of the *Algo* zone, a region in the far ocean. At my request they followed the slave ship you were on to make sure you arrived at Drakens Harbor as planned."

Egorh nodded in astonishment.

Steukhon continued, "I told you that night about your ancient father, the god Darkarh and your mortal mother Nerifa. I also told you before you left that there is more you should know."

"Yes," replied Egorh. "I remember."

"The time has come for you to know all about your destiny."

Chapter 33

#

Steukhon folded his hands together and began to speak. "Zinnia is a powerful sorceress and Arkarrah is her accomplice. She has been searching for you for many years. Your amulet has always protected you."

"And – I lost it," Egorh interrupted.

"I know, but it doesn't matter that much any more. Your own power has become stronger than that of the amulet's, making it less important. For now it will protect your whereabouts from her genies."

"What?" Egorh started, but the priest stopped him.

"Let me start from the beginning, Egorh. Hear me out and then ask your questions. You remember I told you that you are the first-born son of Darkarh and that the beak mark is proof of your special destiny?"

Frowning slightly, Egorh nodded.

"At birth, each son was given a true element by Darkarh that would only manifest itself once each proved himself worthy of it. Yours was the true element of fire, the life force and spiritual energy that is alive within all of us. Without this motivation we would be inactive and die. To Warogh, his second son, Darkarh gave the true element of water. It would have made him the emotional one. Arugh, the third son, received the true element of air, making him the intellectual one. The true element of earth was given to the last-born, Eragh, to be the practical one.

"Then there were the obelisks ... very valuable! To honor his sons, Darkarh had an obelisk made for each of them and had them placed in the four corners of the temple. He instructed the high priest, who happened to be me at that time, to document the lives of all four sons, so that generations to come would know how mighty they were. These obelisks were made of precious metals; orinium, gold, silver and platinum. They were not only valuable, but each one also had a special power known only to Darkarh and myself.

"Darkarh wanted to keep this a secret until his son's twenty-first birthday.

"Your obelisk was made of orinium. This was your father's gift to you. It is a magical metal, consisting of four precious metals and a fifth substance, known only to the metal-god. It can never be duplicated.

"During the *Wizard Wars*, the orinium was woven into a net that was able to draw the essences of true elements into the metal. Its power was so enormous that evildoers could use the orinium to control the worlds by directing wind, water, earth and fire as they pleased. During the wars, innocent people were killed by thirst and fire.

"Villages of defiant and rebellious folks were wiped out with water and earth. It was horrific! All the orinium, except that in the obelisk, was depleted and lost during the *Wizard Wars* and there is now the possibility that the remaining orinium could fall into the wrong hands. Darkarh knew you would be the only one strong enough to withstand the power of greed and the need to rule and dominate others. He believed that you would do good with it.

"As I have already told you, your father loved you the

most and showered you with favors." The priest paused as he recalled those distant days. He cleared his throat and continued. "Your three brothers were extremely jealous of this and aware of the blackness of their own hearts. They knew that their true elements would never manifest. They planned to kill you for your obelisk, to be able to catch the elements and rule. It is stated that the obelisks can only be inherited by the next in line, which would be your brother Warogh."

Steukhon waited a moment before continuing. "Too late, Darkarh discovered their plot to murder you. He was so furious that he cursed his three sons and banished them to the HapLess Sphere to exist in exile as Haffgoss, or half-gods. Here they were trapped in the temple to be tortured by the very same desire they had killed for – the obelisks.

"Darkarh demanded that if your brothers ever wanted to return from exile, they would have to find thirty thousand humans with loving hearts to serve them unconditionally. Darkarh knew that this was an impossible task, especially in the region of exile. What he offered them was not freedom, but a curse. It was hope without hope.

"More trouble started when Zinnia, the evil sorceress was banned from the sorceress-hood because of her evil lust for power. She would stop at nothing to have the magical world at her feet. She learned about the orinium obelisk.

"In her search for this most precious metal, Zinnia broke into the Apse of The Edifice of Secret Knowledge and found the *Book of Records*. From the book she learned about Darkarh, his cursed sons and the four obelisks in the temple. With the orinium she could become the most powerful sorceress and rule earth and the Magic World."

"So my obelisk is the only orinium?" Egorh asked.

"Yes, and now Zinnia seeks your death. We must find the orinium and it must be hidden where it can never be found. To posses orinium is to rule the worlds. This is what Zinnia wants. Possessing the orinium would secure her place on the diamond skeleton throne forever. Your brothers hope to rule again and were willing to trade the orinium for their resurrection, and so this unholy alliance was formed."

Steukhon waited for Egorh to absorb all this information, then he spoke in a gentler tone. "I know this is hard for you to comprehend. Perhaps there is something you'd like to ask?"

"No, I understand. Tell me, what has it to do with Kayrin?" Egorh asked.

"She unfortunately became involved. You have been part of this war since the day you were born. Zinnia is responsible for your earthly-father's death, for the slave trading and now for Kayrin's capture, which was to bring you to Zinnia. Let me explain further," he continued:

In the *Book of Records*, I documented the following:

Jealousy, hate and greed took you to doom and hopelessness,
but thirty-thousand loving, obedient human hearts can restore you.
If you cannot find this, you are not worthy and your souls will tarnish in exile, mingled with greed, lust for hate and power.
Never to live to rule again.

"The recordings made in the secret book, *Sons of Darkarh*, were written in the old language and only I was supposed to know the meaning. I was instructed to take the book to a safe place, The Edifice of Secret Knowledge, where the gnome Jerome looked after it, but with Zinnia's increasing power, she managed to decipher the old language and discovered two flaws in Darkarh's curse.

"The first, your death. The second flaw concerned the flamingos. When Darkarh sent you to earth to release your soul, he placed you amongst the birds and instructed that from that day on you and your descendants would be born on earth

235

as mortals. Using the flamingos, he opened a spiritual portal between them and humans, now connected and bound in spirit.

"As I told you before, Darkarh tried to conceal this flaw by changing their once magnificent blue eyes to a solid yellow and their speech to a mere honk.

"This gave Zinnia an idea, a way to get her evil fingers on the orinium obelisk. She called on the Haffgoss and made a deal with them. She would give them thirty thousand willing, loving human hearts in exchange for the orinium obelisk. The three brothers could not resist the offer and accepted the hearts, for their freedom.

"Zinnia has been capturing people, supposedly as slaves, but in reality she has been taking the hearts from their bodies with her special powers. She turns their hearts into red stones and their physical bodies into flamingos, thus separating the spirit from the physical body, whilst both remain alive. To make her victims loving and obedient, she obtained a potion from a greedy monk, Raleigh, and cunningly deceived them into inhaling it before she stole their hearts."

"What?" exploded Egorh incredulously, "Raleigh the old monk? He is involved with all of this?"

"Yes," said Steukhon. "Zinnia has been harvesting hearts over the years and keeping them alive until her plan is complete. Living around the flamingo lake and releasing more into the colony has raised no suspicion. Now all the indications are that she has almost reached thirty thousand. Her urgency to get to you was why Kayrin was kidnapped.

"Once Zinnia is ready, she will send the harvest to the Haffgoss brothers while the feathered creatures remain alive on earth. The curse will be broken and the Haffgoss restored."

A turmoil of thoughts showed on Egorh's features but when he spoke, he did so with utter control. "So what you are saying is that everything that has happened is because of me and the obelisk? My father's death, the slavery and Kayrin's kidnapping? I have not been blessed by Darkarh – I have been cursed by him."

"You cannot escape your destiny, Egorh," Steukhon reminded him. "You must see that good prevails over evil. You *are* the only descendant of Darkarh who can challenge the Haffgoss, take the orinium and prevent them from ruling again."

"Then take me to this Zinnia! Let me face my destiny, destroy her and free Kayrin!" Egorh demanded.

Steukhon looked down and said, "I am afraid that you may be too late for Kayrin."

"What do you mean?" Egorh whispered, shocked by Steukhon's words.

"Raleigh had your amulet but Bubba managed to reclaim it. He overheard the conversation when Raleigh and Arkarrah discussed kidnapping her. Bubba wanted to warn you of the trap but Arkarrah had blocked all the pathways to the estate. Instead, he followed them all the way here and saw that she and nine other captives were taken into Black Mountain. This was two days ago. I have been watching the openings in the mountain ever since. Ten flamingos have flown from there and I fear they were the group that came in with Kayrin."

"Are you telling me that she is now a bird? That I will never be able to embrace her again? Is this what you are saying?" he asked stunned and angry.

"I am terribly sorry, but it seems that way." Steukhon waited for some time before he spoke again. "Egorh listen to me please. We knew you would come. There is not much time left. Zinnia must be stopped, her work is almost done. If she succeeds and obtains the orinium, the whole of the magic world and this earth, as we know it, will be doomed.

"Now that she has captured Kayrin, she knows you will follow. It will not be easy for you to move around, which is why I sent Bubba to find you and return your amulet.

"We must stop her evil plan and take back your obelisk. It must be melted and given to the rainbow maidens."

"The rainbow maidens. I remember the Dryads' tales of them." Egorh added.

"They calm storms and bring sweet rain. They are also gatherers of information and the ultimate keepers of secrets. The only place the obelisk will be safe is in the pot at the end of the rainbow, where they keep all dangerous secrets and objects. Nothing can ever be retrieved from it."

"Never?" Egorh asked wondering.

"No, never. No one has ever managed to find the end of the rainbow."

Egorh started to pace the room. Steukhon went on, "You are bitter and impatient to seek revenge. You know now what you are up against – the most powerful sorceress and your evil brothers, who will stop at nothing. It is strength you need to show, not anger.

"It was always certain that you would have to take up your destiny. I believe that the time is now." Steukhon smiled gently and said, "This may comfort you slightly. Darkarh gave me a message for you. He said you were the son he loved most and he is sorry if it has caused you pain, but you are the savior of the human and magic worlds. That is why the orinium belongs to you. He knows you will meet the challenges you are facing with bravery and he will watch your victory from the heavens."

Egorh did not reply but resolve settled on him. The three of them spent many more hours talking together, about the Dryads, the upside-down-ear people and their amazing gift, the never-empty quiver.

Chapter 34

Spirit

The next morning, Steukhon shook Egorh by the shoulder and said, "Come, I want to show you something." He followed Steukhon towards the cavern, with Daniel already awake and following close behind. Egorh was distracted, trying to make sense of everything he had been told. The turmoil and mayhem of the past few days showed on his face.

The large pond seemed to end against the cave wall, with smooth granite rock that created a natural barrier to one side. Narrow steps against it led all the way to the bottom, where the wall curved to the left. It seemed as if the stairs continued beneath the pond.

The deafening sound of falling water made Egorh look up from the wet path. "This is water from the pond inside," shouted Steukhon, pointing to a long split running across the cliff. A torrent of water gushed through the opening, leaving just enough space for them to move behind and cross to the other side. Once there, they took a slippery trail to the base of the mountain where the gushing flow changed into a lazy stream. Lush green shrubs grew around the water. The forest that surrounded most of the mountain lay behind them. The smell of decaying leaves, mixed with the faint smell of pine needles, drifted towards them on a light breeze.

They crossed a clearing and a huge lake became visible. Egorh's attention was drawn to the massive black peaks.

"Come," said Steukhon. "Let me show you where Zinnia has been doing her evil work. Maybe then all will be clear."

They turned the corner and stopped. Before them, masses of elegant creatures congregated around the lake. The crimson-pink bodies stretched in a wave all along in the shallow water as far as the eye could see. Gracious necks folded and craned around in strange shapes. Beaks pointed to the sky and then dipped into the water. Their loud cries echoed over the lake. Lean red legs floundered and splashed about, seemingly to dance to the tune of unheard music. Above their heads, the clear sky swarmed with wide spread wings that flapped smoothly and effortlessly, bringing still more birds. It was the chaotic playground of the giant flamingo, an amazing sight.

The bond Egorh felt with these giant birds had never felt as strong as it did at that moment. He stared in silence with an overwhelming feeling of loss. Something told him that this was where he was supposed to be, that this was the place where the battle had been waiting for him. It was here that he would succeed or fail, where his destiny would challenge him.

Memories from his childhood began to rush into his mind. The firm grip of his father's hand as they walked the castle grounds and the rhythm of his voice telling him tales of brave warriors, dragons and sorcerers, his warm breath on his cheek as he wished him goodnight. When a pair of indigo blue eyes swept before him, Egorh thought of Kayrin, and felt his chest tighten with pain. He swallowed a moan before it could escape his lips. The memory of her shocked him back to reality. He looked over the vast sea of birds. Anger and rebellion flared up like wildfire in his eyes. "Dear God! I have lost her! She is now one of these thousands and thousands of birds ... I will never hold her again!"

Daniel stood quietly behind him.

"This was not supposed to be part of my destiny. She had no knowledge of anything," muttered Egorh, shaking his head.

Steukhon calmly answered, "We do not always know what obstacles we will encounter on the path to fulfill our destiny. She became part of it the day you met."

"What will my life be without her?"

"Sometimes fate requires us to be larger than life itself. It gives us the heart to do so, and you too will find your inner strength, Egorh."

Egorh looked to the heavens and it was then that he noticed the dark shadows that had begun to skim the sky although the sun rode high. He shaded his eyes and spotted the enormous eagles that flew in and out of the openings high above in the cliffs.

"Zinnia's eagles," Steukhon said as he followed Egorh's gaze. "Her guard dogs, bred to be ferocious and aggressive, to attack humans. That is how she keeps intruders away from the lake. A man named Sojun is responsible for their training, the same serpent who summoned the vampire bats to attack Kayrin."

"What! She was attacked?"

"Yes, but the Dryads saved her."

Egorh stood motionless for a while, his face silently blank. Steukhon studied him with sympathy, while Daniel waited patiently.

Egorh lifted his head and said, in a voice that resonated with newfound strength, "I *will* save the worlds ... I *will* find this obelisk and capture the orinium. I *will* honor Darkarh's wish." He turned to return to the cave to prepare himself.

He had barely taken a step when a mass of flamingos rushed from around the lake and encircled him. Streaks of thin mist began to swirl as the birds got closer. A faint voice, weakened by great distance, reached his ears. Trapped in the spell, Egorh felt that he could not move or speak. His entire body was paralyzed. He was dimly aware of the pull of his spirit from deep within and he sank down among the crimson-feathered creatures, unable to resist. Soon he was completely cloaked by a thick cloud of pink, white and crimson. His spirit shifted and Egorh felt as though he was floating away, suspended above the water. A great gust of wind stirred and dispersed his spirit, like vapor into the air.

Daniel watched his master in horror. His voice was hoarse, as he asked, "Steukhon, what has happened to him?"

Steukhon stared up in wonder, "Darkarh has summoned the flamingos to send Egorh's spirit to him, almost the same way they brought him to earth! We will just have to be patient and wait for his return. What has just happened was unexpected, but a necessary part of Egorh's quest."

~

As if in a dream, Egorh found himself in a huge open temple, looking down at three men that he knew to be his brothers. Warogh was holding a dagger that dripped blood. Egorh looked at the slain body lying on the floor and realized with a shock that it was his. His heart started to beat faster as he regarded the scene. "They killed me!" Egorh breathed. Then an imposing-looking man rushed onto the scene. "Darkarh ... my father," Egorh whispered again. The man knelt in the blood next to the body, cradled the lifeless form and sobbed as though his heart would break. He then slowly looked up at his sons and spoke in an anguished tone, "You killed him! You killed your own brother!"

Egorh heard Warogh sneer, "Yes! Which now makes me the rightful owner of the orinium obelisk."

Darkarh slowly rose from the body and Egorh saw the anger on his face. He spoke urgently and furiously, his words echoed through the temple. "Your greed and your lust for power have today brought you eternal damnation. I will destroy you and everything you have ever laid eyes on or touched," Darkarh raged.

The temple's pillars and walls started to break apart and crash to the ground. The three brothers reeled in fear and turned to flee, but Darkarh's anger turned into claws, ready to shred them into nothingness as he roared, "Banished are you from the empire to rot in the doom and gloom of the HapLess Sphere!" The three brothers were consumed by fear, as the temple with everything in it began to melt and vanish.

Darkarh gazed at his slain son, threw up his hands to the heavens and commanded, "BIRDS! Take my beloved son's soul and set him free on earth." A flock of giant flamingos immediately engulfed the body and took flight. Darkarh's grief and fury knew no bounds. His pain burst into a roaring blaze that leaped and consumed all evidence of the kingdom and the slayers' existence.

Every fiber tensed with agony as Egorh witnessed how the ancient land of Darkarh was swept with destruction and ruin. The green valleys changed into scourged planes of black and grey ruins where the feeling of death hung low to the ground. His heart was heavy, his features taut with rage and agony at what he had seen and the wrong his brothers had caused him.

Egorh dropped his head in despair. Suddenly from afar he heard someone call his immortal name, "Egoragh!" It suddenly felt as if he was trapped in a tightly spun cocoon. Barely able to breath or move, he began to struggle to free himself. The wall of the cocoon felt soft and he tore frantically at it. It gave way and he experienced the feeling of a huge butterfly escaping through the hole. He darted through the air and flew into the dark sky. Overwhelmed by his freedom he felt as if he could carry on flying forever.

Then suddenly the butterfly changed into a dragon, a huge powerful creature with flames bursting from its nose and mouth, and Egorh felt how he melted and became the roaring creature. The warmth of the flames rippled through his body, comforting and empowering every corner of his being. From deep within, a strength and power started to radiate and engulf him. He became aware of the full strength of the force as he glided between the two worlds.

Slowly, calmness settled and next he was flying with the spirit of a huge bird as its wings stirred the air around him. He suddenly became conscious of time as the mortal world began to embrace him once more. Darkness turned to light as his spirit skimmed the heavens. The lake below reflected the last of the sun's gold rays before it sank below the horizon. Egorh gazed down at his body, sitting motionless at the water's edge, surrounded by his earthly friends. Unquestionably, something meaningful had changed in him and he felt empowered. He had broken free from his bondage. He was now stronger than the amulet. He knew that he was ready to take up his destiny as the son of Darkarh.

~

A day and a night had passed, while Egorh had not moved. Bubba joined Steukhon and Daniel. They remained near the water, watching over him, silent and expectant. It was when a massive silhouette of a bird appeared against the next evening's sunset that Steukhon jutted his wrinkled chin forward and announced solemnly, "He has returned."

The flamingos encompassing the lake began to part as if danger had become visible in their midst. A frenzy of callings filled the atmosphere and their heads lifted towards the sky. The wind and noise calmed when the enormous wings steadied and flared for landing, rippling the wet surface. The birds separated into two crimson-pink waves, leaving a path in the middle. It was dead quiet and not a sound escaped them as they stood waiting.

Egorh felt himself dropping into his body. Something plucked at him, almost as if he had been summoned to awaken.

A gigantic flamingo settled gracefully in the shallow water and approached Egorh with a soft honk. It lowered its neck and dipped its beak, the blue eye disappearing as the yellow color veiled it. Then the bird took flight and vanished like mist into the sky.

Egorh walked towards his friends. Daniel knew this was not the same man of two days ago. He walked taller, with a new confidence and purpose in his stride. There was an impressive power about him. Egorh paused in front of Steukhon, then spoke in a low but firm voice, "Darkarh showed me my brothers. I saw only death and destruction. I saw how the worlds will suffer should the sorceress and my brothers succeed in their evil plan. It can never happen. You have the wisdom of the ages, Steukhon. Will you fight at my side?"

Returning Egorh's stare, Steukhon bowed and nodded, "I shall be honored to do so, son of Darkarh."

He turned to Daniel and Bubba questioningly and they nodded solemnly.

"Then we must prepare to enter the mountain," Egorh said. He took a final look at the flamingos.

Daniel, too, gave a last glance at the mass of birds on the lake. Something shiny in the group nearby caught his eye. As he looked more carefully, he detected a tiny chain dangling from the ankle of a flamingo's webbed foot, as it scratched its head.

But before Daniel could give it another thought, he saw an eagle circling overhead, coming closer and closer. He decided not to linger and quickly followed the others back to the cave.

Chapter 35

The Search

As they walked, Egorh thought about what he had seen: the birds, Darkarh and those terrible scenes from his previous life. A loud yell made him snap out of his reverie. He swung around reaching for his sword. On a rock, Daniel lay sprawled on his back. Chunks of moss clung to his hands and boots. Egorh relaxed and raised an enquiring eyebrow. Daniel reddened with embarrassment and muttered defensively, "It's slippery from the rain." He felt even worse when he saw Egorh struggle to suppress his amusement.

"Maybe you too were daydreaming, Daniel," Egorh said, as he offered him a helping hand.

"Maybe, sir," mumbled Daniel, his mind still dwelling on the image of the chain he had seen on the flamingo's leg.

The cave was inland from the lake, well into the cliffs of the mountain. The path wound along the small riverbank, rock-strewn and interspersed with patches of moss, making it extremely slippery. Egorh followed behind Steukhon, lost in thought, unaware of the soft rain that had spread streaks of grey mist over the valley behind them.

They passed behind the waterfall and entered the cave following the steps leading to the inside. The cave was dark and shadowy. Bubba lit the oil lamps against the walls.

Not far into the rock-shelter, Steukhon was stopped by a group of golden hummingbirds that had suddenly fluttered in from one of the cracks in the cave ceiling. As the cluster wavered in front of him, the priest noticed a scroll held tightly in their tiny talons.

"Ah, word from Jerome," Steukhon said as he gently pulled the scroll from the birds' grip. Their work done they darted away, forming a golden arc as they disappeared.

Steukhon walked to the long table. Maximus woke from where he was lying on the heap of documents and the soft golden nimbus surrounding his body vanished. He stretched, gave a lengthy yawn and, dragging his ears along, he carefully moved to the corner of the table. He heaved another sigh and curled up to sleep again. Steukhon sank into his chair and inspected the roll of writing before breaking the seal. As he began to read, a frown creased his forehead.

Egorh, sensing that Steukhon wanted to be alone, turned his attention to the flamingo at the pond. The bird seemed to be regarding him with interest. Egorh pointed towards it and asked Bubba, "How did this flamingo get here?"

Bubba's features softened slightly and said, "She followed us from the lake one day many years ago and never wanted to leave again. Steukhon has been caring for her ever since." Egorh nodded thoughtfully, then rejoined Daniel who looked preoccupied as he rubbed his bruised elbow.

"Come on Daniel, maybe it's just your ego that's hurt," Egorh smiled.

"It's not that, sir, it's something else that's bothering me."

"Well, let's hear it then. We need to start making plans to enter the Black Mountain."

Daniel looked down and mumbled, "This is going to sound absurd and you'll probably be amused. Maybe it was nothing, but ... but as we left the lake, I think I saw a flamingo with something shiny, like a chain, around its leg. It just seemed so, well, unusual." The words had come out in a rush as Daniel anticipated Egorh's ridicule.

Instead of laughing at him, Egorh asked urgently, "You think you saw WHAT, Daniel? Tell me EXACTLY what you saw."

Daniel spoke with greater confidence. "I thought I saw a chain on the leg of one of the birds this afternoon, but when I looked again it was gone. It must have been my imagination." Daniel shrugged and hoped that Egorh would let the matter go.

"You don't understand what this could mean," Egorh said excitedly. "I gave Kayrin an ankle bracelet on our secret wedding day!"

"You did?" He stared at Egorh as he began to make the connection.

Egorh slapped a hand on his shoulder and asked, "Would you remember exactly where you saw it?"

Daniel clearly understood what this meant and swallowed hard. "I think so. It is directly below the big rock."

"Daniel, we *have* to go there now. We can bring her back here to the cave. She can live here with the other one. At least she will be safe." Egorh was almost beside himself with excitement.

"But it's dark sir and she is a wild bird," Daniel reminded Egorh.

Egorh beat down his impatience. "That does not matter. Show me where you saw her. We can use some bait and lure her to the cave."

Steukhon had followed this conversation without looking up from his papers, "He's right! Flamingos are independent creatures and will not take bait easily. They also don't feed at night."

"There must be a way to get her here!"

Steukhon rubbed his chin thoughtfully, and touched the crystal around his neck.

"We *could* try an enchanted crab," he said.

Egorh stared at him in hope.

"Let me explain. The only way to make sure the bird will follow is if we can get her to eat an enchanted crab. I can use a powerful spell that opens the gates of enchantment. It allows a *worthy* man anything he asks, but you can only request it once, which means we have only one chance to succeed. Magic is given freely for only a few minutes. If the flamingo does not take the crab, I cannot ask again. But it's worth a try."

"Then let's do it!" Egorh urged. He followed Steukhon as he went down one of the corridors and into a second cave.

"Where is the jar of white crabs, Bubba?" Steukhon asked scanning the shelves packed with containers of insects. Bubba indicated to the second shelf.

"Aah ... Here they are!" exclaimed Steukhon and reached for the jar. He removed one crab and placed it in the center of the floor. He rubbed the crystal hanging from his neck, mumbled something ending with, "*Whoever swallows shall follow.*"

A golden light appeared from nowhere and lingered above the crab, coiled and twirled and then entered the small creature's body. The crab became illuminated with golden light. Its golden body lifted off the ground and its legs clawed the air before it dropped to the floor motionless as if it were dead.

Everybody stared, waiting expectantly. Slowly life returned to the creature and the golden crab started to move. Its legs had turned different colors: green, maroon, yellow, red and black. Daniel backed away, amazed at what was happening.

"The colors are to tempt the bird," Steukhon explained.

The crab started to run sideways across the floor, trying to escape. Steukhon yelled, "Quick! Catch it!" Egorh stooped down, scooped the creature up and placed it gently into a jar.

"Good," sighed Steukhon. "We should all get some rest,

we start early in the morning. There's nothing more to be done tonight."

It was with mixed feelings that Egorh found his bed that Bubba had prepared. The flickering flames from the oil lamps threw lively shadows against the walls. Sleep eluded Egorh and images of recent events flitted through his mind: images of Kayrin at the lake in the moonless night and of the evil Zinnia. His stomach knotted and he knew there had been no other time in his life that he had hated so fiercely. He clenched his fists slowly with anger and whispered. "In your search for me Zinnia, you have invited your own death." His thoughts swirled with revenge. He was restless most of the night, drifting in and out of sleep, waiting for the time to pass.

~

Relieved to see the first rays of the sun shine through the cracks of the roof, Egorh leapt up and stretched his limbs, confident as always in his strong body. The scent of the *Amara* flowers hung thick and he took a deep breath.

He was eager to get going and roused the others. He collected the jar with the enchanted crab and waited impatiently.

"Don't forget your magic quiver, Egorh," Steukhon warned him. "We might have to fight the eagles today." Egorh nodded and reached for the quiver, "Let's not waste the day then," He hung it on his back, fastened his sword belt and headed towards the steps.

It was not long before they reached the place where Daniel thought he had seen the flamingo. The men stood as close as they dared to the birds, not wanting to startle them as they began to inspect each bird carefully. The sun had almost reached its peak, but still they had no success.

They watched and waited as the birds moved in and out

of the water. Uncertainty arose in Daniel and he nervously paced the area whilst examining every bird. What if it was my imagination and I was wrong? he thought to himself. Maybe I have given Egorh false hope.

Egorh's face was blank as he crouched to study the hundreds of moving legs. He was fully aware of Daniel's agony, but did not say a word.

Steukhon and Bubba sat further away on a boulder, their eyes scouring every inch for a possible sign. Suddenly, Daniel shouted, "Look over there!"

Egorh swung in the direction Daniel was pointing and he saw a giant flamingo preening and scratching itself. From its webbed foot, something sparkled as it caught the sunlight. Egorh moved cautiously closer and recognized the gold piece. He felt his heart soar.

"That's it, that's the chain I gave her! That *must* be Kayrin," he whispered hoarsely.

"Slowly now," warned Steukhon. "We do not want her to take flight."

Steukhon looked up and noticed black specks in the far sky, pouring out of the rectangular openings in the cliffs. He held up his hand to shade his eyes and saw hundreds of black eagles approaching. Faint echoing screeches could be heard.

"On second thought, Egorh, we must act quickly! I think we have been discovered," Steukhon cautioned, "Look!"

Egorh rose and stared at the black birds in the sky. With a stab of despair, he realized that time was of the essence. His voice was clipped and tense as he said, "Give the bait to Kayrin NOW, Daniel. I will cover you."

As Daniel passed with the crab, Egorh gripped his arm, and his dark eyes bore into him, "Remember, we have only one chance ... Do you understand?" He held Daniel's arm a little longer than he should have, but when he let go, he knew Daniel understood.

251

Daniel's stomach felt hollow as he made his way towards the group of flamingos.

"It's me, Daniel," he spoke gently in an attempt to reassure the birds. The flamingo straightened its neck suspiciously and stalked away a few steps.

"Please don't fly away. Egorh will kill me. Look! I have brought you some food." Daniel nervously dipped his hand into the bottle, grabbed the mysterious crab and tossed it towards the bird. The giant flamingo ruffled its feathers and eyed the creature with curiosity.

Egorh took a slow breath and whispered, "Take it Kayrin, please take it!"

The flamingo watched the crab as it began to move sideways towards the water. Without warning another flamingo rushed forward and snatched the bait away from Kayrin.

"No! No!" Daniel yelled hysterically and waved his arms. The interloper was startled and dropped the crab, but in its effort to get away trampled it into the mud. The crab was nowhere to be seen. Horrified, Daniel knelt in the mud to search for the creature and just in time, saw a huge shadow coming towards him. He fell flat on his stomach and managed to escape the eagle's outstretched talons by a hair's width. He cursed under his breath as he frantically dug around in the mud. His luck held, the colorful legs emerged not far from him and Daniel managed to capture it. Covered in dirt, he pulled himself upright.

"Try AGAIN!" Egorh shouted. "I will stop the eagles. DO IT NOW!" A sudden wind chilled Egorh's face as black wings skimmed close above his head.

He dropped instinctively to one knee and planted the never-empty-quiver before him in the ground. As he drew the arrow, another instantly appeared. He strained his eyes against the brutal sun. The muscle swelled in his right shoulder as he pulled back to stop the first feathered villain. True to Varkin's words, the white-quilled arrows were devastatingly accurate. He sent shaft after shaft into the attacking eagles, where they found their targets before they could reach the men. Death screeches pierced the sky as the eagles came plummeting down. The quiver never emptied.

With renewed effort, Daniel placed the golden crab as close as possible to Kayrin. He held his breath as she slowly extended her neck towards it. Suddenly, she rushed forward and picked it up with the tip of her bill and tossed it down her throat with a jerk of her head.

Daniel pumped his fist and yelled, "Yes!" He stood for a moment with his hands on his knees and his face shone with elation. "We've got you, Kayrin!"

"Come back and take cover, Daniel!" shouted Egorh. When he looked in Kayrin's direction, Daniel saw that she had disappeared amongst the others.

"What now?" Daniel gasped as he rejoined the others.

"Once we move away, she will follow you. Come on!" urged Steukhon. "Zinnia knows we are here now and will soon send her guards."

The four men ran for cover while the remaining eagles continued their attacks. Suddenly, to Egorh and Steukhon's astonishment, the birds broke off and flew back towards the mountain, as if someone had recalled them.

"Go! Go!" ordered Egorh and they hurried towards the waterfall. Egorh looked over his shoulder. One flamingo slowly emerged from the group of birds and began hesitantly to follow them.

"We must hurry," Steukhon reiterated. "Bubba, get ready to lay a false trail to divert Zinnia's henchmen. We must try to throw them off our trail. Wait for my signal. I will clear away our tracks first. Daniel, you go ahead. The magic is such that as long as she can see you, Kayrin will follow. We will keep an eye out for Zinnia's fools. See that you get Kayrin to the cave quickly."

Egorh and Steukhon stood anxiously as they watched the dark figures approaching on horses. It seemed like an eternity to Egorh, but at last he saw Daniel and Kayrin disappear behind the waterfall to safety.

Egorh would have given anything to challenge the riders but he realized that this would have disastrous consequences and urged by Steukhon, rushed towards the waterfall. As they reached it, Steukhon held his arms outstretched over the area in front of him, touched his crystal and loudly intoned, "U-dun-edo. Let nature be untouched again!" An unexpected brown mist rolled out of the sky and skimmed the ground. At once all traces of footprints disappeared as though nothing had ever walked there. Bubba, waiting patiently for Steukhon's signal, then darted back around the mountain, leaving new tracks for their pursuers to follow. Steukhon and Egorh retreated to safety.

Bubba peeked from the foot of the cliffs and saw the riders reach the area near the waterfall. He recognized Arkarrah as he reined his horse, searching on the ground in every direction for tracks. Bubba anxiously chewed his bottom lip, waiting to see if they were going to take the bait of the single track leading his way. He drummed the small silver box with his fingers.

Arkarrah looked puzzled when he saw only a single row of footprints leading away from the lake, around the mountain. Bubba knew he had to hurry when the small group kicked their horses into a canter and headed his way.

He found himself in a narrow canyon. He could hear the pounding hooves behind him as Arkarrah and his riders approached. When he heard the snorting horses, Bubba glanced back again. He could see that Arkarrah rode a fine horse and realized that he could barely stay ahead. He decided it was time to release Shadow. He flipped open the lid of the silver box, the shadow slid out and he ordered, "Lead them away from the door! *Play hide and seek with those I hold in my thoughts!*" Bubba hid behind a rock.

Arkarrah and his men rushed past Bubba, following his shadow further up as it moved over the rocks and disappeared around the side of the mountain, leading the group further and further away. He heard Arkarrah bellow, "Follow him! They must be somewhere around here. We *must* find Egorh."

Once his pursuers were out of sight, Bubba made for the cliff. He took the copper singing bowl and the wooden mallet, gave the magic signal and the mammoth door appeared again in the rock face. Bubba moved quickly as it swung open and ordered his shadow to return. Shadow instantly reappeared and flowed back into the silver box. Bubba snapped its lid shut before running down the stairs. The heavy door slammed closed behind him and faded into the granite cliff just as Arkarrah and his men arrived outside.

Arkarrah eyed the steep, solid walls that surrounded them and the trail that ended against the cliff's face. He was mystified, there was nowhere for anyone to hide here. He turned his horse, cursed loudly and then spurred the animal to follow the trail back.

~

In the cave, Egorh moved slowly towards the flamingo trying not to scare her, as she now stood with the other flamingo at the pond. He stared at her, anxiously waiting for some form of recognition but there was nothing. The bird's yellow eye met his gaze, before she casually started to preen herself. "How can you be a bird?" Egorh asked again for the hundredth time and crushed his disappointment. "Not even a blink of recognition." he whispered, then lowered his eyes to the ground, where he stayed lost in thought.

Daniel wandered around the cave. He looked at a huge book with drawings of insects and writing.

"What is this all about?" he asked Bubba.

"It is Steukhon's research on small creatures, which ones are the best to use for magic."

Bubba changed the subject, "Let's go and feed the flamingo. It is already dark and it may not eat."

Daniel looked at Bubba as he tossed a few insects to the birds and asked, "So, what's with the rice bowl and the shadow?"

255

"It's not a rice bowl, it's a singing bowl." Bubba replied, annoyed.

"I'm sure you did not buy it."

Bubba did not answer.

"I will not tell," Daniel begged.

"Well, if I tell you, promise me that you will not keep on rudely interrupting, as you so often do."

"Promise," replied Daniel and indicated that his lips were airtight.

"I have already told you about the fighting brooms and the witches."

"Oh yes – they caught your shadow!" Daniel exclaimed.

"You have the memory of a tea fly. You gave me your word you would not interrupt."

"Sorry."

"They put Shadow in the little silver box you saw and told me that from that day Shadow would carry all my fears. In addition, I can give him two commands. When I asked them what I should do, they replied, 'Be mindful and use this gift well. The first two commands you ever give your shadow are the only ones it will remember.' I asked them, 'How will I know what commands to give?' but the witches only cackled and left on their brooms without saying another word. I walked around with the box in my pocket for a very long time, thinking about what the witches had said, too nervous to open it.

"Then one day Raleigh burst into the kitchen and ordered me to immediately collect five red poisonous mushrooms for his brew. They grew on the wet riverbanks under the trees in the dense part of the forest. I knew the type he wanted. I was glad to get away from him for a while.

"To get to the mushrooms I had to cross a vast grassland and stumbled upon the most beautiful creature I have ever seen. Her beautiful long chestnut hair shone in the sun, her skin was the color of olive velvet. Her flowing gown looked as if it was made of lace woven with the finest brown copper thread. I noticed that her beautiful hands and feet were webbed and I wondered; is she a human or a bird?

"She was sitting on a boulder, in the middle of a formation that seemed as if it had melted down over millions of years. She was holding a small brass bowl in her slender hand and with a mallet, stirring something in it endlessly, around and around. She looked extremely sad as she glanced at me with her amazing large brown eyes but kept on stirring. I managed to get close enough to peep into the bowl and I saw she was stirring *nothing!*

"She asked me, 'Who are you? Must I be afraid?'

'No don't be. I will not harm you.' I told her. She was quiet and I saw a tear fall from her eye onto the ground and turn into rock. I was astounded and looked around at the many pools in the grassland and wondered, did she cry all these? How long has she been weeping? .

"'Who are you and why are you grief stricken?' I asked softly.

"'I am Naga, the keeper of the nightingales,' she answered. 'I was tricked by the upside-down-ear people. They caught all my birds to take their vocal cords and locked them up. There is no more night singing and when I stir my bowl, no sound is forthcoming because I am too sad.' She lowered her long thick eyelashes and another teardrop fell onto the ground, turning to rock.

"'Please don't cry anymore,' I asked her. 'I will help you find them. My birds are up there, guarded by two of Varkin's strongest men.' I looked up and saw two men standing in front of a cave and wondered, how can I get them away? I sat for a while, then it struck me. 'I can use Shadow! Yes, yes! I can command him to distract them! My first command will be *play hide and seek with those I hold in my thoughts.* That way those guards will follow Shadow and I shall be able to get into the cave. My second command will be, *you win. Return to the silver box.*'

"I hid behind the bushes, took the silver box from my

pocket and slowly opened it. Shadow slipped out to stand next to me and I gave my first instruction.

"Immediately, he started to dart around the two guards, hiding and peeping from behind the rocks. The guards were confused and started to follow. I slipped into the cave and saw hundreds of small brown birds in a massive cage. I opened the cage door and as they flew out, their beautiful sounds filled the heavens.

"When I returned to Naga, she had a smile on her face that could shame the sun and said, 'Thank you. You will never know the extent of your deed today. To show my appreciation I give you my singing bowl as a gift.'

"'No, no! I cannot take it,' I protested, but she insisted. 'You can use the magic sound to move through stone. It will serve you well.' Then she disappeared. I instructed, '*You win. Return to silver box*' and Shadow slipped back into the box."

Daniel was quiet, mesmerized by the story.

Steukhon walked over to where Egorh was sitting, sharpening his dagger on the stone step. He could feel Egorh's misery.

"There is something I want to tell you, but I do not want to raise your hopes too high," Steukhon said quietly. "There is a remote possibility we can save her."

"What do you mean?" asked Egorh, incredulously.

"The scroll I received yesterday was from the Edifice. I have been communicating with Jerome about the power of *Emorph-z*. Jerome says that because of the connection, the heart-stone will glow if it feels the presence of someone treasured – a friend, a lover, a parent or even a loyal servant, the same way you would get excited when you saw someone you loved. If we can find Kayrin's heart among the thousands of stones, I might be able to give it back to her."

"You are not giving me false hope. How would we do this?" Egorh asked with eagerness in his voice.

"It's the same power you have seen me use today. The power

of 'Undo.' I *might* be able to undo what Zinnia has done."

Egorh looked towards Kayrin and spoke with renewed conviction. "That will be part of my quest then, not only to destroy Zinnia but also to find Kayrin's heart-stone."

"Then let me tell you what I know of Black Mountain. None of this is going to be easy and we must be well prepared."

Egorh strode to the table with great confidence. "We have to think every step of the plan through, anticipating every possible problem. We have to find out how Zinnia communicates with the Haffgoss. Once we know how the hearts will travel we will also know the way to the Haffgoss and the obelisk." Steukhon was pleased to see that Egorh had a new sense of purpose.

"Yes, we will use the ring to get there," the priest added.

"What ring?" Egorh asked.

"I will explain later, Egorh. Let's work on our plans first."

They sat in serious conversation for many hours, until long after the oil lamps had died down and only the candle at the table still gave light.

Chapter 36

Algo Pearl

Deep in thought, Egorh paced the floor. Although he had snatched only a few hours of sleep, there was no trace of weariness in his features. Bubba and Daniel were still asleep, wrapped in their blankets on the cave floor.

Steukhon had explained many things to Egorh that night, but he was still hungry to know more. Steukhon stood at the table, slumped over a rough drawing he had made that illustrated the area surrounding Zinnia's fortress. Tapping his forefinger on the map, Steukhon began, "As you can see, the mountain is impossible to reach from the outside ..."

Egorh interrupted, "Tell me what powers she boasts, this Zinnia. Tell me more about this devilish woman. We have only one chance to stop her. What must I beware of?"

Steukhon pushed the map aside, sat at the end of the long table and leaned back as he considered Egorh's questions. "Zinnia was part of the Xyltra sorceress-hood in a land that belonged only to them, on the outskirts of the magical world. The sorceresses worked mostly for the common good. However, if they felt that justice was needed, they did not hesitate to use evil. Part of their practice was that each member would sit on the diamond skeleton throne and rule for one year. The purpose of this was that each should feel the ultimate power of ruling. Because of the strength of their magic powers during this year, the ruling sorceress had to learn how to control her desire for power over everyone and everything, and pass the throne on willingly. This was also to keep the sorceress-hood free from continuous battles and challenges for domination. They took an oath to protect their power and secrets.

"Of course, Zinnia failed this test, as even then, her lust for power was uncontrollable. She was intoxicated by the feeling of the sorceresses bowing to her and she could not let go of the throne. She challenged the others and demanded to rule longer.

"The fight that erupted was furious. The sorceresses fought Zinnia like invisible demons and in the end, they managed to banish her. Zinnia swore she would be back and started her quest, seeking more power wherever she could find it. With her capacity for evil, she used any conceivable way to steal secrets. Anyone standing in her way would be destroyed or cursed. She stole the Pesos spiders and turned the special stones into tiny genies that proved to be remarkably effective. Anyone that refused her anything was cursed."

"Yes, I know. I met Varkin, who would not relinquish the never-empty quiver to her," Egorh commented.

"There are many others. The destruction she has caused is devastating. Worst of all is her power of *Emorph-z*. It can change one substance into another, mostly living flesh to living stone. Her pet black-crested eagle has green stone eyes, her spiders have stone bodies and stone statues of some of her captives can be found everywhere in her chambers."

"I saw the green-eyed eagle when I lost my amulet."

Just then, a loud splash erupted from the large, bubbling, spring-water pool behind them. Daniel and Bubba awoke with a start and rubbed the sleep from their eyes. Egorh and Steukhon spun around. A mermaid emerged from the pool and hovered for a while above its surface, as if examining the area, then called to the water. Another six mermaids appeared, swooping and swimming through the air.

Egorh watched in wonder and awe as the mermaids twisted and whirled closer to form a straight line in front of him.

They were magnificent creatures, with graceful sweeping tails and glittering scales. Strings of pearls adorned their necks and they wore gleaming swords strapped across their chests.

Egorh recognized the mermaid on the far right. She whirled toward him and began to study him with undisguised interest until her eyes rested on the beak mark. Satisfied, she turned to the others and nodded.

The spectacular mermaid then acknowledged Egorh with a small bow and said, "I am Zukressa. I knew your father, son of Darkarh." She fishtailed around him and in a beautiful crooning voice said, "We are the keepers of the *Algo* pearls' secret. We are here to bring you a gift to help you in your battle against the sorceress."

Egorh returned the bow and said, "I am honored, Zukressa."

"Before you can accept it, let me explain the consequences of possessing such a gift." Zukressa swam a full circle in the air in front of Egorh and continued. "There will be risks, trickery, torture and enticement by witches and wizards. They will use their power and ingenuity to try to steal this from you. Do you understand these dangers before you accept our gift?"

Egorh nodded.

Zukressa turned to a mermaid in the middle of the row, stretched out her hand and took from her a large pearl ring. Egorh saw it was identical to the one that Steukhon wore.

Reverently, she offered the ring to him. She continued, "The priest, being honored by us with the same gift, will explain its magic to you. Our time outside the water is over and we must leave."

Egorh took the ring and looked at her earnestly. "Thank you for your trust," he said in a firm voice.

"Then from all oceans and their depths we wish you, son of Darkarh, great strength and honor!" Egorh bowed his head to the mermaids. They hovered for a while and then disappeared back into the water.

"This will make our task much easier!" said Steukhon as Egorh slipped the ring onto his finger. "It has unparalleled and unique powers," Steukhon began to explain. "The pearl is an object that wizards and witches will kill for. Therefore it is important that you speak of it to no-one."

Egorh stared at the ring and said, "What must I know about the pearl, Steukhon?"

"The pearls come from one of the deepest trenches on the ocean floor, the *Algo* zone. A snow-white mollusk, as old as time, lives next to one of the gigantic black smokers in this zone. She makes only *one* pearl every hundred years."

"Black smokers?" asked Egorh.

"Yes, burning sulphide ores erupt from massive holes on the ocean floor, like black chimneys. The only other living creatures that can survive that depth are the giant tube worms. The mermaids use them to harvest each pearl. The zone is too deep for the mermaids to fetch the pearl and the worms cannot rise to the shallows. They suck up the pearl and spit it from the deep waters for Zukressa and the others to catch."

"It is during the transfer from the depths to the surface that the *Algo* pearl obtains its mystical power. It can transfer the wearer from one point to another, as well as move them into another dimension, making them invisible and undetectable."

"Like a magic cloak?" Daniel asked.

"It is much better than that," remarked Bubba, who had seen Steukhon use his pearl many times.

Steukhon smiled. "The secret lies in being able to use it. The pearl takes its instruction from the mind. Whatever image you hold in your mind, the pearl will take you there. The move is instantaneous."

"Then we can enter the mountain this way?" Egorh blurted.

"That would have been ideal, but the problem is that none of us has ever been inside Zinnia's mountain. If you don't know the exact place you want to be, the pearl may place you anywhere and you could risk the danger of being dropped directly into the hornets' nest.

"I have given this some thought and I believe that the safest way to get into Black Mountain will be to disguise ourselves as the men who bring in supplies.

"I have watched them and know exactly where to set an ambush. Normally there are only two. They are mutants whose tongues have been removed so they can never tell what the inside of the fortress is like. I haven't been there for many months, but hopefully the routine has not changed. One of them carries a small bird-whistle to call the gate-watch to open the entrance. Bubba knows how to use it, so he must be with me steering the wagon of supplies."

"Daniel and I could hide in the back, giving me the freedom to fight should we meet with any problems," Egorh said with barely concealed excitement.

"It is the only way to enter the mountain but we must be wary of the eagles. They are well trained to spot intruders," Steukhon warned.

"Do you know how many men we will clash with, once inside?" asked Egorh.

"I believe Zinnia has many guards but exactly how many, I don't know. Arkarrah gives gold to his troops at the entrance. They never enter the mountain and have no information about its interior. We will use the rings' powers to help us escape from dangers, not to get us into the mountain. Egorh, if Daniel travels with you, he can also touch the pearl and you will both be transferred to the place in your mind – in the same way Bubba will travel with me. There's one other thing," Steukhon added.

The priest walked over to where Maximus lay on his book, fully awake, snapping endlessly at a jitterbug. Beside the tall candle was a carved wooden box with remarkable inlays of metal. Egorh watched Steukhon pause with his hand resting

264

on the box. He walked back to Egorh and said, "In this box is the mystic goblet that you will use to bring the orinium back." Steukhon took a leather pouch with velvet lining from the table and handed it to him. "Strap this across your shoulder as a place of safekeeping for the goblet and the glowing heart. This will free both your hands, should it become necessary to fight.

"For now, that is enough. We must start moving soon. The ambush has to happen today or we will have to wait another two weeks. Zinnia only allows two deliveries in thirty days. We leave as soon as everybody is ready."

Chapter 37

#

Steukhon turned to the wall of the cave. He fumbled with his crystal, muttered something under his breath and another staircase appeared in the granite.

"This will be a better way to leave the cave and get to the road. Come Bubba, take the torch and lead the way."

Bubba grabbed the flaming torch from the wall and began to climb the stairs. The other three followed close behind. At the top, a huge door creaked open on its rusty hinges. Looking back, Egorh could see the stairs had already begun to vanish. As they stepped outside, the door slammed shut and melted back into the cliff.

A small canyon stretched before them, bright with the noonday sun. Egorh frowned when he saw the fresh-looking tracks in the ground.

"Don't worry," said Bubba, "Those are the tracks made by Arkarrah's group. They've left the vicinity now."

"He may have left scouts." Egorh worriedly scoured the

tops of the cliffs for any movement. Satisfied that nobody was around, he motioned for them to move ahead and cautiously they made their way between the two peaks.

Daniel took a deep breath, relieved that the giant earthworms had not crossed their path again. Glancing down, he spotted two fat red crickets near his boots and snatched them up to inspect in the light. He then stuffed them into his pocket and murmured, "The birds are going to love these." Since he had been feeding the flamingos in the cave, bugs had taken on a different meaning for Daniel. "Humph ... I am now a creepy-crawly collector."

"Daniel, it's not time to collect bugs now," said Egorh over his shoulder. "You are falling behind again and we need to keep together."
"Sorry ..." Daniel replied and ran to catch up.

Once out of the gully, they swerved into the forest and took a more tortuous route that snaked among the trees towards Black Mountain. Small birds flew around, making warning sounds as they passed.
Along the narrow track, Steukhon suddenly stopped and held up his hand for them to be silent. Behind him, Egorh reached for his sword. Faint noises and the grinding sound of wheels on hard dirt could be heard.
"It's the supply wagon" Steukhon whispered sharply. "Looks as though we're just in time."
They crept forward silently. When they reached the ambush site, they took their places behind the trees and waited. Ancient roots that rutted the path helped to slow down the wagon.
As it came into sight around the sharp bend, Egorh climbed a tree and balanced on an overhanging branch, ready to leap down and attack the drivers. The others would remain hidden until he had got hold of the reins. Steukhon, Daniel and Bubba would strike from the sides. As the supply cart passed

underneath him, Egorh jumped and struck the huge man in the coach driver's seat, but was horrorstruck when the blow from his fist flowed right through the first man, as well as the enormous one next to him. The force of the swing threw Egorh off balance and he went tumbling to the ground. They did not look in his direction but continued on their journey, seemingly oblivious to what had just happened.

Egorh picked himself up and stood in the roadway, baffled by what had just occurred.

He felt Steukhon grab his arm and pull him into the forest. "Take cover quickly!" the priest whispered urgently.

From their hiding place a rattled Egorh asked, "What happened? Those were not real people."

"No. They are ghost riders and part of the Flegos. She must have exchanged her ordinary guards for Flegos!" Steukhon whispered as loudly as he dared.

"THOSE WHERE GHOSTS!" Daniel yelped; the blood draining from his face.

Egorh gave Daniel a warning glance then insisted, "Explain Steukhon!"

"It was a hide-and-seek game the ancient witches used to play. To make the game trickier, they separated the ghost from the flesh and called it Flegos. The ghosts act as decoys. The real bodies follow close behind their ghosts, using the confusion to attack," Steukhon replied in an undertone. His eyes remained on the road while Egorh scanned their surroundings. "Zinnia must have expected an ambush then?" Egorh asked.

"Fortunately for us, there was a bend in the road and the true bodies were not following that closely," muttered Steukhon. "The problem is that we cannot kill them, or their ghosts will report to Zinnia and we will be discovered."

The next moment, two gigantic men, looking identical to the ghosts on the wagon, appeared around the bend.

"Look at the size of them!" breathed Bubba.

They were huge men, taller than any man Egorh had ever seen. Their heads rested on wide shoulders and bulky neck muscles sloped down from their ears to their shoulders, making it hard to believe that it was a neck. Robes covered most of their immense bodies. They wore massive old leather sandals. Curved blades, which looked ancient and heavy, hung at their waists.

Daniel wondered if it was possible to bring such men down. His eyes widened and his throat became dry as the two giants came closer. He mumbled to himself, "Daniel, remember, it's not a matter of size, the correct attitude will win almost any fight."

Egorh moved from behind the tree to the middle of the road. The two Flegos stopped and glared at him with empty eyes.

Egorh was the first to attack, landing the first punch on the temple of the man closest to him, followed quickly with another, sending him senseless to the dirt. The Flegos to the left snorted and leapt forward with a roar, his blade high, ready to strike. His hugeness made him look fearsome but his size meant he was slow to move and Egorh twisted his body to avoid the swinging metal.

Before the assailant could resume his attack, Egorh hammered him on the nose. The giant staggered back, wiping the oozing blood from his face. As he charged forward again, Steukon fumbled with his crystal and murmured something. At once, a thick root from the nearest tree grew across his path, snagging his feet. He growled as he hit the earth and ploughed the soil with his forearms. Before he could drag himself up, roots shot out from every direction and wove him flat against the ground.

The first man lumbered towards Egorh, towering over him, roaring with fury. Egorh backed away and they began to circle one another. Egorh ducked a blow that the Flegos aimed at his head, but the giant managed to grab him by the throat. Daniel and Bubba each scrambled for a branch and with all their might, they went for the back of the titan's knees. The Flegos spun around – head first and body following. This gave Egorh enough time to land a forceful blow on the man's head and he dropped face down on the road, uttering loud cries. Egorh sprang forward and pressed him flat to the ground with his boot, grabbing his arms and pulling them up across his back.

"Bubba! Quickly, tie this one. Daniel, remove their robes," Egorh ordered.

"Then find the whistle, Bubba," Steukhon urged.

They removed the Flegos' filthy brown robes and tied them to trees further into the woods, away from the road.

As Steukhon and Bubba donned the long brown robes, Steukhon suddenly realized that the ghosts were still with the wagon. He rubbed his crystal and intoned a few words. Instantly, the ghosts reappeared next to their bodily hosts and dropped into the flesh.

"Come on! Let's hurry – time is running out," urged Egorh. The abandoned cart was easily found. Without its ghostly drivers, it had run off the road not too far ahead.

"Daniel and I will hide in the back. Warn us of any danger."

When the wagon came to a halt in front of the cliffs, Steukhon elbowed Bubba and whispered, "Now, blow the whistle." Immediately, eagles swept down from the rectangular openings in the towering cliffs. A head appeared high up. Bubba could feel his heartbeat pounding in his chest.

"Just stay calm. The birds can sense if you are afraid or nervous. Remember they are trained eagles," Steukhon said softly from the corner of his mouth. With his hand he signaled a circle and hoped it would be as he remembered. After what seemed like forever the man above bellowed, "Wait!" and disappeared.

"Thank goodness he cannot see our faces, just the brown robes," murmured Steukhon, with a lowered head.

A loud grinding sound began and the solid cliff split open, allowing just enough space for the wagon to squeeze through into a large level area enclosed by more cliffs. Once inside, two men strolled towards them to help with the unloading. Steukhon silently thanked the gods that they appeared to be normal bodies.

"Two guards approaching," muttered Steukhon in a low tone over his shoulder. Egorh and Daniel waited for them to reach the wagon, flew out and slammed into them, knocking both to the ground. Egorh drew his sword and threatened, "If you make a sound today, it will be your last."

Daniel helped to tie and gag the two, threw them into the back of the cart and covered them with bags.

They hid the wagon out of sight and quickly rushed towards the wide steps leading into the inner mountain.

Chapter 38

Iron Door

The four men rushed up the steps leading to a huge opening in the rock. On either side, enormous eagle sculptures held oil lamps and Daniel flinched as he looked at them.

"Come on Daniel! Don't fall behind or you will have a lamp hanging from your talons," Egorh urged, wondering if Kayrin also walked this same path.

The men slowed their pace. "Remember to use the *Algo* pearl if necessary. We must not be seen," warned Steukhon, as they slowly moved forward. The stairway ended in a massive foyer with open arches on either side. Through one, more steps led up to a higher level. The other arch gave entry to a long hall. To the left of the hall was a colonnade of immense pillars that disappeared into the high ceiling.

Opposite them, large crevices near the top of the wall allowed a breeze and some light into the area. At the plinth of each pillar stood human statues, each in a different position, looking almost alive.

Intrigued, Egorh hesitated for a moment and glanced at Steukhon. "They look like humans turned into stone."

Steukhon moved closer to a figurine and whispered, "Diabolical! These are souls turned into stone."

They became aware of voices and the sound of footsteps coming towards them.

"Quick! Use the rings!" hissed Steukhon and they all vanished.

The steps came closer and the four moved behind the columns, where they waited on tenterhooks.

Egorh and Daniel held their breath as someone passed close by. Egorh sneaked a look and was stunned by what he saw. She was a nightmare of beauty and evil, a tall woman in a flowing black dress. Her wild hair was tied with a golden rope and behind her followed an eagle flying from statue to statue.

That *must* be Zinnia, the sorceress, Egorh thought. She was muttering something and he strained his ears to listen.

"It's almost complete," he heard the woman say excitedly. She held a heart-shaped stone in her hand. Egorh noticed her long, gold fingernails, which looked horribly like talons. "My victory is within sight!"

Egorh followed her, dodging from pillar to pillar, Daniel hard on his heels. He noticed a heavy door at the end of the passage. It had no obvious knobs or handles, but to one side it looked as if there were some symbols carved into the flat rock.

Zinnia stopped at the massive iron door and tapped the wall with her nail. Its hinges creaked as it swung open.

Egorh strained to see the opening sequence for the door. He stepped back and accidentally ground Daniel's toe into the floor, causing him to utter a curse.

Zinnia froze and carefully placed the heart-stone in the gold bowl she was carrying. She turned and gazed with narrow eyes in their direction and started to move towards them.

Egorh and Daniel flattened themselves against the gigantic pillar.

Zinnia stopped almost directly in front of them. Breathlessly, they watched as she searched the air with her evil stare. Egorh could see her emerald eyes flickering with demon wickedness. He knew without question that if she should discover them they would know her perpetual wrath. Not trusting her eyes, she trailed her golden nails from side to side as if she knew they were there despite their invisibility.

Egorh instinctively moved his head back as a long nail almost scraped the tip of his nose. Just then Khan swooped down and interrupted Zinnia's intense concentration as he settled on her shoulder.

She is clever, she is REALLY clever, thought Steukhon, who was watching in suspense. It will be a disaster if we are revealed before we find the hearts.

Egorh could see both Zinnia's and the eagle's green eyes looking but not seeing.

His hand slowly reached for his sword. Daniel carefully dug into his pocket for one of the crickets and flicked the bug across the floor, away from them. After what felt like an eternity, it began its usual annoying sound, calling its mate, at first faintly, then more loudly.

Zinnia swung in the direction of the sound. Relaxing as she saw the insect, she murmured, "Hmmm ... Strange. I could have sworn I had visitors." Casually, she squashed the cricket with her golden sandal and headed for the half-open door. Before moving through it, she lifted the stone out of the bowl and held it in front of her. "Extraordinary! The human heart – harboring so many emotions: love ... hate ... despair ... My task is almost done! Come Khan!"

The bird swooped down, gulped the cricket and swept down the long passage, disappearing through the door.

As it shut, they released their fingers from the rings and became visible again.

"Rattle trap, that was close," gasped Daniel, falling back against the pillar.

"Yes, that *was* close ... I am certain *that* is the door that will lead us to the hearts," replied Egorh.

"I wonder which poor soul's heart she's been carrying around," Bubba mused, staring at the closed door.

"Did you hear how she was already convinced that she had won. *'My victory is in sight,'*" mimicked Daniel, still shaken from their recent experience.

"Quiet! We must stay alert," warned Steukhon.

"Is she likely to be coming back?" gulped Daniel.

"She might. Remain watchful," Egorh cautioned with a low voice.

They waited for Zinnia to reappear and when the solid iron door swung open again they made themselves invisible and watched her disappear up the stairs. Once they were certain she had gone, they quickly moved to the huge door.

As they stood before it, they could see an intricate combination of colored lines etched in the stone to the left of the wall, creating three definite contours of blue, green and red.

Steukhon inspected the wall more closely, his nose almost touching it.

"Hmmm ... I wonder what this could mean? Perhaps rivers? Roads?" he mused.

Directly above the horizontal lines was a peculiar pattern, irregular and wavy but clearly resembling a fish skeleton. Gold inlay formed the head and tail and six horizontal silver inlays made up the fish bones on each side.

"Do you not know the meaning of this?" asked Egorh suspiciously.

Without breaking his concentration, Steukhon replied, "No ... I have no inkling."

"What about down here?" Bubba called anxiously. "It is the same writing as in your book."

Steukhon looked to where Bubba was pointing. "Let me see ... Yes! It is written in the old language! It seems to be a riddle," he muttered to himself and began to translate the words.

"Two drops of sweat run from the face of the sun when

turned opposite of horizontal ... four times in a row.
Six sequential tears drop from the eyes of the moon;
pendulums swing lazily before falling.
Half the burden once more.
Run the ring finger in the river that's not flowing ... now
only a name ... but then was something more than a
name
... life."

"Can you crack the riddle?" Egorh asked.

Steukhon rubbed his chin thoughtfully.

Bubba interrupted before Steukhon could answer, "Moon – I remember the songs my mother sang in my childhood. One was about a golden sun and a silver moon."

"That's it! Well done Bubba! But it is the rest that I am not sure of. We must think harder." Steukhon toyed with the crystal hanging around his neck.

Egorh looked nervously towards the arches, not trusting the sudden quietness and added, "Perhaps that means the gold and silver have something to do with the fish skeleton."

"Yes," agreed Steukhon. "The ... hmmm ... *'Two drops of sweat run from the face of the sun'* ... must be the gold fish head – *'when turned opposite of horizontal ...'* Well, the opposite of horizontal is vertical, which could mean above and below, in other words from the head to the tail. *'Four times in a row'* could mean that we must start at the head, then the tail and press each four times."

Again Egorh glanced back and said, "So far so good."

"The silver fish bones must have something to do with the moon," exclaimed Daniel, eager to help, but Steukhon ignored his contribution and continued:

"*'Six sequential tears drop from the eyes of the moon ... pendulums swing lazily before falling.'* *'Sequential'* means one following directly after the other ... *'pendulums swing before falling,'* that is, moving from side to side. Which means we have to start at the top, *'falling'*, and cross sideways six times?

"*Half the burden once more*'... must be ..." continued Steukhon.

"That could mean half of everything again ... in other words, halve the numbers," Egorh interrupted.

"Yes, it *does* seem that way ... do the same, only by half," reiterated Steukhon. They stood quietly as he started to interpret the last line.

"*Run the ring finger in the river that's not flowing ... now only a name ... but then was something more than a name ... life.*' The colored stones obviously represent *something*, but it could be anything." Steukhon murmured thoughtfully.

"*Flowing*' must mean river. Blue water ... giving life," debated Bubba from behind.

"It could mean a river that's dried up ... not flowing ... one that used to give life.

"*Was something more than a name...*' This piece puzzles me. Green forest plants along the river could be life-giving, but the red ... I don't know about the red."

Nervously scanning the arches of the long passage, Egorh said. "Well, we cannot stand here much longer. If it's not the blue, we must try the others until the door opens. It doesn't look as though we have any other option."

"You are right," replied Steukhon. He pressed the gold and silver four times, then the silver crisscross six times. Then twice the gold again and three times the silver. He hesitated at the river, took a deep breath and ran his ring finger along the blue line.

They stood back anxiously, waiting for the door to open. Unexpectedly, the floor gave way beneath their feet and they tumbled down into what seemed to be a dungeon. Looking up, they watched in horror as the surface closed above them.

"Wrong river," commented Steukhon dryly as he looked around. It was eerie and damp but there was enough light to enable them to see. Badly shaken but unharmed by their abrupt fall, they were suspicious and Egorh drew his sword. They could just make out some peculiar sediments in the rocks. Large grey colored bands with whitish rings ran all along the dungeons walls.

"Fossils! I hope this is not what I think it is." Something in Steukhon's tone alerted Egorh.

"What do you mean?"

"Zinnia has possibly used the *Fossils of Time* to guard her prison. Only sorceresses can call on fossils to protect their dungeons. This mountain must have been under water at some stage," Steukhon explained.

Without warning, the grey sediment suddenly became a vicious mass, as if the walls were alive. Egorh saw a gigantic tentacle move out of the granite. He signaled for the others to retreat to the middle of their prison. More giant tentacles began reach out of the wall, all around them.

"Does this mean we are in trouble?" whispered Daniel.

Egorh raised his sword. A tentacle suddenly lashed out, grabbed Steukhon around the ankles and sent him crashing onto the granite with such force that it drove the air from his lungs. His head slammed onto the hard slab and blackness descended on him. The monster began to drag him across the floor.

Another attack from the beast caught Egorh by surprise, grabbing him and causing him to drop his sword. He bellowed, "CUT THE TENTACLE DANIEL!" Daniel darted forward, picked up the sword and slashed into the slimy flesh, managing to hack it halfway through. The creature loosened its grip on Egorh and dropped him, blinding him with the black ink-blood that gushed from its wound.

A terrified Bubba was kicking and yelling in vain as the creature now slowly dragged him towards the wall. Suddenly he heard the old wizard shout. The weakened Steukhon, his hand outstretched in Bubba's direction, hurled a bolt of lightning at the tentacle holding Bubba. The blow caused it to fall motionless to the floor. Bubba, who had been drawn halfway into the stone, escaped its grip and fell from the wall, rolling towards Steukhon. The priest grabbed his hand and yelled, "Daniel, quick! Run for Egorh's ring so we can get back to the iron door."

Daniel dived over and under the sweeping, probing tentacles as the creature tried to entrap him. Swiftly, he moved to where Egorh was staggering, trying to wipe the ink-blood from his eyes. Daniel grabbed his hand and gasped. *"The iron door ... The iron door, take us there ...!"*

The creature was not going to let its prey escape that easily and another tentacle coiled around Daniel's waist, jerking him away. His fingers lost their grip on the ring as he was dragged back across the dirt. Egorh reached for him but suddenly found himself back with Steukhon and Bubba in front of the iron door. He looked around and shouted,

"Where's Daniel? Daniel is not here! I must go back!" He touched the ring and frantically imagined, *"Take me back to the dungeon!"*

"I will go back with you!" shouted Steukhon. "Bubba you stay here!"

Bubba blinked, his eyes wide. "WHAT ME, alone here?" He looked up at the passage then back to Steukhon, but he had already vanished. Bubba ran to hide.

Egorh and Steukhon found themselves back amid the chaos. The octopus held Daniel, whose face was ash-white as the monster tried to squeeze the life out of him.

"HANG ON! HANG ON, DANIEL!" Egorh roared. "I will get you out of here!" Egorh ferociously slashed and hacked in an attempt to reach Daniel. The creature was confused and Steukhon seized the opportunity to throw another lightning bolt. The octopus dropped Daniel and Egorh grabbed his friend. *"Take us to the iron door!"*

"Thank goodness," breathed Egorh with Steukhon behind him.

Daniel, still dazed muttered, "That was a lot of thumping and pushing," and rubbed the back of his head where it had struck the granite.

Egorh's shirt was drenched with the ink-blood of the fossil-beast. He threw his arms in the air and exclaimed, "That's right! I think I've got it!"

Bubba, looking very pale came nearer. "Got what?" he asked.

"Blood! THAT'S IT!" repeated Egorh, while looking at his blood drenched shirt.

"Blood?" asked Steukhon.

"Yes ... blood *flows* ... *blood* is *life* ... blood is *red* ... the river in the riddle refers to the *red* stone, not the blue!" explained Egorh.

"You're right!" Steukhon announced excitedly. *"The red river, blood ... not flowing ... now only a name ... but then was something more than a name ... life!"*

The priest stormed towards the wall and repeated the sequence, only this time he ran his finger along the red line.

They held their breath, anticipating another surprise, then sighed with relief as the iron door slowly creaked and opened.

With every sense alive and every muscle tensed, Egorh inched forward with the others following.

Chapter 39

Demon

As they entered the room, the door slammed shut behind them. They stood back to back and studied every corner, not knowing what to expect next. It felt as though they had entered a mammoth cave. The walls were black and it was empty, cold and gloomy. The sunken floor created a wide gully between them and the staircase on the other side. The bottom of the gully was covered with black pebbles like an empty river bed.

A bridge seemed to be the only way to reach the staircase. A smell of burnt sulphur mixed with mould was quite evident, with no opening anywhere to dissipate it. Egorh's nose itched and he tried to stifle a sneeze brought on by the acid smell. They covered their noses and Egorh could hear the murmured complaints of the others behind him.

Eager to find the hearts, he started to move towards the bridge. "THERE! They must be up there!" he pointed to the stairway and urged the others to follow. "COME!" he yelled and charged forward, but in his way was a large grey-brown boulder. As Egorh sidestepped to pass around it, a glow began to emanate from within, an eerie orange color.

"The seeking stone of fear! Don't look at it!" warned Steukhon from behind and turned to cover his eyes. But his warning was too late for Egorh. He stood stupefied, staring at the glowing boulder as if it was something from either below or beyond the earth.

"The furrow of fear and obstacles," muttered Steukhon.

"What ... what do you mean? Why must we not look at it?" asked Daniel as he saw the sudden glow fade and the stone return to normal. Egorh blinked as if he had just awoken from a trance.

Steukhon paid no attention to Daniel's question and started to pace. With concern, he mumbled, "I cannot believe the knowledge that Zinnia has accumulated. How did she become so powerful?" he mused. "She must have creatures everywhere helping her to collect information. It is impossible that she could have gathered all this by herself."

"I once overheard Arkarrah and Raleigh talking about something Zinnia possessed. Now what was it?" Bubba murmured. "It was ... yes, I remember now ... the Chest of Knowledge. Zinnia has it in her sleeping chamber."

"What? Why have you never told me about this?" asked Steukhon sharply. "What else do you know about this store of information?"

Bubba rubbed his chin thoughtfully and struggled to remember. "She captured the Spirit of Autumn. Yes, that is what Raleigh said." Bubba felt Steukhon's steely gaze bore into him. He wracked his memory for more detail. "Raleigh said ... what was it?" Bubba faltered. Steukhon waited with barely concealed impatience and Bubba continued, "The Spirit of Autumn in the form of autumn leaves could collect all the secrets and knowledge from anyone they encountered as they traveled." Bubba now spoke more confidently as his recollection improved. "Raleigh said that the spirit then took the information back to the Chest of Knowledge where it was stored. Zinnia's genies decipher the information for her. Raleigh was very drunk that afternoon and I had not given it a second thought again until now."

Steukhon nodded, "I have always wondered how Zinnia knew about Egorh's birth on earth. Now I understand." He remembered the night of Egorh's earthly arrival as an infant. The autumn leaves that had been blowing around him. At the time he had thought nothing of it, but now he understood. He sighed, "Much of the knowledge and power the sorceress has accumulated is utterly evil."

"But how does this affect us?" asked Egorh, his head clearing.

"Zinnia has placed these boulders here to protect her vault up there," Steukhon said and a sombre expression settled on his face.

"The boulders can learn your innermost fears and you will not be able to cross the bridge," he said. "It's to do with each one's thoughts of fear and evil. Your fears are collected in your deepest unconscious level and magnified many times. These magnified fears then attack you. It is a devilish way to protect the chamber of hearts. Anybody who tries to enter the chamber must challenge and overcome their fears. The challenge will be different for everyone."

Egorh glanced at the boulder and then at the bridge, adjusted his sword and moved towards it. He spoke in a resolute voice. "There is no time for fear now. We must go and find the hearts and the path to the Haffgoss. We *have* to forge on regardless."

"Wait!" Steukhon called and Egorh stopped.

"If you have fears deep in your heart, you can be sure that Zinnia's demon will find them. Nobody can help you – only you can help yourself."

Egorh pondered for a few seconds, Daniel swallowed and Bubba slowly shook his head.

"Egorh?" asked Steukhon with an arched eyebrow.

"I have none," he answered.

"Then go!"

283

Egorh walked towards the bridge. Almost halfway, he looked back and called, "Come!" He tensed as the pebbles beneath the bridge began to sputter and hiss. They flickered first into small fires and then flared into aggressive flames that spread around and beneath him.

"Quick! Cross over Egorh, before it multiplies," Steukhon yelled.

He hurried on as the flames began to leap higher, twisting around like hungry tongues. To his horror, a demon's face appeared from this fiery mass and drew closer to him. On the evil's cheekbones hung two burning red eyes that glowed intensely while a devilish sneer played upon its thick lips. Its jaw dropped and the mouth became a hole from which deep laughter burst forth. Egorh covered his ears but the sound scraped his nerves and his neck hairs bristled.

The face swayed around Egorh, glaring at him from every angle, hovering around him like a grotesque dragonfly. Egorh jerked backwards as the evil spirit drew a large burning circle with its flaming hands.

A burning carriage broke through the fiery circle and a long-buried memory from Egorh's childhood appeared, the blazing carriage in which his father and Joseph had perished. He felt an overpowering wave of panic spill over him. His face crumpled and he cried out, "NO! Not again!" as the horror of that day was reenacted before him. Egorh turned from the scene in despair and covered his face, begging the demon to stop his torment. Abruptly the flames died, leaving no trace of what had just happened.

Steukhon, watching helplessly, muttered in a low voice, "Egorh's demon has won the first round."

Bubba and Daniel looked on in distress.

"What are we going to do now?" asked Daniel.

"This is not our battle. This one belongs to Egorh alone. We will have to pray that the son of Darkarh is strong enough to overcome his fears, or we will lose," Steukhon muttered, without taking his eyes off the bridge.

Daniel, watching Egorh's agony, clenched his fists and prayed loudly." Egorh, fight this! I know you can win!"

"This is not real." Egorh slowly dragged himself up and started to move towards the middle of the bridge. Again the flames appeared and spread all around him, leaping higher as they melted together to form the wicked devil. Egorh drew his sword, swinging it through the flames and shouted, "You are nothing to me! You live only in my mind!"

The beastly spirit stopped and jerked his head from side to side. He leaned over and peered deeply into Egorh's eyes. It thrashed both its blazing arms above Egorh who ducked as images of buildings came tumbling down, water and mud all around. Wild fires scourged him and thousands of pink flamingos fell from the sky, tumbling into the flames. A torrent of shrieking noises – noises that spoke of death and destruction, deafened him.

"No!" cried Egorh in horror as he remembered the battle of Darkarh and his murderous brothers. Drawing himself away from the inferno and noise, Egorh tried to block his ears and cover his face. He staggered blindly, then skidded off the bridge, just managing to grab hold of a rail, desperately kicking to keep his boots from the leaping fire.

The others watched helplessly as Egorh managed to pull himself back onto the bridge, where he crouched, exhausted.

"I want to talk to him," Daniel said resolutely and with a few faltering steps he lurched over to Egorh, avoiding the flames.

Daniel dropped onto his haunches beside him, cleared his throat and tentatively addressed his master. "Sir, you *have to* beat it."

Egorh ignored him and stared at the empty bridge. Hesitantly, Daniel swallowed and said, "Think of Kayrin, sir."

Egorh blinked and Daniel knew he had hit a chord. He pressed on, "Believe it cannot hurt you."

Egorh lifted his head, stared at the flames and cried, "I cannot. The flames ... the deaths ... the agony ... it's like a thousand daggers ..."

Daniel hesitated and then had an idea. Imitating Egorh's stare into nothingness, he muttered, "Well, come to think of it, sir, you don't *really* have to conquer your demon. We can take Kayrin back home, where she can stay around the lake. We can feed her frogs and grasshoppers every day," Daniel stared nonchalantly at his boots, desperately trying to avoid looking at the flames.

Egorh, shocked by what he had just heard, jumped up and grabbed Daniel by the throat. He was drenched with perspiration and he hissed, "Do you know what you are saying?"

"Go, sir, go! Do it for Kayrin! Follow your heart, not your fear," Daniel croaked. He started to cough as Egorh's grip slowly slacked.

"You are right," Egorh murmured.

Daniel, rubbing his sore throat, returned to where Steukhon and Bubba were standing.

Egorh felt the cold claws of dread in the pit of his stomach and he blinked the sweat from his eyes.

"I will defeat it, Kayrin!"

Then Steukhon thundered, "Egorh, remember, you are the bearer of the beak mark! You have the power of fire within you! Fight!"

The words drifted towards him and images flew through his mind, images he knew he had to fight. He touched the mark on his neck and felt a sudden rush of power wrap itself around him. The flames roared, leaping to trap him, but Egorh stood firm his eyes dark with emotion, as he stared directly into the blaze. He shouted, "You are nothing to me! You will never again BE anything to me! I AM Egorh, THE SON OF DARKARH!"

He watched as the devilish figure convulsed, protesting with the last of its strength, shriveled and disappeared with the receding flames. Egorh knew that something within him had been altered. There would be no more torture of fire. He took a deep breath and ran across the bridge.

He paused at the far side, feeling stunned yet elated.

Perspiration poured from his brow and splashed onto the ground where it turned into tiny puddles of hot sparks. He did not know what it meant, as he watched the flames curl and loop before him. He instinctively touched them and the heat began to fill him with a power he could not explain, a gift he had being waiting for his entire life.

Egorh gazed at the flaming puddles, then gently scraped them together with both hands, creating a ball of fire. He turned to Steukhon, who looked pleased and chuckled.

"Egorh has conquered his fear! He has reclaimed his birthright! The element of fire! Darkarh would be proud."

Bubba and Daniel clung to each other in relief.

With a broad smile on his face, Egorh stood and nodded slowly as he realized what had just happened. "The element of fire. *This* is what Darkarh meant!" He hurled the ball towards the cavern's ceiling. As it hit the rocky surface, sparks and granite particles spun in all directions.

Steukhon whispered, "Egorh has become a worthy adversary."

"Come!" waved Egorh.

"I will go next. I've already been on the bridge and nothing happened," Daniel said eagerly.

"Then go, we will follow." Steukhon knew that Daniel had not tried to cross. Things might be very different for him when he did.

Daniel started confidently but the pebbles beneath the bridge melted together and gigantic tentacles formed. They thrashed all around him, groping and fumbling.

Milk-livered, Daniel reeled back, just in time to escape the swirling arms lashing out at him.

Once he was off the bridge, the tentacles disappeared.

"Hmmm ... your phantom of fear ... Your experience in the dungeon has made the octopus your demon. Did you see any giant earthworms?"

Daniel blushed.

Steukhon set off next. When he was halfway the pebbles

again melted together. Three extremely ugly witches appeared riding their brooms, cackling and screeching as they swooped down on him.

Steukhon halted, smirked and placed his hands on his hips. "You must surely be joking. That was a fear of many lives ago, when I was a boy." He crossed over fearlessly and instantly the witches melted away.

Bubba looked at Daniel, "We have no time to work on your fears. I have none, they are with Shadow in the tin. How about I carry you on my back? Then it will be like you are not crossing. If you close your eyes, you won't see anything and will have no fear."

"This is so embarrassing," mumbled Daniel, reddening at the thought.

"Well, you can remain here and take the chance that Zinnia or Arkarrah might find you."

Daniel didn't hesitate and jumped onto Bubba's back with his eyes tightly shut. Bubba quickly trotted across the bridge to the other side.

Chapter 40

Heart-Stones

Arriving on the other side, Egorh waited and looked around. Sheer walls, broken only by steep granite steps surrounded them. He cautiously signaled for the others to follow. He kept his eyes fixed on the top of the stairway, silently hoping that it would give them some indication of where the heart-stones might be.

As the group ascended, the domed ceiling of the chamber became visible. Egorh adjusted his bow on his shoulder to make sure it was free from any hindrance. Closely followed by Steukhon, he became aware of activity further up. A rectangular window was situated high in the southern wall. Large birds flew in and out of the opening. Raucous sounds flared as they flapped their huge wings, fighting for a spot on the ledge.

"The watchdogs," Egorh whispered indicating the eagles.

"Pray they are there only to protect the sky and not the inside," Steukhon replied.

The head of the stairs opened into an expansive eerie vault. Suddenly Egorh felt his blood turn to ice. What he saw was so strange that he gasped. Shafts of light fell from the high opening illuminating thirty huge, square sandstone blocks, carefully shaped and interlocking, suspended in the air. Carved into the stone were thousands and thousands of little hollows, each holding a heart-stone. The four men stood in silent horror, at the heart harvest before them.

With great sadness, Steukhon shook his head and whispered, "The thirty-thousand hearts ... the book ... the first rule ..."

Egorh walked closer, his eyes swept over the gathered heart-stones and he felt his anger rise. "The brutal malicious witch!" he muttered through clenched teeth. There were no cobwebs, only a fine grey dust that covered the field of hearts like mould on bread. Each heart-stone, cradled in its own hole, lay waiting to be sacrificed to the Haffgoss. Every heart was unique, like the bodies they had once belonged to. Dead, yet alive, they were kept that way by the mystical cord of the flamingo spirit.

"We must try to save these people, Steukhon," Egorh muttered hoarsely.

"I agree," the priest said sadly, "but for now we must find Kayrin's heart-stone and the orinium. We know that Zinnia will not give up the hearts easily."

Egorh drew nearer to the sandstone blocks. He stopped as he realized the enormity of the task. "How on earth will I find her heart-stone among all these?" he asked, with a sinking feeling.

"By the dust, sir," he heard Daniel say quietly behind him.

Egorh was puzzled. "Dust, Daniel? What do you mean?"

"The last hearts that were added will have no dust, sir" Daniel ventured, fearing ridicule.

"Good thinking!" Egorh exclaimed. Daniel flushed with pride. "Take Bubba and search that side. Steukhon and I will search here. If Zinnia still needs hearts and the holes are filled systematically, there could be empty holes near the latest hearts."

"Remember, the heart with which you have a connection will glow when you are close to it," Steukhon reminded them and slowly started to move around the harvest. Silently they got to work. After a few moments Steukhon called, "Quick! Egorh you must see this."

Egorh hesitated a moment before turning reluctantly to Steukhon. "What is so important?"

"A Jade-eye!"

Steukhon stood on the narrow ledge that ran along the rough granite wall. An oval, translucent, blue-green stone with thick inlays of a reddish gold metal protruded from the wall. It looked like a gigantic knob, something either to be pushed or turned.

"This *must* lead to the Haffgoss. This will open the gateway to the Hap*Less* Sphere," Steukhon exclaimed.

"How do you know this Steukhon?" Egorh asked, eager to resume his heart search.

"The Jade-stone is a powerful object of sorcery. It is carved and shaped like an oval eye." Steukhon dragged his finger along the stone's center, "Look ... the two extreme points of the pupil are connected by a metal inlay. Judging by the color of the inlay, it must be tainted with blood."

"Whose blood?" Egorh asked, sensing Steukhon's excitement.

"Most probably Zinnia's, which will make the stone very powerful."

"Meaning?" Egorh asked, looking back towards the field of hearts.

"It means she must have managed to open the channel between her and the Haffgoss." Steukhon nodded, "This is how she will get the hearts to them."

"Are you sure?" Egorh asked skeptically.

"Yes, I am certain."

"Here! Here is an empty hole!" Bubba called out eagerly. Egorh rushed to where Bubba was. Around the hole lay ten dustless stone hearts. Egorh held his hand above them, hoping that he would find the one he was seeking.

Chapter 41

The Battle

Five stones away from Egorh's searching hand, one began to shimmer. As his fingertips moved closer it glowed more strongly, a soft red color.

Egorh beamed. "It's here! I've found you, Kayrin," he whispered. His heart hammered. He reached forward and was about to fold his fingers around the heart-stone when a chilling voice yelled, "Those are mine!"

Stunned, they swung around and saw Zinnia, together with Arkarrah and several guards, standing on a ledge above them. Her face was wild with madness, her irises huge and black in her gleaming green eyes. She was the epitome of everything that was evil, yet beautiful.

"As you can see, there is a hole left, but I will fill it soon with *your* heart," Zinnia rasped.

Egorh's face darkened, "You stole them all, not one of them belongs to you."

Zinnia took a step forward and cackled, "You knew I

was looking for you and if you had not become so stupidly fond of the girl, she would not have ended up here. At least you should know that she gave her heart willingly," Zinnia added cruelly.

Egorh struggled to swallow his rising fury and replied coldly, "You are beyond evil! These hearts *will* be returned to their human bodies and, when I destroy you, your name will be remembered with dishonor and disgrace."

"Hah ... Brave words, son of Darkarh! How do you plan to do that, I wonder," Zinnia sneered. "I see no one powerful enough to challenge me."

"With my help," said Steukhon, stepping forward.

Zinnia stiffened slightly. "Well, well, the old priest," she said sarcastically, a hint of surprise now entering her voice.

"Your powers are no longer a match for mine," she smirked.

"We don't know that for sure, do we?" Steukhon replied.

Egorh seized the opportunity to lunge forward in an attempt to grab the glowing heart, but Zinnia was too fast for him. She ripped the golden rope from her head and her red hair fell around her face and shoulders. Viciously she threw the rope towards Egorh and commanded, "From rope to reptile!"

In mid air, the rope turned into an enormous yellow snake and landed on the glowing heart. It stood upright hissing, venom dripping from its fangs.

Egorh jumped back and reached for his sword. With one hack he sliced off the snake's head, sending a spray of ruby red blood across the heart-stones.

Enraged, Zinnia fumbled to unclip her belt. She removed the frog buckle and sneered, "Let me see how you handle this one, son of Darkarh!" She threw the metal frog high up and as the buckle whizzed through the vast room, it turned into a turquoise frog marked with black spots. The creature landed on the ceiling, where it clung to the granite surface with suction pads on its black feet.

"Send me the power of Khay!" Zinnia commanded loudly and pointed imperiously at the frog.

From the ceiling cracks and walls, thousands of slimy black-spotted frogs appeared, oozing slime.

"Arrow frogs! Keep away from them!" Egorh shouted. "I know these creatures from the forest. They secrete a deadly poison through their skins. If they don't kill you, they will paralyze you!"

Zinnia roared an order and pointed in Egorh's direction. "Leap!" from every wall of the chamber, frogs started to pound down in their thousands.

"Protect yourselves! Don't let them touch you!" yelled Egorh, as the turquoise mass began to rain down on them.

Daniel and Bubba pulled their clothes up over their heads for protection. Egorh instinctively raised his arms. Flames erupted and rolled from his hands, forming a dome of fire above the four men's heads, shielding them. Astonished, Daniel's jaw dropped and Bubba's eyes widened as they watched in disbelief. An indefinable sense of power radiated from Egorh.

Steukhon smiled. "Darkarh's ultimate gift!" he breathed.

The frogs fell onto the flaming shield in their hundreds and slithered down the sides as sizzling pieces of coal. The rank smell of burning frog filled the air.

Steukhon took the crystal from around his neck, held it up and chanted, "Wind! U-dun-edo!"

A strong wind swept in from nowhere, spiraling around them, vaporizing all the frogs. Egorh lowered his arms and the flames died down.

Zinnia's face darkened in fury and she let out a hideous shriek.

"Watch out!" shouted Daniel, when he saw the only remaining frog leap towards Bubba's bare heel.

Bubba brought his sandal down forcefully on the croaker, sending its intestines squirting in all directions.

"You idiot! That was my belt buckle!" Zinnia fumed. She

hurriedly unclipped her spider brooch and placed it on the back of her hand. Her cloak slid to the ground and the brooch became alive. She admired the spider briefly and when it began to crawl on her hand, she hurled it towards them. Again, her voice echoed all around the chamber as she commanded loudly, "Send me the power of Khay!" An invisible hand swept the spider up, spun it around and dropped it onto the floor.

"How many more creatures has she got hanging around her?" whispered Daniel, hiding behind Egorh.

"Let's hope not too many," Egorh replied, keeping his eyes on the spider.

For a moment nothing happened but then the creature began to grow. Egorh, Steukhon, Daniel and Bubba reeled back, speechless as the creature's enormous black silhouette towered above them, its hairy legs waving angrily. Its jaw dropped open and the mouth turned into a cavernous oval, big enough for a man's head to fit into.

At first it seemed like a gush of wind, which rose from inside the creature's belly, but then a torrent of spiders with huge, yellow stone bodies and long, red, hairy legs burst forth. In their thousands, they poured from its mouth and onto the floor. Disoriented, the yellow-bodied spiders crawled around aimlessly before they turned their red eyes towards the four men, ready to pounce.

Stunned, Bubba uttered, "What now!"

Steukhon whispered softly but urgently, "The Charoite spiders! Be careful, their bites are extremely toxic! A victim will suffer forever from unknown fears and sickness. A loving heart will submit to despair and loneliness."

They backed away as the spiders scurried towards them in a venomous wave. Egorh could hear Daniel mumbling a prayer somewhere behind him, mingled with Bubba repeating something in a strange language.

"Move back! Get back!" Egorh warned. He shifted in front of the others and they continued to back away from the creatures.

Daniel jumped with fright when Khan swooped down above their heads and scooped up one of the many spiders. He flew to a ledge, clutching the thrashing spider in his talons, tried to crack the body, then gulped it down.

Daniel petrified, gaped at the eagle, "One! Only one! You have to eat more than *one* to be of any help."

As the first spiders scrabbled towards them, Daniel, in his panic, knocked into Steukhon with such force that the crystal in his hand snapped from its chain and went skidding across the floor, right into the oncoming tide of spiders.

"The crystal!" shouted Steukhon, in horror.

Egorh cupped his hands and again his true element exploded. Flames leaped and coiled as he poured a wall of fire towards the hordes of approaching spiders.

Their stone bodies cracked and melted, thousands of burning legs fueled the blaze as they ran into the flames.

The spiders climbed ferociously over their dead, piling on top of each other, creating a moving wall. Gradually the spider barrage rose and a few of the half burned creatures climbed over the rim of fire. Daniel and Bubba frantically tried to kill them, but more managed to scurry around the side of the blazing wall.

Bubba's sandaled feet were the first to feel the painful bites. He began to stumble, his eyes blurred from the poison and he collapsed to the ground. A small tin skittered out from his pocket and flipped open. Quickly, Shadow swirled out and lingered in the air, waiting for the instruction which never came. Shadow looked at the sea of spiders and quickly zipped high up into the furthest corner of the hall where he tried to flatten himself more than usual.

"Quick!" urged Steukhon, seeing an opportunity. "Let's move to the pillars. I will try to retrieve the crystal! Touch the *Algo* rings!"

"Bubba come!" Daniel shouted. "Come!" But Bubba shook his head and said, "Go! Go! I am surrounded." He desperately tried to kill the spiders on his legs.

"Bubba, just hang in there! I will get the crystal!" yelled

Steukhon, before he, Egorh and Bubba disappeared to reappear outside the fire barrier.

"Scarab-dung!" Zinnia cursed, her eyes flashing with anger as she turned and kicked Arkarrah, shouting, "Where did they disappear to?" Arkarrah crouched in agony, holding his shin.

Zinnia stomped up and down in her frustration and forced herself to think. "I *could* start a war such as these men have never imagined possible, but then I would risk the destruction of the hearts." She continued her pacing, furious at the way things were unfolding.

Arkarrah peered towards the mass of writhing spiders and saw a circle of nothingness moving through them. He grabbed Zinnia's arm and pointed. "There! Look!" The empty circle was moving effortlessly through the spiders, getting closer to the fallen crystal.

"Hah!" Zinnia smirked. She pointed at the invisible sphere and mumbled a hex. A bluish-white bolt surged from her fingernail. "Do you think you can hide from me?" she screamed, holding the current steady. Having reached the safety of the pillars, the shield around Egorh, Steukhon and Daniel exploded. It cracked away like ice, leaving them visible again.

"By the gods ... she cut through the dimension!" Steukhon exclaimed.

Egorh rammed his sword high up into a column and extended his other hand towards Daniel shouting, "Grab my hand!" Daniel jumped but missed and fell back into the spiders. Egorh cast more flames, trying to stop the vicious creatures, but there were too many and they were too close to Daniel.

"We must reverse the spell!" shouted Steukhon as he jumped over the spiders onto a ledge between the pillars. "Egorh, get the crystal."

Zinnia saw Steukhon and snorted in anger, "You old fool!"

She threw another electric bolt at him. He managed to duck behind a pillar as the current crashed into the stone.

Zinnia turned to see Egorh lunge forward to where the crystal was lying.

"Arachnids! The crystal! Stop him!" she screeched hysterically. The surviving spiders turned and scuttled towards it.

Egorh felt them attack, their bites so excruciating that he stumbled, grinding his teeth as he crawled nearer to the crystal.

Dizziness swept over him. It must be the poison. I must act quickly, he thought as he forced his way through the insects, his arms, neck and head now engulfed.

With a final burst of strength, he managed to grab the crystal and with great effort he threw it to Steukhon.

Steukhon lunged forward, snatched it, and commanded, "Wind! U-dun-edo!" As before, a wind spiraled around the chamber sweeping up the blanket of spiders and blowing them into nothingness. The huge spider melted back into the tiny brooch and lay harmless on the floor. Bubba managed to stand, pick up his open tin and stagger over to Daniel.

"Get Egorhagh! The son!" Zinnia angrily commanded Arkarrah and his men. "I don't need his heart. I just want his death!"

"Summon the eagles! Where is Sojun?" Zinnia screamed.

Sojun peered from around a pillar.

"Instruct the eagles to attack those two!" She pointed at Daniel and Bubba "I want them all dead!" she shrieked. "I will take care of the priest once and for all!"

Sojun gave his shrill whistle and within moments the perched eagles swarmed through the hole and started to plunge down, screeching with their curved beaks open.

Guards poured into the chamber and Arkarrah rushed forward.

~

Daniel grabbed Bubba and dashed to take cover under the suspended stone blocks. The eagles attacked, their outstretched talons like daggers ready to shred the skin of their prey.

As the two bent to crawl underneath the blocks, Daniel spotted a glowing heart nestled amongst the many others. He jerked back sharply and gasped. The heart began to glow brightly as he approached and he muttered with excitement, "The heart … it must be Kayrin's!" Daniel carefully reached for it but quickly hid as an eagle attacked.

The space beneath the blocks was too low for the eagles to fly through and they whirled around them. I *have* to get Kayrin's heart, Daniel thought eagerly, watching the eagles. Seizing an opportunity, he dashed out from his hiding place, picked up the heart and slid it into his pocket. An eagle attacked him from behind. It was too late. Daniel felt the bird's talons nail into his skull and he yelled with terror.

Egorh heard the chilling scream and saw the bird's strike on Daniel. He saturated the birds with flames. Feathers swirled around everywhere as the eagles collided trying to escape. In disarray the remaining birds flew around the hall trying to find a place to perch and nurse their scorched feathers. Daniel dived back under the stone.

"Blast! What a mean bird," he groaned as he wiped the warm blood that trickled into his eyes with his sleeve.

"That was a bad one," sympathized Bubba, still slightly dazed and not noticing that Daniel had taken the heart.

Bubba peeped carefully from underneath the stone blocks and muttered, "Where is that shadow?" then shouted, "Shadow, *return to silver box!*" Shadow, who had been glued to the farthest corner, slithered down the side of the wall and across the floor.

"Since when have you been afraid of spiders?" asked Bubba, without showing any pity. Shadow looked down at his feet.

"Ah, you carry my childhood fear – my fear of spiders." Bubba remembered and held the tin open for Shadow to slide into. He smacked the tin closed and slipped it into his pocket.

"Watch out!" yelled Daniel as an eagle suddenly swooped down beneath the stone blocks, talons extended. Bubba kicked frantically at the wide-open beak and it whirled away.

~

"Kill him!" Arkarrah ordered. The guards filtered through the sandstone blocks and surrounded Egorh. Afraid that fire might harm the delicate stones, he drew his sword and waited for the first man to attack. Egorh struck him flat across the cheek with such force that he fell backward into the men behind him. Arkarrah pushed through them screaming, "Kill him!"

The guards began to close in on Egorh. He spun around to confront a man attacking him from behind. He thrust his sword into the assailant's stomach, sliced another at the knee and stabbed a third in the shoulder.

Egorh's body moved instinctively as he lashed and hacked, twisted and leaped. He tore through his attackers, with not one being able to break through his defenses. Egorh, drenched in sweat, his face twisted with rage, suddenly noticed it was only Arkarrah standing before him.

The two men's eyes locked. Arkarrah could see Egorh's anger and hatred. It terrified him.

"I have lost many men because of you," Arkarrah said, breathing heavily. Egorh remained silent, ready to destroy his enemy.

~

From the ledge, a high pitched command escaped Zinnia's lips. She held her hand up and a glimmering silver orb appeared and began to spin on the tip of her long fingernail. With daggers in her eyes, she sneered at Steukhon. "Let's see what you can make of this, old wizard!" She knew that Steukhon was a master

300

at this weapon and it would be a fight to the death, but she had prepared for a day like this. She had mastered the tactics and would make it her business to destroy her enemy.

"Ah! The *Orb of death!* You choose my favorite weapon!" mocked Steukhon in reply, stretching out his palm. Instantly, a purple luminous sphere appeared, spinning on the palm of his hand, emitting tiny lightning bolts from its surface. Steukhon stood visibly tall and planted his feet firmly on the ground. He knew that abnormal concentration and skill were required to control this totally unpredictable weapon. The fight would start with a command and end with a fatal thought that would kill on contact.

Zinnia muttered something and her orb, surrounded by blue sparks, shot in Steukhon's direction. Simultaneously, Steukhon's sphere swept from his palm and blocked the incoming object in mid air. There was a sudden clamor of metal beating on metal and a wave of noise filled the air. The orbs bounced back, hovering on opposite sides, each making short movements to prevent the other from passing.

Steukhon grinned and with a low voice instructed, "*Aggredior!* Attack!" His orb rammed into Zinnia's, sending it flying back and causing streaks of lightning in all directions. Zinnia held up her finger and the weapon returned. "The fight has only just begun!" she crowed.

"A good beginning is half the battle," proclaimed Steukhon as his spinning ball returned to his outstretched hand. Speed was the most important thing now and he changed his orb into a spinning metal oval.

Zinnia yelled, "*Sequitur passim!* Follow, up and down – here and there – repeat!" The orb whizzed like an arrow towards its target. Steukhon blocked the attack and each object tried to outmaneuver its opponent. With more than 366 commands to attack, the *Orb of death* was a lethal weapon in the hands of a master.

Egorh could hear it was a vicious war as their commands whipped through the air but his attention was drawn to Arkarrah rushing towards him. He was the first to attack, but Egorh avoided his sword with ease. Arkarrah began to hack wildly at him. With one skillful movement, Egorh stripped Arkarrah's sword from his hand and sent it twisting away. Arkarrah's snake eyes darted from the lost sword back to Egorh and he knew he was fighting with death itself. He turned to flee. Egorh sheathed his sword and reached for the white-feathered arrow in his never empty quiver. He aimed knowing that the arrow would find its target. As the terrified Arkarrah turned to look back, the arrow shaft plunged deep into the left side of his chest, the force throwing him off his feet and sending him crashing against the wall with blood spurting.

Egorh balanced to leap forward but hesitated when he heard Steukhon's anguished yell, "By the daggers of Hades!" He had just enough time to see a scorching orb spit long flames straight into Steukhon's eyes, blinding him instantly before reeling back to Zinnia's extended hand.

Egorh stared at Steukhon's tortured expression. His face screwed up from the excruciating pain. He staggered backwards, clutching his eyes and collapsed to the ground.
The hall echoed with Zinnia's sardonic cackling. He realized that Steukhon was in great danger as he saw the sorceress spin the iron object, then screaming with raw emotion. "I will kill you priest!"

Steukhon gasped from the floor, "Egorh, the *Orb of death*! Take it and fight back! Instruct it with stronger commands than hers!" Steukhon flung the orb blindly in Egorh's direction.

"Use it!" Steukhon shouted desperately, "or she will destroy us!" His face was like winter as he fought back against the fragments of blinding mist in his eyes. Egorh dived through the air and seized the weapon. It immediately began to spin on his palm. He heard Steukhon whisper urgently, "Remember, your command must always be superior to that of your enemy. Think in extremes!"

302

Egorh felt a powerful surge run through his body. A distant memory of the wizard mind-war, *Orb of death*, flickered into his consciousness. Images and memories rushed into his mind and he answered the priest, "I have not completely forgotten my life with Darkarh and all the teachings of an old wizard." He tightened his jaw when he saw Zinnia standing before him, her face gleaming as she watched him in silence. Anger boiled up from deep down in his chest and he muttered, "Murderer, at last!" This was the moment he had been waiting for. Revenge for all the things she had caused him in his life. This was the moment he was going to free the world of this evil, he thought. Memories from his childhood and Sir Matthew's screams between the flames flashed through his mind. Part of him feasted on the challenge to destroy her. He dispatched the orb with eagerness ignoring his quivering fingers. Despite his pain, Steukhon smiled inwardly when he heard Egorh shout his first *Orb of death* command. The spheres whizzed towards their targets each moving upward, downward and sideways in an attempt to pass the other.

"*Laceratus!* Mutilate!" Zinnia commanded.

"*Leto!* Slay!" Egorh countered.

Steukhon breathed with relief, still half blinded, "That was a superior command."

There was a sudden intensity in the battle as the spheres changed into unpredictable substances of fire, water, iron and lethal fragments of all shapes and sizes, trying to destroy each other. Egorh instructed his ball into a thin sheet of lead bouncing off her heat seeking orb. The thin metal piece ricocheted into the pillar just above her causing a flash as it cut into the granite. Zinnia melted it down as the metal shot in her direction and moved further away from the falling debris that rained down, as more pillars started to crack. She lost her patience and came in fast, the orb bobbing as it rushed towards him. Egorh yelled and his orb blocked hers then turned sharply, leaping up, pouring out strings of flames. Zinnia froze as she saw the flames melt the granite wall above her. "Dragon's breath!" she cursed and furiously spun away to escape the melted rock and hissed between her teeth, "I will finish you, son of Darkarh! *Absorb!*" she commanded, and her orb shot to one side and vanished into the nearest column where it waited. Egorh could sense her frustration seeking a final command.

"Cunning, but not good enough, witch," he retorted and whispered to his spinning sphere *"Acousticum!"* It flattened itself into the shape of an enormous liquid ear and set off in pursuit. It floated up, down and around the pillar, searching soundlessly as it tried to 'listen' for its opponent.

As the reflection of Egorh's orb fell over hers, Zinnia counteracted and yelled, *"Inferno!* Fire!" A strong blaze of fire burst from the pillar, but before it could have any effect, Egorh instructed, *"Aqua!* Water!" Steam rushed upwards as the fire exploded in the liquid ear. Egorh held out his hand and the steam formed a crystal orb on his hand.

Steukhon, partially recovered but with his central vision still fogged, watched how Egorh moved the deadly orb with ultimate confidence almost as if he was locked into the rhythm of war. Time slowed and became non-existent as things turned violently dangerous.

A loud explosion filled the air as the orbs attacked and smashed into each other. Again, Egorh's weapon sent the other reeling into a pillar causing lightning sparks that lit the gloomy room. A massive crack appeared and part of the masonry came plummeting down. Momentarily distracted by the falling debris, Egorh was too slow as Zinnia's weapon swooped up from below, cutting a deep gash across his chest and knuckles. His own orb lunged and forced the other to smash into the granite floor.

Egorh staggered back, reeling, trying to ignore the pain and blood everywhere, then set his jaw against the blistering pain and yelled a command, but somehow the orb would not obey. His heart pounded and sweat broke out on his brow, his legs slowly caved in and he sank to his knees. He knew he was in trouble.

Zinnia sensed her moment of victory. She craned her neck and looked at Egorh kneeling in his own blood and a sneer spread over her face as she throbbed with triumph, "This doesn't have to be a quick death. I can find pleasure in the suffering of the son of Darkarh," she whispered.

Like a praying mantis she waited, as she weighed her next move.

For Egorh time suddenly stood still. A feeling of peace washed over him and he felt as if he was floating on a breeze. Something made him look up from the warm blood that had spread around him and he saw a blurred scattered image drifting towards him. He narrowed his eyes and watched while it came closer and closer. At first the details of the form were dreamlike and rippled before it began to settle. Gradually it became a tangible physical body and the face as clear as crystal. He recognized the hazel eyes that bore into him as if they wanted to touch his soul. In front of him stood Darkarh upright, strong and proud and Egorh smiled.

"Father, why are you here?" he heard himself say.

"Egorh, you are stronger than you think. Use your special gifts and fulfill your destiny. Remember, you were the chosen one, my son."

Egorh could not answer. A memory of long ago flashed through his mind, the blood on the temple floor, his three brothers and Darkarh's arms around him. This is not happening again, this cannot be happening again, he thought.

He searched his father's eyes and felt a powerful energy radiating from them. A mighty force began to crawl and twirl into every fibre of his being. Then Darkarh nodded his head and slowly moved away to disappear in a mist of nothingness.

Egorh emerged from his trancelike state and became aware of his surroundings. He looked down at his gaping bleeding wound. He took a deep breath and somehow knew what he had to do. When he rose, his hazel eyes were bleak with pain. He cupped his hand and carefully poured flames onto the cut. The pain was excruciating. The wound and blood turned black from the scourge, and his screams rippled through the mountain sending the eagles scattering away through the openings.

Another voice came to his ears and he remembered it to be Sir Matthew's from that morning of their last skirmish long ago: 'A trained mind is more important in battle than just skill with weapons.'

With his eyes locked on Zinnia, he took a deep breath then slowly blew out his anger. He felt a wave of calmness wash over him and he muttered, "No anger, no revenge, Egorh, and you will surely kill the witch. Good will reign over evil this day!" He held out his hand for his orb to return. He felt his grip slippery with blood, but empowered now by the ancient gifts, he gave the fatal command. As both spheres shot forward on a collision course, he whispered *"Hoax-uneno"* and out manoeuvred Zinnia's by appearing in its path, first above then below, causing total confusion. His orb shot straight past and hovered in front of Zinnia's eyes. She was mad with fury but knew the vicious object would strike at any movement. At that moment Zinnia realized she had overplayed her hand.

Egorh saw victory and used all his concentration to hold the weapon in position. Incapable of counterattack, Zinnia's orb crashed to the ground and shattered into a million pieces of powerless debris.

Just then one of Sojun's eagles swooped down behind the sorceress, causing Egorh to lose his focus for a second. The weapon picked up the eagle's movement and struck, not at Zinnia, but towards the bird. Zinnia seized the opportunity to escape and sprang away.

Egorh summoned his powers. The orb reshaped into a spinning metal wedge, turned and attacked the sorceress. Two of the genie bangles on her arm clattered to the ground as the sharp metal tore through them slashing into the flesh of her arm.

Her gleaming green eyes widened with shock and she uttered a scream of pain. She clutched the wound, cursing loudly. Egorh strained to see where he wounded her. The speed and heat of the weapon had burned into the open wound. No blood came from the ugly cut that ran almost the full length of her arm. She fell back from the impact and staggered sideways against the wall and into the Jade-eye.

There was a strange sound as the eye split in half, revealing a huge light-blue vortex. For a moment it felt as if all and everything was frozen. Then a beam of blinding light shot out straight from the eye, into the center of the stone blocks and disappeared again. The loud grinding noise of stone rubbing against stone erupted as the blocks began to shift and slide into position.

~

Daniel and Bubba dashed out from their shelter beneath the moving stones and awestruck, they all watched how the slabs assembled into a huge, perfect cube. Zinnia scrambled to her feet and leaped towards the heart-stones, yelling "No! No! It is not complete!" But as she tried to raise her arms to conjure up the necessary command, she found her muscles were too weak as her one arm hung useless at her side.

"There are a few hearts missing! I cannot lose everything because of that!" she bellowed in agony. Gradually the huge cube began to pivot, picking up an astonishing high speed for such a heavy structure. As the movement reached its peak, the cube became invisible and disappeared with the harvest. "Steukhon! Quick! We must do something! We cannot let the hearts go!" Egorh shouted frantically as he realized what was happening.

Keep the image of the stone cube firmly in your mind and use the *Algo* pearl! We will follow," the priest exclaimed.

"Daniel, Bubba, get out of here, leave the mountain," Egorh yelled as he vanished.

Zinnia watched Egorh and Steukhon touch their rings and disappear. Her face twisted horribly when she realized that she had no power to stop the vanishing sandstone blocks. She cackled and screeched, "Victory *will* be mine, son of Darkarh!" She turned and scanned the battlefield behind her, boiling with rage as if all the chaos before her eyes was mirrored in her black soul. Frantically she thought, I must find a few more hearts to complete the thirty-thousand. If the Haffgoss manage to kill Egorh, our deal can still stand.

She flung herself sideways as a pillar cracked above her head. Statues and walls collapsed all around her as the mountain began to crumble. She knew she had to get out and, scooping up her genie bangles, she fled from the hall.

Arkarrah rushed past Zinnia and stumbled, completely worn out. He slid down onto the floor, clutching at the arrow embedded in his chest. Blood spread all over his shirt and cloak. He whimpered pathetically, "I am wounded!"

Zinnia stared at him blankly. She lifted her dress and climbed over him, glaring angrily at him and snarled, "You and all your so-called thugs! You could not even bring one man down! You're pathetic!" She bent over Arkarrah and maliciously jerked the arrow from his body, tossing it unceremoniously aside and muttered with contempt, "Stupid fool! There is no time for bleeding wounds now! Get up, we have work to do!" Arkarrah cowered.

Zinnia turned from him and muttered, "I have to get out of this crumbling mess! Maybe the Haffgoss will be happy with the hearts."

Arkarrah watched as Zinnia disappeared, then looked at his wound. With a puzzled expression he mumbled, "No pain?" He gingerly slid his hand inside his cloak and lifted it to check the wound. A smile spread over his face as he realized that the shaft had hit the gold coins in his pocket and the blood was from his dead bat. He tossed the lifeless body of Horris away.

Arkarrah, Sojun and Dwarf dashed after Zinnia.

Bubba hurried back down the stairs and Daniel tried to follow but did not see the huge falling pillar. It struck him and sent him tumbling to the ground. As more stones and rubble hit him, everything turned black.

Chapter 42

The Old Witch

Zinnia ran to her chambers to see what she could salvage before it was too late. Cracks had already begun to appear in the granite floor. She managed to grab Kep, who was lying on the table, the spiders on their webs and her old witches' book. She glanced at the Chest of Knowledge and hesitated for a moment, but when the floor groaned and shook beneath her she knew she had to leave.

There was only one way out and that was from the narrow ledge at the highest point, leading straight down past the lake to the north. The forest was dense there and she would be concealed.

As she was leaving the chamber, Arkarrah, Sojun and Dwarf joined her. Sojun was holding his dilapidated cage with the two bats and Dwarf was carrying Hooter. They followed her down the passage to a low doorway. Her mind whirled. Maybe all is not lost.

She ordered Arkarrah to smash the door open. They found themselves outside on a narrow ledge, where rocks crashed down from above and the ground heaved under their feet. Around them the sky was filled with smoke and a black-crested eagle shrieked from one of the peaks.

"We must get down from here Arkarrah!" Zinnia was now on the brink of hysteria. "We have work to do!" I want the orinium and I want that pearl!" She was out of breath, wracked with pain and consumed with rage. "We must find another place where there are flocks of flamingos." She turned her rage to Sojun." And you, miserable wretch, call the eagles and see how many have survived. It takes too long to train new ones."

The miserable group moved slowly down the path. Suddenly Zinnia stopped.

"What is it?"Arkarrah asked from behind, his snake eyes filled with panic.

"Listen! Do you hear that?"

The path trembled beneath them. From the cliffs came a rumble like distant thunder.

As Zinnia took another step the rocks gave way beneath her feet. Loud noises from above made her look up. Huge boulders came crashing down and she tried to shield herself, rocking uncontrollably on the unstable ground. Arkarrah reached out to grab her as the rock split. Zinnia lunged desperately to catch hold of his hand but missed. She fell backwards and tried frantically to grasp at anything she could with her uninjured arm. Where there had been malice in her evil eyes, there was now only hopeless terror.

She made no cry as she fell, her hair fluttering wildly and her long golden fingernails flashing in the eerie light. The horrified Arkarrah and Sojun sank to their knees and peered down, but she was gone, engulfed in black ash from the huge explosion that had rocked the mountain.

As the melted rock spewed from the mountain top they slid, clawed, jumped and ran as fast as they could down the trembling path.

~

Zinnia tumbled into the shallows of the river that fed the lake and realized that her fall had somehow been broken by the dense foliage. She lay there for a few minutes to get her breath back, bruised and battered, but exhilarated by the fact that she was still alive.

"Damn the son of Darkarh," she moaned as a sharp pain shot up the swollen arm hanging limply at her side. She realized she was in serious trouble. No power could flow between her hands. She was powerless with the use of only one arm.

She crawled to the river bank and fell back. A huge scroll of black smoke in the sky reminded her of her defeat. She swore through gritted teeth, but suddenly sat upright as she remembered; "Orta, the one eyed witch! I must get to her. She lives somewhere near the river." She stumbled along the river bank. After what seemed like hours, grimacing in pain, she saw the dilapidated log house not far away.

She banged on the door with all her remaining strength. "Orta are you there! Open the door – you must help me. OPEN!"

The door slowly opened and a little old weathered face with one eye peeped out. "Zinnia, what do you want?"

"You must help me. I am hurt."

The woman stared at Zinnia's injured arm and said, "Go away!" She tried to close the door but Zinnia's foot prevented her.

"I will give you your eye back if you help me."

"Why should I believe you? You are a liar." The old witch could see the veins in Zinnia's arm had been severed and found it very hard not to gloat. Her arm was in a bad way and the flesh would soon begin to rot.

"Maybe not this time," Zinnia scowled.

Her one eye rolled as Orta thought for a moment. Reluctantly she opened the door and gestured for Zinnia to come in. "The bloodletting will be painful."

"Do you think I care? I need my arm," Zinnia snapped.

"Sit there." She nodded to and old chair in the corner, "I

will be back soon." She disappeared through the door, grabbing a bucket next to the stove as she went.

Zinnia fell back in the chair and her face paled as she looked at the long purple-edged gash on her arm.

"Where is the old hag? I cannot lose this arm," she mumbled impatiently. After what felt like forever, the entrance of the door darkened and Orta stumbled into the house with the bucket, slopping water onto the floor. She knelt next to Zinnia, picked up a piece of wood, wiped it on her dirty skirt and mumbled, "Bite on this."

Zinnia hesitated and the witch said, "I told you it will be painful. You could lose the arm."

"Not if you want your eye back," said Zinnia and bit down on the wood.

The witch bent over the bucket and with bony fingers scooped a handful of slimy black leeches out of the water. As they squirmed on her palm, she picked out the largest ones and began to apply them all along the gash. Zinnia winced as the creatures attached themselves and began to suck the blood from the enflamed wound.

"Don't worry. Unlike you, they are merciful creatures. The mucus they secrete will numb the flesh."

Zinnia sighed with relief as the pain began to subside. The old lady sat hunched at her side and watched as the creatures filled their bellies with blood before they detached and fell to the ground. She picked them up and dropped them into another container, placing fresh ones on the wound until the purple swelling was gone and blood began to flow freely from the gash.

"Your wound will bleed for a while because of the blood thinning poison, Hyrundyn in their saliva, but the moving of blood is good," she mumbled.

Zinnia stared with hollow eyes at the old witch, not knowing if she could trust her, but she knew she had no option and just nodded weakly.

Orta mixed dark green herbs into a soft paste with which

she poulticed the wound and then wrapped it with cloth. Zinnia felt desperately tired. As she drifted off, she vaguely wondered if the old witch had put something in the herbs to make her sleep.

With her back to Zinnia the old woman grinned as she took the leeches and milked the blood from their bodies into a black glass bottle.

She smiled as she dropped the last lifeless leech into the bucket and then sealed the bottle with wax. Her eyes glowed hatred as she held the liquid high and cackled softly, "The sorceress's blood – more precious than any gold. She can keep the eye."

Chapter 43

Haffgoss

In the center of the temple floor three creatures lay sleeping, oblivious to their surroundings. As a rule they were either animal or human, but since their exile they had been more beast than man.

As Eragh lay sprawled on the marble floor, the breath from his huge nostrils moved the dust in front of his nose. Draped over a wide ledge, Arugh used his inhuman fangs to anchor his head into the stone, unable to close his monstrous mouth. Heaps of slime leaked from the corners of his lips and saturated the wall all the way down to the floor.

The only movement in the ill-omened temple was from the tail of Warogh, where he lay stretched out on the steps. The scales of his tail glittered as it swept slowly to and fro in a catlike manner. His scaly belly was pressed flat on the marble floor and his ivory seahorse earring scraped back and forth as he snored. In this manner the brothers slept their cursed lives away, waiting for the day when the sorceress would send them the hearts.

Barely visible, in the corners of this gloomy place, stood four tall obelisks: orinium, silver, gold and black platinum. Although covered in dust, they were still able to attract and hypnotize both mortals and immortals. Slightly taller than a man, each magnificent obelisk stood bejeweled and engraved. Precious stones, familiar and unfamiliar to most men, filled the inlays. Each son's history was engraved in an ancient language. Unknown to them, each obelisk had magical powers.

On the silver obelisk, which belonged to Warogh, twelve huge pearls could be seen, three on each side. They bulged out from the silver surface and changed the air to floating water, creating the illusion of moving water.

Intriguing and strange was Eragh's gold obelisk, which was covered in rubies. From the top of the obelisk, red liquid flowed from a gaping, wound-like opening. As it reached the bottom of the obelisk, it fused and turned into magnificent rubies, which lingered for a few seconds before disappearing, giving the impression of a fountain of blood. In the opposite corner, stood Arugh's solid black platinum obelisk, dull and rigid like a gravestone; the surface so smooth that not even the smallest particle of dust clung to it. But strangest of all was the orinium obelisk that glimmered eerily in the grey light.

~

An unfamiliar sound made the beasts stir. Mystified, they drew their limbs closer to their bodies and sat up straight. Warogh grabbed his ears as the deafening sound came nearer and a breeze curled up a tunnel of dust. A huge spinning stone cube appeared. It gradually slowed and then floated above the floor.

There was the loud grinding and screeching sound of stone on stone. The massive block separated into smaller components, exposing the multitude of heart-stones, each in its own little hollow.

Curious, the Haffgoss shuffled forward, hissing and spitting.

"It's the hearts! Zinnia has sent the hearts!" yelled Arugh and he lunged forward to pick one up with his claw. Holding it high, he inspected it with undisguised delight.

The others lurched forward and roared, "Our freedom! Our power! The obedient hearts at last!"

The three creatures lumbered along beside the suspended blocks, wild with excitement, until Arugh abruptly stopped. Staring closely at the harvest, he bellowed to the others, "Some are missing! The deal is unfinished."

"It's unfinished, it's incomplete," echoed the other two, staring at the empty hollows. They jerked their heads up as another deafening sound sent them rushing to seek cover. Their beastly shapes changed to human in the space of a few seconds and they stood quietly, barely breathing.

~

Egorh and Steukhon dropped onto the suspended stone blocks. The dust created by the landing spiraled upwards and they covered their noses. Watchful and ready to act, they leaped down and stood back-to-back as they scanned the area.

"What kind of place is this?" Egorh whispered and strained his eyes into the gloom. "Some kind of temple? Is it night or day?"

Steukhon murmured, "It's the temple where Darkarh exiled his sons. I am amazed that not everything was destroyed with his wrath. The two-paneled altarpiece, the murals, all untouched! There are the four obelisks." Steukhon pointed. "That is the orinium."

Egorh stared at the obelisk and his eyes filled with wonder. What he saw was so extraordinary that he gazed mesmerized, lost in the obelisk's beauty and the strange feeling of familiarity it induced in him. It was as if the obelisk was alive. The magical particles of the metal vibrated and moved. They collided with each other, producing metallic colors of gold, red copper and silver. There were other magnificent colors that Egorh had never seen before.

"It is incredible!" he breathed.

"Yes, and powerful! The metal has always managed to awaken the avarice in the hearts of dwarves and dragons, especially in the hearts of those wizards and sorcerers that knew its ultimate magic power. It is for this that Zinnia wants your life, Egorh," the priest quietly said.

Faint sounds came from the gloom of the temple. "I sense we are not alone," Steukhon whispered. Egorh tore his eyes away from the obelisk and focused his attention. "Let's make for the obelisk while we have the chance," Steukhon urged.

As they sneaked forward, Egorh caught sight of something glowing not far from where they were standing. "Steukhon! Wait!" He pointed at the soft glowing heart. "It *must* be Kayrin's heart!" and moved nearer.

Steukhon also leaned in closer. "You are right, it's glowing. The gods are on our side, Egorh. Take it, I will watch out."

With his heart hammering with excitement, Egorh carefully reached out and gently picked up the heart and slid it into his leather pouch, then turned back to where Steukhon stood, unable to keep the moment of joy from his eyes.

Steukhon nodded and then gestured for Egorh to come. As the two men drew closer to the orinium obelisk, they became aware of loud whispers and movement in the background.

"It's the priest and our brother," Egorh heard a voice whisper.

Three men in long robes shuffled out of the darkness towards them. From the corner of his mouth, Steukhon warned, "The fallen brothers! Be careful! Remember, they are not as they seem."

Egorh tensed at the sight of his murderers. He swallowed hard to suppress the anger that flared up within him.

Eragh, feigning friendliness rasped, "Ah! Our erstwhile priest and esteemed brother!" He bowed slightly, the long brown curls falling over his face, his jewels sparkling dimly with the movement.

"Perhaps you don't remember, but we are your brothers. I am Eragh, and this is Arugh and Warogh."

"You are NO brothers of mine! You are murderers," Egorh hissed, his eyes riveted on Eragh, who had started to pace in front of them. "You stuck a blade in me and robbed my father of the son he loved."

Eragh's smile was replaced by a mask of annoyance. He moved forward, his beady eyes cold as he snarled, "So *here* is the boy that our father favored. *He* is the reason for our banishment."

Steukhon's mouth tightened. "Let's not waste time," he interjected. "We know of the deal between you and the sorceress."

"The sanctimonious priest," sneered Eragh.

"Collaborator and spy for Darkarh!" added Warogh.

Egorh felt his anger break free and drew his sword. But Steukhon laid his hand on Egorh's arm and whispered, "Wait, today we will have to fight like wizards." Egorh paused, but kept his sword ready.

Sneering at Egorh, Eragh cried "Hah! Look at him! What does *he* have that Darkarh abandoned and exiled us for?" Standing together now, they mocked and sniggered at Egorh.

Steukhon glowered at them. "Everything your father could not find in you! Honor, trust, nobility and compassion, the lack of lust for power!

"Look at the three of you," he continued, incensed. "Eragh, your element of earth was supposed to bring stability and strength to your father's kingdom, but everything you touched became dirt because of the blackness in your heart. And you,

Arugh, your element of air was supposed to bring innocence and freedom, but instead you brought guilt, intolerance and harshness over his kingdom." Steukhon stood up straighter and his voice became clipped and tense. "Warogh, your gift was the element of water, giving life. Yet, you planned your brother's death and you still wonder at your father's wrath? You disgraced and dishonored Darkarh before the gods!" Steukhon glared at each of them, his blue-grey eyes flashing with anger.

Warogh hissed, "We do not care, old priest. We will take what belongs to us."

"I saw you take a heart, *brother*," Eragh sneered. "It belongs to us. Put it back!"

"Why don't you come and get it?" Egorh taunted.

Eragh glanced at the others, uncertain what to do. The muscles and tendons of his neck swelled as he started to burn with rage. Arugh clenched his left fist so hard that it made his arm shake. Then, as if contagious, the anger flared up in all three and Egorh watched as they started to change from their human shapes into demonic creatures. Their bodies bulged. They grew short arms and legs and their scales glimmered.

As Eragh swelled, his taloned forefeet slammed into the marble. Warogh's triple tongue flickered and Arugh's wings rustled as the three pressed closer to Egorh and Steukhon.

Egorh stared at the evil that stood before them. Readying himself, he clenched his sword and whispered with a sting of sarcasm, "Steukhon, have I managed to provoke them?"

"This is who they really are, vile and evil. They are showing their dark side. Be ready," Steukhon warned. "Soon they will unleash their corrupt powers with a vengeance."

Steadily, the beasts inched closer to Egorh and Steukhon.

"So you want to challenge us ... *brother*!" hissed Arugh.

"*If* you know of our plan, you should know that you must die. Your obelisk is ours!" Eragh spat.

Egorh placed his feet wide apart as Eragh opened his jaws and charged. He swung his sword for the creature's neck, but it bit into the thick leather collar Eragh wore. With one swipe of his huge foot, Eragh sent the sword spinning away.

"Did you think you could challenge me with a piece of steel?" Eragh scoffed.

"No, I just wanted your head as a souvenir."

Egorh could feel how they circled from behind, their breath foul and hot.

He cupped his hands and a ball of fire erupted. He turned to meet them. They staggered back petrified by the flames.

Before they could recover, Steukhon cut the air with a blue current that caught Arugh on his side, leaving a deep wound. He screamed in agony and retreated, then crawled away to a corner to lick the oozing blood from the wound.

The other two resumed their vicious attack. Eragh, enraged, scooped up a large boulder, which he sent flying towards Egorh.

"Melt it!" shouted Steukhon. Egorh extended his arms as the boulder careened towards him and melted it effortlessly, leaving a glowing path of molten rock on the floor.

He saw Warogh conjure up a globule of water. Arugh limped back to rejoin the fight. He called up a strong wind, freezing the water and transforming it into razor-sharp icicles. With a gesture, Egorh melted these missiles as they came towards him.

"To beat them we must channel our powers to one at a time," Steukhon yelled.

Egorh nodded. They directed flashing lightning and tongues of fire towards one brother at a time. The battle was ferocious. Snarling, the three creatures began to retreat, heckling and spitting to hide in the dark corners of their domain.

Egorh saw his chance and shouted, "Cover me, Steukhon! I am going for the orinium!"

He ran to the obelisk and pulled the mystic goblet from the leather bag and placed it on the floor. He melted the metal with flames from his free hand. Like wax from a huge candle, the orinium poured into the never-full cup. As the last drop fell, the goblet sealed itself and Egorh slid it back into the leather bag with the heart, and hurried back to rejoin Steukhon.

Egorh and Steukhon watched the Haffgoss slowly turn into their human forms. Their red eyes alerted Steukhon to a new danger. The three brothers clustered together, their faces horrifying.

"This is what Darkarh was always afraid of," warned Steukhon. "The Haffgoss are thoroughly evil and feed on each other's power."

"What do you mean?" Egorh whispered.

"When they stand together as humans with their evil thoughts, they are violent and unbelievably powerful," the priest explained.

Egorh watched as the three Haffgoss put their hands together and poured out a stream of mud and rust. Arugh's eyes became black as he blew the mass into a tornado not higher than himself extending partially from the ground. A loud roar like thunder developed as the whirlwind snaked and turned faster and faster, transforming into a black fiend. It started to spin in Egorh and Steukhon's direction demolishing everything in its path.

"We cannot risk fighting their demon. It is too strong. We must get the orinium to a safe place!" muttered Steukhon.

They jumped away just in time, as the thundering form tore straight through the center of the blocks, where the hearts were nested. They saw the stone blocks crack and disintegrate. The tornado slammed into the opposite wall, melting it. They witnessed the collapse of the massive wall and watched in horror as the burning mud engulfed most of the hearts.

As the demon turned again, Steukhon bellowed, "Let's get out of here! Use the pearl!"

"Doomed you will stay," yelled Egorh and they disappeared just as the dark spinning cloud cut through the floor in front of them.

The Haffgoss released their thoughts and the devilish shadow vanished. Wounded, the three limped closer to where the hearts had been. Eragh's gaze fastened on the destruction.

"The hearts ... they are destroyed!" he bellowed in frustration. "We cannot escape this region of *doom and hopelessness!*"

Warogh, his face a mask of rage, leapt forward to the mass of broken hearts and frantically tried to salvage the few undamaged ones. The temple quivered as the brothers lifted their heads in unison and howled their anguish in a black wave of despair.

Chapter 44

The Flamingo Curse

The fortress in Black Mountain was a ruin when Egorh and Steukhon reappeared. Egorh glanced at the unstable pillars that shook and leaned at dangerous angles. The granite floors had split open beneath them. Steam and gouts of fire spewed up from the earth below. Behind them a pillar shuddered and fell, crashing to the floor and causing it to shake beneath their feet.

"We must hurry! We *have* to find Daniel and Bubba." Egorh was frantic with worry for his two friends. "The mountain is going to blow," he warned and began to run with Steukhon following hard on his heels. They kept on probing the area for any sign of the two.

Flames erupted all around them. With a roar, the floor swelled and ripped open a huge cleft amongst the fallen pillars. Fragments of rock spat into the air as the chasm spouted molten lava, radiating a fierce heat. They ran as fast as they could, trying to escape the falling rubble from the last of the pillars as the walls began to give way.

Steukhon stopped to look around when they reached the

courtyard. He tried to suppress a feeling of dread. "They are not here either."

"Let's use the rings to return to the cave. Surely they managed to escape and they may be waiting for us there," Egorh suggested, although he too felt desperate.

Steukhon nodded his agreement. "We have succeeded, Egorh. The orinium is safe and we can only hope that our friends are too."

"Let's get the heart to Kayrin, then you can call on the rainbow maidens." Egorh urged.

They visualized the cave, touched their rings and disappeared.

~

"Daniel? Bubba?" Steukhon called, once they were back inside the cave. His eyes darkened with worry as he turned to Egorh.

"They are not here!"

"I am sure they soon will be, Steukhon. Let's go to Kayrin."

Egorh carefully removed the leather bag from around his neck and slid his hand into the thick velvet lining. He gently cradled the stone for a moment, then held it in front of the flamingo that he knew to be Kayrin and whispered, "I have your stolen heart!"

The stone began to glow and Egorh's heart hammered in his chest as he passed it to Steukhon. Kayrin approached and gave a soft honk, almost as if she understood.

"Come, Steukhon! Undo the deed!" Egorh urged impatiently, his eyes glowing with excitement.

The priest held the heart in the air and inspected it for a few moments. "The power of *Emorph-z*. How did the sorceress get it? I wonder. I must send the hummingbirds out and request information from the gnome on this subject."

"Steukhon!" growled Egorh.

"All right, all right." The priest cleared his throat, then stridently commanded, "U-dun-edo!"

Unblinking, the two men stared at the heart. A tiny, pink streak of mist began to twirl from it and twisted in different directions, as if seeking its owner. Egorh moved slightly forward, following the mist as it glided towards Kayrin.

Standing silently, he waited for the mist to reach her. But the twirling streak made a surprising detour, passed Kayrin and weaved its way to settle on the flamingo behind her.

"No! That's the wrong bird! *This* is the bird, not that one!" Egorh shouted, ready to jump forward to intervene. Steukhon quickly grabbed his arm and said quietly, "Wait. Let the heart find its own." Aghast, Egorh dropped his arms to his sides and watched the pink mist wrap itself around the other flamingo's body, expanding until it had engulfed the bird.

"What's happening? This cannot be!" he whispered in anguish.

"It is not Kayrin's heart!" Steukhon breathed, as he realized what had happened.

"What do you mean, it's not Kayrin's heart?" Egorh demanded, distraught.

At that moment, the men saw a pair of dainty feet appear. An amazing transformation was taking place. Despite his misery and anguish, Egorh stared and watched as two perfectly shaped human legs followed.

Steukhon called out, "Quick! Bring a cloak, Egorh! The girl has no clothes!" With her back to them, the girl's long, thick, black hair covered most of her body.

Egorh watched, transfixed by the metamorphosis. Steukhon grabbed a cover lying on one of the benches and draped it over the girl's shoulders.

He was puzzled by the appearance of the young girl, "You have been with me as a flamingo for such a long time ... Who are you?"

The two men held their breath as the girl slowly turned

around. Her beautiful brown eyes seemed bewildered. She stretched her arms out in wonder, admiring them, realizing she was no longer a bird. She looked up at Egorh and said, "Thank you! Thank you for my heart!"

Steukhon again softly asked, "Who are you?"

She smiled and said, "My name is Rangi."

"Where do you come from? Where is your family?"

"My village was raided and I was taken by the slave traders. I was separated from my brother, Bubba. He is my only family."

"Bubba's sister!" exclaimed Egorh.

"You know Bubba?"

"But why did your heart glow?" Egorh asked, ignoring her question.

"It was not for you, it was for me. We stood together in the temple." Steukhon gasped astonished.

"Where is Bubba?" she asked again.

Steukhon sighed, "Bubba and our friend Daniel are missing. Much has happened. I will explain later."

Egorh realized the reality of the situation and said in anguish, "I have lost her!" He turned away.

Rangi frowned and looked at Steukhon questioningly as she saw Egorh's pain. The priest shook his head slightly and pressed a warning finger to his lips. She understood that something was terribly wrong and remained silent.

"I am going back to the mountain to find Daniel and Bubba," Egorh said after a pause. The cave now felt cold and claustrophobic. He grabbed his cloak, threw it around his shoulders and prepared to leave.

"I will come with you, but first we must call the rainbow maidens to fetch the orinium before it is known that you have taken it," Steukhon reminded him.

"And I will come too," Rangi added. "I must find my brother." Wrapped in only a blanket, she followed them out of the cave, back towards the lake.

A honk behind him startled Egorh and he swung around.

"Kayrin! You followed me?" Puzzled, his first thought was to take the flamingo back, but he realized that it no longer mattered. Looking into her yellow eyes he said quietly, "I am sorry. I have failed you!"

The bird trumpeted again and dipped her bill. She turned and stalked away towards the edge of the water. Egorh followed her and watched helplessly as she spread her wings and took flight. Her wings beat in harmony as she skimmed the lake, her neck and slender legs outstretched. The chain dangling from her ankle flashed as it caught the sun. His eyes were empty as he watched her go.

He wanted to stop her but could only whisper helplessly, "No! Please don't go! Don't leave me!" but the bird had disappeared. Maybe it is better for her to be free, Egorh thought, his head bent in sorrow. Steukhon and Rangi watched Egorh's agony in silence. Then Egorh spoke again. "Steukhon, before you call the maidens, let's go back to the lake and the mountain once more to see if we can find Daniel and Bubba." Steukhon nodded and they began to scan the area and skirted the lake back towards the Black Mountain to search.

~

Near the lake, Steukhon gasped and grabbed Egorh's arm, his eyes widening at the scene in front of them. "By the gods! It is happening."

Horrorstruck, the two men froze. In the space of a few seconds everything had started to change. Thousands of the beautiful flamingos began to stumble, their long red legs giving way. Their bodies, one after the other, slumped to the ground. They trampled each other in confusion and screeched hysterically. Magnificent birds lay motionless where they had fallen with their heads buried. Rangi turned her face away, her eyes full of tears.

Anguish filled both men's hearts. The rumbling of the mountain had died away and an eerie silence settled all around them. Only the cloud of smoke in the sky spoke of the recent battle.

"Their heart cords have been severed," Steukhon murmured sadly.

They remained silent, helpless witnesses to the carnage.

Egorh shook his head and whispered, "So utterly evil. All this destruction in the name of greed!" He sighed desolately, "And I could have saved them all."

Steukhon turned to him. "I know you feel you could have done more, but you have given life to our worlds. In the midst of great danger, I saw your courage triumph! By being alive, you have saved the worlds from damnation. The magical orinium is secure and your brothers cannot claim it. You, Egorh, have prevented the triumph of evil. These beautiful birds have traded their lives so that Zinnia will not rule."

With his eyes resting on the heaps of dead flamingos, Egorh said sadly, "Then I shall remember them as brave warriors, though they shall never know."

"We can do nothing more here," Steukhon said softly. He placed a comforting arm around Rangi's shoulders and started to walk in silence.

Egorh held back slightly, reluctant to leave the lake and the lifeless flamingos. It appeared as if a crimson-pink blanket had been loosely tossed all along the edge of the lake. "My father loved me but his love cursed the flamingos," he whispered.

Egorh's head snapped up when he heard a voice calling, "Help! Help me!"

"Bubba? Daniel?" he called out and rushed forward. Bubba was carrying the motionless body of Daniel, hanging over his shoulder.

"He is injured and unconscious," gasped the exhausted Bubba. "I think he is hurt badly." He laid Daniel on the ground.

His face was covered with dry blood and a massive wound gaped on his leg.

Bubba looked up and saw Rangi. For a moment he stared at her, not registering who she really was, then a look of utter disbelief spread across his face. He jumped up, grabbed her hands and yelled, "Rangi! Rangi!" He touched her cheek and whispered, "Are you real?"

"Yes, it's me!" she exclaimed and embraced her brother. Despite his joy, he sensed something was terribly wrong. Noticing the look of despair on Egorh's face as he kneeled beside Daniel, Bubba looked quizzically at Steukhon.

"It was Rangi's heart that Egorh brought back from the Hap*Less* Sphere," the priest quietly explained, "He saved your sister."

"And Kayrin? Where is Kayrin?" asked Bubba.

Steukhon's eyes followed the horizon where the bird had disappeared and he sighed deeply. "She flew away."

"What do you mean, she flew away? She was in the cave!"

"She followed us out and took flight. I think she knew we had not managed to save her heart and decided to leave."

Bubba lowered his head, his happiness suddenly dampened as he thought of Kayrin. "But she is alive and that means her heart is still somewhere and can be found," he exclaimed hopefully.

Steukhon agreed. "A few hearts must have been buried in the mud and enclosed by rocks. It is impossible to reach them. Those flamingos will live as birds until they die. I'm afraid that Kayrin is one of them."

Daniel groaned and Egorh raised him slightly when he saw his lips moving. "I think he wants to say something. It's all right, Daniel, don't speak, we will take care of you," Egorh tried to reassure him, but Daniel continued his struggle to bring forth words. Before Egorh could hear what he was trying to say, Daniel had drifted off again.

"We must get him to the cave," said Steukhon.

Egorh bent to pick Daniel up as he resumed his mumbling.

"He has been trying to say something since I rescued him. He's been muttering the same words over and over, about something he found," Bubba explained.

Egorh looked down at Daniel and this time he heard him whisper, "In my pocket."

"Pocket?" but Daniel had drifted away again. "Don't die on me! Don't die!" Egorh pleaded, shaking his friend. "Bring him some water," Egorh ordered. Daniel spluttered as Egorh dripped water onto his cracked lips.

"It glowed ... so I took it," Daniel managed, barely moving his lips.

Egorh frowned and patted his friend's pockets. He felt something hard and pulled the object out. Egorh gasped when he realized it was a glowing heart-stone.

Steukhon stormed forward, "A heart?"

"Do you think it could be Kayrin's?" Egorh asked doubtfully.

"The heart is glowing. Rangi's heart glowed for me because I took care of her in the cave."

Steukhon spoke excitedly, "Think about it, Egorh! Who else would Daniel know, other than Kayrin?"

Egorh frowned. "Even if it is her heart, I cannot give it to her. She has flown away." He turned towards the lake staring at the glowing heart in his cupped hands. He fell to his knees and yelled towards the empty horizon, "Kayrin!"

They all stood quietly. From far away, a tiny black speck appeared in the sky, growing gradually larger. A flicker of hope danced in Egorh's eyes and he slowly stood up.

"Could it be ...?" Breathless, the group stared as the black dot came closer. "It *is* a flamingo! Please, dear God, let it be Kayrin," Egorh prayed aloud.

The bird slowly glided over the lake towards them, flapping its magnificent wings. As the red legs extended to land, a gold sparkle reflected in the sun.

Egorh gazed transfixed as the flamingo landed in the

water. He could no longer contain his joy. He leaped into the air shouting, "It's her! It's Kayrin!" He grabbed Steukhon's arm and holding the heart-stone in his other hand, pulled the priest towards the lake. "Come quickly, before she flies away again. Take the heart and say what you have to!" Egorh was almost beside himself with joy.

Steukhon took the heart, held it in the air and intoned, "U-dun-edo!"

As before, Egorh watched as a tiny pink streak of mist emerged from the heart, twirled around, circled a few times and glided towards the flamingo where it wrapped itself around the bird. The waiting was agonizing. Egorh watched the pink mist finally engulf the flamingo's body.

Again, first the feet and legs appeared. Egorh ripped the cloak from his shoulders to cover her naked body as Kayrin stood knee deep in the water.

As she emerged, the bird's yellow eyes turned into those unbelievably blue eyes that reminded him of the indigo bunting bird. Egorh remembered how he had loved those eyes from the first time he saw her standing on the steps of her father's house. Their eyes locked, then he gently pulled her closer. She trailed her fingers across his muscular forearms, overwhelmed to be in his embrace again. He tenderly took her face in his hands and kissed her sweet lips.

"My beloved Kayrin," Egorh whispered. "You are safe now. I have been tortured being without you. I thought I would never see you again. Surely by now the gods must know that you are my reason for living!"

Kayrin clung tightly to him and her eyes brimmed with tears. "Egorh, my love, you came for me. I've been so frightened but I held onto your promise of that day, when you told me: if somehow fate tricks us, send a message with the wind for me to catch and I'll be there. I love you, Egorh." They remained wrapped in each other's arms, oblivious to anyone else's presence.

Steukhon, forgotten in all the excitement, coughed politely to get their attention. "I should call on the rainbow maidens now. We must hurry and give the orinium to them to store for all eternity."

They watched as Steukhon walked a short distance, stopped and raised his arms to the sky and called out in a strange language none of them could understand.

A soft rain began to fall and instinctively everyone fell silent. Gradually the rain turned into mist and a rainbow appeared in the sky over the lake. Its end split open and its magnificent colors changed into the seven imposing maidens. Their splendid hair and garments fluttered around them gracefully in the breeze, as delicate and intricate as lace woven from silk and gold. Each maiden wore a golden sun on her forehead, and each sun held a colored stone in its center. Their glowing skins looked soft and new. They were almost too beautiful to look at.

"They are here," Steukhon announced as he walked back to where the others stood.

The maidens gazed around sadly. It was Sapphire, powerful and strong, who first moved forward. Her striking blue skin shimmered in the mist while her indigo lace hair flowed loosely around her shoulders. She clutched a cobalt-colored vase under her arm and her stunning dark eyes sparkled. The others followed, hovering slightly above the ground.

"Look!" said Amethyst. "The priest!" They lowered their eyes to where Steukhon was standing and Emerald's strong voice asked, "You called us?"

Citrine and Ruby floated forward with their vases under their arms and asked. "Why?"

"The son of Darkarh has saved our worlds! He has taken the magic orinium away from the Haffgoss and needs to place it in the rainbow pot, never to be found again. Only then can we be sure it will be safe from wizards, witches and sorcerers."

The maidens moved back to the end of the rainbow where they conjured up an enormous golden pot with their slender hands. The pot changed shape continuously to how the mind of anybody perceived it to be. No shape was the same. Its true shape was a secret and only known to the maidens.

"Come," beckoned Sapphire. "Pour the orinium in here."

Egorh took the mystic goblet and as he tilted it, it opened and the magical metal disappeared as it fell into the pot.

Steukhon put his hand on Egorh's shoulder and whispered, "Your destiny is fulfilled, son of Darkarh."

The maidens turned away and looked at the lake with its dead flamingos. They moved to the lifeless birds, lingering here and there.

"What are they doing?" whispered Kayrin.

"They are gathering information and evidence for the gods, for they will have to report the deaths," Steukhon replied.

Their work done, the rainbow and its maidens vanished as quickly as they had come.

Kayrin noticed a grey figure with a glass box under her arm floating away from the Black Mountain.

"The Sorrow-queen," she murmured.

"The *who*?" Steukhon asked.

When the Sorrow-queen heard Steukhon's voice, she hid behind the nearest rock.

"She collected my sorrows," Kayrin continued.

Intrigued, the others watched as blue-grey knuckles appeared around the rock, followed by a pair of huge eyes.

Sorrow-queen recognized Kayrin, emerged slightly and then groaned. "My pot broke," she whined.

Kayrin could not help but smile. "Really?"

Sorrow-queen's eyes lingered on the lakeshore littered with the dead flamingos and she mumbled, "At least they had no sorrows. They helped me fill my box. My box of sorrows is only half full." She emerged completely from behind the rock, swayed in front of them and announced, "I have to go now, back to my old pot in the graveyard." Almost gone, she darted back and asked, "Do you have any sorrows for me?"

"No, no. We are fine," Kayrin assured her. Sorrow-queen tucked her glass box under her arm and vanished.

Daniel groaned and Kayrin rushed over and knelt down beside him. "You are hurt!" she exclaimed when she saw his wounds.

Daniel put on a brave face. "No ... no, it's nothing ... just a few scratches," he gasped and tried to raise himself onto his elbows, wincing with pain.

"You saved me." Kayrin said to him.

"I did?" whispered Daniel casually.

Egorh smiled at Daniel's bravado and said earnestly, "Thank you a thousand times over, my friend."

"Who are *you*?" asked Daniel when he saw the lovely Rangi, but Bubba interrupted before she could reply. "It's a long story; your wounds must be treated first."

Egorh hugged Kayrin and said, "Come, we must head home. We have a wedding to plan at Old Falcon Place. We must find Vector and take Daniel home."

Bubba and Egorh gently picked Daniel up and Steukhon muttered, "I have to send a message with the hummingbirds to the gnome. It must all be documented: the battle, the victory and the carnage!"

Turning back towards the mountain, Steukhon wondered, could Zinnia and her cohorts have survived? He followed the others and muttered, "I hope not. I hope the gods have favored us and buried her in the mountain with the evil she created! Bubba and Rangi, will you come with me?" Bubba and his sister nodded without hesitation.

From the North, scores of marabou storks, the 'undertaker birds', were landing around the lake. The black-coated scavengers stood with an air of propriety over the remains of the dead giant flamingos.

Epilogue

In recent years scientists have noted that mass deaths of flamingos, which used to occur sporadically along the Rift Valley lakes, are more frequent. In the past few months, more than 30,000 flamingos were found dead along the shores of Lake Nakuru. A local newspaper has since described the place as a "flamingo death camp."

Most scientific attention has focused on the environmental changes to the lakes. Water levels have lowered and concentrations of soda in the water have increased. This increases the risk of toxic bacteria growing there, say scientists.

However, researchers say other causes could be involved and have urged an investigation of the deaths.